She had to get out of there before she said something she regretted.

Or before *he* did, because the intensity of his gaze was almost…unnerving. Just the sight of Javier lying in bed, watching her like that, as if he was going to slide over to make room for her to join him…

Oh, for the love of Pete. The man was recuperating from near-fatal injuries. He certainly wasn't having those kinds of thoughts.

So why in creation was she?

Dear Reader,

I hope you like this new FORTUNES OF TEXAS series as much as I do. It was fun to return to Red Rock and revisit old "friends" as well as meet some new ones.

In *A Real Live Cowboy*, JR Fortune fell in love with Isabella Mendoza. I'd mentioned that she had a brother, Javier. So you can imagine how exciting it was to be able to tell Javier's story and help him find his own happy ever after.

Of course, the poor man nearly died when the tornado struck Red Rock two months ago. The near-death experience and the long road back to recovery have taken an emotional toll on him, and the only bright spot in his day is when Leah Roberts, a lovely auburn-haired Florence Nightingale, enters his room.

As Leah's handsome patient heals, he begins to revert back to the man he once was—the kind of man who could prove to be the worst thing to ever happen to her… or the best.

So sit back and enjoy the romance that's about to unfold.

Happy reading!

Judy

MENDOZA'S MIRACLE

BY
JUDY DUARTE

First published in Great Britain 2013
by Mills & Boon, an imprint of Harlequin (UK) Limited,
Eton House, 18-24 Paradise Road, Richmond, Surrey TW9 1SR

© Harlequin Books S.A. 2012

Special thanks and acknowledgment to Judy Duarte for her contribution to The Fortunes of Texas: Whirlwind Romance continuity.

ISBN: 978 0 263 90084 2
ebook ISBN: 978 1 472 00441 3

23-0213

Harlequin (UK) policy is to use papers that are natural, renewable and recyclable products and made from wood grown in sustainable forests. The logging and manufacturing processes conform to the legal environmental regulations of the country of origin.

Printed and bound in Spain
by Blackprint CPI, Barcelona

Judy Duarte always knew there was a book inside her, but since English was her least-favorite subject in school, she never considered herself a writer. An avid reader who enjoys a happy ending, Judy couldn't shake the dream of creating a book of her own.

Her dream became a reality when Mills & Boon released her first book, *Cowboy Courage*. Since then she has published more than twenty novels.

Her stories have touched the hearts of readers around the world. And in July 2005 Judy won a prestigious Readers' Choice Award for *The Rich Man's Son*.

Judy makes her home near the beach in Southern California. When she's not cooped up in her writing cave, she's spending time with her somewhat enormous but delightfully close family.

To the other authors who took part in this series:
Karen Templeton, Marie Ferrarella, Susan Crosby,
Nancy Robards Thompson and Allison Leigh.

Chapter One

Javier Mendoza might have been a little irritable and short-tempered with his family just moments ago, but all he really wanted was for them to go home and leave him alone.

When they finally got the hint and left his hospital room, he was relieved. That is, until they gathered out in the hall and began to whisper.

"Maybe it's time for us to call in a psychologist," his father said.

Luis Mendoza might have lowered his voice, thinking he couldn't be overheard, but Javier wasn't deaf.

He glanced at Leah Roberts, who stood at the foot of his bed. From the expression on his personal Florence Nightingale's pretty face, he realized the comments they'd both overheard had struck a sympathetic chord in her.

"They mean well," Leah said, her own voice lowering to a whisper so the family members who'd gathered in the hall couldn't hear her words.

She was right. His father and siblings had held prayer vigils while he'd been in the ICU and had continued to visit regularly, even after his condition had been upgraded and he'd been moved to a regular room. He was grateful for their love and concern, of course, but there wasn't anything wrong with his mental state. Dragging this whole thing out any longer than necessary wasn't going to get him back on his feet any sooner.

Two months ago, a tornado had struck Red Rock, and in the blink of an eye Javier's life had been permanently altered.

Of course, all he knew about that fateful day— and for the next three to four weeks after—was what others had told him and what he'd read in the old newspapers Leah had brought for him to read.

In fact, there was very little he recalled after the December day his brother Marcos had married Wendy Fortune. The two families had celebrated the Christmas holiday together, then the Atlanta-based Fortunes had planned to fly home to attend a New Year's Eve party.

It had taken several vehicles to deliver them all to the airport, and Javier had been one of the drivers.

The wind had kicked up and the clouds had grown dark, threatening to ground all the flights. So the travelers had hoped to get out of Red Rock before they were forced to wait out the storm.

Then the unthinkable happened. A tornado struck, killing several people and injuring others.

Javier, who'd almost gotten a one-way ticket to the Pearly Gates, had been one of the "lucky ones," which was what more than one medical professional had told him. In fact, his injuries had been so serious that it had been weeks before anyone knew if he'd pull through or not.

He supposed he had his family's prayers and the skill of one of the top neurosurgeons in the country to thank for that.

Still, he'd been in a coma for over a month, which had been medically induced for part of that time, and had finally regained consciousness in February.

His family and the many specialists who'd treated him had been relieved to learn he hadn't suffered any lasting brain damage, although he'd suffered a lot of confusion those first few days.

His recovery was going to be far from easy. He still faced some physical hurdles, since multiple fractures in both of his legs would require extensive rehab in the facility attached to the hospital, but at least he'd be able to walk again. For a while, doctors hadn't been sure.

Jeremy Fortune, Javier's orthopedic surgeon, as

well as a longtime family friend, had been honest about what the future would bring. The physical therapy would be grueling, but it was necessary for Javier to regain full body function.

"You're young," Jeremy had said. "And you're strong. With rehab, you'll eventually be as good as new."

But Javier wasn't convinced of that. He'd lost a lot of time, not to mention a once-in-a-lifetime business opportunity that had slipped through his fingers while he'd been out of commission. And thanks to the blasted confusion—which was better but still lingered—there'd been countless other details and opportunities lost to him.

Sure, the brain fog had cleared some, and with time, he'd probably regain his physical strength. But deep inside, where no one could see, something had changed.

Javier was different.

His family seemed to think he was depressed. Okay, so maybe he was—a little. Who wouldn't be?

For all of his thirty-one years, he'd relied on quick wit and keen business savvy to see him through. But after the injury and weeks of recovery, he feared the healing had stopped.

What if he never got his mental mojo back?

The question itself struck fear deep into his battered bones. And it was something he'd never admit to anyone, not even to a shrink.

Javier again looked at Leah, whose long, auburn hair was pulled back with a clip, whose expressive hazel eyes seemed to know what he was thinking and feeling most days without him ever having to say a word.

She was the only person whose presence didn't make him want to scream. Maybe that was because she hadn't known him before and didn't have any pre-conceived notions of how he "should" react to things. Or maybe he just appreciated the fact that she didn't walk on eggshells around him and act cheerful when she wasn't.

Then again, she was a beautiful woman, inside and out. How could he not want to be one hundred percent whenever he was around her? After all, he might be wounded, but he wasn't dead. And certain parts of his body weren't in need of any rehab at all.

Leah made her way to the head of his bed and rested her hand on the railing. Her fingers were long and tapered, her nails neatly manicured. Her touch, as he'd come to expect, was light yet steady and competent.

He was tempted to reach out to her, to place his hand over hers. But before he could ponder the wisdom—or the repercussions—of doing so, she said, "I'll ask them to continue their discussion in one of the conference rooms."

That would help. "Thanks."

She nodded, then left his room to join his family in the hall.

The last voice he heard was Leah's saying, "Why don't you come with me."

As Leah led the Mendoza family past the nurses' station, their footsteps clicking upon the tile floor, she said, "Javier was listening to your conversation, so I thought it would be best if you finished your discussion in private."

"Aw, man." Luis, Javier's dad, raked a hand through his hair. "I didn't mean for him to overhear what we were saying. It's just that we've been worried about him."

Leah had been concerned, too. She'd noticed the change in Javier's attitude whenever his family came to visit. She'd even asked him about it one day, although he'd shrugged it off as no big deal and then changed the subject.

"Being incapacitated is a big blow to a man like him," Leah said as she walked along the hall.

They all nodded in agreement.

"It's too bad you didn't know him before he was injured," Luis said.

Leah would have liked knowing him before. Even in his injured condition, she'd found him to be intriguing. And if truth be told, she stopped by to visit him even on those days when she'd been assigned to other rooms and patients.

"Javier is a contractor and a real estate developer," Luis added as he strode next to Leah. "And he's always been enthusiastic about whatever project he was working on. In fact, those deals always seemed to energize him. But now, if we mention anything about business or properties, he changes the subject."

Leah had picked up quite a few details about her patient, including the fact that he'd been very successful with his land dealings and that he had a nice house in one of the better areas of Red Rock—custom-built just for him.

"He's also a part-time musician," Isabella, his older sister, added. "And he's an athlete. He played both tennis and golf before his accident. But if we mention music or sports, he clamps his lips tight and his expression turns grim."

"I'm sure, in time, he'll play golf and tennis again." Leah opened the door of the conference room that was located just beyond the nurses' station and waited for Luis Mendoza to enter, followed by his son, Rafe. Next came Rafe's wife, Melina, and Isabella.

"My brother has always been positive and energetic," Isabella said. "So it's heartbreaking to see him depressed."

"I'm sure it is." From everything Leah had gathered, Javier Mendoza was bright, ambitious and successful. She'd also overheard his family mention that he had an active social life and that he was one of Red Rock's most eligible bachelors.

To be honest, if Leah had run into him before the accident—and if he'd given her the time of day—she would have found him more than a little appealing herself.

Actually, she did now—even when he was stretched out on a hospital bed or seated in a wheelchair.

"I'm an occupational therapist," Melina said. "So I understand where Javier is coming from. I've worked with many accident victims, some of whom had to face the reality of never being the men or women they once were. It's tough to face your own mortality and frailties, so Javier's depression is only natural. Besides, he's a competitor at heart. And he's always prided himself on being the best. So dealing with his incapacitation—even one that's temporary—is going to be especially tough for him."

"That's what I'm talking about." Luis looked at Leah as though appealing for her agreement. "Don't you think it would be good if he talked to a psychologist or a counselor?"

"Yes, I do," she admitted. "And once he's moved into a room at the rehab facility, he'll have an opportunity to speak to a professional."

"So you're saying we should back off?" Luis asked.

If there's one thing Leah had learned about Javier Mendoza, it was that he didn't like to be pushed—whether it was to eat a bit more of his meal or to take some medication to help him sleep.

"I would wait a bit longer," she said. "He has a lot to deal with right now. Time is really your best ally."

The family seemed to ponder her suggestion, which she hoped was the right one. When Dr. Fortune ordered Javier's transfer to the rehab unit, she'd be sure to mention the family's concern in her report.

"You know," Rafe said, "I've been thinking. We've asked his friends and business associates to refrain from coming to see him. After all, he was in a drug-induced coma for a month. And then they brought him out of it slowly. For a while, he suffered some confusion, so we knew he wouldn't want to see anyone other than family. But maybe it's time to let people know that he'd like to have visitors."

"I don't know about that," Isabella said. "His mood is difficult enough for *us* to deal with."

"I'm not saying that we should encourage *everyone* to visit, but what about one of those women he used to date?" Rafe reached for Melina's hand. "My lady always puts a smile on my face."

At that, everyone in the room broke into a grin.

Everyone except Leah.

Somehow, she didn't like to think of the women Javier used to date before his injury and hospitalization. And why was that?

It wasn't as though she had plans to date him herself. She'd never get involved with one of her patients.

Oh, no? a small inner voice asked. Then why did

her heart drop each time she saw that Javier's room had been assigned to another nurse?

She didn't have an answer to that—only to argue that she'd grown fond of Javier. She understood the uphill battle he'd been waging and seemed to have bonded with him somehow.

The fact that he was not only handsome, but personable, and that she found him attractive had nothing to do with it.

That's not true, that pesky little voice said.

As much as she wanted to object, to defend herself and her feelings, she had to admit that there was something about Javier Mendoza that called to her.

Something she couldn't explain.

Javier had been surfing the channels on the television in his hospital room for several minutes, but he couldn't seem to find any shows that interested him.

A tennis match only made him resent the fact that he wouldn't be able to play for months, if not years. And the news stations reminded him of how much he'd missed during the time he'd spent in the ICU.

Hell, he could hardly remember what his life had been like outside these white walls, and as he thought of his hospitalization and the long road to recovery, frustration swooped down on him again like a hungry vulture unable to wait for his hope to completely expire.

With the dark shadow came the urge to throw the

remote across the room, even though he'd never been prone to displays of temper. Instead, he placed his index finger over the red power button, shutting off the TV.

As the screen faded to black, Leah entered the room. Just the sight of his pretty nurse was enough to make his frustration ease and his mood take flight.

Talk about a nice diversion…

A grin tugged at his lips, softening what had been a grimace only moments ago.

At first glance, Leah, who stood about five foot four, wasn't what Javier would call a striking woman. After all, he'd never seen her wearing anything other than hospital scrubs and a matching pair of Crocs on her feet. But with each passing day, as he looked beyond the loose-fitting clothing that masked her femininity, he'd found a lot to admire.

Her long, straight hair was a pretty shade of auburn, although she usually kept it pulled back with a clip or woven in a single braid. She wore very little makeup—if any. But she had such a wholesome beauty that she really didn't need any of the usual female props.

He wondered what she looked like on her days off or when she spent a night on the town. In fact, he'd like to know a lot of things about her, like what her life was like outside the hospital.

Was she married?

He certainly hoped not.

As she moved through his room, he wondered if she was dating someone special. It was difficult to imagine men not clamoring to be her one and only. How many women were as comforting, as gentle, as sweet?

A couple of times he'd been tempted to ask if she was single and unattached, but he hadn't, and he wasn't sure why. He supposed he hadn't wanted his nurse to know that he found her that attractive. If he hadn't been laid up—and barely able to walk— it might be a different story. In fact, the old Javier wouldn't have thought twice about asking her out. But he was a far cry from the man he used to be.

"I take it there's nothing good on television," she said.

"Nope." He set the remote aside.

"The dinner cart will be here shortly," she added.

"I can hardly wait."

Catching his sarcastic tone, she turned to him and smiled. "You're lucky. The food at San Antonio General is actually pretty good."

Maybe it was, but his appetite had yet to return. In fact, the only reason he even looked forward to mealtime was because it helped to pass the time from morning to night, making him come one day closer to discharge.

But why focus on all that mundane reality when he had Leah with him?

"Hey, Florence," he said, using the nickname he'd

dubbed her with when he'd first began to see her as a woman and not as his nurse. "I have a question for you."

"What's that?" She neared his bed, checking the ice and water level in the small plastic pitcher that sat on his portable tray.

"What does your husband do for a living? Is he in the medical field, too?"

She paused as if his comment had thrown her for a loop. "My *husband?* I'm not married."

Javier fought the urge to smile at that news. "Oh, no? I just assumed that a woman like you would have a man in her life."

Her hand lifted to the boxy pink top she wore and she fingered the stitching along the V-neck.

Was she nervous? Off balance? Flattered maybe?

He liked to think so, even though he wasn't in a position to follow through at this point.

Before either of them could speak, a woman's voice sounded in the doorway.

At the cheery "Hello," both Javier and Leah turned to see a tall, willowy blonde walk into the room carrying an arrangement of spring flowers that hid her face.

Savannah Bennett?

As the blonde lowered the multicolored blooms, he realized that's exactly who'd come to visit.

"I hope you don't mind me stopping by," Savannah said. "I'd been wanting to see you for weeks, but

I'd heard that your visitors had been limited to family members."

No one had told Javier that only his relatives were allowed to see him, although he hadn't much cared either way. In fact, he'd rather not deal with visitors at all—whether they be family or friends.

"But then I ran into Rafe at the grocery store this afternoon," Savannah said. "He told me you were eager to have company. So here I am."

Eager? That was a crock, and Rafe knew it.

More irritated at his brother's interference than Savannah's surprise visit, he forced himself to be polite. "Thanks for stopping by."

He wondered if Savannah noticed that his tone lacked sincerity. After all, they hadn't dated in a couple of months—well, make that four or five, since they'd split up way before the tornado had struck Red Rock.

Savannah had wanted more from him than he'd been able to give her—like a commitment. And while he'd made no bones about being a happy bachelor, she seemed to think that she was the one woman who would eventually change his mind. So there'd been a few tears on her part, but he'd suspected she would have been a lot more hurt and disappointed if he'd strung her along.

Of course, Rafe had no way of knowing any of that. Javier had never been one to kiss and tell—or to break up and vent.

Leah, who'd been standing by his bed, took a step back, as though trying to bow out graciously.

She wasn't going to leave him alone with Savannah, was she? Not that it mattered, he supposed. It's just that he… Well, he didn't want Leah to go. Not when she provided the only upbeat moments in his day.

"Hey, Florence," he said, trying to recapture the playful moment they'd been having—or that they'd been about to have before Savannah's arrival.

Leah paused, her expression unreadable. "Yes?"

For a moment he was at a loss for words. But he wanted to let both women know he and the blonde weren't romantically involved, at least not any longer.

"I'd like to introduce you to a friend of mine," he told his nurse. "Savannah's a paralegal at a local law firm. Or she was, the last time we talked." He turned to his unexpected visitor. "Are you still working for Higgins and Lamphier?"

Savannah nodded, her demeanor a bit stiff and a frown creasing her brow.

"It's nice to meet you," Leah said with a casual smile. Then she nodded toward the doorway. "I'd better get back to work and let you two chat."

Javier could have argued, asked her not to leave. But then what? His obvious attraction to his nurse would have only complicated any future discussion he had with Savannah.

And his life was complicated enough as it was.

Chapter Two

As Leah slipped into the hall, a whisper of uneasiness breezed through her. She could have sworn that Javier had been about to ask whether she was single and maybe even…

Available?

Okay. So maybe she'd only imagined that's what he'd been getting at.

When it came right down to it, she wasn't sure why he'd asked those questions or what he'd meant by them. The minute Savannah what's-her-name had entered the room, their conversation had ended before it even had a chance to take off, so all bets were off.

And really, wasn't she better off not knowing what Javier had planned to say next? The last thing she needed to do was to create any unnecessary workday drama.

Still, the line of questioning had taken her aback and made her face the fact that, in spite of her efforts to remain completely professional, she was growing a little too fond of one of her patients.

Of course, she would never act on her attraction. She was too committed to her job to let anything like that get out of hand.

As she made her way to the nurses' station, glad to be back on the job and out of Javier's room, she held her head high, her shoulders straight. Yet disappointment threatened to drag her down for the count. She was sorry about the way things had played out.

And why was that? she wondered.

Probably because she cared more for her patient than she should. So for that reason alone she really ought to be glad that Savannah's arrival had interrupted their conversation.

And she *was*.

Yet she'd flinched when the beautiful blonde had entered Javier's room, and she'd found her emotional reaction to the visit more than a little bothersome. After all, Javier was a handsome bachelor. He probably had a slew of women in his pre-hospital life. How could he not?

So why would one woman's visit surprise her? And why would it leave her so unsettled, so uneasy?

She supposed that was because, at least up until

now, only his family had come to see him. And she hadn't given his love life much thought.

Well, now…that wasn't entirely true. She'd thought about the women he might have dated in the past, but in all of her musings they'd been faceless beauties.

Of course, that was no longer the case. Now one of them had a face—a pretty one that suggested Javier liked tall, sophisticated blondes who dressed to the nines and were skilled at applying makeup and styling their own hair.

Leah clicked her tongue, scolding herself for making that kind of assumption. Maybe she was connecting all the wrong dots. How did she know that Savannah and Javier had actually dated? Hadn't he downplayed that possibility?

If he had no idea whether she still held the same job, how could he and Savannah be romantically involved? Clearly, he hadn't seen her in a while.

Leah's uneasiness began to lift at that conclusion—until she realized he'd spent more than two months in the hospital. He'd also been in a coma for nearly half that time. And he'd suffered some confusion and memory loss when he'd first come to.

Then, to make matters worse, she remembered what his brother Rafe had suggested to the family earlier this morning.

So it was easy to conclude that Savannah's hospital visit hadn't been a coincidence. In fact, Rafe had set it into motion when he'd run into her at the grocery store earlier today.

It hadn't taken much of a leap for Leah to realize that, even if Javier had made it sound as if he and Savannah were merely friends, that hadn't always been the case. At one time, they must have been more involved than that.

As Leah took a seat behind the desk, she had to admit that she didn't like the idea of Javier having a girlfriend, which meant that her feelings had grown to the point that they bordered on that fine line between sympathetic and inappropriate.

Bordered? She was afraid that she might have crossed the line already, and that she was more attracted to her patient than a nurse ought to be.

So the way she saw it, she would either have to request a transfer to another floor or fight her feelings so she wouldn't compromise her professional ethics.

With the dilemma still weighing on her mind, she reached for a chart belonging to another of her patients and tried to pretend she was busy. Yet even though she studied the paperwork in front of her, her thoughts were a million miles away.

Okay, so they weren't all that far away. They were just down the hall, with Javier and the attractive blonde who'd come to visit him. A frown slowly stretched across her face as she realized she had no one to blame for her green-eyed uneasiness but herself.

For some reason, while he'd been on the third floor at San Antonio General, she'd come to think of him as…

Well, unattached, she supposed. And even pondering his romantic status had been the first hint that her interest in him was out of line.

So now what? Should she request a transfer to either the obstetric or pediatric ward? That might help.

Trouble was, Javier's mood lifted whenever she was around. And Margie Graybill, who worked the night shift, had told his family that Javier never cracked a smile, no matter how hard she tried to coax one out of him.

"You must have a special touch," Javier's father had said to Leah the other day. "His attitude is much better whenever you're on duty."

She liked to think that she had managed to reach him when other nurses hadn't. So if she was one of a few who had the ability to draw him out of his somber mood, how could she ask for a transfer?

What kind of nurse would she be if she gave up on her patient when he needed her most?

Leah had lucked out. She'd finished the rest of her shift without having to go back into Javier's room. But that didn't mean she wasn't aware of who went in or came out.

Savannah had left the hospital shortly after she'd

arrived, which had pleased Leah more than it should have, especially since she'd made up her mind to maintain a professional attitude when it came to Javier. But there wasn't anything remotely professional about the rush of relief she'd felt when the blonde had left his room after only a few minutes— five or six at the most.

Leah glanced at her wristwatch, realizing it was about time for the shift change. Thank goodness she didn't have to work tomorrow. Taking a break from her handsome patient would help tremendously. She'd shake those inappropriate thoughts and feelings that surfaced whenever she was near him.

As she opened the last patient's chart and prepared to make a note before leaving the hospital for the next couple of days, Leanne Beattie, the nurse's aide who delivered meals to the third floor, said, "The guy in three-fourteen doesn't seem to like anything we serve him."

The guy in 314 was Javier.

Leah glanced up from the note she was writing, "What do you mean?"

"Well, he hasn't eaten much of anything today. He didn't touch his breakfast and only picked at his lunch. As far as I can tell, he left everything except the chocolate ice cream on his dinner tray. So I thought I should mention it."

"Thanks, Leanne. Loss of appetite is a side effect

of one of the new medications he's on, so I'll be sure to tell his doctor."

Of course, the depression his family had been concerned about might also contribute to him not eating, although Leah wasn't convinced that they were right. Whatever was bothering him only seemed to flare up when he had visitors.

But either way, she'd like to see him start eating better. He was going to need his strength when he moved to the rehab unit and his physical therapy became more vigorous than it was now.

On her drive home that night, she thought about her own dinner and what she'd like to eat. For the most part, she avoided red meat, fats and processed foods. But she'd had the munchies ever since she'd left Savannah and Javier alone in his room, so she decided to give in to temptation and pick up a cheeseburger and fries.

She didn't allow herself those kinds of indulgences very often, but she figured the fast food would be filling—and it was better than fixing herself a salad with low-fat dressing, then popping open the freezer and wolfing down the rest of a carton of rocky road ice cream, which was what she'd probably end up doing when the veggies didn't hit the spot.

And on a night like this, she didn't think a salad was going to be enough to hold back temptation.

As she pulled into the drive-through of her favorite fast-food restaurant, she realized that people sometimes craved foods that they'd grown up eating. There were days when nothing else would do the trick.

At that thought, a game plan began to unfold.

She didn't have to work tomorrow. Why not take lunch to Javier? She could pick up something tasty that was a change from the usual hospital fare he'd been served. Maybe that would spark his appetite and entice him to eat a full meal.

So the next morning, after cleaning her small apartment, she took a shower and slipped into her favorite jeans and the new black sweater Aunt Connie had given her for her birthday. Then, after applying a little makeup, brushing out her hair and pulling it back in a ponytail, she drove to the most popular Mexican restaurant in Red Rock, which Jose and Maria Mendoza owned.

Jose was related to Javier's father, Luis, although Leah wasn't entirely sure of the exact connection. They might be cousins, she supposed. Either way, it was probably safe to assume the entire Mendoza clan spent a good deal of time eating at Red.

Actually, she was surprised that none of Javier's relatives had come up with the idea before. But she wouldn't think about that now. Instead, she would surprise him by taking him lunch.

At a few minutes after eleven, Leah arrived at Red and parked her car out front. So far, not many people had gathered, but she knew it was only a matter of time before the lunch crowd would begin to roll in.

She'd only eaten at the restaurant once before, and that was several years ago. But she'd been impressed by the historic building, which had once been a hacienda.

The Mendozas had done a great job decorating with nineteenth-century photographs, antiques and Southwestern artwork that lined the walls.

In fact, while waiting for her order to be prepared, she might even sit in the courtyard, with its rustic old fountain, lush plants and the colorful umbrellas that shaded pine tables and chairs. There she'd listen to the soft sounds of mariachi music coming from the lounge, as well as the relaxing gurgle of the water in the fountain while sitting amidst the bougainvillea that bloomed in shades of fuchsia, purple and gold.

As Leah entered the door, a dark-haired hostess greeted her. "One for lunch? Or are you meeting someone?"

"Actually, I'd like to place an order to go."

The woman reached for a menu. "Do you already know what you'd like? Or would you like to see what we have to offer?"

Leah took the menu. "I'll need a moment or two to decide. But can you tell me if Marcos Mendoza is here today?"

Javier's brother managed the restaurant. And if anyone knew what Leah should order, it would be him.

"Yes, Marcos is here. I think he's in the kitchen. I'll get him for you."

From what Leah had heard, Marcos used to spend a great deal of time at Red, making sure that everything ran smoothly. But he actually kept a regular schedule now that he and Wendy had a new baby. Their little girl, who had been born a month early but was doing well now, was expected to be released from the neonatal intensive care unit soon.

Leah knew all this because she'd taken to stopping by the NICU to see Mary Anne Mendoza and the other preemies…and wondering what it would be like to have a baby of her own.

Sure, the neonatal unit housed the most seriously ill newborns, but while some didn't make it, many of them did. And as a nurse she was proud of the success rate.

In fact, each year, the NICU staff put on a reunion party for the children who'd once been patients and who'd gone home healthy. The oldest were about ten years old now, and some of the parents had created play groups that were still going strong.

While waiting for Javier's brother, Leah opened the menu and studied her options. Marcos might know what Javier would like to eat, but she planned to choose something for herself.

Who knew what might happen when she surprised him with his favorite Mexican meal. He might even ask her to join him for lunch. And if he did? She'd agree. Otherwise, she'd take her food home and eat it there.

"Can I help you?" Marcos asked upon his approach.

When she looked up from the menu and smiled, recognition dawned on his face. "What a surprise, Leah. I didn't realize who you were in street clothes."

"That's not surprising. I practically live in scrubs."

"How are things going?" Marcos asked. "I didn't get a chance to stop by and see my brother last night. Wendy and I wanted to talk to the neonatologist when he made his morning rounds, so I had to work late to make up for being gone."

Wendy, who'd once worked at Red, too, had been expecting a baby this month, but she'd gone into premature labor back in January. The doctors had managed to stave off her contractions, then they'd put her on bed rest. She'd eventually given birth at home in early February, which had to be a real worry for them. But the baby girl was small but healthy and now thriving.

At least, that's the last Leah had heard. "Mary Anne's still doing okay, isn't she?"

"Yes, everything is great. She's been gaining weight, and the doctor is pleased with her progress." A broad smile told Leah that the new father couldn't be happier.

"I'm glad to hear that," she said.

"It was a little scary for a while," Marcos admitted, "but we're all doing great. In fact, now that Mary Anne is out of the woods, Wendy and I are settling into parenthood. We've even been thinking about having a party soon to celebrate our daughter's birth."

With the size of the Fortune and Mendoza families, that would probably be some party. And Leah couldn't help but smile.

The two families had been through a lot lately, first with the tornado and Javier's injury, then with Wendy's baby. So now that everyone was on the road to health and wellness, they had a lot to celebrate.

"The hostess said you wanted to talk to me," Marcos said. "Is everything all right?"

He was worried about Javier, Leah realized, so she shot him a smile to put his mind at ease. "Your brother is coming along just fine, but I have a feeling that he's getting tired of the hospital food. So I thought I'd surprise him with something different for a change. Do you have any suggestions? What does he usually order when he comes here?"

Marcos chuckled. "I don't suppose they'd let you sneak him an ice-cold beer and lime."

"I'm afraid not," Leah said, enjoying the brotherly humor.

"Well, he'll be happy with the carne asada, which is what he usually orders."

"Then I'll take a plate to go."

"How about you?" Marcos asked. "Aren't you going to have lunch with him?"

The thought had certainly crossed Leah's mind, but she wasn't so sure it was a good idea any longer.

Marcos must have read her indecision, because he added, "My brother seems to really like you, and I'm sure he'll be more likely to enjoy his meal if you share it with him."

He had a point, she supposed. "All right. I'll take the small chicken taco salad."

She reached into her purse.

"Oh, no you don't," Marcos said, placing a hand on her arm. "Put your money away. After all you've done for Javier, this order is on the house."

She wanted to object, to tell him she'd just been doing her job, that she'd fully intended to pay for lunch, that she hadn't chosen the family's restaurant hoping to get a freebie. But both appreciation and sincerity lit up his smile, so she released her wallet and thanked him instead.

"Is there anything else you need? Dessert maybe? Javier likes the flan. I can also pack up napkins, silverware—whatever else you might need."

She was going to say that the takeout order was enough, then another idea struck. A *good* one.

"You know," she said, "I just might need a little more help from you after all."

When she told Marcos what she had in mind, he grinned and nodded his head in agreement. Then he turned to the hostess. "Give her whatever she wants."

Five minutes later, as Leah waited for her order, she went into the courtyard to cut a few sprigs of the fuchsia-colored bougainvillea with the scissors the hostess had given her.

As she took the last cutting, she wondered how Javier would react to her surprise.

The man was a little moody at times and hard to read, so it was anyone's guess. But the idea had certainly put a bounce in her step and a smile on her face. She just hoped it did the same for him.

Javier had just talked to Jeremy Fortune, who'd told him he'd be sending him to the rehab unit tomorrow or the next day, depending upon when they had a bed available.

"You won't have to stay very long," Jeremy added. "After you're discharged, you can do the rest of your rehab as an outpatient."

"That's the best news I've had in months." Javier blew out a weary sigh, glad to see some light at the end of the tunnel, even if he still had a long road to full recovery and a life he'd have to recreate in many ways. "You have no idea how badly I want to get out of here."

"I can imagine." Jeremy placed a hand on Javier's shoulder. "You've been through a lot these past two months. In fact, if you ever feel the need to talk to a professional, I can refer you to someone."

Javier stiffened and clucked his tongue. "Did my family put you up to that?"

"No, they didn't. Do they think you need counseling?"

"It was suggested," Javier admitted, before making his own opinion clear. "But I *don't* need it."

"I'm not saying that you do. Just know that it's available should you change your mind. And that if you do decide to talk to someone, it wouldn't be a sign of weakness."

Maybe not, but Javier already felt like a ninety-pound weakling going up against a UFC fighter in a championship bout, and that's what frustrated the hell out of him.

Still, Jeremy had a point—and Javier knew that his family had reason to be concerned, too.

"Well, I've still got several patients yet to see," Jeremy said, "so I'd better finish my rounds."

"I…uh…" Javier heaved another sigh. "I'm sorry, Doc."

"What for?" Jeremy asked.

"For snapping at you." Javier ran his hand through his hair, which was shorter than he was used to, thanks to the neurosurgery he'd had two months back. "I've been pretty quick-tempered lately, and you don't deserve to be the target of my frustration."

Of course, neither did his family. Maybe he really *should* talk to a counselor, someone he could unload on instead of the people who loved him the most.

"Don't worry about it," Jeremy said. "You've got every reason to be irritable. You nearly died, spent a month of your life in a coma, woke up in pain and confusion. And now that you're facing some intensive physical therapy… It's enough to make anyone touchy."

Yeah, well maybe Javier had better figure out a way to shake that dark cloud that hovered over him. His future might be messed up, but he didn't need to make everyone else's life miserable, too.

"I'll see you tomorrow," Jeremy said as he turned to go. Then he stopped in his tracks, allowing someone to enter the room.

But not just any someone. It was Leah.

What was she doing here? She was supposed to be off today.

She was definitely not on the clock since she was wearing regular clothes—a black sweater and jeans. Her glossy auburn hair had been pulled back in a soft, loose ponytail.

She'd draped a striped, brightly colored serape over her shoulder. What was she doing with a Mexican blanket that looked a lot like one his sister Isabella might have woven?

Leah greeted Jeremy first. "Hello, Dr. Fortune."

"Do you need any help?" he asked. "It looks like you've got a full load."

That was for sure. In one hand, she held a heat-insulated bag with the familiar Red logo, and in the other, she held a couple of sprigs of bougainvillea.

"Thanks for the offer, Doctor. But I've got everything balanced just right."

As she placed the insulated bag on the chair near Javier's bed, Jeremy stepped out of the hospital room and into the hall, leaving the two of them alone.

"What's all this?" Javier asked.

"I decided to surprise you with a picnic."

In the hospital? Was she kidding?

"I would have taken you out into the rose garden in a wheelchair," she added, "but I figured this was better for now."

"What's in the bag?"

"Carne asada, rice, beans, chips, salsa, guacamole… And a taco salad for me."

Javier didn't know what to say. Nor could he get over the sight of her in a form-fitting sweater and a pair of tight jeans, rather than those blousy hospital scrubs he was used to seeing her wear. More than once he'd tried to imagine what she hid behind the loose-fitting fabric, but now…?

Dang. There wasn't much need to guess. Denim didn't lie. At least, hers certainly didn't.

She draped the serape over the portable bed table. Next, she pulled out a small vase and filled it with a couple of sprigs of the bougainvillea that he suspected she'd found growing in one of the clay pots in the courtyard of his family's restaurant. Then she placed it on top of the serape-covered table.

For a moment, he almost forgot that he was in a hospital—and that he'd been there for ages.

He nodded toward the Cinco-de-Mayo-style decorations. "That's a nice touch."

"I thought so." Her smile nearly turned him inside out. He'd always considered her attractive when she'd tended him as his nurse, but now?

His head was almost spinning as he tried to take it all in, tried to take *her* all in. He'd never seen hair that color—a rusty shade of auburn—and wondered if she ever wore it loose and wild.

He'd only seen it pulled back and out of her face, but he could imagine it splayed across a white pillow...

Cut it out, he told himself. Thoughts like that weren't going to do him any good in a place like this.

He was tempted to call her Florence, to try and put some lighthearted humor into the situation, but all he could think of was one of the oldies but goodies his dad used to play on the radio in the car. "Just look at her in those blue jeans, her hair in a pony tail."

She could be Venus, as far as he was concerned.

He hadn't even been alive when that song had first come out, but he was tempted to hum the tune or even belt out the lyrics—something he'd been known to do when the mood struck him.

And it was the first time the mood had struck him since last Christmas Eve, when he'd sung "Grandma

Got Run Over by a Reindeer" just to make the kids laugh.

"I hope you don't mind me bringing lunch," Leah said.

"Not at all." Heck, right now, he didn't care if she poked him with a hypodermic needle. "It was a really nice thing for you to do. Thanks for thinking of me."

How many nurses went above and beyond the call of duty like that?

He reached for the button that lifted the head of his bed higher, then adjusted the pillows so that he was sitting up.

As Leah removed the food from the red bag, he caught a whiff of beef and spices, of cilantro and chili, and his stomach actually growled.

"This is going to be some picnic," he said as his eyes scanned the food she set out on the serape-covered table.

"Eating outdoors would have been nice," she said. "But look at it this way, at least we don't need to worry about avoiding ants or using sunblock."

"You've got a point there."

Moments later, with the table set, she pulled up a chair to sit beside his bed and they began to eat.

Javier stuck his fork into a piece of marinated beef and popped it into his mouth.

Dang. When was the last time he'd tasted meat so tender, so tasty?

After relishing another bite, he said, "I can't tell

you how much I appreciate this. How'd you come up with an idea like this?"

"It just struck me on the way home last night. You've been eating at the hospital for weeks on end, and while I think the food is pretty good, I can see where you might get tired of it."

He'd gotten tired of just about everything in the hospital. Everything except his nurse.

"I asked Marcos which meal was your favorite," she said, "and he suggested the carne asada. Would you have preferred the chile rellenos? Or maybe the tamales? He said you liked them, too."

"No, this is perfect. If I'm still in this room tomorrow, maybe I can have someone at Red deliver us another meal. I owe you one now."

"You don't owe me anything."

That's not the way he saw it. If not for Leah, he might have gone stir-crazy weeks ago.

They finished their meals in silence, but that didn't mean Javier's mind wasn't going a jillion miles an hour—plotting and planning—much like it used to do before the injury.

Finally he said, "I'm going to be transferred to the rehab unit within the next couple of days."

She paused, her fork in midmotion. Her pretty eyes, a whiskey shade of hazel, widened. Then she smiled. "That's good news. You're getting closer to being able to go home. I bet you can't wait."

He wanted to leave the hospital; that was a given.

But he wasn't keen on the idea of never seeing Leah again.

Why had she done all of this for him? And on her day off?

He could read all kinds of things into her effort to surprise him, he supposed. But he wouldn't. Instead, he planned to enjoy the meal and the nurse who'd brought a bit of sunshine on a mundane day, the beautiful Florence Nightingale who'd provided him with a taste of the real world he was about to reenter.

Chapter Three

The next morning, while Dr. Fortune was making his rounds, Javier learned that he would be transferred to the rehab unit within the next hour or so.

After two long months, he would finally put that devastating, life-altering tragedy behind him. But leaving the third floor also meant leaving Leah.

He supposed he could always look her up after he was discharged from the hospital completely, but not until he was back on his feet and had a better grip on just who the post-tornado Javier really was—and where his future lay.

Still, he hoped to see her before he left, to say goodbye, to talk one last time. But he might not get the chance since Karen, one of the other third-floor nurses, had already come in and told him she'd been assigned to his room for the day.

Karen was nice enough, but she wasn't...

Well, she wasn't Leah.

Javier had just turned on the television to watch the midday news when his dad, Rafe and Isabella entered his room.

Determined to be a little more upbeat and better tempered than he'd been in the past, he greeted them, then reached for the remote and shut off the power to the TV.

"How's it going?" his dad asked.

Javier gave them the good news that he was moving to rehab, which meant he was one step closer to being discharged and sent home.

"That's great," Isabella said.

Rafe and his father broke into smiles, too, clearly in agreement. Then his dad pointed toward the serape that was now draped over the back of the chair by his bed. "What's that doing here?"

Javier smiled, thinking about the lunch he'd shared with Leah. "I had a surprise visitor yesterday and she brought that to me, along with some carne asada, which beat the heck out of what I've been eating."

"So Savannah came by to see you," Rafe said with a grin—no doubt pleased with himself for setting it all up.

"Yes, she came by. And she gave me those flowers by the window. But Leah's the one who brought the serape and the food I hadn't realized I'd been craving."

"That was nice of her," Luis said. "The entire nursing staff has been great, but I gotta admit, Leah's one of my favorites."

She was one of Javier's, too.

"When will they transfer you to your new room?" Isabella asked.

"Probably within the next hour." Javier studied his sister, with her long brown hair and big brown eyes. She was actually his half sister, a young woman he'd only met seven years ago.

Javier's father had married young and divorced shortly thereafter. He'd been very involved in Isabella's life, but when his ex-wife remarried and relocated to California, she took Isabella with her and disappeared under the radar for more than fifteen years.

Javier's dad had been devastated to lose contact with his daughter, and even after he married Elena, Javier's mom, and started a new family, he'd never forgotten his "little girl."

When Javier was born, Luis had been thrilled to have a son. Yet he hadn't made a secret of the fact that he would never truly be happy until Isabella was found.

Javier and his brothers knew they were loved, of course. And that they each had a secure position in the family. Still Javier had always gone out of his way to make his father proud and to fill the hole in his heart created by Isabella's loss.

Deep inside, Javier had hoped that his achievements would enable his dad to forget Isabella and to get on with his life.

Of course, Luis had always been incredibly proud of Javier—of all his sons, for that matter. But he'd never forgotten his firstborn or given up hope that they'd be reconciled someday.

By the time Javier finally understood the depth of his father's love for *all* his children, the need to win and come out on top had become so ingrained in his character that Isabella's memory no longer had anything to do with it.

When Isabella finally reached adulthood and found Luis, the entire family welcomed her with open arms, including Javier, who actually liked having a big sister, especially one who was as artistic and talented as she was sweet. And he couldn't imagine what their lives would have been like if she'd never come back home to San Antonio.

Isabella, who'd married J. R. Fortune a few years back, was a talented Tejana craftswoman, as well as an interior designer. So it wasn't a surprise that the handwoven blanket had caught her interest.

"That's amazing." Isabella made her way to the chair and lifted the serape, carefully looking it over. "This is one of mine. Where did Leah find it?"

"I don't know. My guess is that Marcos gave it to

her when she was at Red. She brought that vase and the bougainvillea, too."

If anyone thought the nurse had gone above and beyond, they didn't say it, and Javier was glad. He'd been doing a little too much thinking about what might or might not be going on between the two of them as it was.

"I'll have to ask Leah about it when I see her," Isabella said. "Is she working today?"

"I think so, but I haven't seen her yet."

Javier and his family made small talk for a while, and he did his best to act interested in everything they had to say, especially about what was going on outside the hospital walls. Since he could finally see some light at the end of the tunnel, he was going to have to play catch-up if he was ever going to recreate—or, more likely, reinvent—his life.

Just as his family was saying their goodbyes, Leah entered his room.

She wore a pair of light blue scrubs today, so she was obviously working. And the fact that she'd made the effort to stop by to see him, especially when she didn't have to, brought a smile to his lips.

The Mendozas greeted her, then excused themselves and headed for the door.

When they were gone, Leah said, "You have a nice family. They're so loving and supportive."

Javier merely nodded his agreement.

"I've noticed that you're not always happy to see them," Leah added.

A stab of guilt robbed him of his smile. "It's not that I'm unhappy when they stop by."

"Then what is it? Do you have issues with them?"

"No, it's just that… I don't know. I guess you could say that I feel as though I've failed them somehow."

"How? I don't understand."

By not being at the top of his game…

By being flawed and less than perfect…

By him needing their help instead of it being the other way around…

Javier had always been the one to step up to the plate, the one who'd had money to loan, advice to give, but he didn't feel like admitting any of those things. Instead, he said, "I guess it's their sympathetic expressions that bother me. Sometimes, I wanted to climb the walls—and probably would have, if I could have gotten out of the damn bed."

"They love you, Javier. You can't blame them for being worried about you. First because they thought they would lose you, and now because they sense you're wrestling with something."

She was right on all counts, he supposed. But how did he admit that the struggle was in the realization that he was less than the best—something he wasn't sure he'd ever get used to?

Competition and winning had always come easily for him, whether it was in academics, sports, business…or even romance. But now he wasn't anywhere near as confident about anything, and that bothered him more than he cared to admit to anyone—even to Leah.

"Your family would like to help," she said. "But they can't unless you let them."

He hated feeling helpless, something he'd felt ever since regaining consciousness. But instead of making that admission, he said, "Some roads are meant to be traveled alone."

Leah eased closer to his bed and placed her hand on his arm. "Most of the time, it's nice to have someone at your side or in your corner."

Their gazes met and locked. For a moment, he wondered if she was offering *her* support even though he was about to leave her care. But before he could make any real assumptions, she withdrew her hand and took a step back, as if she'd realized that she'd overstepped her boundaries.

And maybe she had. Javier wasn't up for a relationship until he was back on top, and God only knew when that would be.

While the patients ate lunch and Leah manned the nurses' station, the call Javier had been waiting for finally came in. An orderly was on the way to get him and take him to the rehab unit.

Leah hated to see him go, but it was really for the

best. Hopefully, she'd find the old saying to be true—
out of sight, out of mind.

She took some comfort in that thought until another old adage came to mind. What if absence made
the heart grow fonder?

At that possibility, she clucked her tongue, then
told herself no. Once Javier was gone, she was determined to put him out of her mind and to focus on her
work and the other patients.

Still, she was glad that she would be the one to give
him the news that an orderly was coming to get him,
even though it was Karen's job to do that today. But
Karen had taken an early lunch break and Leah was
covering for her.

So she turned to Brenna, the LVN who was working at the desk with her. "I'm going to step away for
a minute or two. Will you get the phone if it rings?"

When Brenna agreed, Leah went to Javier's room,
where she found him wearing a grimace as he carefully set aside a pair of crutches he'd been using for
balance and then climbed back into bed. Earlier in the
week, Dr. Fortune had surgically removed several of
the pins that had held his broken bones in place until
they healed, leaving some that would remain permanently. So now Javier could stand and bear his full
weight, although it was still painful for him to do so.

"Are you okay?" she asked. "Do you need any
help?"

"No...thanks." His grimace morphed into a pain-streaked scowl, and his words came out in labored huffs. "I've…got it."

She hoped so. He'd just started to use those crutches, thanks to the seriousness of his fractures. He'd been through a lot physically, so there were going to be some tough days ahead. She wasn't sure if he carried any scars beyond what she could see, but she understood why his family had suggested that he get some counseling.

Since she'd already made a note of it in his chart, she wouldn't bring it up to him again.

"Does your family know you're moving to rehab today?" she asked.

"Yeah." He shifted his hips in bed, lifting the sheets and moving his legs to get into a better position. As he did so, he stopped and closed his eyes for a moment, clearly dealing with the effort and pain. "I told them about it yesterday, although I wasn't sure when the bed would open up."

She watched him move again, straightening his legs out a little more.

"Do you want me to call anyone and let them know which room you'll be going to?" she asked.

"No, that's not necessary. They're going to check with rehab before their next visit."

She waited a beat before adding, "I'm a little envious of you and your family. I know there's a downside to having so many people in your life, but there must be some wonderful perks, too."

"Yeah, there are." His expression softened, indicating that the pain he'd suffered from his trek to the bathroom had finally eased. "I take it you don't have many brothers or sisters."

"I just have one—a brother. But Justin and I aren't very close."

"Why is that?"

"I don't know." She moved toward the serape that was draped over the chair, then began to fold it so he could take it with him. "I suppose it's because he's nearly ten years older than I am. He also lives out of state, so we don't see each other very often."

"That's a pretty big age difference. Is he only a half brother?"

Leah could understand why he'd think so. Javier wasn't the first to make that assumption, especially since she and Justin didn't bear much resemblance to each other.

"Our parents got married young," she said. "They loved each other, but they separated and reconciled off and on for years. They finally got it together when he was nine, so they decided to have me."

"It sounds as though your childhood was probably a lot happier than your brother's must have been."

"In some ways it was. But when I was four, my mom was diagnosed with cancer."

"I'm sorry."

Leah didn't usually share that memory unless it was with a patient she wanted to help come to grips with his or her own tragedy, so she wasn't sure what to say.

It had been a long time ago, but she still remembered that sad and lonely period in her life, even though she'd tried hard to put it behind her.

"My mom lived another four years," she said, "although the last six months were especially rough."

"I lost my mother last year, and it was tough on all of us. I can't imagine how difficult it must have been for you as a child."

"It was a sad time, but things happen that are out of our control. And to be honest, it was almost a relief when she passed. She'd suffered a lot, especially at the end."

There'd been another good thing to come of it, she supposed. When her mom had been sick and in the hospital—the surgeries, the chemo, the radiation—Leah had grown close to some of the nursing staff, who'd offered a great deal of comfort and support to her mother, as well as to her. As a result, Leah had decided on a medical career while still a little girl. In fact, she'd never considered anything else.

"Were you close to your dad?" Javier asked.

One might think that would be the case, but that's not the way it had worked out.

"My father never was very good at dealing with his emotions—or with anyone else's. That's part of the reason he and my mom had those marital troubles in the early years. So he found it easier to go to work than to spend much time at home."

"He left you alone?"

"No, we had a housekeeper. But pouring himself into his business made it easier to deal with his loss and easier not to deal with mine."

Silence stretched between them as he pondered either her comment or his response. Then he said, "I've escaped into my work in the past. But I don't have kids."

Leah didn't need him to complete the chain of thought to realize they were on the same page. Being a father required a man to put his children ahead of himself. At least, that's the way it was supposed to happen.

"Don't get me wrong," Leah added. "My dad might not have been home much, but he loved my brother and me. He also provided all the nicer things in life. Justin and I were both able to attend a private college without having to work or get student loans. And I had a closet full of clothes and shelves loaded with toys and books."

Still, the "things" her dad had given her hadn't been able to make up for not having him around. Or for a house that was never really a home.

Even when Justin came back to Red Rock during his summer vacations, he didn't spend much time with Leah. He had a lot of friends he wanted to see while he was in town, so she was left on her own more often than not.

Of course, things really perked up whenever Aunt Connie came to visit. Her mom's sister came to Red Rock each Christmas and once during the summer. It was only natural that Leah had gravitated to the single woman who'd been a loving mother figure. Had Connie lived in Texas, rather than in Florida, things might have been different. *Better.*

Not that her childhood was all that bad.

Leah glanced at Javier, saw him watching her. A thought-provoking silence stretched between them as the seconds ticked by.

Goodness. What was she doing? Lollygagging and reminiscing while she was supposed to be working with other patients?

She glanced at the clock on the wall. How long had she been here? Just a couple of minutes, she supposed, but she couldn't stay. She had to get out of here before she said something she regretted.

Or before *he* did, because the intensity in his gaze was almost…unnerving.

Just the sight of him lying in bed, watching her like that, like he was going to slide over to make room for her to join him…

Oh, for the love of Pete. The man was recuperating from near-fatal injuries. He certainly wasn't having those kinds of thoughts.

So why in creation was she?

As she took a step back, preparing to return to work, Javier lobbed an easygoing grin her way. "You're spoiling me, Florence. I hope the nursing staff in the rehab unit is as good to me as you are."

Her heart warmed at the affectionate tease, yet her pulse rate slipped into overdrive, too. This particular patient was going to be her undoing, if she'd let him. But that was her secret.

So she returned his lighthearted smile, as well as his tease. "You're in luck. The rehab nurses are incredibly competent. The only one you need to watch out for is Brunhilda. They say she ran a torture chamber in a past life and isn't fond of men. So I hear tell she can be brutal at times."

"I'll keep that in mind." Javier zeroed in on Leah, saw the glimmer that lit her eyes, revealing a playful side he hadn't always been privy to.

He couldn't help but add, "Then maybe I ought to refuse to go and just stay here, where the nurses are fond of their male patients."

Her smile drifted away and she bit down on her bottom lip as if he'd struck a sensitive spot.

Was *she* fond of him?

Before she could respond, an orderly with a wheelchair entered the room, followed by a candy striper pushing a small cart.

For a moment, Javier wondered if Leah had been relieved by the interruption or sorry for it.

"Javier Mendoza?" the orderly asked.

"Yes, you've come to the right place," Leah said. Then she turned to Javier. "It looks like your ride is here. Do you have everything ready to go?"

"Pretty much." Javier threw off the covers, then made the effort to swing his legs over the edge of the mattress and sit up in bed.

He wasn't sure what was going on with Leah—or if they'd merely shared a few flirtatious but meaningless moments during his stay.

Either way, he'd always looked forward to her visits, even if it was to give him medication or run some test. And he hoped he'd see her again.

As he prepared to stand, he wondered what the old Javier would have said to her at a time like this. Without a doubt, that Javier would have jumped on the chance to ask her out, even at the risk of hearing her say no. But the new Javier wasn't sure which of his limitations were going to improve remarkably with rehab and which he'd be stuck with for life.

So he'd be damned if he'd pursue anything with her at this point. What man wanted his lover to double as his nurse or caregiver?

Not many.

And certainly not him.

He stole a glance at Leah, watched as she placed the folded serape in a white plastic bag that bore the blue hospital logo. She wore a quiet expression, a pensive one he'd give anything to read.

Did it bother her to see him leaving? Was she going to miss him?

Before Javier got a chance to either give it some serious thought or to shake it off completely, the orderly pushed the wheelchair closer. "Do you need my help?"

Javier would rather fall to the ground than to admit that he wasn't able to do something so simple on his own.

"No," he said, his movements slow and deliberate. "I can do it."

As he turned so he could lower his backside in the chair, Leah asked, "Are your things packed?"

"Not yet, but I don't have much to take. My shaving gear is in the bathroom, and I've got a few things in that closet."

"I'll get it for you." Leah headed to the bathroom, where she picked up his toiletries. Then she went to the closet and packed the extra pair of pajamas Rafe had brought, along with a pair of goofy-looking socks that served as slippers.

For a guy who'd always slept in the raw, the PJs were enough to make Javier feel as helpless as a child, which cast a dark shadow on his mood.

After Leah placed the bag on the cart, she gathered the rest of his things, including the flowers Savannah had brought him the other day. The other floral arrangements he'd received after his transfer from ICU to the third floor had died and been thrown out long ago, but the potted plants still thrived.

As Leah tiptoed to reach a philodendron from one of the shelves near the window, he watched her top pull up a tad. Too bad it wasn't short enough to show some skin....

Damn, it would have been nice to see her wearing that pair of tight jeans again, rather than those boxy scrubs. Still, she moved with a natural grace and style, no matter what she wore. In fact, there was something classy about Leah. And something sexy that the shapeless medical garment couldn't hide.

If the orderly and the candy striper hadn't been in the room, Javier might have uttered something flirty again. But it was best that he didn't.

Once the cart was loaded and he was seated in the wheelchair, he was tempted to ask Leah if she would come to visit him in rehab, but the question seemed a little too...needy. A little too weak. And for a guy who'd held the world by a string just two months ago, he wasn't about to do anything that made him feel any less of a man than he already did.

Besides, he had too much on his plate right now to be thinking about romance.

Yet he couldn't help wishing that she would come by to see him on her own.

Chapter Four

After the orderly wheeled Javier to the rehab unit, Leah remained standing in his empty room, taking a moment to feel the loss of the man who'd just left.

Talk about crazy. She rolled her eyes and started back to the nurses' station, only to find the doorway blocked by a petite brunette carrying what appeared to be a box of chocolates.

"Excuse me," the woman said. "I'm looking for Javier Mendoza. I could have sworn his brother told me he was in three-fourteen."

"Up until a few minutes ago, this was his room. You just missed him. He's been transferred to the rehab unit."

The attractive visitor knit her brow as though confused or disappointed.

"That's actually good news," Leah said, offering some reassurance. "After he spends a week in rehab, he'll be released from the hospital altogether."

The woman's striking blue eyes, which had been enhanced by a thick application of mascara, lit up. "*Oh*. Then that *is* good news."

Leah scanned the well-dressed visitor, who was in her mid to late twenties, wishing she could find fault with her appearance or her style, but she couldn't.

"Can you tell me how to find the rehab unit?" the brunette asked. "I've been waiting to visit until the family gave the okay."

"It's on the east side of the hospital. You'll need to go down to the second floor, which is the only access from here. Then follow the signs. You shouldn't have any trouble finding it."

Her perfect smile gleamed. "Thanks so much. You've been a great help."

"No problem." Leah returned the woman's smile, although her own fell short of sincere.

As she watched the brunette turn and walk away, her hips swaying, her high heels clicking upon the hospital floor, Leah realized she was the second beautiful woman who'd come to see Javier in the past three days. And since Rafe had obviously orchestrated both visits, it seemed like a natural jump to assume they were both old lovers—or maybe even current ones.

A green-eyed twinge, which felt a bit too much like jealousy, rose up inside of her, but she did her best to tamp it down. Why should she give a darn if women were clamoring for an opportunity to offer Javier some tender loving care?

The only explanation she could come up with was that some transference was taking place, the psychological phenomena that occurred when a medical professional found him- or herself attracted to a patient—or vice versa. They often imagined themselves in love when it was just a fleeting attachment taking place. And she wasn't going to fall into that trap.

So she shook off those lingering, inappropriate thoughts and feelings, as she headed back to the nurses' station, determined to focus on her work.

She'd barely taken a seat behind the desk when the phone rang. She answered it. "Third floor nurses' station."

"I'm sorry to bother you, but I just called Javier Mendoza in room three-fourteen, and he isn't answering. I spoke to his brother last night and he suggested I stop by to visit. But once I arrived in the lobby, I realized that I should have called first and made sure that it was…you know, okay with him. Is now a bad time?"

Probably, since the brunette who'd just come looking for him was probably arriving in Javier's new room about now. But Leah wasn't about to help the man juggle his lovers, so she said, "Mr. Mendoza has been moved to the rehab unit. It's on the east side of the hospital. Take the lobby elevator to the second floor, then follow the signs."

"Thank you *so* much."

Something told her that Javier wouldn't be anywhere near as thankful for her answer as the caller had been, but if he'd been dishonest in his relationships, then it served him right.

As Leah hung up the receiver, she couldn't help wishing that there really was a rehab nurse named Brunhilda—and that she'd been cracking her knuckles, waiting for Javier to arrive.

Oh, for Pete's sake. What kind of adolescent thought was that?

Still, in spite of a decision to put Javier Mendoza out of her mind for good, she couldn't help wondering how many women he'd been seeing.

More than he could keep track of, no doubt. Before the tornado struck Red Rock, he'd probably had a different woman on his arm every night of the week. And if that were the case, Leah was lucky he was gone. She'd never trusted cocky, overconfident men who refused to make a commitment or to keep their promises.

Just like Stephen Gardner, the man who'd broken Aunt Connie's heart.

When Leah was a teenager, Connie had spent a summer in San Antonio, where she'd met a handsome and charismatic attorney. She'd fallen hard and fast for him. And why wouldn't she? The man had wined and dined her until she was walking on clouds.

One night, she'd come home and told Leah how deliriously happy she was. "I'm calling a Realtor in the morning and putting my house on the market."

Leah had been thrilled, not only for Connie but for herself. She adored her aunt and hadn't been able to think of anything better than having her nearby so they could see each other daily. But before Connie could list her condo in Palm Beach or give notice at work, Stephen had ended things—over the telephone.

"I care for you," he'd told her, "but I think it's best if we take things slow."

Connie had been crushed, of course, but she'd decided to let him have a little space and time, hoping that he'd come to realize what she'd already known— that their relationship was meant to be.

Then, just days later, while Connie and Leah had gone out to dinner to celebrate Leah's birthday, they'd seen Stephen out on the town with another woman.

Connie was heartbroken, to say the least. And she'd immediately canceled her plans to move to Texas. When Leah had dropped her off at the airport, they'd both cried their eyes out—saddened by what would never be.

And even now, years later, Connie was different— more somber. The whole Stephen thing had changed her.

But enough of that. Leah wasn't going to stew over

the past, so she reached for the file of one of her patients. She wanted to double check the dosage of the new antibiotic Dr. Wang had ordered.

Before she could open it, Brenna, the LVN, approached the desk. "Have you got a minute? I'd like to ask you a question."

Leah looked up from her work. "Sure. What is it?"

"Do you know anything about Brice McNally, the new intern on the fourth floor?"

"No, not really. Just that he came here from Johns Hopkins and that he's supposed to be sharp. Why?"

Brenna bit down on her bottom lip, then shrugged. "I don't know. He…well, he asked me out. And I told him I'd think about it."

"Are you looking for advice?"

Brenna nodded. "Yes, I guess so."

"For what it's worth, I try to make it a practice not to date anyone I work with. It makes life easier that way."

"I had a feeling you'd say that." Brenna blew out a wobbly sigh. "And you're probably right. I need this job, and I don't want to have any problems at work."

Leah studied the young woman, saw the dilemma in her eyes.

"It's just that…" Brenna shrugged a single shoulder. "He's amazing, and I was so flattered when he asked me out. But I can see where things could get awkward. I'm not the only woman who's interested in him. Know what I mean?"

Leah nodded her agreement. Since she spent so much time at the hospital, both of her relationships had been with men she'd met on the job. And that's what had made things a little more complicated when they hadn't panned out.

"Sometimes those workplace romances can turn awkward," she said.

Brenna paused a beat, then asked, "Have you ever had one?"

"Yes, but it didn't last very long." About six months after Leah had landed the job at San Antonio General, she'd been attracted to one of the interns, too. They'd dated for a while, but the flirtatious doctor was too caught up in himself to settle down.

"If the opportunity came up again, would you reconsider?" Brenna asked.

"I actually did give it another try about a year ago, although that relationship bit the dust before it even had a chance to blossom." Several months after the breakup, Leah had agreed to go out to dinner with a radiologist she'd met in the hospital cafeteria. The guy was solid, dependable and family-minded, but he was also incredibly dull, and she hadn't been able to imagine living the rest of her life with him.

Sadly enough, she couldn't imagine living the rest of her life alone, either. But she'd come to think that having a husband and a baby might not be in her future. But that was okay. Her job and her patients had become her life's plan.

Brenna frowned, then shrugged again. "But what if I don't go out with Brice, and he turns out to be…"

"The *one?*" Leah asked.

Brenna nodded.

"That's the risk you'll have to take. I can only tell you what's right for me." And that's why she needed to steer clear of Javier—and not just because he was a patient. She had reason to believe that he wasn't the kind of guy to go the distance in a relationship. So Leah would be a fool to get involved with someone like him no matter how handsome he was, how charming his smile.

At the sound of rubber-soled footsteps, Leah looked to the left and spotted Karen, the RN who'd been assigned to Javier's room today, returning to the desk.

"I'm sorry for taking so long," Karen said. "First, I was at lunch, then I was called into an emergency situation in room three-twenty-one. What's going on?"

"Javier Mendoza has gone to rehab," Leah said, "so his bed is now empty. But other than that, things have been quiet."

"Good."

Karen was clearly glad to know that the floor hadn't been left shorthanded, while Leah couldn't help thinking it was "good" that Javier was gone.

Of course, she'd been left with a Texas-size hole in her day. And in spite of her resolve to steer clear of the man, the next morning, curiosity—or whatever else it might be—got the better of her and she decided to stop by the rehab unit during her lunch break to see how he was doing.

Javier, his head still damp with sweat, had stretched out on his bed after returning to his room following a difficult workout. He'd done all the therapist had asked and more, hoping to shorten his time in the rehab unit and return home. He'd be in therapy for quite some time, but at least he'd be out of the hospital.

Interestingly, his drive had returned, and he'd found himself pushing through the pain with a goal in mind. And *that* had felt good.

He glanced around his new room, which was smaller than the one he'd had on the third floor. That didn't matter, though. If all went according to plan, he'd be headed home in less than a week.

As his gaze landed on the clock on the wall, he realized that Leah would be taking her lunch break soon. If he was still on the third floor, she'd probably stop by to see him on her way to the cafeteria. She'd tell him that another nurse would be checking in on him while she was gone. But instead of slipping off, she'd hang around for a while, refilling his pitcher of water, making small talk.

He wondered if she was as dedicated to all her patients. Or if she'd found something special about him.

Damn. He was going to miss her.

But that wasn't going to get him anywhere. He had a goal in mind now, and that was to heal as quickly as possible and get back on his feet. Even if Leah felt the least bit interested in him, there wasn't anything appealing about a man who could barely walk on his own.

Still, in spite of his determination to heal and get back into the swing of his life, he couldn't help wondering what was going on back on the third floor. And wondering what Leah was up to.

He missed her smile, the lilt of her voice, the glimmer that lit those pretty hazel eyes—a shade that turned golden whenever she wore a green top.

The desire to see her again was hard to explain unless he admitted the obvious: he was missing Leah a hell of a lot more than he'd ever thought he would.

"Hey, there," a woman's voice sounded from the doorway. But it wasn't just any voice. It belonged to the nurse who'd captured his thoughts more often than not. And the dazzling smile she offered him was a far better gift than chocolate or flowers.

As she entered his room, Javier's mood lightened like a bouquet of helium balloons.

"Hey yourself," he said.

Leah made a quick scan of his new surroundings. "Well, what do you know? You're alone. I can't believe it."

"Yeah, well, it seems that they don't check on the

patients nearly as much in here as they did on the third floor. Or maybe the nurses aren't as competent."

"I wasn't talking about the medical staff," Leah said. "I expected you to have visitors. After all, I can't count how many women called or stopped by to see you, even after you were transferred." She wore a grin, but the way her eyes had flared, the tone of her voice...

Was she *jealous?*

Javier liked thinking that she might be, but he didn't want to play games about something like that.

"There couldn't have been more than three," he said, making light of the visits from Savannah and Maria, as well as the one from Jessica. "And they're just friends."

At least, they weren't any more than that now.

"As soon as I get my walking papers," he added, "the first thing I'm going to do is hunt down my brother and chew him out for sending every woman he meets to visit me."

The glimmer in Leah's eyes softened, as though she'd taken some comfort in his explanation.

"Nevertheless," she said, "I have a feeling things got a little awkward for you yesterday."

A smile stretched one corner of his lips. "Just a bit. But I've always found honesty to be the best policy. So there weren't any catfights, if that's what you're thinking."

She eased closer to the bed, but not quite close

enough. "I had a feeling you were a player in your pre-hospital days. So I'm sure you had no trouble soothing ruffled feathers—or rather, fur."

There it went again—that flicker in her eyes that seemed to chastise him for something she knew nothing about, something she thought he'd done, even though he hadn't.

"I dated two of those ladies," Javier admitted. "And while it might appear that they didn't know about each other, they did. I've always been up front and honest in my relationships."

"Which means what?" Leah asked, folding her arms in front of her as if protecting herself.

"I dated Savannah in the fall and Maria was a summer fling. But I never made either of them any promises."

"So you only date one woman at a time?"

"Usually. But if not, I've always told them that they weren't the only women in my life. If they weren't okay with that, then they'd find someone else."

"So you're a commitment-phobe."

"Not at all. I just haven't met anyone who made me want to settle down and have a serious relationship."

The truth of that statement struck something deep inside, something tender and raw. To be honest, and Javier wasn't ready to open up that much to anyone, he'd been reevaluating his life over the last few weeks.

He'd come pretty close to meeting his maker, and while he still had a long road ahead when it came to recovery, he'd taken a good hard look at his family. The fact that Rafe and Isabella had found love and were starting families reminded him of something he didn't have. Something he hadn't realized he wanted.

"So you'd settle down if you met the right woman?" Leah asked.

"Sure." But even if he actually found that particular lady, he couldn't very well settle down until he was back to his fighting weight.

That same dark shadow that had plagued him since coming out of the coma settled over him again, reminding him that life as he'd known it was over.

The two things he'd always counted on—his body and his brain—had failed him. And while he knew he'd see some improvement with time, he wasn't sure how much. That in itself was hard enough to deal with, but how was he supposed to get by without his mojo?

In the past, he'd been gifted with an inherent streak of luck, but it had run out on him the day that tornado struck Red Rock. And he feared he'd never get it back, that he'd never be back on top again.

"What's wrong?" Leah asked.

What was he supposed to tell her? That he missed the old Javier? That he might even be feeling sorry for himself?

Nope, he wasn't going to do that. So he conjured a phony smile and gave a half-assed shrug. "I guess the therapy took more out of me than I thought."

Then he risked a glance at her face to see if she'd bought his excuse, only to recognize sympathy as well as skepticism in her eyes. Great. Just what he needed. The only woman he'd found the least bit appealing in the past two months saw him as a wimp.

But maybe that was for the best. He wasn't anywhere near ready for a relationship—and who knew when or if that would change.

As Leah studied Javier at rest, his hair still damp from the physical workout he'd had earlier, her heart went out to him. She didn't doubt that he'd just gone through a grueling therapy session, but the pain he'd suffered and the effort he'd gone through hadn't put that shadow in his eyes. Something else was bothering him—that same something his family had noticed.

Unable to help herself, she eased closer to the bed and placed her hand over his. It was just a sympathetic touch, a gentle reminder that he had people who cared about him and a boatload of support. But when her fingers grazed his skin, a zap of heat shot clear to her bone and kicked her heart rate into overdrive.

As their eyes met and their gazes locked, something warm and charged with energy stirred between them. And for a moment, their brief connection melded into a solid and palpable bond.

Afraid to acknowledge whatever was simmering between them, she addressed his mood instead.

"What's really bothering you?" she asked.

He didn't respond right away. About the time that she was giving up hope that he would, he chuffed. "I'm not used to being laid up, crippled or weak, so I'm struggling with it, okay?"

His disclosure, his vulnerability, struck something deep inside her. The dedicated nurse within— or maybe it was the lonely woman—ran her fingers over his knuckles, along his wrist and settled on his muscular forearm. "There's nothing weak about you, Javier. You're recovering from life-threatening injuries that might have killed a man who wasn't in top physical condition. But you survived. And not only did you pull through, that strength and drive that made you successful before is going to make you better than ever."

With that, she removed her hand altogether, releasing the patient who'd stirred her in ways no one else ever had, and took a step back. She knew what to expect from the professional side of her, but those womanly thoughts and urges left her a little unbalanced and seeking a quick escape.

"Thanks for the vote of confidence," he said. "I've always been an optimist, but after the injury…"

Again, the nurse spoke up. "It's only natural that you'd focus on your limitations, but instead, look at how far you've come. Two months ago, your family called in a priest to give you last rites. And you've continued to improve to the point you can now walk. It's just a matter of time. You'll be home before you know it, and you'll hold the world by a string once again."

He didn't argue, but she wasn't sure that he was entirely convinced.

Still, that was reason enough for her to leave, to let him get back to the life he had once led. Because she didn't want to witness him morphing back into the successful real estate developer and entrepreneur who'd charmed attractive women right and left. Not that Leah had any real evidence that Javier was that kind of man—just a suspicion, a hunch.

Of course, even if he was a player at heart, maybe the accident had brought about a change in him, a good one.

Or was that merely wishful thinking on her part, brought about by transference?

She hoped that's all it was, since patients sometimes fell for their doctors—or their nurses, as the case may be—but that feeling was supposed to be fleeting. And the more time Leah spent with Javier Mendoza, the stronger her attraction grew.

"You're good at that," he said.

"At what?"

"Putting things in perspective, forcing me to see the whole picture."

Maybe so, but she wished she could actually take her own advice. She needed to take a big step back and let the rehab nurses do their jobs. Still, she thanked him for the compliment.

"So tell me," Javier said as the shadow in his eyes faded, leaving the whiskey-brown as clear and intoxicating as a double shot of Scotch. "How did you manage to get by this long without someone slipping a diamond on your finger?"

The crooked slant of his smile, the teasing tone of his voice, set off a buzz in her bloodstream and a sexual longing deep in her core. And by the intensity in his gaze, she suspected that she wasn't the only one feeling a rush of desire.

But she had to cut it off before it got out of hand, so she said, "I haven't met the right guy yet. And since I take my job seriously, I don't get many chances to meet eligible bachelors."

For a moment, she thought Javier would jump on the "eligible bachelor" line, but he didn't.

"You don't have to go out on the town to meet someone," he said. "There's got to be a doctor, lab technician or medical professional who's caught your attention."

Yes, once upon a time there had been. But neither of those relationships had worked out. And something told her that flirting with Javier Mendoza wouldn't work out so well either.

"I make it a point not to fish off the hospital pier," she said, even though her opportunity to "fish" anywhere else was limited due to her work schedule.

"That's too bad," he said.

Was it? The glimmer in his eye and his boyish grin

suggested that he might be imagining himself as one of those fish; she certainly was. But Javier Mendoza was off-limits to her—no matter where or how she'd met him.

"I'll settle down someday," she said. Then she added, "When the time is right."

And the timing couldn't be any worse than it was right now, even if transference or hormones argued otherwise. So she'd have to get her head out of the clouds, since a down-to-earth woman like her wasn't anywhere near ready to enter the high-speed dating world of an "eligible bachelor" like Javier Mendoza.

In fact, there were probably a lot of reasons she ought to refuse to go out with him. And as she began to ponder the first of them so she'd be ready with a quick response if he came out and asked her, she realized that she shouldn't have bothered.

In the end, no matter what she'd read in his body language or heard in the flirtatious tone of his voice, Javier let the subject drop, as if he'd never planned to ask her out or to see her again once he was discharged and went home.

Chapter Five

Five days had passed since Javier had entered the rehab unit and four since he'd last seen Leah. To say that he missed her visits was putting it lightly.

Their paths had crossed daily while he'd been on the third floor, yet with his move to the east side of the hospital, he might as well be on a deserted island.

He wasn't sure what that meant, but the truth was, as nice as the other nursing staff had been to him, he hadn't given anyone else a passing thought. The hospitalization and the long road back to recovery had taken an emotional toll on him, but Leah had managed to begin a healing process on the inside, on something he couldn't see.

So he would look her up as soon as he could walk

across the room without the use of crutches or a cane—a decision that gave him another reason to push harder during his physical therapy sessions.

Sure, she'd claimed that she didn't "fish off the hospital pier," but Javier wasn't a coworker. And he wouldn't be a patient at San Antonio General much longer if that bothered her.

So where was she now? Was she working today? Or was she trying to avoid him?

The thought that she might be distancing herself from him didn't sit well, even it if was probably for the best at this point in time. After all, he still grimaced in pain when he walked, still had to steady himself with a cane or crutches, still required time to recover from the effort to move from his bed to the bathroom, which he needed to do now. So there was no way that he'd ask her out until he was back on top of his game.

But when would he be fully mobile? What if by the time he did get back to fighting weight, she got involved with someone else?

And why did it seem to matter so much if she did?

Grumbling under his breath, he threw off the covers, rolled to the side and slowly swung his feet over the edge of the mattress. Then he reached for his cane and made his way to the bathroom.

Thanks to Isabella, who'd brought sweat pants and T-shirts for him to wear while in rehab, he no longer needed to wear those blasted PJs. So, in a sense, he'd taken one more step toward his goal of getting out of here and going home, where he could recover on his own.

After washing up at the sink, he splashed water on his face, then dried off with a towel before making the slow trek back to bed. Once he'd gotten settled on the mattress and the pain of walking had subsided, he tried to imagine himself at home, stretched out on the sofa, watching a ball game. But he'd been away so long. Two months seemed like an eon, and even now, when he was nearing the end of his hospitalization, the minutes ticked by at a snail's pace.

As he reached for the television remote, he heard footsteps moving down the hall and slowing at his doorway.

He wished he could say that a pair of Crocs had made the sound, but whoever it was wore a pair of street shoes. Still, he turned to the door just as his father entered the room carrying a familiar guitar case.

"What are you doing?" Javier asked, reaching for the remote to turn down the television volume. "Why'd you bring that here?"

"I thought you might like having it around." Luis carried the instrument to the window ledge and leaned it against the wall. Then he turned to Javier and smiled, looking for a moment like the man he'd once been before his wife's unexpected death had knocked him to his knees.

When Elena Mendoza died of pneumonia last year, the entire family had been heartbroken, but none as much as Luis. The couple had been exceptionally close and happy, so Luis now bore the ragged marks of grief that had deepened the fine lines on his face into wrinkles.

Not that he was bent or stooped, but his dark hair had also begun to gray at the sideburns and he no longer wore an easy smile.

At fifty-eight, he still had the physique of a younger man, but his shoulders didn't seem nearly as broad as they'd once been.

Had the fear of losing Javier so soon after his wife's death created additional stress on him?

Of course it had. And with that realization, a pang of guilt shot right through Javier, making him want to do whatever he could to ease his old man's worry.

"Thanks for thinking about me," Javier said.

"Yeah, well, music helps you relax. And you've been through a lot, first with your mom…and then the accident."

After his mother died, each of her sons had grieved in different ways. Javier had closed himself off to the world with only his guitar for company. And his music had helped a lot during those first few days after the funeral. But he'd soon found that focusing on his business deals had worked the best to ease the pain and to get him back into the swing of things.

Thankfully, his family had managed to rally, supporting each other, just as they'd done during Javier's recovery from near-fatal injuries.

"I would have brought your guitar to you sooner," Luis said, "but I didn't think they'd let you play when you were on the third floor."

"That's for sure. And the rehab nursing staff will have my hide if I create a racket."

Strumming the chords always took his mind off his troubles, but he wasn't about to play the thing while he was in the hospital. While tempted to ask his dad to bring the case closer, to open it up, he didn't.

"No one's going to complain if they hear you play, *mijo,* especially if the songs are soft and soothing. The other patients will probably enjoy hearing it."

Maybe so. He'd always found music to be therapeutic. Whenever business pressures built in the past, Javier would pick up his guitar and find a quiet place to play. Before long, a calming sense of peace would settle over him, leaving him relaxed and ready to face whatever challenges came his way.

Everyone who knew him—his family, teachers and friends—claimed he had the talent to pursue a career on the stage, but music was more of a hobby to him.

Instead, when given an opportunity to work with Roberto Mendoza, a distant cousin who had a thriving real estate business, Javier had jumped at the chance. And he'd never been sorry. His drive and ambition had served him well, leading to financial success and the purchase of quite a few properties he'd developed himself.

"Have you heard from Roberto?" Javier asked his dad. "I haven't seen him for a while."

"He's in Austin, putting together another real estate venture, but he'll be home soon."

"I'll bet he's missing Frannie and the kids."

"Without a doubt. He adores his family."

A couple of years back, Roberto had married Frannie Fortune, his old high school sweetheart. They were now raising their grandson Brandon, who was just a few months older than Maribel, their three-year-old daughter.

"I'm sure you're eager to get back to the office," Luis said, although an arched brow suggested he wasn't so sure about anything Javier was thinking or feeling. And he wasn't.

No one knew that he still struggled with being less than perfect, less than the best. As far as he'd been concerned, the guy who came in second was merely the first loser.

But Javier's father had suffered enough already, so he said, "You're right, Dad. I'm ready."

Maybe instead of strumming the guitar strings he ought to call someone and have them bring his laptop so he could access the internet, check a zillion emails and ease himself back to work.

Getting into the swing of things at the office might help him forget about Leah, too.

* * *

After Leah's last visit to the rehab unit, she'd forced herself to stay away from Javier for nearly a week, yet thoughts of him continued to plague her, especially when she knew he was only a five-minute walk down the hospital corridor. And as far as she knew, his time at San Antonio General was nearing an end.

What was she going to do when he was discharged and left the hospital for good?

She had no idea. Even with him being out of sight, he'd been on her mind more than ever. So in spite of her better judgment, she took some time during her lunch hour to visit him one last time.

With each stride she took toward the rehab unit, her steps grew peppier, her heart lighter—until she reached his room and found his door shut.

She would have turned away, but the guitar music coming from inside caught her by surprise.

Was he watching television?

There was only one way to find out, so she knocked lightly.

The strumming stopped, and the rich, baritone sound of Javier's voice said, "Come on in. It's open."

Leah reached for the knob, gave it a turn, then let herself inside his room. But the sight of Javier, sitting up in bed, with a guitar in his lap, stopped her in her tracks.

The past few days in rehab had given him a casual,

comfortable air. If he hadn't been in a hospital room, she might have forgotten that he was still a patient.

"Well, sing of the devil," he said, his deep and sensual voice wrapping her in a velvet embrace. "I thought you'd left me for good, Florence."

For the first time since he'd been transferred to her care, she was struck speechless from… What? Longing? Attraction? Desire?

His boyish grin and whiskey-colored gaze were almost mesmerizing, and it was easy to see how a woman could lose her head around him. In fact, Leah wondered just how many actually had.

She certainly struggled to stay in control.

In order to break the arousing eye contact and to end the awkward silence, she nodded toward the guitar he held. "I had no idea you were a musician."

"I'm not really. It's just a hobby."

The chords she'd heard hadn't sounded like those of a beginner or a hobbyist, but she let the comment go and made her way to his bedside, kicking herself as she did so.

Just as she'd feared, absence seemed to have made her heart grow fonder. And whatever she'd been fighting while in his presence had only grown stronger, more difficult to tamp down and keep under control.

"So how's it going?" she asked.

"It's all right. I guess I lucked out while being here."

"What do you mean?"

"I haven't seen hide nor tail of a nurse named Brunhilda. She must have quit right before they transferred me to rehab."

Again came that lazy grin, that teasing glimmer in his eyes.

Leah smiled, soothed by his easy manner while lured by the aura of sexual attraction that had built with each step he'd made toward full recovery.

What was she going to do about that? Hope that it ran its course before she fell in too deep?

Or maybe let it unfold naturally and see where it went?

"That *is* good news," she said. "So I take it the nurses have treated you well."

"Well, not as good as you did. But I don't have any complaints. I just wish that I could say the same thing about my physical therapist. He's an old military man, so he pushes hard. But he reminds me of my high school football coach, who used the same approach, which ought to be just as effective. With some hard work and perseverance, I'll be back up to speed in no time at all."

She certainly hoped so. He'd been through so much already.

As she scanned his room, which didn't have anywhere near as much medical equipment as his old one, she noticed quite a few get-well cards that had been prominently displayed along the window ledge.

"Isabella did that," he said. "And I didn't have the

heart to tell her I didn't want that stuff displayed for all the world to see."

The fact that he hadn't wanted to hurt his sister's feelings or to argue was a good sign.

"You didn't have that many cards before. Apparently, your many friends and admirers are coming out of the woodwork."

"Thanks to my brother. Rafe must have told everyone in town that I need cheering up."

Every *woman,* most likely.

Leah managed a smile. "It must be working. You're looking more upbeat."

"It's the music. It always does that to me." He strummed the guitar for a moment, again lulling her while luring her with slow but seductive chords. Then he looked up, smiled and nodded toward the door. "Would you mind closing that for me?"

"Not at all."

When she'd done as he asked and turned back toward him, he said, "Have a seat."

As she settled into the chair by his bed, he began to play a familiar tune, and she found herself drawn by both the man and his music. While he sang, telling the tale of a lady who was down on love and the cowboy who set out to mend her broken heart, the soul-stirring lyrics and music touched something deep within her.

When he finished, it took a moment to find her breath, let alone her voice.

"That was beautiful," she finally said. "I had no idea you were so talented. Have you ever sung professionally?"

"No."

"Have you ever considered it?"

"Not for longer than a moment or two. My family sometimes ropes me into singing for them at birthday parties and get-togethers, but not very often."

"I can see why they'd want you to sing."

He paused for a moment, then said, "Don't get me wrong. I don't mind doing it. But if performing was a job, it wouldn't be fun anymore."

Too bad, she thought. He had a wonderful voice— rich and seductive—as well as a great command of the guitar. It wouldn't take him long to build a fan base. But if getting on stage wasn't his thing, then he'd made the right decision.

She let the subject of his talent drop and said, "You're looking good. You even have a little color in your cheeks."

"My therapist and I worked outside for a while today. And I'm glad we did. Being in the sunshine and breathing in the fresh air felt great."

Maybe that's all he needed—to be out of the hospital and back on his feet. She'd have to mention that to his family if they brought up the idea of a counselor again.

Leah noticed an open laptop resting on Javier's tray table, which was a pretty good indication that he'd begun to move into the real world again. "I see you've been doing more than watching television these days."

He nodded. "I asked my dad to bring in a few things for me. I'm trying to play catch-up, but it's going to take a while. I must have a million emails to wade through, not to mention some online banking I needed to do. If I hadn't made two payments to the utility companies, I would've had turn-on fees—and no power or water when I got home."

She supposed his family had been too worried about him to think about making sure his bills had been paid while he was out of commission. From what she understood, his finances were solid, so he wasn't in debt, just behind on sending out checks.

"How much longer are you going to be here?" she asked.

"A day or so maybe. Jeremy wanted to consult with my neurologist. He's going to let me know what's going on when he makes his rounds today."

"I'll bet your family is planning a huge celebration when you're discharged," she said, knowing how concerned they'd been, how supportive of him.

"I wouldn't be surprised, but I'm not up for any parties. I just want to go home and sleep in my own bed for a change."

She couldn't imagine being hospitalized for more than two months, but before she could comment, a knock sounded at the door.

"Come on in," Javier called out.

Jeremy Fortune entered. When he spotted Leah, he seemed a little surprised.

"I thought I'd stop by and visit Javier," she said. "I'd heard you were going to release him soon, and I wanted to say goodbye and wish him the best."

Jeremy nodded as if her explanation made total sense. But why wouldn't it? No one knew what she was thinking, what she was feeling.

Goodness, how could they when *she* didn't even have a clue?

"Looks like Leah stopped by just in the nick of time if she wants to say goodbye." Jeremy scanned Javier's room, then broke into a smile. "We're going to send you home, which we'd better do before you nest in here for good."

"I take it that I've been given the green light," Javier said.

"Yes, you have. We have another test we'd like to run before we cut you loose, but nothing major. I see no reason you can't go home this evening—unless you want to hold off until morning."

"No, I'd like to go as soon as I can. I'll call around and see if I can find a ride home."

"I'm off duty at six," Leah said before she could consider what she was offering.

"You wouldn't mind taking me home?" he asked.

She certainly ought to mind. What had she been thinking?

Visiting him at the hospital was one thing; she

could explain that to herself and whoever might ask. But if she knew where he lived, if she delivered him home, she'd be tempted to stop by to see him again. And then where would she be?

Of course, it was too late to backpedal now. "No, I don't mind at all. That is, unless you'd rather ask someone else to take you."

Javier tossed her a bright-eyed grin. "To be honest, I'd actually like going home with you."

Going home with her?

She knew what he meant. He was talking about the ride she'd offered. But she couldn't help thinking about getting him in her car, driving straight to her house, putting him in her bedroom and continuing to monitor his recovery and care.

But that was the most absurd and inappropriate musing she'd had in days. Still, she managed to conjure a carefree smile and said, "Great." Then she nodded toward the open doorway. "I'd better get back to work. I'll see you around six."

"Good deal."

Was it? She wasn't so sure. But as she slipped out his door and started down the corridor, she found herself wearing a silly grin and humming the tune Javier had just sung to her.

After Javier signed the discharge paperwork, he called his family to give them the good news: he was

finally going home. Needless to say, they'd been over-
joyed.

While he'd talked to Isabella she'd suggested that
she and J.R. throw a party for him at their ranch, but
Javier had asked her not to bother planning anything.
He'd certainly regained some strength and built up a
bit of endurance over the past week in rehab, but he
had a long way to go until he felt the least bit normal.

As far as he was concerned, there was no real
cause for celebration yet. He might be walking again,
but he had a limp. And he still struggled to stay on
top of the feeling that his once charmed life had been
stolen from him.

His dad and his brothers, including Miguel,
who'd flown in from New York City two days ago,
and Marcos, who was spending all of his free time
at home with Wendy and their newborn daughter,
offered to pick him up at the hospital and take him
anywhere he wanted to go. But Javier told them he
already had a ride lined up.

He just hoped it hadn't been a mistake to accept
Leah's offer. But she'd been the one person he'd
looked forward to seeing, the only one who seemed
to understand how he felt and what he'd been through,
the one who had a ready smile and drew one from him
without fail.

In fact, he'd been tempted to ask her out several
times after he moved from ICU to the third floor—
and again after he was sent to the rehab unit. But he

hadn't broached the subject. After all, she deserved a man who had his life together, his future mapped out. And Javier wasn't there yet.

Since he'd packed his belongings a couple of minutes ago, including the guitar, he took a seat in the chair near the bed until Leah got off work and came for him.

Fortunately, he didn't have to wait very long.

"Hey there," Leah said as she walked into his room. "I just clocked out, so I'm free to leave. Is everything still a go? Are they still discharging you this evening?"

"Everything's done. All I have to do is ask for an orderly to wheel me out to the curb."

"Then I'll get my car and meet you there."

Five minutes later, Javier was carefully maneuvering himself from the wheelchair and into the passenger seat of Leah's black Honda Civic. "I appreciate your offer to take me home."

"No problem. Just tell me where we're going."

His first thought was to suggest they go out on the town, maybe have a drink at his favorite upscale country-and-western bar, but the old Javier was still out of commission. It would be a while before he stepped out on a dance floor again or heard another bartender announce last call.

"I probably ought to stop by the pharmacy," he said. "I've got a couple of prescriptions to pick up."

"Should we swing by the market, too? If you

haven't been home in months, you'll probably need to stock up on some food."

"Actually, I should be okay. I have a lady who comes in regularly—at least, she did before I was laid up. I called her yesterday and asked her to clean out the fridge, then to stock it for me." He'd also asked her to stop by tomorrow so he could pay her, and she'd insisted upon helping him to settle in.

"Sounds like you've got everything under control," Leah said as she gripped the wheel.

Not like before. But he nodded and said, "It's an old habit."

"You mentioned doing some online banking. I hope you paid your cable bill. You're going to need your TV."

He didn't know about that. He'd watched enough television over the past few weeks to last him a lifetime. And while it had helped the days to pass, he'd gotten pretty sick and tired of watching game shows and old movies, although he still enjoyed *Pawn Stars*.

Even ESPN, which had always been a favorite cable network, hadn't done much for him other than remind him of his physical shortcomings, so he'd steered clear of that channel.

So once he got home, he'd probably avoid TV for a while. He had a state-of-the-art entertainment center and looked forward to listening to some good music for a change.

"The utilities are working, and the house is in

order. So I've got everything under control." He stole a glance across the console, wondering if Leah was buying him being on top of it all.

Sure, his bills had been paid and Margarita had stocked his fridge and pantry with food. The TV worked and so did the surround sound system.

But the things he'd really enjoyed doing like morning runs, biking and playing tennis were lost to him. At least for the unforeseeable future. Still, he had Leah to himself for the next few miles. And he planned to enjoy every minute of their time together.

Chapter Six

After stopping by the pharmacy, Leah followed Javier's directions to his gated community and pulled up in front of the condominium he pointed out as his.

She had to admit that she was a bit surprised at the part of town in which he lived. Sure, she'd known that he'd been successful and financially secure, but she hadn't realized he lived in one of the more exclusive areas of Red Rock, which was impressive by anyone's standards. And she couldn't help commenting on what he'd probably heard a hundred times. "This is a great neighborhood."

"Thanks. It was one of the first developments my cousin Roberto and I worked on. I liked the location and the builder, and had been offered my choice of units. So I snatched this one because it's on the green-belt and close to the pool and the biking trails."

She couldn't help wondering if he was going to invite her into his home, and not just because she was eager to see what it looked like on the inside.

"If you unlock the door," she said, "I'll bring in your things."

"I'll carry something."

"How are you going to do that? You're walking with a cane, remember?"

He grew silent. She hadn't meant to remind him of his limitations, but he was just getting to the point where he could walk from point A to point B. Why risk a fall now?

Minutes later, Javier opened up the door and turned on the lights.

"What a beautiful painting," Leah said as she spotted the brightly colored artwork he'd purchased in San Antonio.

"Thanks. The artist is especially talented. Isabella knows him and suggested I check out his work when I was decorating the place."

"It was a great suggestion," Leah said. "And you made a good choice."

After dropping off the first load of his things on the floor near the sofa, she returned to the car for the rest of them, the last of which were two potted plants he'd received during his stay on the third floor.

"Do you mind if I place these on the kitchen counter for now?" she asked.

"That's fine. Thanks."

While in the kitchen, she scanned the interior, taking note of the black granite counters and the stainless steel appliances that would be up to Emeril's standards. Then she returned to the living area, picking up on the scent of lemon oil and cleaning products, as well as noting the professional decor.

With its modern leather furniture and touches of chrome and glass, it could have been one of the models in the presale days.

In the living room, where Javier had settled on the sofa, she spotted a state-of-the-art entertainment center. And she couldn't help thinking the interior decorating had been customized with a bachelor in mind. Still, it required a comment of some kind.

"Your home is beautiful," she said. "And spotless. It hardly looks lived in."

"That's probably because it's been vacant for months."

That's not what she'd meant. But she let it go. He'd mentioned having a cleaning lady, so the woman had probably had plenty of time to spend polishing the place while he'd been gone.

"Have you had dinner?" she asked. "Do you want me to fix you something to eat?"

"That sounds good—if you'll join me. You've got to be hungry, too."

She was. And while the smartest thing to do would be to fix him a quick sandwich, throw back the covers on his bed, then skedaddle, she found herself saying, "Sure, why not?"

And that's the attitude she maintained for the next thirty minutes as she took a couple of chicken breasts from the freezer and defrosted them in the microwave. She found pasta and spices in the pantry, which she used to create a flavorsome dinner for two.

When she entered the living room to tell him dinner was ready and ask where he wanted them to eat, she found music playing on the stereo and the blinds opened to reveal a beautiful array of city lights.

Clearly, she'd been right about this being a bachelor pad. And about Javier knowing how to set the stage for romance.

Of course, with her wearing a pair of hospital scrubs, it was hard to imagine him having romance on his mind. And while that should be a relief, she couldn't quite muster a smile.

"Why don't we eat in here," Javier said, indicating the dining room table. "I haven't had a meal with any ambiance since... Well, since last year."

The tornado had occurred at the end of December, and while that had been a couple of months ago, technically he was right. But a second thought struck her.

He hadn't mentioned the tornado. Was that on purpose? Was he trying to put it out of his mind while he dealt with the aftereffects and his recovery?

Or was she reading way too much into it?

"I'll bring in our plates," she said, deciding to drop the subject completely. "What would you like to drink?"

"I'd like a glass of wine, but with the medication I'm on, I'll have to pass. But you can open a bottle for yourself."

She wouldn't do that. She still had a ten-minute drive home, and… Well, a glass of wine, added to a view of the city lights and a handsome dinner companion, made this meal seem way more than it was.

Again disappointment flared and raked over her like the needles on a cactus.

"I spotted some lemons in the kitchen. Why don't I make us some lemonade?"

"Sounds good to me."

Moments later, they sat down to eat at the formal dining room table, which provided an amazing view of the city. If she'd been dressed differently, if she'd worn some makeup or had done her hair, it might have felt like a date of sorts.

As it was, it was a quiet dinner for two between friends.

After they finished eating, she helped him settle in on the sofa. "I'll put the leftovers in the fridge. There should be enough for your lunch tomorrow."

"Thanks, Leah. I really appreciate this—the ride home, the meal, the pleasant company."

"You're welcome. It was nice, wasn't it?" She

nodded toward the kitchen. "I'm going to take the plates to the sink. I'll be back in a few minutes."

"Don't bother washing the dishes," he said. "The cleaning lady is coming by tomorrow to see if I need anything. So I'll have her take care of that."

Leah slowed her steps, then turned to face him. "I'm not leaving the mess for someone else to do."

"Margarita will be happy to have something to do once she gets here," Javier said.

Leah doubted that. She'd never had the luxury of having hired help. At least, not after growing up, moving out of her dad's house and getting a place of her own. But rather than make that comment, she said, "I'm not comfortable having someone else pick up after me."

"Believe it or not, neither am I. But you don't know Margarita. Trust me on this. She'll be delighted to have something to keep her busy."

Leah found that hard to believe. "Why do you say that?"

"It's who she is. When I was a teenager and our family lived in San Antonio, she was a neighbor. She didn't have kids of her own, so she kind of took to my brothers and me, making us cookies, taking us to the movies and that sort of thing. When her husband died, leaving her in a financial bind, she had trouble finding a job. By that time, my parents had already moved out to the ranch, where my dad works now, so I made a job for her, even though I'm not home very often. In fact, sometimes I leave a mess just so she has something to do when she arrives."

Leah tried to wrap her mind around what he was saying. He hired a woman for a job he didn't need, then went so far as to find things to keep her busy?

"She likes fussing over me," Javier added. "And it's kind of nice knowing that we're doing each other a favor. Besides, my mom asked me to look out for her, and since it was the last favor my mother ever asked of me, I plan to keep Margarita both busy and employed."

Leah waited for him to continue, but the conversation seemed to have stalled. And a whisper of sadness crossed his face.

Was he thinking about the promise he'd made to his mom? Or was he still struggling with her loss? How long had she been gone?

"When did your mother die?" she asked.

He paused for a moment, then said, "Two years ago this month."

His eyes glistened and he glanced out the window, as if searching for something in the city skyline. But she figured the only thing he was really looking for was an escape from his grief, from the memory.

"I'm sorry," she said.

"Yeah. Me, too. It was quite a blow."

Instead of remaining in the center of the room, Leah returned to the sofa and took a seat next to him—not too close, yet within an arm's distance.

"What happened?" she asked. "How did she die?"

"She had a chest cold and a cough. She expected it to run its course, but it only got worse. When we finally insisted that she see a doctor, she was running a high fever. We all figured a shot of penicillin or something like that would make all the difference, but it didn't. Apparently, her cold had developed into pneumonia—an exceptionally virulent strain that didn't respond to antibiotics.

"The doctor called an ambulance while she was still at his office. And they took her directly to the hospital. But by the time she got there, her fever had topped one hundred and five. And nothing brought it down. In spite of everything they did, she died that evening."

The story, the sadness, draped over Leah like an old cloak she'd worn once herself.

"We wish that we'd insisted she seek medical care sooner," Javier said. "But I guess that's water under the bridge now."

"Sometimes medical care isn't enough," Leah said, thinking about some of her patients who'd died in spite of medication, surgery or the latest treatments.

"My dad took it hard," Javier added. "I guess we all did. But he's kicking himself for not insisting that she see a doctor a few days earlier, when they might have been able to help her."

Was Javier feeling the same way his father did? Or

was he blaming someone—his father, the doctor or himself?

Leah reached over and placed her hand over his, giving it a gentle squeeze, trying to offer compassion, sympathy…friendship. "I didn't mean to dig up old memories."

"Don't worry about it. I've come to grips with her loss. But it's tough sometimes. We were actually pretty close, so I really miss her. And that's why Margarita thinks she has to look out for me. And why you need to leave some of the mess for her to take care of tomorrow."

Again Leah faced the possibility that she might have made false assumptions about Javier. She couldn't quite grasp how a man who juggled his romantic relationships would be the kind of man who'd call his mother his friend and grieve her loss two years later. A man who would create a job for a woman who'd made cookies for him as a child.

"So go ahead and put the leftovers in the fridge," he said, "but leave the dishes. Okay?"

"Can I at least let them soak in the sink?" she asked.

A smile spread across his face, chasing away the shadows of grief. "You drive a hard bargain, Florence."

Leah smiled, then reached across the seat and patted his hand one last time. "Why don't you stretch out and put your feet up for a while. I'll be back in a minute or two."

True to her word, she placed the leftover chicken and pasta in a plastic container before refrigerating it. Then she filled the sink with hot, soapy water and left the dishes to soak.

But there was no way she'd leave the kitchen without making sure she'd wiped down the countertops. What if she actually met Margarita some day? She wouldn't want the woman to think she was irresponsible or messy.

When she returned to the living room and spotted Javier lying on the sofa, she nodded toward the doorway that had to lead to his bedroom. "Do you want me to turn down the covers for you?"

"No, that's not necessary. I can handle it."

She supposed he could, so she said, "If there's nothing else I can do, then I'll head home."

"I don't need anything else—unless you'd like to hang out for a while. I like having you around."

She was tempted to stay and chat longer, but knew it wasn't a good idea.

"I've got a cat to check on," she said, even though Miss Kitty was probably fine.

Yet she still didn't move toward the door. Why was she dragging her feet?

She really ought to say her goodbyes and get out of here. But her reasons for dashing off no longer held any merit. After all, she hadn't known that Javier had such a tender heart. Nor had she realized there was much more to the man that just a handsome face, a sexy smile…and an incredible musical talent.

He'd loved his mother and had called her his friend. And he had a strong, loyal streak, not to mention a generous nature.

"Well," she said, "I should get out of here so you can get some rest. Do you have anyone who can stay with you tonight?"

"No, I don't need anyone here. I'll be fine."

Still she found herself hanging out, hanging on. And she wasn't sure why. At a loss as to what to say or where to go from here, she threw a question his way—one she couldn't help asking, "Would you like me to swing by tomorrow and check on you?"

Javier hadn't expected Leah to take such a personal interest in him, and he wondered what she would have suggested had he told her he didn't feel good about spending the night alone.

He wasn't the least bit uneasy about it, though. That's why they'd had him stay an extra week in rehab—to make sure that he'd do fine on his own.

So he said, "Sure. That would be nice if you stopped by tomorrow. But if something comes up, I understand."

"I've got a couple of days off and no real plans other than reorganizing my garage."

As Leah strode toward her purse, which she'd left

on his recliner, Javier got to his feet and reached for his cane.

"Where are you going?" she asked.

"To walk you out to your car."

"You don't need to do that."

"I know. But it's dark out there."

She smiled, revealing a pair of dimples he hadn't noticed while he'd been hospitalized. "That's what porch lights are for."

Still, as he got to his feet, she waited. Then she slowly made her way to the door, as if making sure she didn't get too far ahead of him.

At least that's what he told himself. Yet as he followed behind her, trying to catch a glimpse of her silhouette through those boxy scrubs and not lucking out, he couldn't help remembering she was a nurse. A woman who was only doing what came naturally to her—taking care of the sick and wounded.

Like it or not, he was one of her wounded, one of her patients. And while he liked the idea of her coming by again to check on him tomorrow, he realized she was doing it out of sympathy.

Sure, there *might* be something else going on, too. But nothing he wanted to cultivate just yet.

He probably ought to tell her not to bother going out of her way. He had more family and friends than he knew what to do with, and each one would be calling or stopping by to check on him.

But none of them was Leah. And she was the one he preferred having around.

He'd dated more than his share of women in the past—some just for dinner, others for more than that. Yet none of them had looked out for him the way Leah had. Or maybe he hadn't let anyone else see his vulnerable side or get this close to him before.

Who knew what was really going on, but he opted to go with the feeling, the desire to see her again.

When they reached his front door, she opened it. Then she flipped on the porch light. "See? I can make it on my own."

Yeah, and so could he—even if he wasn't at one hundred percent yet and had no idea if he ever would be again.

"I owe you," he said.

"No, you don't. I'm glad I could help."

They stood like that for a moment, his legs aching from the workout he'd had before leaving the hospital and threatening to give out on him. But he was willing to take the risk, just to stand upright—and next to Leah. To see her eye to eye, to see how her head matched up to his. How his lips would fit over hers.

"I'll see you tomorrow," she said, her voice soft, husky.

Her gaze locked on his and her spring floral scent swirled around overhead.

It took all his willpower to refrain from reaching

out and running the knuckles of his hand along her cheek, to seek the softness.

The struggle between lust and love was nearly killing him as he fought the urge to remove the clip from her hair, to free those silky auburn strands and watch them tumble down her back.

With the smallest effort, he could tip her chin up and press his lips against hers....

But he had a long way to go before he won the right to do that, and in spite of all the hormones and pheromone pumping between them, he kept his hands to himself and said, "Thanks for the ride and for fixing my dinner."

"It was my pleasure."

No, it had been *his*. And one of these days, if he pushed himself hard enough in physical therapy, he would do everything in his power to earn the right to pleasure them both—and in more ways than one.

As Leah turned and walked away, Javier leaned against the doorjamb, trying to support himself and to keep from collapsing.

Yet he was unwilling to turn around and close the door until she was gone.

All the way home from Javier's condo, Leah had gripped the steering wheel as though she could ensure staying in control of both her vehicle as well as life as she knew it.

Their evening together had been surreal, ending

with what seemed to be a romantic moment only to dissipate as quickly as it had risen. When Javier had walked her to his door to say goodbye, she could have sworn that he'd been sorely tempted to kiss her. Or maybe she'd just hoped that he would.

To be honest, she wasn't sure if she would have let him or not.

Okay, that in itself wasn't true. Last night, as they'd stood in the doorway, as his eyes had zeroed in on hers, she knew exactly what she would have done if he'd lowered his mouth to hers.

She would have kissed him.

But he hadn't kissed her. And to make matters worse, she'd asked herself why all the way home. Had she merely imagined their attraction? Was it only one-sided?

If that were the case, she'd really gone out on a limb when she told him she'd return the next day.

Once she'd gotten home last night, she'd gone through the motions of feeding Miss Kitty and giving her the meds the vet had prescribed for arthritis. Then she'd turned on the television, only to find her thoughts a million miles away.

Well, not quite that far. They were across town, with Javier.

She'd dreamt about him off and on that night and finally woke a little after seven with Miss Kitty snuggled at her feet and the morning sunlight filtering through her blinds.

If truth be told, she was sorry she'd volunteered to check on Javier. After all, it's not as though he was an only child and all alone in the world. He had a big support system, including a number of concerned family members lining up to visit him and to make sure he had everything he needed.

She'd met them all at least once while he'd been hospitalized and under her care, including the brother who lived in New York City.

Okay, so she'd committed herself to driving back to his house today for a visit. But that didn't mean she had to rush over first thing in the morning, which would make her appear much too eager to be a part of his life.

But isn't where all of this was heading? She blew out an exasperated sigh.

Too bad he hadn't mentioned anything about his feelings for her—whatever they might or might not be. It would have made it easier for her to deal with her own feelings.

She'd give anything to be able to compartmental- ize her thoughts into a neat little box marked as inap- propriate and out of reach.

After a light breakfast of fruit and yogurt, she threw a load of colored clothes into the washer, then went for a run.

When she returned, she took a shower and sham- pooed her hair, using the new products she'd pur- chased at the salon last week. She took care to choose a special outfit—something more feminine than the hospital scrubs she seemed to wear more often than not—and settled upon black slacks and a pale blue knit top.

Then she blow-dried her hair with a rounded brush, adding body and a little curl to the ends. When she was finished and pleased with the results, she applied a dab of mascara to lengthen her lashes, as well as a light shade of lipstick.

It was just after noon when she climbed into her car and drove to La Montana Vista, the complex where Javier lived. He'd given her the gate code last night, as well as the number of his unit, and she hadn't forgotten.

After parking at the curb, she made her way up the walk, then rang his bell.

She'd expected Javier to answer or to call for her to come inside, but a silver-haired woman in her late sixties swung open the door.

Leah might have worried that she'd transposed the house number had she not recognized the Spanish-tiled entry and the colorful Southwestern painting that hung on the wall.

"You must be Margarita," Leah said.

The woman nodded. "And you are…?"

"Leah Roberts. I was Javier's nurse."

The older woman brightened, then reached out her hand in greeting. "It's so nice to meet you, Leah.

Javier mentioned that you brought him home last night and prepared his dinner."

Leah's cheeks flushed warm. "I'm sorry for not cleaning up after myself."

"Oh, pshaw. Javier told me that he insisted you leave them. Please don't give it another thought. It only took me a moment or two to load the dishwasher."

"Well, good. I'm glad to hear it. And speaking of Javier, is he up to having company this afternoon?"

"I'm sure he would be, if he were here. But Rafe just picked him up and took him to his physical therapy appointment."

Since Leah hadn't mentioned what time she'd be stopping by or asked about Javier's appointment schedule, she couldn't blame anyone for missing him but herself.

"I probably should have called first," she told Margarita. "Would you let him know that I stopped by to see him?"

"Of course. He'll be sorry he missed you."

Was that true? Leah wasn't so sure. And the embarrassment, the uneasiness, only made her wish she'd kept her mouth shut last night, that she hadn't told him she'd stop by today.

As she turned away and headed to her car, the door shut behind her. Yet she still couldn't shake the lingering disappointment that she'd missed seeing Javier—or the stark realization that she might never see him again.

Chapter Seven

The wind was cool and breezy, the perfect March day for kite flying—if a guy was still into that sort of thing. But Javier had given up kid games and activities a long time ago.

It would have been a good afternoon for a run or a bike ride, too. Instead, he climbed behind the wheel of his Expedition and drove himself to rehab. Ever since his discharge from the hospital, he'd been relying on everyone else to do things for him, which had been a real pain. He'd always prided himself on being self-sufficient, in being one to offer aid to others.

So today he'd taken another step toward independence and control of his life again.

He'd had a standing twelve-thirty appointment

with his physical therapist all week, but he left his house early today, hoping to stop by the third floor to visit the nurses who'd been so good to him and drop off a box of chocolates.

Okay, so he was actually only looking forward to seeing one of them—Leah. And the candy was merely a ploy to make his visit look legit.

Margarita had told him that Leah had stopped by to see him that first morning after he'd gotten home from the hospital, but as far as he knew, she hadn't come back. He probably should have looked her up sooner, but he'd been determined to stand firm on his decision. He didn't want to strike up any kind of romantic relationship until he was back to normal—or at least until he was walking steadily without the use of a cane.

He was definitely improving and getting a little better, a little stronger, each day. But he still wasn't recovering as quickly as he wanted to. Yet after waking this morning, after spending another dream-filled night with Leah, he'd decided to talk to her again, whether he was limping or primed and ready to run a marathon.

So here he was parking in the visitor's lot, getting out of the car and reaching for his cane. He still had months to go before feeling even remotely like the man he'd once been, the man who'd been on top of his game, his career, his life. But Javier wasn't going to let another day go by without seeing Leah.

Moments later, after limping through the lobby and making his way to the elevator, he got out on the third floor and headed for the nurses' station.

Brenna, one of the LVNs who worked with Leah, was talking on the telephone and taking notes. When her call ended, she looked up at him and, as recognition dawned on her face, she broke into a welcoming smile. "What a nice surprise. You're *back*—and all in one piece."

"Well, not quite yet. But I am getting around on my own now, so I thought I'd stop by and say hello to the best nursing staff in all of San Antonio." He handed over the gold-foil covered box. "And to give you this as a token of my appreciation."

"Well, thank you," Brenna said. "Aren't you sweet?" Then she looked up at someone walking their way and called out, "Hey, Leah. Look who's here."

Javier expected the same reaction he'd gotten from Brenna, a bright-eyed smile that announced his visit had been a welcome surprise. But instead, Leah's lips parted and her eyes widened in a way that seemed...

Hell, he'd seen that expression once before. On the face of an old lover when they'd accidentally run into each other on the street. He'd always prided himself in being honest, in not dating a woman who cared more for him than he did for them, although that required a woman to be honest with him, too.

But he and Leah hadn't been lovers or even occasional dates.

Just what had been going on between them? And when had it ended?

"Hey," he said, for lack of a better opening. "I'm not faster than a speeding bullet or able to leap tall buildings at a single bound yet, but at least I'm mobile and driving again."

"I can see that." She finally smiled, but it didn't quite reach her eyes.

Was she sorry to see him?

Again he was struck with that old-lover feeling, the awkwardness. Too bad he didn't have any sexually explicit memories to go along with that I-didn't-mean-to-hurt-you feeling as well.

Leah had on a new pair of scrubs today—a pair of lime green pants and a matching floral print top. Her glossy auburn hair had been pulled back into a single braid that hung down her back. As usual, she wore very little makeup, although she was one of the few women who were beautiful without any of the usual enhancements.

Her natural beauty, those expressive hazel eyes, full lips…

Damn. When had she become so much more to him than a nurse? And why did he feel as though he'd somehow dropped the ball?

"It's good to see you up and around," Leah told him.

Was it?

"How are you doing?" she asked. "How's rehab?"

"It's tough, but going well."

She smiled, her eyes finally showing a sign of the warmth he'd missed seeing.

However, what he'd really like to see again was the expression her face when she'd left his house that night, when the pheromones had swarmed in the porch light. Maybe he should have kissed her when he'd had the chance, but he'd felt as weak as a newborn foal and had feared he'd fall on his face.

And no way did he want Leah to continue seeing him as weak and damaged.

But if he wanted to set things to right, to get back where they'd once been, he'd have to get her alone.

"When can you take a break?" he asked.

Again, her lips parted as if his question had surprised her even more than his arrival had. But she glanced at her wristwatch—one of those no-nonsense styles with a leather band. As she did, he found himself focusing on her delicate wrist, thinking that it ought to sport a diamond bracelet instead.

"Actually," she said, looking up, "I can probably take a break now. Let me check with Marie, who'll have to cover for me."

Javier gripped the counter of the nurses' desk and watched as Leah headed down the hall. Moments later, she returned.

"I've got about ten or fifteen minutes," she said. "Do you want me to find an empty conference room?"

"No," he said. "Let's go out to the rose garden instead. It's only an elevator ride and a short walk from here."

Her eyes finally sparked, as if his suggestion had been a good one, and she nodded.

Five minutes later, they'd left the hospital and began the trek outside to the rose garden, moving slowly thanks to Javier's limp and dependence on a cane.

"It's nice to see the buds opening up," Leah said. "It's usually a beautiful garden, but it's been pretty stark all winter long."

"Now that spring is here, it should be looking good again in another few weeks."

She nodded, scanning the quiet grounds. "When the flowers are in full bloom, it's a beautiful place to reflect or to steal a few quiet moments."

Javier wasn't so much interested in the colors or the beauty the rose garden provided as he was the privacy. He'd just wanted to get Leah alone, but now that he'd done that, he'd be damned if he knew what he would say to her.

His first thought was to ask her out, even though he was a far cry from being completely healed. And while the wisest thing for him to do would be to hold off a while longer, he'd missed seeing her over the past week and didn't want to lose out on what they had—whatever it was.

So he sat in one of the benches, with its green slatted seats and black wrought-iron frame.

Leah took a seat, too.

"I stopped by to thank you for everything you've done for me," he began. "Not just for doing your job, but for understanding where I was coming from, even when I wasn't sure myself."

"No problem. I'm glad I was able to help."

"I know, but it was more than help. You went above and beyond." He didn't dare tell her how he'd waited each day for her to show up in his room, how the hours lugged by whenever she wasn't working.

Leah glanced down at her feet and at the Crocs that matched her scrubs. He had no idea how many pairs she owned, but he suspected it was four or five—each one coordinating with several different professional outfits.

He imagined her wearing a pair of spiky heels and a slinky black dress, with her hair swept up in a stylish twist. What he wouldn't give to see her let loose a little, to be a woman for a change, instead of just a nurse.

They sat like that for a moment, with him tempted to say the words that revealed his thoughts and feelings rather than those that made more sense. Words that would be safer, wiser…

He couldn't go so far as to ask her out.

Or could he?

On numerous occasions, when their conversations had taken a personal turn, he'd noticed how she would smile one minute then turn shy the next. It was almost as if she'd been struggling with her feelings for him, as if torn between woman and nurse.

And wasn't that exactly how he was feeling? Torn between being a man and a patient?

So now what? He had her alone for a few minutes longer. Where did they go from here?

"What did you want to talk to me about?" she asked.

"Mostly, I wanted to thank you for driving me home last week, for fixing my dinner. And also for stopping by to see me again the next day. I'm sorry I missed you. I tried to call but your number is unlisted. I'd kind of hoped you'd come back or leave a number where I could get a hold of you, but you didn't."

There. How was that for letting her know that he'd wanted to see her again without committing to anything else? Was it enough? He certainly hoped so.

The late morning breeze kicked up a bit, blowing a loose strand of hair across her cheek. As she swiped it away, she said, "I just stopped by your house because I'd told you I would. But I didn't see any reason to go back. You were in good hands. Margarita seemed both caring and competent. And your family was obviously taking you to your appointments."

Did she think he no longer had need of her? When it came to being his nurse, that might be true. But when push came to shove, he'd quit thinking about her as his personal Florence Nightingale a week ago— maybe even longer.

He turned to the right, his knee brushing against hers and jolting them both with a surge of physical awareness.

Yes, they'd both been jolted, because she'd been studying those ugly green shoes of hers, then the moment their legs had touched, she'd shot a glance his way and zeroed in on him.

As their gazes met and locked, that same swirl of pheromones kicked up again, urging him to reach out to her, to draw her close, to kiss her or to make some kind of romantic move.

But then what?

He couldn't afford to be that bold right now, especially when he had no idea if and when he would fully recover. Yet in spite of his best intentions and his conflicting thoughts, he couldn't help seeking out some middle ground.

"I'd like to take you out to dinner some night," he said.

"You don't need to do that." She brushed aside that same pesky strand of hair from her cheek again. "I was just doing my job."

They both knew she'd gone the extra mile time and again. And that the seeds of something sexual or romantic hovered over them—both then and now. And while he had no doubts about his ability to make love with her—and to make it good for both of them—he couldn't offer her much more than great sex and a less than perfect body.

Still, he pressed on, wanting her to know the direction his thoughts were heading.

"I'm not asking you to dinner as a token of my appreciation," he said. "I just thought it might be nice to see you wearing something other than scrubs. To sit across a candlelit table. Maybe to toast the future—whatever it might bring."

There. He'd done it. Laid his cards on the table, just to see what she'd say. And if she threw it right back in his face, he wasn't sure what he'd do. He'd never had to deal with something like that before.

"You want to date me?" she asked, lips parting again, her eyes growing wide.

Her expression—disbelief or whatever it was—set his heart on end, and he figured he'd better backpedal. It was one thing knowing that he wasn't good enough for her yet and another to know she was thinking the very same thing.

Still, it's not as though his ego couldn't handle rejection. So he said, "Yes, I suppose you could call it a date."

When she didn't immediately respond, he added, "Not right away, of course. I've got a lot of work to do in rehab yet."

Damn. Why had he admitted that he wanted to go out with her before he was ready to? He hated laying his vulnerability on the line like that.

But he didn't want to lose his opportunity to be with her either. And that was just plumb crazy since he'd never lacked having a romantic interest in his life. And he'd have someone again—as soon as he was walking without that damned cane.

Yet no other woman interested him right now.

"I don't know what to say," Leah said. "I've never dated a patient before."

"Yeah, well, I've never dated a nurse before either. But for the record, I'm not your patient anymore."

So why wasn't she jumping at the chance to go out with him? Her hesitancy was a first for him.

Of course, that's probably because he only asked women out who appeared to be interested in him.

And while he'd sensed there was something brewing between him and Leah, he might have been wrong. Damn. Had he lost his touch with women, with his ability to sense their romantic interest?

He wasn't sure. But he wasn't going to grovel or spin his wheels any longer, so he reached for his cane and, using the bench's armrest to steady himself, got to his feet.

"Give it some thought, Florence. But there isn't any rush. By the time I'm actually ready to take a woman out to dinner again, you'll probably be married with a couple of kids."

She merely sat there, her eyes still wide, her lips parted.

Okay, so he'd definitely lost his touch completely. He could have sworn Leah was feeling something for him, even though they'd never talked about it.

A slow smile slid across her face. "I doubt that I'll be married for a long, long time. My job is my life."

She hadn't said yes or no to his question, and he couldn't help wishing he'd held his tongue, that he'd kept his thoughts to himself.

After all, why would someone as perfect as Leah want to get involved with someone who was only a shadow of the man he'd once been?

Rather than let her sense his vulnerability, he slapped on a happy-go-lucky grin and shrugged it off. "Relax, Florence. It was just a wild-ass idea. Maybe I'll stop by the hospital to see you in a couple of months. We can play things by ear."

Then he forced a chuckle, as if he'd been joking all along, and glanced at his wristwatch. "We'll, I'd better go. I've got a rehab appointment in a couple of minutes, and I'm not as quick on my feet as I used to be. Thanks again for being such a top-notch nurse. You deserve one heck of a raise."

Then he turned and walked away, pushing himself to increase his pace, just so he didn't have to risk another conversation with her.

Or to give her the idea that her reluctance to respond had been a lot more painful than telling him the truth—that she didn't want to go out with him.

As Javier limped away, Leah sat dumbstruck on the bench. She hadn't known what to expect when he'd asked to talk to her in private. Or why he'd suggested they walk out to the hospital rose garden, the one place that she chose when she needed to commune with God or nature, the one place she allowed herself to reminisce about the past and to dream about the future.

She'd thought he might have a medical question for her, something he hadn't wanted to discuss with anyone else. But he'd just asked her out on a date.

At least, she'd thought that's what he'd done. He'd also implied that he wanted to have dinner with her several months down the road.

Why was that?

And why not now?

Sure, the question had taken her aback. He'd asked her in such a roundabout way that she hadn't known what to say, how to respond. And when she'd been tempted to agree—whether that was wise on her part or not—he'd treated the whole thing like a joke.

At that point, he'd dropped the subject as though he'd reached out and grabbed the heated end of a curling iron.

Or course, even if he'd asked her out with a bottle of chilled champagne sitting in an ice bucket, along with two crystal flutes and a bouquet of roses, she would have been even more surprised, more speechless.

And she wasn't entirely sure what why was. While he'd been in the hospital and under her care, he'd flirted with her at times, but he'd never gone further than that.

And he hadn't actually done so now.

Either way, he'd just walked off, leaving her to solve the puzzle on her own.

Or had her hesitancy caused him to retract his question altogether?

Something told her he'd gotten the wrong message from her. Or maybe she'd been the one to confuse the issue.

For a woman who'd sat on this very bench on more than one occasion, wondering if she'd ever meet a special man, she'd certainly botched things up with Javier.

Not that he was the kind of man she ought to date. But he was definitely appealing in more ways than one.

She couldn't let him go without explaining herself and her hesitation. So she got to her feet and started toward him. "Javier? Wait up."

He stopped and turned. "What is it?"

She nearly froze for a moment, then pressed on.

"I'm sorry for not speaking up sooner. I guess the whole idea was a little surprising. But I'd like to go out to dinner with you. That is, if you're serious about it."

He studied her for a moment, as if she might be lying, as if she might be stringing him along. "It was just a thought I'd had."

And one she found irresistible.

"I probably should have called ahead and let you know I was going to stop by," he added. "My visit had to throw you off stride, especially since we haven't seen each other in a week or so."

"I was surprised to see you," she admitted.

"I'm not sure why you didn't come back to my house—unless you're trying to avoid me. And if you'd rather we not see each other again, that's fine, too. Just say the word."

"I made it a point to stay away, but not because I'd been trying to avoid you."

Okay, so that wasn't entirely true. She'd been trying to *forget* him, although it hadn't worked. No matter how many books she picked up or how many TV movies she'd tried to watch, Javier had remained on her mind.

"You don't have to explain, Florence. No harm, no foul."

"I think you're missing the point."

He stood there, as if daring her to explain. So she finally admitted what she'd been fighting for weeks on end.

"I care about you, Javier. Probably more than I should. And I'm not sure it would be in either of our best interests if we dated."

His eye twitched ever so slightly.

"You lead an active social life, and I'm pretty much a work and homebody."

"Yeah, well, my life has been curtailed as of late, and I'm not sure if that's going to ever change."

"Of course it will. You'll be back to your old self in no time at all."

He nodded as if he agreed. But something in his eye, in the way he tensed his lips, said, *Yeah, right*.

"For whatever it's worth," she added, "I'd like to go to dinner with you whenever you're up for it. And I doubt I'll be married by then."

As much as she worried that they were both making a big mistake, that he would be better off with a classier woman, that he ran in a different social circle than she did, she reached into her pocket and pulled out a small notepad and pen she kept handy.

"I'll give you my number, and you can do whatever you want with it." She looked up, caught his eye, then gave him a little wink. "Well, other than give it to someone else."

"You don't have to do that," he said.

What? Give him her number?

Even with the many doubts she had, she still had to admit that she felt something for him. And that it might be a bigger mistake not to give it to him.

What if she *could* trust her feelings? What if the two of them were better suited than she thought?

No closer to an answer, she scratched out her telephone number on a blank sheet, then tore it from the pad and handed it to him.

Javier took the paper from Leah, glad to have a

way of contacting her outside the hospital, yet realizing she hadn't given it freely to him.

"I'm not looking for your pity," he said.

"Pity is the last thing I feel for you."

He searched her gaze, her expression, looking for a sign of truth. "So you admit to feeling something?"

"Yes, but I'm not sure what it is. There's some definite attraction, but I'm afraid it might only be a case of transference on one or both of our parts."

"What's that?"

"It's a psychological phenomenon that occurs when a medical professional finds himself or herself attracted to a patient and vice versa. And it's way more common than you might think… Some patients actually think that they're falling for their doctors or nurses but the feeling isn't lasting. And it's not real." She took a moment to catch her breath, then continued, the words flowing from her mouth in a nervous rush. "It's not ethical for medical professionals to get involved with their patients, so I thought it was best to let those feelings run their course. And so I stayed away for a week…. But it's still a struggle. And I'm not sure why that is."

Javier took a step closer, reached out with his free hand and gripped her shoulder. "You're rambling, Florence. And I've never seen you like this. What's going on?"

She took a deep breath, then slowly blew it out as though she could banish her nervousness and reel in her jabbering. "Being around you is making me this way. I'm attracted to you. And I'm struggling with it, okay? I want to do the right thing, and I'm not sure what that is. And so I'm…"

Javier had no idea what had set her off like that. But the one thing he did gather was that she was attracted to him and fighting it for some reason. Although she was blaming it on transference or some crazy thing, rather than taking it for what it was.

She was flat-out flustered by their conversation— and so damn cute—that he couldn't help but grin.

Nor could he keep from removing his hand from her shoulder, cupping her jaw and drawing her mouth to his.

Chapter Eight

Leah's heart skipped a beat the moment Javier touched her shoulder, let alone her cheek. And she nearly flatlined as their lips met, as their breaths mingled. She reached out for his waist to steady herself, even though he was the one who held a cane.

The kiss, which had started out both sweet and sensual, deepened, their mouths opening just as though they'd been lovers for years. Just as though the dreams she'd been having about him every night for the past two weeks had decided to come true right this moment.

Still, she continued to kiss him—to brush her tongue against his, to dip, to taste. For a moment, she forgot who she was, let alone where she was—

outside the hospital, where any one of her colleagues might glance out a window and see her. But having witnesses didn't seem to matter one little bit right now. Not while she was making note of the fact that Javier Mendoza was the most talented kisser she'd ever known.

Not that she was an expert in the art of foreplay by any means, but just the same, she knew what she liked and how it affected her. And this one?

Oh, wow. What a kiss. Talk about fireworks—and it wasn't anywhere near July.

She leaned into him, knowing better yet yearning for more of the wet and wild heated assault of her mouth.

As he slipped his arms around her, drawing her close, his cane slammed onto the ground, bringing her to her senses.

Bringing them both to their senses.

She slowly pulled her mouth from his, placing her hands on his chest and gripping his shirt as if she could push him away and hold him close at the same time.

What was she doing?

Her cheeks flushed warm with embarrassment— or maybe as a result of raw desire. She had no idea what it was, but she had to gain control of herself. Goodness gracious. She'd have to go back to work in a matter of minutes.

Ignoring the awkward now-what discussion that

was bound to come up, she bent to pick up his cane. After all, what if he fell? What if he hurt himself all over again?

She tried to brace herself and Javier at the same time as she dropped down in front of him, past his belt, over his...

Of for Pete's sake. As she made eye contact with his fly, as she grew aware of a stirring erection, she swallowed—hard. Her heart began to pound like a jackhammer and she didn't know what to do, what to say.

For the second time in minutes the man had left her speechless and nearly brain-dead.

She reached for his cane, then rose to her feet and handed it to him, this time focusing on anything but the man in front of her. Yet her head was still spinning.

"Well, I guess that answers one question," he said.

She had no idea what he was talking about because, when it came to questions, she had a ton of them herself and didn't know where to begin.

"What's that?" she asked, finally making eye contact and hoping her cheeks weren't flushed as deeply as she suspected they were.

"You were right, Florence. You are feeling more than pity for me."

"I don't know what I'm feeling, remember?" She took a step back and crossed her arms.

"Well, there's definitely some chemistry brewing between us."

She couldn't argue that point.

"Maybe we should try kissing again, just to make sure it was the real thing."

Her cheeks heated even more, setting off a rosy flush. no doubt. But it had all been real—the kiss, the arousal, the desire for more. Yet now it was her turn to shrug off the feelings, the magic.

"We'll see about that. But not here."

He scanned the rose garden. "What's wrong with this place?"

"Nothing. It's actually a special place." And now, each time she came back out here, she would think of him and the best kiss she'd ever had.

He cocked his head slightly. "Do you come out here very often?"

She nodded. "Sometimes during my breaks I'll come out here to read, to eat lunch and to reflect." She turned and scanned the bushes that were just starting to bud and show a bit of color. "A few months ago, I had a patient who reminded me of my mother. She had cancer, too. And after we had to tell her that the treatments weren't working, that she was going to die in a matter of weeks, I came out here to keep from bawling my eyes out in front of her."

"Did it help?"

She nodded. "Yes, some."

"So it's a sacred place."

"No, it's not that. I've had a lot of quiet times out here, lost in my thoughts and dreams." And now those dreams were going to include Javier, whether she wanted them to or not.

And even if she never saw him again, every time she walked out to the rose garden, she'd relive that kiss again in her memory.

"I'm not the only one who takes refuge out here," she said, hoping to steer the conversation away from what the rose garden was going to mean to her from here on out. "And it can be seen from the windows of half the rooms in the hospital."

"So you're concerned that someone may have seen us?"

She didn't know what concerned her the most. She just needed to get her thoughts back on track. So she glanced at her wristwatch, noting the time. "We're going to have to talk about all of this later. I have to go back to work now."

"I don't suppose you'd like a kiss goodbye." He cracked a boyish grin.

"To be honest?" A smile crept across her face, matching the one on his. "I'd like that—a lot. But that's not going to happen. I'm going to have a hard time keeping my mind on my patients as it is. And that's not good."

"Okay, I'll tell you what. Go on back to work and do your best to put it out of your mind. We can talk about it tonight over dinner at my place. Nothing fancy."

She didn't know what to say, which was bothersome in itself. She'd never felt so indecisive in her life.

"I'll see you around seven," he added, clearly assuming that she would say yes.

And maybe he knew her better than she thought, because she found herself nodding in agreement as she turned around and walked back to the hospital.

Javier had never planned to kiss Leah—at least, not yet. He'd wanted to wait until she met the man he once was. And while kissing her had complicated things, it had also convinced him that he needed to resort to Plan B, an option he hadn't come up with before.

As much as he'd wanted to be one hundred percent when he asked her out, he couldn't put that off any longer. No way did he want to risk her hooking up with someone else in the meantime. And the kiss— as mind-blowing as it had been—had convinced him to alter his plans.

So he'd asked her to come to his house for dinner tonight, hoping to buy some time to figure out what he wanted to do about her. And kissing her again was definitely on the top of his list.

Damn. He'd known it would be good between them, he just hadn't realized how good. They'd definitely be sexually compatible if things progressed that far. And right now, he couldn't see any reason they wouldn't—as long as he kept improving.

So after she'd gone back to work, he'd made the trek from the rose garden to the rehab unit, where he'd had one heck of a workout session, pushing himself hard, wanting to get better as fast as he could.

And then he'd gone home and crashed for a while.

He hadn't given dinner much thought when he'd invited her. If he'd been steadier on his feet, he might have thought about grilling something.

Too bad Margarita had taken the afternoon off to visit her sister, who was visiting from Guadalajara. He would have asked her to whip up one of her specialties before going home and leaving him and Leah alone.

As it was, he decided to drive to Red and order takeout. After getting out of his car, he limped to the entry of the family-owned restaurant his brother Marcos managed. He'd barely reached the hostess desk when Marcos spotted him and broke out in a smile.

"It's good to see you up and around, Javier. We're going to have to schedule a golf match soon."

"I don't know about that. The only thing I've been able to swing these days is my cane."

"That may be the case, but it's great to see you standing upright. You're looking good." Marcos reached for a menu. "Are you meeting anyone? Or is it just you?"

"Actually, I just want to order some takeout."

"We can do that. What'll you have?"

As Marcos handed over the menu, he said, "By the way, Wendy and I are having a little party next Friday night. Now that Mary Anne is home, we're inviting everyone to stop by for an open house. I hope you can make it."

"I wouldn't miss it for the world. Would you mind if I brought a friend?"

"Not at all. Who is she?"

"What makes you think I'm bringing a woman?"

"Because you'd never bring one of your golf buddies or your business partners to a family gathering. In fact, you'd never bring a regular date, either. This woman must be special. Who is she?"

Javier wasn't sure how to address the idea that Leah was special, even though she was. He wasn't sure if he wanted to let his family know that he'd found someone worth dating for a while exclusively.

"It's Leah Roberts, my nurse."

Marcos grinned. "I had a feeling something was going on between you two, but I kept quiet so I didn't jinx it. Now that I'm happily married, I'd like to see all my brothers find what I've found with Wendy."

"I don't know if things are going in that direction," Javier admitted. "We're really just…tiptoeing around the idea of a relationship. But she knows most of you anyway. And—"

Marcos gave Javier a little jab. "Don't stumble over

an explanation on my account. We'd love to see Leah, so feel free to bring her along. I won't mention anything to anyone about you guys dating, although I'm not the only one who noticed the way you looked at each other."

Javier ought to object, but the truth was, he'd looked at Leah differently than he had the other nurses. And she'd been looking at him in the same way.

He had no idea what would become of them as a couple, he just knew that being with her felt right.

Leah couldn't explain why she'd agreed to have dinner with Javier, since she had good reason not to get any further involved with him than she was. But the simple fact of the matter was their kiss had changed things.

So after getting off work, she quickly stopped by her house to change into street clothes.

If she'd listened to her head instead of her hormones, she wouldn't have gone to the trouble. As it was, after she'd freshened up, she chose a pair of low-waisted khaki slacks and a green top, as well as a lightweight sweater. Then she drove to his house, arriving a minute or two before seven.

Javier must have been watching for her because he opened the door before she had a chance to ring the bell.

He cast an appreciative gaze over her, then smiled. "You look great, Leah."

"Thanks." As much as she'd wanted to claim that kiss hadn't affected her as deeply as it had, that she was immune to his charm and that dazzling smile, she warmed at his praise, which she'd secretly been seeking all along.

"Come on in," he said, stepping aside for her, then closing the door once she'd gotten inside.

"You must be hungry." He led her to the dining room table, with the large bay window providing a romantic view of the city lights. "And since I picked up food for us, it's probably best if we eat first. We can talk over dinner."

Minutes later, they sat across the candlelit table with a Mexican feast spread before them. Javier had chosen grilled chicken, lightly seasoned, along with Spanish rice and a salad with what appeared to be a light sprinkle of cotija cheese over an avocado-cilantro dressing.

"This looks delicious," she said.

"I hope you like it."

"I'm sure I will."

After they'd both picked up forks, he said, "I want you to know that I didn't plan on kissing you in the rose garden today."

She certainly hadn't planned it, either. Nor had she expected him to launch right into the subject before she'd gotten a bite into her mouth. But that's why he'd invited her and why she'd agreed to come.

"I'm not in a position to jump into a romantic relationship with anyone right now," he added. "I've got to focus on my rehab."

That was good, wasn't it? She ought to be pleased to hear it, but an unwelcome stab of disappointment struck hard.

Was he giving her a breakup line before they'd even discussed dating?

"But when I'm ready for one," he added, "I'd like it to be with you."

Leah's heart leapt as a thrill shot through her. Was he indicating that if and when the time came he'd choose her exclusively? That the women who'd come by to visit him in the hospital, called on the phone and sent all those get-well cards would be history? That his days of playing the field would be over?

Aunt Connie had bought that line once, when she'd believed a happy bachelor had found her special and unlike the other women he'd been dating. And that false belief had only led to heartbreak.

Or was Leah reading too much into his simple comment? He'd only mentioned that he wanted to have a relationship in the future. Not now.

"You're not saying anything," he said.

Goodness. She'd been fighting her feelings for him for so long, convincing herself that her emotions couldn't be trusted, that she didn't know quite how to respond.

What if transference had nothing to do with any of this? What if her feelings for him were real?

"I'm…" She set her fork down on her plate. "I'm not sure what to say, Javier."

"There's something going on between us," he said. "Something too big to ignore. I've known it for some time, and I think you have, too. That kiss we shared this afternoon, along with your response to it, are proof enough for me that whatever we're feeling is mutual."

He had a point. The physical attraction—at least on her part—was nearly blinding with intensity. But was it also blinding her from reality? Was she seeing Javier clearly? Could she trust him when he said he was feeling it, too?

"That kiss was amazing," she finally said. "I'll grant you that. And I'm attracted to you. But you're right. Jumping into something at this point in time isn't going to do either of us any good."

"Then we're in agreement there."

Were they?

Then why was she tempted to ask when she'd see him again, when they'd have another opportunity to kiss?

And why did she fear that he only wanted a friendship or a relationship with her to help see him through rehab, when he'd be back to the old Javier?

And who was the old Javier? Her instincts told her he was a lot like the man Aunt Connie had fallen for, a lot like the intern Leah had once dated—a dyed-in-the-wool bachelor who moved from one woman to the next with the ease of changing his socks.

A man she'd be wise to avoid.

Instead, she opted to change the subject. "This chicken is out of this world. You'll have to give my compliments to the chef. It tastes even better than it looks."

"I'm glad you like it," Javier said. "I'll tell Marcos. He's thinking about adding it to the menu."

"Speaking of Marcos, how are things going with him? Are Wendy and the baby doing well?"

"Yes, they're all great. Apparently, Mary Anne is thriving and gaining weight. I haven't seen her yet, so I'm looking forward to visiting them soon."

"Mary Anne's a cutie," Leah said. "I went to the NICU a couple of times and saw her through the window. I know your family was worried about her for a while, so it's nice that she's home now and doing well."

"I hadn't realized you checked on her, but I'm glad you did."

Leah smiled. "I don't always get that close to a patient's family, but in your case, it was easy to do. Your dad is a great guy. And your brothers and sister are nice, too. In fact after hearing so much about Wendy and their concern for her, I went to the maternity ward a few times to visit with her and to give her a report on your progress. Then, after the baby was born, I stopped by the NICU to take a peek at her."

Javier seemed to ponder that for a while, then said, "Wendy and Marcos are hosting an open house on Friday. Why don't you come with me? You'd get a chance to see my family again. The baby, too."

Leah hadn't mentioned that she'd visited the neonatal unit nearly every day after Mary Anne's birth, just for a chance to look at the tiny babies, to watch the mommies and daddies peering into isolettes, reaching in and stroking a tiny foot or hand.

She'd like to see Mary Anne, now that she was healthy and at home. She'd been so tiny, so fragile at birth. Yet so precious, too.

But more than that, attending the party meant that Leah would see Javier again.

Afraid to tip her hand, to reveal her yearning, she said, "I don't know. I'm not a family member, so I'd hate to intrude on a special celebration."

"My family knows how helpful and supportive you've been to me, as well as to them during my hospitalization. And they think of you as a friend. I know they'd be happy to see you there."

What about Javier? Would he be happy to have her there with him? Was that why he was including her?

"I'll think about it." Yet even as the vague, noncommittal words rolled off her tongue, she realized that, deep inside, she actually wanted to go.

She'd always enjoyed being around loving families since she really hadn't had one of her own. In fact, sometimes she wondered if getting married and having children was even in her future. Her own experience as a child, as well as her two attempts at having a romantic relationship as an adult, had resulted in one disillusion after another.

Maybe that's why it was so easy to remain dedicated to her patients. Nursing provided her with an opportunity to nurture others almost daily without risking disappointment and heartbreak.

She stole a glance at Javier, watched him cut into his chicken and take a bite. She'd better focus on the meal in front of her, rather than on dreams that might never come true.

When they finished eating, Javier pushed aside his plate and tossed her a smile. "How about some ice cream? I've got chocolate and strawberry to choose from. And even some raspberry sherbet."

She hadn't left much room for dessert, but she wasn't in any hurry to leave just yet. So she said, "A little sherbet sounds good. Why don't you stay seated? I'll get it. Just tell me which flavor you want."

"Thanks. I'll have the chocolate."

When Leah returned and placed his bowl in front of him, he thanked her again, then added, "I don't usually expect people to wait on me."

"Don't give it another thought. I don't mind at all." Leah took her seat and dug into her sherbet, relishing the sweet, tangy raspberry taste.

As she dipped her spoon in for a second bite, she asked, "What's the first thing you want to do when you're discharged completely?"

"Besides taking you out on the town?"

She smiled, wondering if he really planned to ask her out. Sure, he'd said that he wanted to. But what if he turned out to be as insincere as the lawyer who dumped Aunt Connie and broke her heart?

Leah had nearly fallen for a man like that once, and she'd been determined to avoid playboy bachelors ever since.

Would Javier prove to be different from the man she suspected he'd been before the accident?

She hoped so, because a failed romance with Javier would be a lot harder to bounce back from than either of the two relationships she'd had in the past.

Of course, she hadn't invested all that much emotion in them, and she found herself caring for Javier a little more each day.

While finishing their dessert, they made small talk for a while. Then, when both bowls were empty, Leah stood to clear the table.

"Don't bother doing the dishes. Margarita's coming again tomorrow, and I want her to have plenty to keep her busy."

He'd told her the same thing last time, but just like before, Leah refused to let his housekeeper clean up after her—no matter how badly Javier wanted to provide the older woman with work.

Fortunately, they'd had takeout, so there weren't any pots and pans to wash or countertops to be wiped down. She merely had to fill the sink with soapy water, then she compromised again by leaving the dishes to soak.

When she returned to the dining room, Javier was just getting to his feet. A grimace on his face let her know that it had been a long day and probably a painful one.

"Don't get up," she said. "I can see myself out."

He seemed to rally and lobbed a boyish grin her way. "Just like making sure I saved room for dessert, I managed to save enough energy to walk you to the door."

She returned his smile, wondering if he had plans to kiss her again. While it probably wasn't a good idea, she decided not to put up a fight if he made a move in that direction.

As they walked through the living room, she stopped to pick up her purse. Then they headed to the door.

"Thanks again for dinner," she said. "It was a nice treat."

"I'll have to grill for you someday."

There he went again with the "someday" talk. Why

did he seem to put everything off to the future? Why not give her an actual date to look forward to—like next Saturday or even three weeks from whenever?

She had no idea, other than to think he wanted to take things slowly, and that was probably for the best.

As she opened the front door and stepped out on the stoop, he stopped her with a question.

"Are you working on Friday?"

"No, I've got the weekend off. Why?"

"Because I won't have to wait until seven to pick you up. I'll come for you around six."

"Where are we going?"

"To Marcos and Wendy's house."

She was about to remind him that she'd said she would think about going, but maybe he could read her a lot better than she'd thought he could. Either way, she wasn't going to fight him on the party.

"All right," she said. "I'll be ready."

She gave him her address although he didn't write it down.

He nodded and his eyes glimmered. "I'll see you then."

Apparently so.

But before she could turn to go, he slipped his free arm around her waist and drew her toward him.

Her heart rate spiked as anticipation soared.

Only a fool would turn down a kiss from Javier

Mendoza. So she wrapped her arms around his neck and leaned toward him.

As his lips touched hers, she was lost in a burst of fireworks, this time even better than the last.

Chapter Nine

Four long days had passed since Javier kissed Leah on the porch and set the stars spinning, yet not an hour went by without her thinking about his lips pressed on hers, his tongue sweeping the inside of her mouth, seeking hers for a lovers' tryst.

She'd tried to attribute her mindless arousal to the fact that she'd been suppressing her physical needs and desires. After all, it had been ages since she'd felt a man's embrace. But the truth was, until she'd met Javier, she hadn't obsessed about sex at all. So there was only one explanation that made sense. Now that she'd had a taste of what was to come, what she would experience in his slow, expert hands, she hungered for more.

She hadn't talked to him since that night at his house, and when Friday finally rolled around, she'd spent the afternoon fixing her hair—putting it up, then leaving it down. After getting dressed and applying her makeup, she settled on wearing a soft and feminine look.

As it grew close to six o'clock, the time Javier was supposed to arrive, she reminded herself that attending the open house wouldn't be a date. It was only a chance for her to see the Mendoza family again and to wish Wendy, Marcos and the baby her best.

But she wasn't so sure about that. Not when she was looking forward to seeing Javier again, to being with him.

When the doorbell rang, she took one last look in the mirror, then went to answer the door.

"Wow," Javier said, his eyes lighting up with appreciation. "You look great, Leah. I've been waiting to see your hair down and loose."

"Thanks. You look nice, too."

His hair, which was still growing out, had been trimmed and styled. He'd also shaved and splashed on some woodsy cologne that set her senses reeling. She didn't recognize the brand or the scent, but it was no doubt as expensive as it was alluring.

He wore a light blue button-down shirt, open at the collar, and a pair of black slacks with a matching jacket. He seemed so strong, so vital, so whole, that anyone who was unaware of what he'd suffered, what he'd been through, would think the cane was only a prop.

"Are you ready to go?" he asked.

"Yes." She locked the door, then walked with him to his SUV.

Less than ten minutes later, Javier pulled along the curb and parked in front of Marcos and Wendy's modest three-bedroom house.

"It doesn't look like anyone's here yet," he said, scanning the street and the driveway. "But that's bound to change soon."

"Are they expecting a lot of people?" Leah asked.

"If you'd ever attended a Mendoza get-together, you'd realize what a big family I have. And when you add the Fortunes from Red Rock, as well as those from Atlanta, well…" He grinned. "There will probably be a slew of them, but with it being an open house, people will be coming and going all evening."

Leah and Javier climbed from the car, then made their way to the front door, where Marcos welcomed them.

"Are we the first ones here?" Javier asked.

"Yes, unless you count Emily, Wendy's sister."

From what Leah had heard, Emily Fortune had flown in from Atlanta to help care for the baby. It must be nice to have a sister, she thought, especially at times like this.

At that moment, the new mommy entered the living room wearing a brightly colored gypsy skirt and a matching red top, as well as a full apron to protect the fabric from kitchen spills and splatters.

Wendy welcomed Javier with a hug, then turned and embraced Leah as well. "I'm so glad y'all are here."

"Thanks for inviting me to tag along," Leah said.

"I would have been disappointed if you hadn't. You have no idea how much I appreciated your visits while I was in the hospital. You not only kept me in the loop, letting me know about Javier's condition, you also helped me feel better about my own situation."

"It was my pleasure," Leah said. "How's the baby? It must be wonderful to finally have her home."

"She's doing great. I'll take you to see her in the nursery. Emily's changing her diaper."

Wendy led Leah through the living room, which was an eclectic mix of a contemporary style with a bit of cozy chic added here and there. From what she'd been told, Wendy was a fashionista, and it showed both in her clothing and her house.

"I like your decor," Leah said.

"Thanks." Wendy chuckled. "I did what I could with what Marcos had. This place used to be a bachelor pad, with lots of leather and chrome that centered around a big-screen TV. But I added my own little touches here and there, and this is what we ended up with."

"Well, I'm impressed. You certainly did an amazing job."

"Thanks." Wendy led Leah down the hall, stopping near an open doorway. "Here it is."

Leah peered into the nursery, where Emily Fortune stood at the changing table with the tiny baby who was still the size of a small newborn.

"Have you met my sister?" Wendy asked.

"Yes, several times." Leah smiled at Emily. "It's nice to see you again."

Emily laughed. "I'd shake your hand, but I'm a little tied up at the moment."

"I can see that." Leah eased into the room.

"Well, if you two don't mind," Wendy said, nodding toward the hallway, "I have something in the oven and need to check on it."

After Wendy took off down the hall, Leah scanned the nursery, with its white walls and furniture. The curtains, a tropical fabric with fuchsia, orange and lemon-yellow flowers on a bright aqua background, as well as a hand-painted border with the same floral print, added a blast of color to the room.

And so did a white glider and ottoman upholstered in a matching bright aqua.

"The nursery is darling," Leah said. "Your sister has a real talent with decor."

"Yes, she does. She's becoming a real domestic goddess." Emily Fortune, the oldest of the Atlanta Fortune daughters, was the director of advertising for FortuneSouth Enterprises.

At five foot seven, with long blond hair and green

eyes, Emily had a sophisticated air about her—maybe due in part to the glasses she often wore.

Leah had thought of her as a career woman, but standing here in the nursery, changing a newborn's diaper, gave her a whole different look.

"I'm just about done here," Emily said as she put a second little foot into the pink sleeper. "And once this last snap is done, I'll let you hold her if you'd like."

"I'd love to," Leah said.

After taking the baby, Leah sat in the rocker and began to glide back and forth while Emily looked on with a loving smile.

From what Leah had heard, Emily had been buried alive during the tornado. But unlike Javier, she'd come out without any serious injuries.

Leah studied the baby in her arms. "She's precious. And while she's still small, she's a lot bigger than when she was in the neonatal intensive care unit."

"She's hungry all the time," Emily added. "I have a feeling she'll be outgrowing her preemie clothes in no time at all."

Leah reached for the child's small foot, felt her little toes inside the pretty pink sleeper. She'd worked in the NICU briefly after she'd graduated from nursing school, so she'd handled preemies. But this was different. Mary Anne was healthy and thriving.

"You look good with a baby in your arms," Emily said. "If Javier saw you like that, he'd be in awe—and undoubtedly thinking about the future."

Leah cocked her head slightly. "What do you mean?"

"Rumor has it that there might be another Mendoza wedding one of these days."

Seriously? Was Emily talking about *Javier?*

And *Leah?*

What did she mean by "rumor"? Where would anyone get an idea like that? After all, Leah wasn't even sure what she and Javier were dancing around.

"I can't imagine how a rumor like that might get started," Leah finally said. "It's way too early in our friendship to even think about something so far off as marriage. Besides, Javier has lived the life of a happy bachelor for years. I'm not so sure he'll ever want to settle down."

"I don't know about that," Emily said. "I've always been career focused, even when I was a freshman in high school. But being in a tornado, fearing for my life, has made me reevaluate a lot of things."

Leah could see where a near-death experience could open a person's eyes. Is that what was going on with Javier? Was he actually reexamining his life and planning to make some changes, too?

She hoped so.

Mary Anne began to squirm, to scrunch up her tiny face and fuss.

"What's the matter?" Leah asked. "Do you think she's hungry?"

"Actually, Wendy just fed her a few minutes ago. Maybe she needs to burp."

As Mary Anne continued to cry, Leah put her up on her shoulder and began to pat her back to no avail.

"Let me give it a try," Emily said, taking the baby from Leah. She paced the nursery floor, patting the child's back lightly.

Moments later, as a burp sounded, Mary Anne stopped her fussing and settled down. Once she was quiet and still, Emily handed her back to Leah, taking time to stroke her little cheek, to look at her with love and longing.

"I imagine being around this precious baby makes a woman wish she could get married and start a family of her own," Leah said.

"Yes, I'll admit that it makes motherhood appealing. But I'm not thinking about marriage. I've given up waiting for Mr. Right to come along. What I really want is to have a baby."

Leah liked the idea, too. But she'd nearly given up on having a child, on becoming a mother.

"My brother, Blake, inspired me to come up with a plan to make it happen," Emily said.

"A plan?"

"Yes, and it's a good one. I compiled a spreadsheet of fertility clinics with their success rate percentages, as well as a list of exclusive sperm banks that use only Ivy League, Mensa and Nobel Prize–winning donors.

I also have the names of several well-recommended adoption attorneys who promise fast results."

Leah didn't know what to say about that. Talk about coming up with a family plan and seeing it to fruition....

Still, as much as Leah might like to have a little one of her own, she'd rather conceive a baby the old-fashioned way.

With that thought came a vision of her and Javier, stretched out in bed together, naked and kissing and stroking...

Whoa. Talk about inappropriate times and places.

Leah quickly squelched the amazing, blood-stirring thought and returned her attention to the baby in her arms.

"Emily?" Marcos called from the doorway. When both women looked up, he said, "Wendy would like your help with something in the kitchen."

"I'll be right there." Emily reached down and caressed the baby's head, running her hand along the soft tufts of dark hair. Then she excused herself, leaving Leah alone with the baby.

Emily hadn't been gone long when Leah sensed someone watching her. When she glanced up, she spotted Javier in the doorway, a wistful smile on his face.

For a moment, something bound them together—a thought, a look, an unspoken dream.

Or had searching his expression while she held

a baby in her arms set her imagination off on a tangent, seeking a pot of gold at the end of a rainbow that didn't exist?

Leah tamped down her musing, which was probably a result of the "rumors" Emily had mentioned. But that didn't mean she could ignore the fact that Javier stood in the doorway, looking at her in a way that touched her very core.

Javier had been so blown away by the sight of Leah holding a baby, so amazed to see the maternal side of her that he'd stood in the doorway, unable to move or to speak.

"Have you met your niece yet?" she asked.

"No, but I'd like to." Still, it took him a moment to make that first step, to cross the carpeted nursery floor with his cane in hand. But once he did, he peered at his brother's firstborn baby, nearly dumbstruck with awe.

"Do you want to hold her?" Leah asked.

"No, I'll just look at her. She's so tiny. And I'm not very good on my feet yet. I'd hate to drop her."

"You can have my chair."

"Please don't get up."

Leah looked so good like that, rocking a sleeping newborn. She was going to make one heck of a mother; he was sure of it.

When the doorbell rang and voices sounded in the

living room, Javier realized that the other guests had begun to arrive.

"Looks like the open house is finally getting under way," he said.

"Then I'd better take Mary Anne to her mommy and daddy." Leah carefully got to her feet. "I need to let someone else hold her for a while."

Javier took a step back, even though he hated to see Leah leave the nursery. Seeing her with a child in her arms—so serene, so loving—was enough to make him wonder what she'd look like holding a baby of her own.

His baby.

But Javier wouldn't allow himself to have those kinds of thoughts before he could comfortably walk the floor with a fussy baby, take a toddler to the park or show a boy how to ride a bike or hit a baseball.

A *boy?*

Somehow, that didn't seem to matter. If he were to have a daughter, he'd teach her how to do those things, too.

With Leah on her feet, he took the time to get a closer look at his brother's newborn, the tiny angel who'd come to bless their lives.

"I can see a lot of Wendy in her," he said. "But she's got my brother's eyes. She's beautiful, isn't she?"

"Absolutely."

As they reached the doorway, Javier let Leah and

the baby go first, then he followed them into the living room, where the Atlanta Fortunes had gathered.

He greeted Wendy's brother Blake and his fiancée, Katie Wallace, first. Then he took the time to introduce the couple to Leah.

Blake, who was the head of marketing for FortuneSouth Enterprises, and Katie had been childhood friends. She'd been in love with him for years, and the two had recently become engaged.

Javier's mother, if she were still alive, would have announced that love was in the air. And maybe she would have been right, because next in line for introductions was Wendy's brother Scott and his fiancée, Christina Hastings.

Scott, the vice president of FourtuneSouth Enterprises, had been trapped with Christina during the tornado. And within the first few weeks in January, he and the pretty waitress had fallen in love.

Leah, who'd met the couple while Javier had been in the hospital, greeted them.

By the time Javier got around to introducing Wendy's parents, Virginia Alice and John Michael, everyone had gathered around Leah, who still held Mary Anne.

"I think it's time for her grandmother to take her," Leah said, handing over the baby to the silver-haired woman.

Virginia Alice beamed as she took the child,

clearly thrilled to see her newest grandbaby again, this time without all the NICU monitors attached.

Leah took a step back, getting out of the way of the crowd, and Javier couldn't blame her for that. There were a lot of people in the room, and even more would be passing through the door this evening.

Still, she'd handled it well, greeting each of them with grace and style. But he'd make an excuse to leave pretty soon. Once they'd had a drink and eaten a couple of the appetizers Wendy had made, Javier would tell everyone he was tired. Then he and Leah could escape.

Just the thought of having her to himself again brought a smile to his face.

As the women continued to coo over the baby, Javier turned to John Michael, the patriarch of the Atlanta Fortunes. "When did you get in?"

"Just a few hours ago. Scott picked us up at the airport, then drove us to his and Christina's place."

Marcos had mentioned that Scott and Christina had a seven-bedroom home, so there had to be plenty of room for guests.

"Would anyone like a drink?" Marcos asked his guests. "I have a bar set up in the patio."

"I'll take you up on that." John Michael patted his son-in-law on the back, then followed him out of the living room.

At six feet four inches and with salt-and-pepper hair, John Michael was not only distinguished, but imposing as well. Javier suspected a lot of that had to do with the fact that he'd created FortuneSouth Enterprises, a huge telecommunications company, and had become a millionaire by the time he was thirty.

He was sixty-two now and had only refined his blunt, aggressive approach to both business and life.

He and his wife had been married for nearly forty years, although Javier suspected she deserved a lot of credit for holding down the home front while he commandeered the business.

Virginia Alice was the epitome of a genteel, Southern woman—an authentic steel magnolia. She was also as soft-spoken as her husband was blunt.

From what Marcos had told Javier, the woman had raised their six children single-handedly and didn't believe in nannies.

Jordana, Wendy's sister, was the last to step through the threshold, and when Javier tried to introduce the two women, Leah said, "We met one day at the hospital. It's good to see you again, Jordana."

"Yes, it is."

"The last time we talked," Leah said, "you were getting ready to fly back to Atlanta."

"And now I'm back." Jordana smiled. "I couldn't miss this party—and a chance to see my niece again."

Jordana Fortune, the assistant director of research and development for FortuneSouth Enterprises, was a bright woman with blond hair and brown eyes. She also had a shy demeanor.

Javier shot a glance at Leah, saw that she was holding her own with the ladies, so he said, "I'll be back shortly. Can I bring you a drink?"

"A diet soda, if they have one."

Javier nodded, then followed the men out to the patio. He was looking forward to having a quick drink with his friends and family. Then he would take Leah back home, where he planned to kiss her one more time.

And maybe take things a little further than that…

Leah doubted that she'd be able to keep all the Fortunes straight, but at least she knew Javier's family from having seen them regularly at the hospital.

Luis had been the first Mendoza to arrive, followed by Rafe and Melina.

Apparently Isabella had an art show of some kind today. From what Leah had been told, Isabella and J.R. would definitely attend the open house, but they'd be arriving late.

After taking time to chat with Javier's father and siblings, Leah scanned the small but cozy living room and found herself envying the close-knit group. Javier might complain about his siblings at times, but it was clear that they all loved and supported each other.

The Fortunes, too, for better or worse, seemed closely involved in one another's lives. And for a moment, Leah tried to imagine having a family like that.

And having a husband like Javier.

She'd seen him with the baby, watched him with his friends and siblings. Had she been wrong about him being a Casanova?

There was so much she had yet to learn about the man, so much she wanted to learn.

Before she knew it, he was at her side.

"Are you ready to go?"

She wouldn't mind staying a while longer or leaving, but she suspected he was getting tired. So she said, "I'm ready whenever you are."

"I think we've stayed long enough."

Leah stood, then said her goodbyes to the hosts, as well as the people she'd met. Everyone seemed glad that she'd come with Javier and sorry that they had to leave, but they understood.

What they didn't realize—and Leah did—was that she was actually looking forward to the drive home and spending some quiet time with Javier. She might even invite him into her house for a cup of coffee or whatever else he might want.

Her thoughts took another sexual turn, and she tried to shake them off. It's not as though their relationship had progressed beyond a good-night kiss.

As Leah and Javier left the house, they spotted Jordana Fortune standing just off the porch, looking a little green around the gills.

"Are you okay?" Leah asked.

The woman nodded. "Yes, I'm fine. It was just a little warm and crowded in there."

"You don't look fine," Javier said. "Maybe you should go inside and lie down."

"No, I don't want to go back in the house."

"Maybe you should let Leah look at you," Javier said, as he leaned against his cane. "You might need to see a doctor."

"I'm fine," Jordana said. *"Really."* Her gaze quickly sought Leah's. "It's nothing contagious. And it'll pass soon."

It didn't take much of a leap for Leah to realize that Jordana might be pregnant.

"Would you like me to get you some saltines? Or maybe some ginger ale?"

"That might help. But please don't mention that it's for me. Or that you saw me out here, okay?"

Realizing that her assumption might prove to be right, Leah nodded. "If there's one thing I've learned how to do since becoming a nurse, it's to be discreet. This will be our little secret."

Leah glanced at Javier, indicating that he was in on the secret, too. And while she didn't think he'd come to the same conclusion she had, he nodded in agreement.

Moments later, Leah returned outside with the soft drink and crackers, only to find Javier out near the street, talking to J.R. and Isabella, who'd just arrived.

Jordana had moved, too. Now she stood near the tree at the side of the house, talking to someone on her cell phone.

Leah wasn't sure if she should stand back, giving the woman her privacy, or let her know she'd returned. As it was, she drew closer, only to catch a bit of conversation.

"What do you mean I'm not the only one with unfinished business in Red Rock?" Jordana asked.

Leah's steps froze. Surely this was a conversation she wasn't meant to hear. So she turned to walk away, just as Jordana said, "How do you plan to make things right, Victoria?" She paused. "Okay. Then I'll wait in Red Rock until you fly in."

As Leah reached the porch, Javier returned with J.R. and Isabella. The couples greeted each other, making the typical small talk, then the Fortunes entered the house.

Javier looked at the drink and crackers in Leah's hand. "Where's Jordana?"

"She's over there." Leah nodded toward the tree.

"What's she doing?"

"She's on her cell phone, talking with someone named Victoria."

"Her cousin?"

"I suppose so. As soon as she hangs up, I'll give her the soda and crackers. Then we can go home."

Moments later, Jordana returned to the porch, looking just as pale and nauseous as she'd been before—maybe even more so.

Something told Leah the conversation with Victoria had upset Jordana, but she wasn't about to pry into someone else's business. Besides, Javier had been on his feet long enough today. And she was eager to go home, where the two of them would be alone.

And where she might kiss him again.

Chapter Ten

It was almost eight o'clock when Leah and Javier finally left the party and headed back to her house.

After parking in the driveway, Javier opened the driver's door.

"You don't have to get out," Leah said. "Unless you want to. I know how tired you must be. It's been a busy day for you."

"I'm fine."

They climbed from his SUV and made their way to the front door, the porch light illuminating their path along the sidewalk.

Leah had been fighting a growing attraction to Javier ever since she'd first laid eyes on him in his hospital bed. As long as he'd been on the third floor and under her care, she'd refused to even consider becoming romantically involved with a patient, which was a matter of ethics. But now that he'd been discharged, that was no longer a reason to hold back.

Okay, so he was still technically under the care of San Antonio General as an outpatient at the attached rehab facility. But she could easily argue that it wasn't the same thing. And that it wouldn't be a violation of any kind.

Next she'd worried about him being a player, a perpetual bachelor who had no plans to ever get married or to settle down. But she now had evidence to dispute that belief, too.

Either way, she'd come to the conclusion that her feelings for Javier had grown too strong to fight. And that she'd already lost the battle.

By the time they reached her front door, her heart soared with anticipation.

Yet she couldn't help noting that Javier had been walking slower than before.

Was he reluctant to say goodbye to her and end their night together?

Or had he pushed himself too hard and grown tired at the party?

As she reached for her key, she asked, "Would you like to come in? I can make us some tea or coffee. I also have some soft drinks and a bottle of wine."

"Decaf sounds good if you have it."

"I do." She let him inside, then closed the door

and turned on the light. Everything was just as she'd left it. Even Miss Kitty was still snoozing on the blue chintz love seat, her favorite resting spot.

The cat looked up, but only for a moment. Apparently the old gray tabby didn't care that Leah had brought home a guest. But then again, at her age, she didn't worry much as long as she had a little peace and quiet.

"Why don't you have a seat while I brew a pot of decaf," Leah said.

"All right."

She left Javier in the living room, then made her way to the kitchen, where she filled the carafe with water. As she shut off the faucet, she heard music playing—something soft, slow and seductive.

Was he trying to set up a romantic ambiance while they ended their evening together? A part of her hoped that he was. But she doubted that was the case.

Javier had to be exhausted. And since he'd told her that music relaxed him, he was probably trying to unwind after an afternoon at rehab and an evening spent at his brother's open house.

Yet as Leah finished placing the coffee grounds into the filter-lined basket and turned on the power to start the brewing process, she couldn't help wondering what awaited her in the other part of the house— even if it was just a tall, dark and handsome man stretched out on her sofa.

While the water gurgled and dribbled into the pot,

she returned to the living room, only to find Javier seated on her love seat next to Miss Kitty. He stroked the cat, who seemed rather indifferent about having company. But at least she wasn't hissing at him.

"I hope you don't mind that I put on some music," he said. "It was pretty quiet in here, and your cat wasn't much company."

She smiled. "That's not surprising. Miss Kitty is nearly nineteen years old, so she's content to sleep most of the day and night. And no, I don't mind the music at all."

Still, she wasn't sure what had compelled him to choose that particular radio station. Did it have anything to do with the romantic ballad that was playing?

She listened to the lyrics for a moment, as well as the sound of a lonely fiddle, then said, "I like this song."

"I do, too. Why don't we dance to it?"

His question came as a complete surprise, and while she thought it was a nice idea, he had to be worn out from the day's activities.

"How are you feeling?" she asked. "Are you really up to it?"

"Probably not." He tossed her a boyish grin as he slowly got to his feet, biting back a grimace. "But the way I see it, if I drop in my tracks, I'm with the right person. You'll know just what to do."

He took a step away from the sofa, letting the cane

lean against the armrest. Then he held out his arms in an invitation to give it a whirl.

"This probably isn't a very good idea," Leah said, mindful of the severity of his injuries, of the long road he had to full recovery. Yet she still made her way toward him.

"No need to worry about me," he said. "I have it all figured out."

She couldn't see any reason to argue or to point out his weakness, so she stepped into his embrace, leaned her body into his and offered her support.

The woodsy scent of his cologne mingled with the pheromones overhead, creating an arousing spell that was too strong to resist. So she placed her cheek against his chest, relishing the warmth of his body, the steady beat of his heart.

Did he feel it, too—the sexual thrill, the rush of desire, the longing for more than an embrace?

They swayed to the music, although they didn't actually dance. Yet that didn't matter. All Leah wanted to do was to hold Javier close for as long as she had the chance.

When the song ended, he continued to sway on his feet, then dipped slightly. She held him tight, determined to support him, to keep him steady and upright.

Was he in pain? Was his strength giving out?

Or had a stumble been part of a plan to gain her sympathy, to weaken her defenses, to get her into bed?

Oh, for heaven's sake. Enough of that already. Not every handsome, eligible bachelor was a playboy whose only goal was to score.

Leah took a step back, intending to retrieve Javier's cane so he could support himself better, so he could make his way back to the love seat. But before she could turn away, he caught her chin with his finger, then tilted her face upward.

She saw the kiss coming in his eyes, felt it in the pounding of her heart. As their mouths met, their lips parted and the kiss deepened, just as though their bodies knew right where they'd left off. Only this time, the intimacy of it all intensified as their hands explored, stroked and caressed until Leah could scarcely breathe.

When Javier's hand reached her breast, when he palmed the soft mound, he skimmed his thumb across her nipple—once, twice, a third time.

Her breath caught and her senses spun out of control.

The man was a master when it came to romance— the absolute best. And while she knew she ought to be leery of him, her desire and curiosity mounted until she wanted nothing more than to learn what she was going to experience in his arms next.

Kissing Javier suddenly seemed to be the best decision she'd ever made—or *not* made, since her brain was no longer in charge of her actions.

As he worked his magic with his hands, his mouth

and tongue, an ache settled low in her core, reminding her of just how long it had been since she'd had sex, how empty she'd become. And that sweet ache merely grew until her head swam and her knees threatened to buckle.

But no way could she allow herself to become unsteady on her feet. If that happened, she might not be able to keep Javier from falling if the need arose.

So she drew her lips from his, knowing she was doing the best and wisest thing, even though every cell in her body screamed out in complaint.

"I need to get off my feet," she said, rather than admit that her real concern was for him. Javier, like most men, probably wouldn't like having his weakness pointed out.

"Do you want to take a seat?" he asked. "Or maybe…lie down?"

Javier clearly knew how to wine and dine and charm a woman into bed. Yet Leah would throw caution aside and listen to her hormones—just this once.

"The sofa could get awkward," she said. "Maybe we should go into my room and stretch out on the bed."

When Javier didn't answer right away, she feared she'd gotten the wrong message.

Had she misunderstood his intentions?

Javier could hardly believe what Leah had just agreed to, and while he ought to backpedal on the whole let's-take-this-to-the-bedroom thing, it was too late to do that now. Everything he needed to make love—his libido, his hormones, his erection—had escaped injury in the tornado. So he was primed and ready for love.

"Lying down sounds like a good idea to me," he said.

As Leah stooped to reach for the discarded cane, a kindness on her part that reminded Javier that she was well aware of his physical shortcomings, his gut clenched.

He remembered the decision he'd made to maintain a platonic relationship with her until he'd fully recovered. But what was he supposed to do? Turn around and limp away?

Let her see how far he still had to go before making a full recovery?

But he had one thing going for him—his skill as a lover. And that was something the tornado hadn't stolen from him.

After that last kiss he and Leah had shared, after those amazing moments of foreplay, he was willing to change his game plan at this point. After all, the rest of his body might be struggling to walk without the aid of a cane, but there were certain parts of him that worked just fine—especially if he would be lying down.

He might not be able to make her any promises about the future, but there was one thing he knew for sure. He was going to do everything in his power to make things good for her tonight. And, if all went as he hoped they would, he would take her to a sexual place no other man had ever taken her before.

As Leah led Javier to the bedroom, he followed her, convinced he was doing the right thing. And thanking his lucky stars that he'd been in the habit of carrying a condom with him.

Once they reached her bed, he kissed her again. Then after he kicked off his loafers, he looked to her for either approval or objection.

Damn. Where had the doubt come from?

But it didn't last long. As she slipped out of her heels, he knew they were on the same page.

He took off his black sports coat and, after removing the condom he kept in the inside pocket, he draped the jacket over the bedpost. Then he left the foil packet on the nightstand.

The seconds ticked slowly as they continued to undress, one garment at a time.

She lifted the hem of her top, then pulled it over her head and let it drop to the floor.

He unbuttoned his shirt, then moved on to the cuffs. All the while, sometimes out of the corner of his eye and at others straight on, he watched every seductive movement she made, following her step by step.

She undid the button on her slacks, then tugged

down the zipper. When she was done, she peeled the black fabric over her hips, then wiggled out of them.

He removed his pants as well.

All the while their eyes remained on each other, watching, gazing with both longing and appreciation.

When they'd finally discarded their clothing and stood before each other naked, her pure beauty struck him hard and low.

"I had no idea how beautiful you really are."

She thanked him as if she didn't quite believe him but was too polite to argue. He was going to have to do something about that. And the first step was to take her in his arms again, to let her feel his skin on hers. As her breasts pressed against his chest, he kissed her like there was no tomorrow.

Sure, they'd have to face the consequences of their actions after the night was over, but he wasn't going to think about any of that now.

His hands slid along the curve of her back, then down the slopes of her hips. As he drew her close, a surge of desire shot right through him.

When he doubted that his once-broken legs could hold out much longer, he ended the kiss, nodded toward the bed and said, "After you."

She drew back the covers, then climbed onto the mattress. As much as he wanted to join her, he couldn't help taking in the sight of her as she lay naked and lovely.

Her legs were long and shapely, her breasts full,

her nipples peaked. Her eyes watching him with as much appreciation as he watched her.

They'd kissed off the last of her lipstick, leaving her lips red and plump. And with her head on the pillows, those long, glossy strands of auburn hair were splayed against the white cotton pillowcase—just as he'd imagined so many times before.

Unable to hold off a moment longer, he slid into bed beside her. And as they lay together, he kissed her again—this time with all the hunger, all the passion rushing through his veins.

She whimpered, then arched forward, revealing her own need, her own arousal.

As she skimmed her nails across his chest, sending a shiver through him and a surge of heat zipping through his veins, he knew he couldn't prolong their first joining indefinitely.

But that didn't mean he wouldn't take the time to kiss her breasts until she was begging to have him fill her to the brim.

So he leaned over her and took the first dusky pink tip into his mouth.

Leah gasped in pleasure, yet Javier continued to taunt her, to make her yearn for more. Then he turned his attention to the other side until she gripped his arms, making crescent dents into his skin with her nails.

"I'm not sure how much more of this I can take,"

she said. "I need you inside me or I'm going to scream."

A smile stretched across his face. "When that happens, you just might cry out in pleasure anyway."

Her smile turned sultry, then she reached for the condom on the nightstand and tore into it. When she'd helped him roll it in place, he turned to the side and hovered over her.

At this very moment in time, there was no place else he longed to be, no one else he wanted to be with. And he was sorely tempted to tell her so.

While the unspoken words stalled in his throat, words he'd never uttered to another woman in his life, he did his best to choke them back. It was too soon to utter promises he wasn't quite ready to make.

But one thing was certain. Javier belonged to Leah—at least for tonight.

As she opened for him, he entered her slowly, deliberately, relishing the experience of two lovers becoming one for the first time.

And as her body responded to his, as she arched up to meet each of his thrusts, he couldn't recall anyone else ever taking him to such a soaring height.

Hell, he couldn't even remember any other lover's name. And for some reason, he doubted that he ever would again.

When he reached a peak, she arched up, dug her nails into his back and cried out with her climax, setting off one of his own.

They came together, as a blast of colors burst somewhere in his mind, and he held her tight until the last sexual wave eased.

He wanted to speak, to again tell her how beautiful she was, how good they were together, how much he...

Damn. It was way, *way* too early to mutter emotions best left alone until he was back to normal, until he had a chance to determine if they were really true, if what he felt right this moment might actually last.

But double damn. Making love with Leah had been awesome, amazing and...unreal.

Javier might not be anywhere near one hundred percent physically, but tell that to his libido, which still worked like a charm. Tonight he'd been on top of his sexual game.

Still, he had no idea where the relationship would go from here.

As it was, he'd sleep on it until dawn's first light. Maybe then he'd have an idea about what he wanted to do about this.

He'd always considered himself doing a solo gig in life, and up until now, it had worked out just fine. And while the injuries he'd suffered in the tornado had set him back for months, they'd also opened his eyes to a lot of things.

For the first time in his life, he could imagine himself settling down and having a family. But not now. Not until he was back on his feet without the aid of a cane. Not until he'd gone back to work at the office and had a couple of deals cooking.

Not until he could shoot par at the Red Rock Country Club again.

Not until he knew he was number one.

Sure, he knew he could spill his guts, share his fears about all of that with Leah and he knew she'd tell him that she liked him just the way he was.

But Javier didn't like himself. And he wasn't going to let an awesome night of lovemaking convince him that he'd be number one again at everything he tackled.

So instead of saying anything at all to Leah and tipping his hand, he held her close, afraid to let her go.

Or to face whatever reality the morning brought.

Chapter Eleven

The rising sun peered through the spaces in the shutter slats and cast dawn's muted light in Leah's room, where she lay in bed, more asleep than awake.

She'd just spent the most incredible night of her life with Javier, who'd proven to be an amazing lover, even better than in her dreams. And she looked forward to what the new day would bring.

So she reached for him, hoping to stroke his arm and whisper good morning. But the only thing she touched was the cool expanse of mattress and a rumpled sheet.

At first she thought that he was in the bathroom, but she didn't hear any water running.

Where was he?

Surely he hadn't slipped away in the middle of the night. She sat up in bed, scanned the faintly lit room and spotted her discarded clothes lying in a pile on the floor.

But Javier's weren't anywhere to be seen.

Her heart dropped to her stomach with a cold, hard thump—until she took a whiff and caught the aroma of fresh-brewed coffee.

Was he fixing breakfast for her?

She ought to be the one in the kitchen, cooking for him—not the other way around. He was her guest, and an injured one at that. So she threw off the covers, climbed from the bed and removed her pink chenille robe from the closet. Then she padded into the kitchen where, sure enough, he stood near the stove, his cane leaning against the counter, his jacket hung over the back of a chair.

His hair was damp and stylishly mussed as he lifted the lid of the frying pan and peered into whatever he had cooking in it.

"Good morning," she said. "You're up early."

He turned and smiled. "Yeah, well I couldn't sleep. So I showered. And since neither of us had much for dinner last night, I thought I'd come in here and whip up some scrambled eggs. You didn't have bacon, but I found some red potatoes and English muffins. I hope that's okay."

"It's fine." In fact, it was great. Not only was he a good lover, but he knew his way around a kitchen.

He was also thoughtful. If he'd already showered and dressed, he must have gone out of his way to keep quiet.

She appreciated his consideration, until she imagined him as a bachelor again, with more women coming in and out of his life than he could count. And if that were the case, then he'd probably had a lot of practice getting out of bed quietly and slipping away in the middle of the night.

But the moment that thought arose, she tamped it down and scolded herself for making such a negative, not to mention unfair, assumption. After all, Javier *hadn't* taken off while she'd slept. He'd merely surprised her by fixing breakfast.

"Can I help?" she asked.

"I've got everything under control, although you could pour us each a cup of coffee."

She strode to the cupboard, pulled out two blue mugs, then filled them with the fresh morning brew. She remembered the decaf she'd made last night and smiled. They'd forgotten all about it in the heat of the moment, so he must have thrown it out this morning and started from scratch.

"Do you take cream or sugar?" she asked as she filled the cups.

"No. I like mine black."

She handed him the first mug, then added a bit of sweetener to hers, as well as a dab of creamer.

As she reached for a spoon, she wondered how

to broach the subject of the future. And to ask one of several questions she had, the most important of which was, "Where do we go from here?"

Instead, she kept things light. "How did you sleep?"

"Not too bad."

That wasn't quite the answer she'd wanted to hear. Not that she expected him to wax on about how wonderful last night had been or how refreshed he'd awakened.

Goodness, she'd only gotten a few hours of sleep herself. But once she'd nodded off, nestled in Javier's arms, she'd slept like a baby.

Again, she tried to shrug off her disappointment, but it wasn't easy.

Was it wrong for her to want to hear him say that making love with her had been every bit as special to him as it had been to her? She didn't think so.

After stirring her coffee and setting the spoon in the sink, she took a sip. Javier certainly knew how to brew a good cup of java. In fact, after last night, she'd learned firsthand some of the other skills he had.

"What do you have going on today?" she asked.

He turned from the stove and faced her, yet he still kept his eye on the eggs. "I've got physical therapy this afternoon. Pete, my therapist, said I could take the weekend off, but I'd rather not. I'm tired of being laid up. It's hell to feel like only half a man."

Her lips quirked into a smile. "You weren't half a man last night."

His eyes sparked and he smiled. Then he returned to watch the pan on the stove, using a spatula to keep the eggs from sticking.

"I thought I'd do some laundry today," she added. "Then I probably ought to run a few errands."

He didn't respond, although she supposed he didn't need to. So she decided to take a more direct approach.

"Would you like to have dinner with me tonight? I thought I could fix chicken."

The light in his eyes dimmed. "I'd like to, but I'm not sure that's a good idea."

What wasn't a good idea? Her stomach clenched. Them having dinner together? Or him returning to her house once he left?

Slow down, she told herself. She was jumping to conclusions. After all, he was fixing breakfast for her. If he'd meant to make a hasty exit, wouldn't he have done so while she'd been sleeping?

Still, her heart, which had been soaring with hope when she first entered the kitchen, sputtered and threatened to stall. "Why isn't it a good idea?"

"Well, because…as good as it was last night—as good as we were together—I think we should take things slowly for now."

He might be right about not rushing into anything, but she couldn't help feeling as though he was giving her the morning-after brush off. And in spite of wanting to give him the benefit of the doubt, she bristled. "I see."

After removing the egg pan from the flame, he turned to face her again, resting his backside against the cupboard. "It's not what you think, baby."

Baby? Under normal circumstances, she might be touched by the term of endearment. But didn't bachelors often refer to their lovers as baby or sweetheart or honey so they didn't have to worry about calling someone by the wrong name?

"Then what should I think?" she asked.

Again he paused, as if choosing his words carefully. And who could blame him? If he wasn't planning to make a commitment, yet wanted to sleep with her again, he'd have to be careful how he handled things now, wouldn't he?

"Last night was great," he said. "*We* were great. But I have a long way to go before I can make any promises or plans for the future."

What was he talking about? Didn't he realize that, at least in some ways, he was as good as he'd ever been? And that even after he was fully healed, she didn't expect perfection?

As badly as she wanted to explain it all away—his attitude, his inability to make a commitment—she realized that she'd been right about him all along. Javier was a playboy bachelor, and there was nothing she could do to change that.

Their romantic night of lovemaking might have meant the world to her. But to him, it had only been the means to an end.

The same thing had happened when she'd dated Jason Novachek, the internist who'd taken her out and charmed her into bed. And while she'd been disappointed that things hadn't worked out the way she'd wanted, that Jason hadn't been the man she'd expected him to be, she hadn't loved him. Not like she...

Oh, God. She took a step back at the realization: she *loved* Javier.

And just like Aunt Connie, she'd fallen hook, line and sinker for a charming but dedicated bachelor whose only real interest in her had been a sexual romp.

Connie had been so devastated by the breakup that she'd never been the same again.

And neither would Leah.

Sure, she was stronger than Aunt Connie. She wouldn't cry and carry on—at least, not in public. She wouldn't go to bed and curl into a fetal position for days on end.

No, Leah would go back to the hospital on Sunday and throw herself into her work. And, with time, she'd get over the pain, over the crushing disappointment.

But when it came to getting involved in another relationship?

She'd trust her instincts next time. And she'd *never*

let some smooth-talking Casanova charm her into bed again.

As badly as she wanted to throw her mug across the kitchen, to hear the ceramic shatter like a heart breaking, to watch the coffee splash and spill down the wall like tears, she held fast to her temper.

And as tempted as she was to scream and demand that Javier get the hell out of her life, she bit her tongue.

After all, she really had no one to blame for any of this but herself. She'd known all along that her handsome patient would recover one day and revert back to the man he'd once been.

Her initial assessment of him had proven to be right. She just hadn't wanted it to be.

"So," she said, "let me see if I understand this. You want to take things slowly until you finish rehab?"

He turned away from the stove to face her again, nodding. "I think it's for the best."

Best for who? Him?

Nevertheless, she continued to lay it on the line. "And you don't want to think about the future until that time?"

He gave a half shrug. "I don't mind thinking about the future. But I don't want to make any plans until I can kiss this cane goodbye."

"And making 'future' plans or commitments includes having dinner with me tonight?"

"You're angry," he said.

No, it was much worse than that. She was ready to throw him and his damn cane out the front door.

He took a step forward. "I care for you, Leah. A lot. And I don't mind dating you."

He didn't *mind?*

She took a step back, maintaining her distance. Then she grabbed hold of the lapels of her robe, holding the edges together, shielding herself from his view. "Maybe you're right, Javier."

He scrunched his face as if he was trying to make sense of her tone, of her words. But a man like him would never understand.

"Once I'm done with rehab," he explained, "we can take up where we left off. It shouldn't be long. A few months maybe. I'll work hard."

Yeah, right. She knew when she was being cut loose. And while she felt the tears welling in her eyes, she refused to cry. Not in front of him.

Take the power position, she'd told Aunt Connie when the attorney told her he wanted to date other women. *Don't call him. Don't grovel. Don't let him think you need him in the least.*

Connie hadn't taken Leah's advice, and look where that had left her.

But Leah wasn't going to let that happen to her. She was going to stand tall. And she was going to end things completely before Javier had the chance to do it himself—whether he'd finished rehab or not.

"You know," she said, "I'm not the least bit hungry.

Instead, I'm going to take a shower and then run those errands I told you about. In the meantime why don't you enjoy your coffee and eggs."

His head cocked to the side, as if he knew she was going to lower the boom. And his instincts were right.

"Just be sure you're gone by the time I'm ready to leave."

Then she turned on her heel and padded out of the kitchen, coffee mug still in her hand.

She might have taken it back to the sink, since her stomach was tied up in so many knots that she wouldn't be able to drink a single drop, but there was no way she'd return and risk undermining the dramatic exit she'd just made.

You'd think that she'd be feeling a little smug, yet disappointment filled her chest. Somewhere, deep inside, she wished that Javier would follow her, that he would stop her and explain that she was wrong, that she'd misunderstood him.

That he loved her, just as she loved him.

But that didn't happen.

As she stepped into the bathroom and closed the door, the tears she'd been holding back began to fill her eyes to the brim until they overflowed and rolled down her cheeks.

Still, she pulled back the shower curtain, turned on the spigot and waited for the noise of the flowing water to drown out any sobs she might make.

Then she dropped to her knees next to the tub and

pressed her hands against her chest—as if that might hold the cracks in her heart from shattering into a million pieces.

Javier had never been asked to leave anyone's house before—especially not that of a woman he'd just made love to. And the fact that the woman in question was Leah made it all the worse.

He'd been tempted to follow her to the bathroom, to knock on the door, to tell her he'd reconsidered. That he wanted to offer himself to her just as he was. And for as long as he lived.

But until he was back on top of his game, he couldn't allow himself to give in. He'd be strapping her with a cripple, and she deserved so much more than that.

When he offered himself to her—body, heart and soul—he would be standing on his own two feet and able to carry her over the threshold. He'd tried to explain that to her.

What if she grew to resent him and his physical limitations? Hell, not a day went by that he didn't resent them himself. Couldn't she see how important it was for them to start out on even footing?

When he'd been in the hospital, Leah had always understood where he was coming from, even when he hadn't come out and said anything.

So why didn't she get it now?

Hell, maybe because he had a hard time wrapping his mind around the reality of it all.

Last night, after the last wave of their climax had ended, after they lay spent in each other's arms, he'd expected to doze off with a sated smile on his face. But he hadn't.

How'd you sleep? she'd asked him earlier.

Not too bad, he'd said. But the truth was, he'd slept like crap. He'd stayed too long at the party last night and had probably overdone it.

He'd been in a lot of pain this morning. So he'd gotten out of bed while she was still asleep, while she couldn't see him reach for his cane, hobble to where he'd left his clothes, then take them to the bathroom.

Once inside, he'd removed his prescription bottle and downed a pain pill before climbing in the shower.

He could have left at that time, he supposed. But when he'd seen her lying in bed, he hadn't been able to go without talking to her this morning. Without explaining why a relationship with him would have to wait. Not until he'd given her his promise to bust his ass in therapy until he was back on top.

But how did that work for you? a small voice asked.

Not good. Not good at all.

Javier glanced down at the eggs he'd fixed, at the fried potatoes he'd placed on a serving platter, ready for someone to eat. And while he'd only munched on appetizers last night, he no longer felt the least bit hungry now.

Instead, he piled everything on one plate and covered it with plastic wrap. Then he put it in her refrigerator.

Next, after he washed the pots and utensils he'd used, he put them back in the cupboard in which he'd found them.

By the time the water had stopped running in the pipes and her shower was apparently over, he had slipped on his sports jacket and was headed for the door.

When he reached for the knob, he had second thoughts about leaving. But only for a moment. Only until he remembered coming through this very door with her last night.

They'd shared a slow dance, wrapped in each other's arms. And when the song had ended, when it had come time to separate, he'd stumbled. And he'd have fallen to the floor if she hadn't offered her support.

If he hadn't been so all-fired enamored with her and so determined to prove that he wasn't a complete cripple, he would have called it a night and limped away.

Instead, he'd proven to her that he could be the man she deserved in bed. And soon, he'd be man enough for her in all the other ways.

He just hoped she'd give him a chance when that day finally came around.

Javier went home long enough to change into his workout clothes, then drove straight to the rehab facility at San Antonio General. He was madder than hell at just about everyone in the world, starting with Mother Nature for sending that blasted tornado through town and having it strike right where he was standing.

And he was angry at Leah for not understanding the one thing that was most important to him.

He needed to be number one in her life, and he couldn't win that position until he'd reached it again in his own.

As he pulled into the parking lot, he found an empty space close to the front door. Then he shut off the ignition, reached across the seat for his gym bag and locked the door.

Once inside, he took a quick scan of the facility and the people inside, noting that Pete hadn't arrived yet. But that didn't matter. Javier knew the routine and would start working out on his own.

He would push himself, too. Even harder than Pete pushed.

After all, he wasn't going to lollygag around and risk having his recovery take longer than necessary. Once he took command of his body and his life again, once he was at a hundred percent, he would set his relationship with Leah back to right.

He would even plan a romantic evening to tell her how he was feeling. He'd never been in love before, but he suspected that's where all of this was heading. His feelings for Leah were too strong not to be the real deal.

"Hey there," Jeremy Fortune called out as he crossed the room to greet Javier. "I'm glad to see you up and around these days. Pete says you're doing great."

Not as great as he'd like to be. But he thanked Jeremy just the same.

"I didn't see you at the open house last night. Kirsten and I arrived late because I was on call and had an emergency. But I heard you and Leah were there."

Javier nodded. "It was a nice party, but we didn't stay very long."

His thoughts drifted to Leah, to the night they'd spent making love. It was only a natural progression to this morning, when everything had come to a head.

"Leah's a great lady," Jeremy said.

That she was. And as wonderful as she was, that lady was pretty damn angry with him right now. He'd never seen her like that, had never suspected she would react like that.

"Are you two dating?" Jeremy asked.

"Not exactly. I have a long way to go before I can think about romance."

"You'd know best," Jeremy said.

That's what Javier kept telling himself. But he'd begun to have his doubts. What if he agreed to have dinner with Leah tonight—assuming she'd accept his apology and reissue the invitation?

And what if they continued to date, even though he wasn't running any marathons yet?

"Well, I'd better go," Jeremy said. "I wanted to check on the progress of one of my other patients, but I need to head back to the office. I have a full afternoon scheduled."

After the men shook hands once again, Javier told his friend and doctor goodbye. Then he began his workout.

He started out slowly, with some stretches and easy exercises. Then he took it a step further, pushing harder, willing his muscles and tendons to strengthen, willing himself to heal.

Working out helped, he decided. It also proved to be a good outlet for his anger and frustration.

As he pushed through the pain, as he fought to become whole once again, his breath came out in ragged huffs. Perspiration beaded upon his brow.

His head grew light.

Still, he didn't let up.

He didn't quit.

As he moved from one of the chair exercises to another, his knees shook, wobbled. His vision blurred, and without warning he found himself falling.

His ears were ringing, but he heard someone yell, "Call for Dr. Fortune. *Stat!*"

As Javier collapsed, his head struck something hard, and everything went black.

Chapter Twelve

After Leah returned home from running her errands, she parked her car in the garage. Then she entered the house through the laundry room.

She might have had the last word with Javier this morning and taken the power position, but she'd never once felt like the winner. Not when she'd lost what few hopes and dreams she'd dared to harbor.

From the time she'd holed up in the bathroom this morning, with the water running to hide her cries, she'd tried to make sense of it all.

How could he make love to her like that—with a slow hand that seemed to know all the right places to touch, to stroke, to caress? It had seemed as though her needs and desires had been more important to him that night than his own. Yet he'd given her every reason to believe that she'd been an amazing lover, too.

She supposed he'd had a lot of practice with that sort of thing. But that didn't make losing him any easier.

Even when she'd dressed and returned to the kitchen, she'd held the briefest of hopes that he would be waiting for her, that he'd be eager to explain, to tell her the words she'd wanted to hear.

But she'd found him gone, the dishes washed and put away as if he'd never been there at all.

Yet he'd been there all right. She had an ache in her heart and a fist-size knot in her stomach to prove it.

It was nearing lunchtime now, but she still wasn't any hungrier than she'd been this morning when she'd told him to leave.

After making two trips to the car to bring in all of the shopping bags, she began to put everything where it belonged—frozen food in the freezer, perishables in the fridge and canned goods in the pantry.

She'd just folded the recyclable shopping bags and put them away when the telephone rang.

She closed the cupboard door, then answered on the second ring. "Hello?"

"Leah? I hope I'm not bothering you, but this is Pete Hopkins from the rehab unit."

She stiffened. Why would Javier's PT call her at home?

"What can I do for you?" she asked.

"I'm afraid there's been a little accident."

Her heart, which she'd thought had already been broken beyond measure, dropped to the floor. "What are you talking about? What happened?"

"Javier Mendoza collapsed while working out today. We rushed him to the E.R., and they've admitted him for observation."

"Oh, my God. How did that happen?"

"I wish I could tell you, but I wasn't there at the time. From what I understand, he didn't get much sleep last night. He also went without breakfast this morning, so his blood sugar was low. Then he pushed himself too hard in therapy. When he fell, he hit his head on the floor and blacked out."

His head? Oh, no. She grabbed her purse and keys before hearing anything else.

"Is he going to be all right?" she asked.

"I hope so. You'll have to talk to Dr. Fortune, who was the first to arrive in rehab. He called in the resident neurologist to make sure."

"Thanks, Pete. I'll be right there."

"Dr. Fortune thought you'd say that."

She didn't give a whole lot of thought about what Dr. Fortune might have said or why. She just knew that she had to get to the hospital.

And she had to see Javier for herself.

Javier lay on a gurney in the E.R., awaiting word that he'd been admitted to San Antonio General.

He was lucky, he supposed. His collapse and fall hadn't caused any permanent damage. But because of the head injury and the surgery he'd had in January, the neurologist ordered a CT scan and made the decision to keep him overnight for observation.

After Javier had passed out on the rehab floor, Jeremy had rushed to his aid, then had him placed on a gurney and taken to the E.R. And while he had a good-size knot on his head, Javier had come to fairly quickly, although things had been abuzz for a while. But he'd been assured that he hadn't suffered anything more than a mild concussion.

"You shouldn't be pushing yourself so hard," Jeremy had told him once the crisis was over.

"I'm sick and tired of being laid up. I want to get better."

"You *are* better, Javier. And each day you make a little more progress toward a full recovery. But you can't expect any more miracles than the one you've already had."

Javier figured that Jeremy was talking about the fact that he'd nearly died those first days after the tornado. Yet he'd still lived to tell about it. And he was probably right. The doctors and specialists who'd met with his family had all given them the same advice: hope for the best, but be prepared for the worst.

"Don't forget that there were some serious concerns about brain damage after the head injury you suffered. And at that point, your internal injuries and fractures had only been minor inconveniences in the scheme of things." Jeremy crossed his arms. "Who's been pushing you so hard?"

"No one. Just me."

Jeremy clucked his tongue and shook his head. "Then I'll give you the same advice I'd give anyone else who'd encouraged you to work out that hard. And on an empty stomach at that. *Knock it off.* You've got several more months of therapy ahead of you, and as long as you give it your all—letting Pete be the one to push you—you'll be fine. But if you refuse to listen to medical advice and continue with that macho attitude of yours, you might end up suffering a major setback. And then where will that leave you?"

In a place much worse than the one he was in right now, he supposed.

"Before you know it, probably by the end of summer, you'll be back on the golf course and flying across the country, wheeling and dealing again."

"You think so?" Javier asked, wishing it was sooner but glad to have some kind of date to set his sights on.

"Unless you try to rush the natural course of things. And if that happens, then it's anyone's guess."

"I'll take it easy," Javier said. "But tell me, Doc. What are the odds of me making a complete and full recovery by…say, September?"

"I'd say a hundred to one."

"Six months, huh?"

"Can you deal with that?"

When Javier nodded his agreement, Jeremy patted him on the shoulder, then glanced out the door. "I'm going to call for an orderly."

Jeremy had no more than stepped away from the gurney when someone else approached. But not just any someone.

It was Leah.

And she looked like hell. Her hair was windblown, her face was pale.

"What's the matter?" he asked.

"You're asking *me?*" Her pretty hazel eyes grew wide. "What in the world happened to you?"

"I told you I didn't like being laid up, so I was trying to hurry things along."

"That was a crazy thing to do."

"Yeah, that's what my orthopedic surgeon just told me—at least in so many words." Javier gave a little shrug, then studied the nurse who wasn't on duty today, yet obviously came running to the E.R. on a moment's notice. And the fact that she had almost made his collapse from exhaustion worthwhile.

"How did you know where I was?" he asked.

"Pete called me. Apparently, Jeremy thought I should know."

"Thanks for coming. I'm glad you did."

"You are? Why is that?"

Javier wasn't sure what he should say at this point. *I'm sorry* came to mind. And so did *We need to talk.*

Instead, he said, "Because you've been the best friend I've ever had. And the fact that you've been so annoyed with me, yet you still cared enough to come see about me proves that I'm your friend, too."

She paused for a beat, then crossed her arms. "Pete said you missed breakfast. And then you overdid it during your therapy workout. What in the world were you trying to do? Kill yourself?"

He liked that spark of life that lit her eyes—even when it had been fueled by anger, like it had been this morning.

"I wasn't lying when I told you that I didn't want to make a commitment to you until I was completely healed."

"And that's why you pushed yourself so hard?" She appeared skeptical.

"I was also trying to get well enough to tell you something I probably should have admitted this morning."

"What's that?"

Damn. It had come to mind so easily before. Why was he having such a difficult time confessing it now?

He took in a deep, fortifying breath, then said, "When I told you that I wanted to take things slowly, it wasn't because I was questioning what I felt for you or because I wanted to see other women. You're the only one I want to be with—now or in the future."

Her lips parted and her head cocked slightly to the side.

He supposed she didn't understand what he was getting at. Did he have to spell it out and tell her he loved her when he hadn't quite gotten used to the idea himself?

"I'll make a commitment to you just as soon as I can carry you to bed. I don't want to have to rely on you to get me there."

"You didn't need any help once you were lying down," she said. "And I hope you're not saying that you don't want to make love again until you can run a footrace."

"No, I'm not saying that. I want to see you, to be with you, to sleep with you. It's just that…" Hell, right this minute, it didn't seem to matter anymore.

"Why would your physical condition even come into play?" she asked. "I consider you whole—with or without that cane."

"Thanks, I appreciate that. But before we start talking about rings and that sort of thing, I not only want to be walking on my own, I want to be back at work, buying and selling property, turning a profit, investing. And I'm just not there yet."

"So why didn't you just come out and say that this morning?"

"I couldn't admit it, I guess. Maybe because you deserve so much more than the man I am right now. But I swear to you, honey. I'll be that man again before you know it. Jeremy said it would take another six months. Can you wait for me?"

"Are you *kidding?*" She crossed her arms and scrunched her brow.

Why would he kid about something like that? His feelings for her and the fear of losing her for good were all he'd been thinking about since leaving her house this morning.

"You mean to tell me that you don't want to have anything to do with me for six months?" she asked, her eyes sparking again, the furrow in her brow deepening.

"I didn't say that." In fact, after making love with her, he wasn't so sure he wanted to wait more than a day or two for another repeat of their romantic evening.

"But you turned down my dinner invitation tonight," she reminded him. "Why is that?"

"I don't know. Mostly because I needed some time to sort through all that I'm feeling for you. So I didn't want to rush into things. It seemed like the right idea at the time."

"How does it sound now?"

"Not so good, Leah. I want to have dinner with you every night for the rest of my life. I think I'm falling in love with you."

The furrow that had marred her brow disappeared, and she unfolded her arms. As her eyes sought his, she reached for his forehead, where he now sported a nasty bump thanks to the fall, and carefully probed around the tender spot with gentle fingers.

Did she think that having his brain jarred again had caused him to imagine feelings he didn't have? If so, he needed to set her straight. "Leah, I've been falling for you for a long time—probably since the first day you walked into my room and introduced yourself. But I've never said those words to anyone other than my family members. So no, it didn't just roll off my tongue without a whole lot of forethought and consideration."

A smile stretched across her face, lighting her eyes.

Did that mean she was going to cut him some slack? He sure hoped so.

"I've never felt this way before," he added, "so all of this is new to me. I'm bound to say the wrong thing on occasion. But I'll get it right. I promise."

"You're not the only one who's on uncharted ground. I'm afraid to lay my heart on the line and have it thrown back at me."

"Is that what you thought I was doing this morning? Throwing your feelings right back at you?"

"Weren't you?"

He really hadn't meant to do that. "I'm sorry, Leah. When I get out of here, we can go back to your house and do things right."

"I'd like that," she said. "To be honest, I've probably been a little too sensitive. Ever since a couple of your old girlfriends came to visit you in the hospital, I realized that I could never compete with them. And I was afraid that when you fully recovered and

regained your strength, you'd revert back to the man
you were and the life you had before."

"First of all, for the record, those women could
never compete with you in any respect, honey. You'd
blow them out of the water. And secondly, other than
having stiff and aching legs, I'm still that same guy."

Leah seemed to think on that for a moment, as
though she needed to let his words and the reality
sink in before she believed it.

But then again, Javier needed to let those words
sink in, too.

Other than having stiff and aching legs, I'm still
that same guy.

As the truth struck home, something clicked inside.
Something he'd struggled with for far too long. He
wasn't perfect—and it didn't matter that he wasn't.
He didn't have to prove anything to anyone, especially
not to Leah.

He might have suffered some physical setbacks,
but deep down inside his heart, he was still the same
man he'd always been.

"So what do you think?" he asked. "Can you give
the old me with bum legs and a cane another chance?"

"I'd been afraid that you were the worst guy in the
world for me to fall in love with."

"And what do you think now?"

"That you're probably the best." Then she bent
down and placed a loving kiss on his lips.

After she straightened, she added, "As much as I'd

like to stay and talk to you more about this, I'm going to take off and let you get some rest. That's why Dr. Fortune wanted you to stay the night."

"All right. But I need to clarify one more thing."

"What's that?"

"You didn't actually say that you were falling for me, too."

"I tried my best not to, but I'm afraid I fell head over heels in love with you the day they wheeled you into your room on the third floor."

He slid a boyish grin her way. "Even before I could get out of bed on my own?"

"Even when you were snippy and moody with your family." She reached for his hand and gave it a squeeze. "I don't want a perfect man, Javier. I just want you."

He laughed. "Why do I get the feeling that you meant that as a compliment?"

"Because I did."

Before he could respond, the orderly showed up to take Javier to his room.

"I'm getting out of here tomorrow," Javier told Leah. "And since you're not working, will you pick me up?"

"I'd be happy to."

"Great. As soon as they get the paperwork in order, I'll give you a call and let you know when to come."

"All right. But why don't I just come early? I can hang out with you until you're released."

"No, I'd rather you waited for me to call. But I wouldn't mind having you fix that dinner you were going to make for me tonight."

"All right. You've got it. Should I plan on having you stay over for breakfast, too?"

"I'd be disappointed if you didn't."

When he finally reached his room, she kissed him again—this time as a goodbye. "I'd stay, but you need to get some rest."

She was right about that. He also wanted to have a minute to himself. He had a couple of phone calls to make in preparation for what he planned to do when she came for him tomorrow.

When Leah arrived at San Antonio General to take Javier home, she spotted Luis Mendoza in the lobby and stopped to greet the man, who was grinning from ear to ear.

"How's he doing?" she asked.

"He's got a bump on his noggin, but other than that, I don't think I've ever seen him better." Then Luis reached out and took both of Leah's hands in his, giving them a warm clasp before letting them go. "He said you're going to take him home. And I think that's really nice."

Okay. Something seemed a little off. But maybe it's because she hadn't ever seen Javier's father so happy. Had he and Javier received good news?

She made her way to the elevator, then took it up to the third floor.

But when she entered 310, the room he'd been assigned last night, she found his bed empty. So she went to the nurses' station, where Brenna sat.

"Where's Javier?" she asked.

Brenna burst into a grin nearly as bright as the one Luis had worn. "Dr. Fortune took him outside in a wheelchair. And they said to tell you, if you came looking for him, that you'd find him in the rose garden."

After thanking Brenna, Leah made her way to the garden.

She only walked a short way before spotting Javier sitting on one of the benches, his cane resting beside him. In his hands, he held his guitar.

Is that why Luis had been smiling? Because Javier had asked for his guitar?

That seemed like an odd request, especially since he was supposed to be going home today, but she decided not to dwell on it. Instead, she approached the bench on which Javier sat.

She hadn't seen it at first, but a glass vase filled with red roses sat at his feet.

"What's going on?" she asked.

He strummed a couple of chords, then asked her to take a seat. As she did so, he began to play a familiar tune—Anne Murray's "Could I Have This Dance."

She'd always loved that song and had heard it used

at several weddings. As Javier sang the words as though they'd been written especially for her, asking her to dance with him for the rest of his life, her heart swelled to the point that she thought she might float away.

And she found herself falling in love with him all over again.

When he'd sung his heart out, when the beautiful words had rung true, her eyes filled with tears.

"I'd wanted to wait to ask you to be my wife until I was back to fighting weight. And Jeremy assures me that I'll be as good as new by fall. So I was wondering how you'd feel about a September wedding?"

She couldn't believe he was doing this for her, sharing his talent, touching her heart.

"I think that would be perfect. Do you have a day in mind?"

"No, I'll let you settle on one. And while you're at it, why don't you see if you can take a couple weeks off for a honeymoon."

"I'm sure that I can. I've got a lot of time on the books." Up until this point, she'd been so focused on work that she had a lot of vacations she'd failed to take.

"Then marry me, Leah. Be my friend, my lover, my wife."

The tears welled in her eyes, and as she nodded her answer, one droplet slid down her cheek, followed by another. "Yes," she finally managed to say. "I'll marry you, Javier."

He placed the guitar to the side, then wrapped her in his arms and kissed her with all the love in his heart.

When the kiss ended, when they came up for air in the garden where Leah had first dreamed of having a home and family of her own, she realized that Javier had just made her dreams come true—and in such a wonderful, romantic way.

"I love you," she said. "More than you'll ever know."

"I've got a pretty good idea, honey. Because I love you more than I ever thought possible." He glanced at his watch. "Come on, we'd better get home before the phone starts ringing."

"Are you expecting a call?"

"A whole slew of them. You see, my dad brought my guitar and the bouquet of roses to me this morning."

"So he knows about this, about us?"

"Yes, and he's probably spread the news to everyone in the family by now."

"I hope they'll be happy."

"They'll be thrilled," he said. "And they'll probably start gearing up for our big day in September. So I hope you like big weddings."

"I'll like ours."

Then right there, in the center of the hospital rose

garden, with new blooms bursting with new life, Javier kissed Leah again. When their kiss ended, Leah said, "Come on. Let's go home."

"There's nothing I'd like better." As he reached for his cane, he wobbled a bit. She stood by to grab him if he needed her to, but she didn't make an issue of it.

"You know," Javier said, as they started down the walkway. "Jeremy mentioned that my survival after that tornado had been nothing short of a miracle."

"That's true," she said.

"And he implied that miracles are often a once-in-a-lifetime occurrence. But next time I see him, I'm going to tell him he's wrong."

"What makes you say that?"

"Because I've been more fortunate than most people ever are. I've experienced two of them within the past three months. And falling in love with you and having you love me back is the biggest miracle of all."

He was right about that.

Leah slipped her free hand into Javier's and walked toward the parking lot where she'd left her car.

She'd been blessed beyond measure, too.

What they'd found in each other's arms was nothing short of miraculous. And she planned to love and cherish him for the rest of her life.

* * * * *

"I came here to thank you for saving my life."

"You told me three months ago."

"No, I didn't."

"You kissed me. Pretty much said it all. Can't say it was the best kiss I've ever had planted on me, but I got what you were meaning by it."

She narrowed her eyes. "If I'd wanted to kiss you in a memorable way, I would've, but I guarantee you I put more emotion into that one kiss than any other I've given."

"Well, isn't that a sorry state of affairs."

"I'm a good kisser!"

"If you say so, ma'am." He touched the brim of his hat. "Have a safe drive back to town." He walked away from her.

Dear Reader,

Anniversary celebrations aren't just for marriages. And as I write this, I'm marking the anniversary of being offered my first book contract, eighteen years ago. Since then I've written thirty-six books. It still amazes me, every single day. The pleasure and privilege of creating a piece of work for others to read never fades.

Creating this particular book has been especially gratifying. Taking an independent Texas cowboy who's much happier among stray dogs and horses, and pairing him with a society-born much younger woman was fun and challenging. I love that Garrett Stone is clear about what he wants and doesn't want in life. Even more, I love how Victoria Fortune makes him change his very set mind.

I hope you enjoy taking their journey with them.

Susan Crosby

FORTUNE'S HERO

BY
SUSAN CROSBY

First published in Great Britain 2013
by Mills & Boon, an imprint of Harlequin (UK) Limited,
Eton House, 18-24 Paradise Road, Richmond, Surrey TW9 1SR

© Harlequin Books S.A. 2012

Special thanks and acknowledgment to Susan Crosby for her contribution to The Fortunes of Texas: Whirlwind Romance continuity.

ISBN: 978 0 263 90084 2
ebook ISBN: 978 1 472 00442 0

23-0213

Harlequin (UK) policy is to use papers that are natural, renewable and recyclable products and made from wood grown in sustainable forests. The logging and manufacturing processes conform to the legal environmental regulations of the country of origin.

Printed and bound in Spain
by Blackprint CPI, Barcelona

Susan Crosby believes in the value of setting goals, but also in the magic of making wishes, which often do come true—as long as she works hard enough. Along life's journey she's done a lot of the usual things—married, had children, attended college a little later than the average co-ed and earned a BA in English. Then she dove off the deep end into a full-time writing career, a wish come true.

Susan enjoys writing about people who take a chance on love, sometimes against all odds. She loves warm, strong heroes and good-hearted, self-reliant heroines, and she will always believe in happily-ever-after.

More can be learned about her at www.susancrosby.com.

For Bobbie and Ernie, The Cowgirl and Her Prince.
You wrote your own romance,
and you did it so well! With love to you both.

Chapter One

"Keep away from those cowboys, they're ramblin' men..."

The lyrics to the country song popped into her head the moment she saw the tall, blue-eyed man striding past her in the terminal of the small and private, but busy, Red Rock, Texas, airport.

He caught her staring, hesitated a second, then winked. Definitely the rambling type and one to stay away from. He touched a finger to his black Stetson and just like that he was gone, the moment over.

Then the tornado hit. That black hat was the last thing she saw before the roof was ripped from above her, the roar of air sucking everything within, including her, pulling her, dragging her. Around her, wood and metal flew and crashed, ricocheted and bounced.

Pain hit first, then panic. She couldn't catch her breath, couldn't fill her lungs enough to scream. Noise. So much noise. Then suddenly no sound at all.

The quiet was almost as frightening. Gradually she heard crying, someone screaming, others calling out.

Her face was pressed against the cold concrete floor. She tried to move but couldn't. The sound of someone running toward her crept into her awareness. A man flattened himself next to her, his face in shadows—her hero, whoever he was.

"You okay?" he asked.

"My legs hurt," she managed to say, wiggling her toes and feeling them move inside her high-heeled boots, the rubble preventing leg movement.

He sprang up.

She grabbed for him, caught thin air. "Don't leave me. Please, don't—"

But he didn't leave. Weight was lifted from her, twisted metal, lumber and laminate.

"Can you drag yourself out?" he asked, this giant of a man who'd single-handedly raised the wreckage. "Hurry. There's not much time. You can do it, sweetheart. Try."

There was nothing to grab. Her useless polished fingernails dug but found no traction. She caught her breath against the unexpected pain of moving and exerted herself a little more, tried to belly crawl like a solider. Just when she thought she was going to be stuck there forever, he gripped her arm and yanked her from under the debris. Her feet cleared the mess a second before it came tumbling down. He scooped her into his strong arms and rushed away as the whole building creaked and moaned.

Panic set in. "My family...?" she asked.

He angled his head. "Over there."

She'd just started identifying relatives when part of the building they'd left crumbled with a final *whoomph*. If he'd been a minute later, she'd have been buried alive. She clenched him tighter, too shocked to say anything.

"I've got you," the stranger said. "You're safe."

The cowboy, she realized finally. The man who'd winked at her. She hadn't recognized him without his hat.

"Help will come soon," he said, his voice comforting.

She looked up as he set her down. An eerily calm sky replaced portions of the roof of the two-story structure. She'd been sitting on the other side of the room. How far had she been pulled—or thrown?

"You think you can stand on your own?" he asked.

"I think so." Her eyes were level with his chest. She focused hypnotically on the bolo tie he wore, silver and onyx, before looking up at him.

"You'll be okay," he said, releasing her, understanding in his eyes.

Before he could abandon her, she grabbed him

by his bolo and tugged him down for a quick, hard, thank-you-for-saving-me kiss, over as soon as it started. Her heart lodged in her throat, damming up the words trapped inside. She couldn't even ask his name—or tell him hers.

He cupped her shoulders and moved back. For an instant his eyes met hers, then he was running away from her. Paralyzed, she didn't budge for a minute, then she finally focused on her surroundings. It looked like a war zone. Some of her family were sitting in shock; some were running around. Suitcases were scattered everywhere. What had once been a small plane lay nose-down not twenty feet from where she'd been sitting before the tornado hit.

When she turned back to the terminal she saw no sign of the cowboy. Transfixed, she moved toward the luggage, thinking to stack it all together, needing something to do. Then she heard sirens approach and she staggered toward the sound, waving—

Victoria Fortune jerked awake, sweating, her sheets tangled, her long, dark hair stuck to her skin. She'd had the dream again, the same vivid but increasingly detailed dream. The tornado had struck on December 30 in Red Rock, Texas. She'd been headed home after being a bridesmaid in her cousin Wendy's wedding. Now, three months later, Victoria was safe in her own bed, in her own condo, in her hometown of Atlanta, Georgia. Three months, and she was still dreaming about it.

And *him*. She didn't even know his name, never

even thanked him, the man who could've died with her that day but who'd rescued her without regard to his own safety.

She was sick of it, physically ill from the constant nightmares and loss of sleep. Even during the day she was assaulted by visions of the destruction and the surreal feel of the tornado sweeping her across the floor.

Maybe it'd been even worse this time because she'd talked to her cousin Jordana last night, who'd suffered her own traumas, and they'd agreed Victoria should go to Red Rock so they could deal with their problems together. Support each other. Be there for each other.

Victoria glanced at the clock then threw off the covers, realizing she needed to start packing for her late-morning flight. She was going to face the past and deal with her near-death experience. She also needed to thank her hero, which was long overdue.

But first she called her parents to tell them she wouldn't be attending the requisite family Sunday brunch.

"The pew was mostly empty this morning," her father, James Marshall Fortune, said when he answered the phone.

"I'm sorry, Daddy. I overslept."

"You party too much," he said gruffly but softly. As the youngest child and only daughter, Victoria got away with more than her four brothers could. Occasionally she used that to her advantage.

"What constitutes 'too much'?" Victoria asked

sweetly, making an effort with her beloved father.
Even he had been openly worried about her.

"Ha! We'll wait for you. Your brothers aren't all
here yet, either. Only Shane."

Victoria wandered onto the balcony off her
bedroom. She was on the fifteenth floor. "I'm not
coming at all, Daddy. I'm heading to Red Rock in
a couple of hours."

"I thought you'd decided to skip that party."

"I did skip it. The party was last night, but Jordana and Emily are still at Wendy's house. We're
going to have a little girl time, just us four cousins.
Well, plus Wendy's new husband and baby. Please
tell Shane I'm taking a few days of vacation, all
right?"

"Your brother is your boss. If you need time off,
you need to square it with him yourself. And I'm
sure your mother will have something to say."

"Yes, sir." Her father made it sound like she was
a sixteen-year-old kid instead of a twenty-four-year-old college graduate who lived alone and held down
a good job—if she could hold on to it. She hadn't
been pulling her own weight for a while now.

"Shane overheard and says that's good news," her
mother said, coming onto the line. "What's going
on, honey?"

Victoria repeated what she'd said to her father.

"You're still having bad dreams," her mother
said.

"Yes, ma'am. They're not going away on their
own."

"What about that man—that cowboy who rescued you? Are you going to see him?"

"I need to thank him. It's been haunting me that I haven't. I think that's part of my problem."

"I can see where it could help. Are you taking the company jet?"

Victoria closed her eyes. "I'd have to land at Red Rock Airport, and I'm not ready for that. I'll fly into San Antonio and rent a car."

"Call me if you need me. I think it's good you're doing this, sugar. Important. You've looked so tired."

"Thanks, Mom." But it was more than *good,* Victoria thought. It was necessary. She hadn't been able to deal with molehills lately, much less mountains.

Hours later she drove into downtown Red Rock, then pulled up in front of Marcos and Wendy Mendoza's pretty three-bedroom house. Wendy had been working her magic on the place, transforming it from bachelor pad to family home, a fun mix of contemporary and cottage styles. She'd been gardening, too, Victoria could tell. What had been barren at the time of the wedding in December now bloomed with welcoming spring beauty.

Wendy burst onto the front porch. At twenty-two, she was two years younger than Victoria, and she sported the same long brown hair and eyes. She was more openly bubbly than Victoria, but as first cousins, they'd been as close as sisters. So were Jordana and Emily, Wendy's sisters.

"Where's the star of this show?" Victoria asked, hugging Wendy.

"Sleeping. Finally," Wendy answered. "Marcos is working."

"And your sisters?" Victoria asked as they stepped into the house.

"Emily went for a walk. Jordana left."

Victoria stopped. "She left? When? Why? I talked to her just last night. She said she would wait for me."

"I don't know what happened. She took off right after lunch. Honestly, Vicki, Jordana was acting weird the whole time she was here. Em noticed it, too. We're worried about her. Did she tell you what's going on?"

She had, but Victoria couldn't tell Jordana's secrets. Victoria made a noncommittal sound as she checked her cell phone for messages, finding none from Jordana.

"You can bunk with Em instead of at the hotel now that Jordana's gone. Would you like some tea?" Wendy asked. "We could sit on the sunporch for a while."

"Yes, fine," Victoria said, trying to drum up some enthusiasm for Wendy's sake.

"Meet you on the porch in a minute." She laid a hand on Victoria's arm. "Are you all right?"

"I'm fine. Just fine. Why is everyone asking me that?" She closed her eyes and gritted her teeth. "I'm sorry, Wendy. I really am. I don't know if I'm all right. I know I haven't been myself. I'm hoping this trip will be the vacation I need."

Victoria carried her suitcase into the guest room. How could Jordana leave without a word to her? They needed each other.

And she needed the name of her rescuer. Needed to see him, thank him. She wasn't in the mood for idle chitchat, but she knew good manners indicated she should spend time with her hostess first.

Victoria peeked into the baby's room, caught a glimpse of a tiny pink bundle in the bassinet, then tiptoed out, afraid of waking six-week-old Mary-Anne.

"I'm surprised that Emily is still here," Victoria said to Wendy as they sat in the glassed-in sunporch. "She's been staying with you for weeks. How long can she stay away from work?"

"I've stopped asking her that question. I figure she knows what she's doing. She's been a huge help since we brought MaryAnne home. She was so tiny, you know, as premature as she was, but so perfect. Emily's a natural mom. She steadied me." Wendy looked around. "Honestly, though, I think Marcos is looking forward to the three of us becoming a family on our own."

Victoria sat up straight. "Of course he wants that. You must, too." Just like all she wanted was to talk to the stranger who'd saved her. "I'll encourage Em to go home, and I'll move to the hotel. We're being so—"

"Stop. Please, Vicki, I didn't mean right this

second. Marcos is glad I've had company since he works such long hours at the restaurant. I just meant that I think we're both ready to establish our own routine. But not this week. Not yet."

"Well, I only plan to stay a few days. I'll get Em to leave with me, too."

"It's not necessary, Vicki. Really. I think she's hiding out here, but I'm not sure why. And then there's Jordana—"

"Who is the biggest mystery of all," Emily said, coming into the room. She was tall, blonde and green-eyed, yet she also had the Fortune look about her. "Hey, Vicki." She bent to give her cousin a hug while eyeing Wendy. "I'm not hiding out here, sister mine. I've been helping. I've also been working from here. You look like crap, Vicki."

"Thank you so much."

Emily shrugged. "Is MaryAnne still sleeping?"

"Like a baby," Wendy said with a grin.

The women settled into conversation, as they had all their lives. Their fathers were brothers, highly successful, self-made financial geniuses in Atlanta, each owning separate companies that weren't in competition with each other. It was amazing, actually, that the cousins got along so well, considering that their fathers did not. At family events, the brothers ignored each other. Only the two men knew what was behind their estrangement.

"So, Vicki," Emily said, "why did you come today instead of in time for the party last night?"

Because my sanity depended on it. "Jordana and

I talked last night, and it just seemed like the right time."

"Did she tell you what's going on with her?"

"Going on?" Victoria asked innocently.

Wendy and Emily exchanged glances. "She doesn't look well," Emily said. "In fact, she looks worse than you. We're really worried."

"I think she's fine," Victoria answered. "She's dealing with some stuff. No, don't ask. She's not sick. Wendy," she said, changing the subject. She couldn't wait a second longer. "Did Marcos ever figure out who got me out from under the debris? I would like to talk to him."

"He's pretty sure it must have been Garrett Stone."

Garrett Stone. Her heart skipped a beat or two. She finally had a name to put to him, a strong name, solid. Heroic. "Where does he live?"

"He's got a ranch—although I'm using the term loosely—outside town called Pete's Retreat. He's born-and-bred Red Rock, but he's left town a couple of times, for several years at a time. There've been rumors about him, apparently."

"Like what?"

"For one thing, he was involved in some kind of scandal years ago with a young woman. That forced him to leave town the first time. For another, no one knows how he makes a living. Plus he's a loner. He's got dogs and a few horses. Strays gravitate to him."

Victoria remembered he was a man of few words, and also how his hands had been gentle on her.

Now that she was here, she wanted to get it over with. To see him. To thank him. To take back her life. "Could you give me directions to his place? I'd like to go there now."

"I can call Marcos and ask," Wendy said. "But I think it would be better if one of us went with you."

"Why?"

"In case he's rude or something."

"Standing-on-the-porch-holding-a-shotgun rude or just brusque? He can't be totally without civility. He saved my life, after all. And besides, I'm not without charm, you know," she added, fluttering her eyelashes.

"I doubt anything in your past has prepared you for Garrett Stone," Wendy said. "Face it, Vicki, the easy appeal you have comes from having led a charmed life. We all have. If you're expecting him to welcome you with open arms and listen to you shower him with gratitude, you're deluded. I gather people don't venture out to his ranch. There must be a reason for that. I'm not sure he'll be nice to you."

"I'm not a princess," Victoria said, crossing her arms. "If he doesn't want to hear what I have to say, so be it. At least I will have done what I need to."

"Wow. You've really gotten snippy."

Victoria dug for patience. "I'm sorry for my attitude. It's just been weighing on me."

"I see that. What I think is that you've got a big ol' case of hero worship, some big fantasy you've worked up in your head about him without knowing the whole truth," Emily said. "And although we may not wear crowns, we Fortune daughters have been protected and pampered since birth. You can't deny that. But the men of Red Rock are different from the men in our social circle back home."

"Meaning what?"

"Have you ever been rejected, Vicki?"

"Of course I have. But it's not like this is a love connection, you know. I just have a few things to say." Except that she'd been fantasizing about him, too, that he'd carried her far away, her hero.

Emily raised her hands in surrender. "Okay, then. At least you'll know what to expect if you go there."

Victoria frowned, thinking it over. She *had* been rejected. Maybe not by anyone who mattered, but then she'd never been in love, either. Perhaps because she'd never developed any long-term relationships, something that had irked her parents to no end. As old-fashioned as the notion was, she'd been expected to find a future husband while she was in college. Her parents were old-school, with traditional expectations, and she hadn't lived up to them. It was different for her four older brothers, who were still single, their martial status not even an issue.

Armed with directions from Marcos, Victoria headed out twenty minutes later. She'd brought a bottle of eighteen-year-old single-malt, award-winning Scotch whiskey. She'd never tasted it herself, preferring sweet, fruity drinks, but the whiskey was praised by most men she knew.

It wasn't a long drive, but an increasingly des-

olate one. Why anyone would want to live so far
from civilization puzzled her. She liked her creature comforts, which meant shops and restaurants
within walking distance and the theater and opera
close enough to attend frequently. It was the reason
why she lived in a condo in downtown Atlanta. She
loved the action.

Finally she saw the mailbox Marcos had told her
to watch for. She turned into the property. There
was no sign announcing she'd arrived at Pete's Retreat, no welcoming fence-lined driveway, just a
long dirt path. After a minute, she spotted a corral
with three horses, then some dogs began to bark,
several rushing up to her car. She slowed way down,
afraid of accidentally hitting one. Garrett Stone may
take in strays, but he sure didn't train them well. Or
maybe he wasn't home to call them off—

No. There he was, coming from a barn. Stroll-
ing, actually. Or maybe moseying, that slim-hipped
stride she associated with cowboys, no-nonsense
and no-hurry at the same time. He was as tall as
she remembered, a foot taller than she, and she was
five-four.

She stopped the car in front of his house, an old
but well-maintained, single-story ranch style. He
came to a halt in front of her vehicle and stared at
her through the windshield, apparently not recog-
nizing her. He still hadn't called off the dogs, who
barked and jumped. She felt imprisoned in her car.

Finally he made a motion with his hand and the
dogs dropped to all fours and stopped barking. They

sidled closer to him. With another hand motion, all
but two dogs headed toward a barn.

Victoria opened the window and called out, "Hi!
You probably don't remember me. I'm Victoria Fortune. From the airport? The tornado?"

"I remember." His face was shadowed by his
hat, so she couldn't judge his reaction, except she
thought he was frowning.

"Will your dogs attack me if I get out of the car?"

"Probably not."

She expected him to wink, as he had at the airport, but his expression never changed, no sign to
indicate whether or not he was joking. Even though
she felt unsure of her welcome, she grabbed her gift
and opened the door. When the dogs didn't growl,
she climbed out, grateful she'd changed into jeans
and boots so that she fit in better. Still he didn't
move.

"I was in the neighborhood…" she began. Nervous now, she brushed at some dust on her jeans,
giving herself something to do, wishing he would
pick up the conversation.

His mouth quirked, but whether it was a sign of
annoyance or humor, she didn't know.

She thrust the whiskey at him, apparently a little
too hard. It hit him in the stomach and bounced off
obviously strong abs. He grabbed for the container.
The bottle fell—

He caught it at his knees.

"Whew!" she said, grinning. "Good catch."

He eyed the container. If he knew how expensive

it was, he didn't indicate it; he just waited for her to speak. Or leave, she guessed.

"Maybe we could go inside?" she asked.

"Why?" he asked.

"I—I'd like to talk to you."

"Here's as good a place as any. You're interrupting my work."

"What do you do?"

"This 'n that."

She crossed her arms. He might look exactly like the man from the airport, but he no longer seemed like the winking type. "You're loving this, aren't you?"

"What?"

"Being the taciturn cowboy. Keeping the myth alive."

"Taciturn. That's a mighty big word, ma'am."

Aha! There *was* a glimmer in his gorgeous blue eyes. He was just playing with her. He'd probably decided she was just another pretty face. "Something tells me you know its definition, but okay. You win. I came here to thank you for saving my life."

"You told me three months ago."

"No, I didn't."

"You kissed me. Pretty much said it all. Can't say it was the best kiss I've ever had planted on me, but I got what you were meaning by it."

She narrowed her eyes. "If I'd wanted to kiss you in a memorable way, I would've, but I guarantee you I put more emotion into that one kiss than any other I've given."

"Well, isn't that a sorry state of affairs."

"I'm a good kisser!"

"If you say so, ma'am." He touched the brim of his hat. "Have a safe drive back to town." He walked away from her.

She called out, "You know, cowboy, where I come from, it's rude to walk out on a visitor."

"Where I come from, princess," he said over his shoulder, "it's rude to drop in uninvited."

Chapter Two

Garrett didn't slow his stride. His old hound Pete trotted beside him and kept looking back at the woman who'd audibly gasped her indignation at his abrupt dismissal. Truth was, she tempted him mightily, and he was afraid if he invited her in, even for just a second, he would fall under her spell. It was obvious that she was trouble with a capital *T*.

The moment he'd caught sight of her at the airport three months ago, he'd felt gut punched. A few seconds later he'd recovered enough to wink at her, but had kept walking because he'd been inclined to start up a conversation, which would've been a big mistake. She wasn't his type at all, which had made it all the more baffling. Two birthdays from now he would turn forty. She looked barely out of college.

She was petite and dark-haired, and he was partial to blonde and tall, or at least closer to his own six foot four than she was. She wore designer-chic clothes, even her jeans and boots had probably come from a boutique or something, and she'd already turned up her nose at the good Texas dust that had settled on her jeans as if she'd been contaminated.

He'd met plenty of high-maintenance women in his life. He'd learned to avoid them, especially after an experience a couple of years back with a woman named Crystal, one he'd like to forget, except for the lesson learned.

But he also liked women with curves. Give him more than a handful of a woman in his big bed and he was happy, especially if she was just passing through. He didn't date women looking for long-term, and felt no need for conversation or companionship on a regular basis.

Sure, the petite Ms. Victoria Fortune of the Atlanta Fortunes was wife material—but not for him. She'd had stars in her eyes when she'd arrived a few minutes ago. He wasn't sure what had caused them. Glorification of him as her hero, maybe? He'd never been a hero in anyone's eyes before. Just the opposite, in fact. He'd been blamed for lots he didn't do, just because people expected it.

He'd been a rabble-rouser in his youth, prone to bar fights and speeding tickets, but that'd been years ago. And then there was that incident with Jenny Kirkpatrick....

It hadn't mattered that he'd been a teenager at the

time—nor had he been the guilty party. Some reputations couldn't be lived down, however, so he'd stopped trying.

Pete assumed his usual dog-sentinel post on the porch as Garrett let himself into his house. He decided to wait until Victoria was gone before resuming his work. When he didn't hear her car start up, he set down the bottle of fine whiskey, peeked out a window and saw her leaning against her car, arms crossed, staring his direction. His collie-mix mutt, Abel, plopped next to her, his tail wagging, dust flying. Idly she petted him, then crouched and gave him a good scratch behind his ears, something Abel loved more than anything except a good belly rub. What male didn't?

Picturing her hands sliding over his own body knotted him up good—and how the hell long was she gonna hang around when he'd specifically dismissed her?

Everyone knew Fortune women liked their luxuries, and they probably always got their way, too. Maybe she wouldn't leave until he forced her off his property.

Well, she wouldn't get her way here. Not with him.

Choking off a colorful oath, he opened his front door, jammed on his hat and strode across his yard. Abel stood and wagged his tail, looking a little guilty at being caught getting attention from another human.

And *that* human was looking at him like he was a rock star or something. Aw, hell.

"Why are you still here?" he asked.

"I'm not a princess," she said calmly. "I came here because I dream about you every night."

Gut punched again, he said nothing. He'd had a few dreams himself....

"Nightmares, really," she added.

So much for hero worship. "You need professional help with that. You're not gonna find that here."

"I'm sure you're right. But I've never been that close to death, Mr. Stone. So I decided to come see you, to thank you, with the hope that I can stop thinking about it, obsessing about it really. I would appreciate it if you would acknowledge the fact you saved my life and let me thank you properly for doing so. I'm sure I'll be able to move on then."

"And just how long does it take to say thank you?"

She cocked her head. "How long does it take to pour a glass of whiskey?"

She had sass, he gave her that. Sometimes that was a good quality in a woman.

"Are you of legal drinking age?"

"I'm twenty-four."

"Are you expected back right away?" he asked.

"I suppose my family will worry after a little while. Why?"

"Before we break open that whiskey, we need to go for a drive."

"Where?" she asked, a touch of suspicion in her voice.

He angled closer. "Well, now, if you don't trust me..."

Her eyes shimmered, eyes the color of chocolate diamonds and just as deep. "Let's just say my entire family knows I'm here, so I don't think trust is an issue," she said.

"C'mon, then." He crossed the yard to where his pickup sat, he could hear her boots crunching against the hard ground. He got into his truck, expecting she would climb in the passenger side on her own, since she wasn't a princess. He smiled a little at that.

"Buckle up," he said when she settled next to him.

They made the trip in silence, and he could feel her tension rise with every mile. Then when he made the last turn into Red Rock Airport, her fingers dug into the seat. Her eyes were glued on the structures ahead as he paused.

He sat still, letting her take in the view, letting her adjust to seeing the place where she'd almost been buried alive. Seeing the airport rebuilt should help her rebuild her own life.

"Let's go inside," he said, keeping his voice soft and low, treating her the same as any wounded animal who'd landed on his property.

She nodded. He admired her for that, for not making him coax her, for facing her demons. He came around the truck as she dropped onto the ground, then he walked toward the terminal. She caught up with him in a couple of seconds and gripped his hand, keeping up with him.

"The airport's back to being used all the time," he said. "They're close to finishing the rebuilding."

"How many people died?" she asked.

"Three." He eyed her. "Could've been a whole lot worse."

"What were you doing here?"

"Picking up a shipment that'd been airfreighted to me." He opened the glass door to the terminal and took her inside with him. She squeezed his hand tighter, if that was even possible. "Clear skies, Victoria. Don't worry."

"Hey, Garrett!"

"Boyd," Garrett said, acknowledging the jack-of-all-trades airport worker he'd known since grade school.

"Need somethin'?"

"I'm showing off the construction."

Boyd waved a hand then walked away.

"It's just a building," Garrett said, feeling her start to shake.

"It was almost my tomb."

His, too, but he didn't remind her of that. He'd been able to tuck it away in his memories.

It was dark by the time they'd walked the entire place. She never let go of his hand, and he had to admit it was kinda nice holding it. Every now and then he noticed the sparkle of her nail polish, felt the softness of her skin against his rough hand and

how small it was compared to his—all indicators of
how different they were.

She was just as quiet on the drive back to his
ranch. He hadn't expected a miraculous recovery
for her, but he'd thought maybe she would chat him
up a bit. She petted Pete and Abel after she climbed
out of his truck, crooning to them. Garrett wouldn't
admit to being jealous, but he felt…something.

"You still want that whiskey?" he asked.

She looked up at him. Her smile was calmer than
when she'd first arrived. "Rain check?"

He didn't answer because he didn't expect to see
her again. He walked her to her car, opened her door
and waited for her to get inside and go. He was in
a hurry for her to leave him in peace. He'd thought
he'd buried his own memories, but being at the airport with her had brought them back in full. He
could toss six feet of dirt over them again, but he
needed quiet to do that. And for Ms. Victoria Fortune to be out of his sight.

"Thank you," she said, a little quaver to her
voice.

Aw, hell. She wasn't gonna cry, was she? *That* he
couldn't deal with at all. "You drive safe now."

She was staring at him, at his chest anyway. "You
were wearing a bolo tie that day," she said. "Silver
and onyx. It was gorgeous."

What he remembered was how she'd grabbed his
tie and pulled him down to kiss him. He also remembered her perfume, sweet and spicy. She didn't
wear any today, and he liked that, too.

Finally she raised her gaze to connect with his, searching his eyes.

"Thank you for taking me there." Then, surprising him, she reached up, locked her arms behind his neck and tugged him down as she raised up on tiptoe. He could've easily set her aside. Instead, he met her halfway and accepted her final gesture of appreciation. Her lips were soft, her mouth hot. When she tightened her hold on him, he did the same, pulling her body next to his, wrapping his arms around her, sliding his hands down to cup her rear.

Then Abel jumped up on him from behind and her cell phone rang at the same time, a double jolt of awareness to the situation they'd been about to put themselves in.

"I'd better answer that," she said, stepping back to dig into her pocket, her hands shaking. "Someone's probably worried."

He backed off as she took the call, telling the person on the other end that she was on her way home. Then she tucked her phone away. He had no idea what to say, so he left it to her because his next move would be to haul her to bed.

"I should go," she said. She climbed into her car and started the engine. Her smile turned mischievous, the dull glaze in her eyes replaced with more clarity. "I didn't want you to think I wasn't a good kisser," she said pertly, then she gave him an indecipherable look through the windshield as she backed up to turn around. She waved as she drove off.

His body was like granite. He hadn't been this on edge for a long time. He was usually the one with the last word, too. She'd caught him off guard. That was also rare.

Maybe he'd helped her with her post-tornado trauma, but she'd given him something to dream about.

It was the last thing he wanted.

Red Rock's most upscale restaurant, Red, was situated in the heart of downtown. Wendy's husband, Marcos Mendoza, managed the restaurant that was owned by his aunt and uncle. It was where Marcos and Wendy had met. She'd been exiled, as she referred to it, from the family business in Atlanta and sent to Red Rock to work for one of the Fortune businesses to discover her talent. She eventually ended up at Red, first as a waitress, then finding her calling as a dessert chef.

The original building was a converted, very old hacienda rumored to have belonged to relatives of the infamous General Santa Anna. It had been rebuilt after a fire but still featured an inside courtyard with a water fountain and several dining areas, both public and private.

Stepping into the main dining room, Victoria admired the rich, colorful decor and peaceful aura. Wendy had urged her and Emily to get out of the house for a while, and Marcos had insisted they have a spectacular dessert on him at Red. They'd argued it was unnecessary, but Wendy had prevailed. She couldn't take MaryAnne out in public for at least two more weeks, according to the pediatrician. She would go to bed when the baby did, and she wanted Emily and Victoria to have some fun.

They sat at the bar, where they had a good view of the restaurant that was a little too understated to be called a "fun" spot. It was a place to gather or go on a date, but not a mix-and-mingle hot spot, nor was there a dance floor in the main room.

"So," Emily said after taking a taste of a creamy dessert called Heavenly Sin and licking her spoon clean. "You've been awfully quiet since you got back from seeing Garrett Stone."

Victoria took a bite of a black-and-white pudding that melted in her mouth. She closed her eyes, savoring it before she spoke. "There's not much to say. I thanked him. He decided I needed to see the airport and took me there, as some kind of therapy, I expect."

"Was he right? Did it help?"

"I suppose I'll find out tonight. If the dream doesn't return, I'll call it a success."

"And was the cowboy rough around the edges or gorgeous?"

"Both."

Emily's brows went up. "Do tell."

"He's different" was all she said.

He came across as a man who didn't rile easily, was in fact paternal and protective, but he also simmered with passion. He just kept a tight rein on it. She could tell when he'd been restraining himself.

That kind of self-control, Victoria thought, was even sexier. And it made her want to break through it.

She dipped her spoon into the pudding again just as the cowboy in question took a seat at the bar, not close enough to talk to, but close enough to exchange glances. The bartender drew a draft and set it in front of Garrett without any words being spoken. He lifted his glass toward Victoria, took a sip and looked away.

"You're blushing," Emily said then looked around, her gaze landing on Garrett, who steadfastly stared at the wall of bottles behind the bartender. "Is that *him?*" Emily whispered.

"Who?"

Emily gave her a tolerant look. "Your therapist."

"Yes. And don't you dare put him on your Baby Plan list."

Emily turned again and caught him studying them. "He'd make great babies, don't you think? Tall and lean, and those ooh-la-la blue eyes."

"Off-limits," Victoria said, feeling her face heat up even more. "Anyway, I thought you were looking to adopt. At least that was your plan a week ago."

"That was originally my goal, but looking at Cowboy Freud here, I don't know…." She grinned. "Don't fret, Vicki. I can see you've got the hots for him. I won't unleash my considerable charms on your man."

"He's not my man." She scraped her bowl for the last taste of pudding.

"Yet."

"I'll be going home in a couple of days."

"I didn't hear you say you weren't attracted."

Victoria shrugged. Attracted? What a mild word…

Garrett stood then and moved to sit next to Emily. They made a beautiful couple. She was several inches taller than Victoria. Her blond hair was more golden than his darker blond, but they fit together.

So much for his being a loner. She tried to remember why she'd labeled him that in her mind.

"Evenin', Ms. Fortune," he said, looking at Victoria.

"Hello, Mr. Stone." The fact they'd shared a passionate kiss and were being so formal with each other made her heart beat faster, as if she was hiding something, when usually her life was an open book. She introduced him to her cousin.

"You following me?" he asked Victoria over the rim of his glass.

She arched her brows. "I believe we were sitting right here when you arrived," she said, pointing out the obvious, not appreciating Emily's curious and rather amused expression.

"Everyone knows I'm here every Sunday night 'round this time."

"I'm new in town. No one thought to add me to the Garrett Stone Sunday Routine loop."

Marcos came up to them and shook Garrett's hand, welcoming him. No, she hadn't known, but

Marcos certainly must have, and he'd issued the command performance to come to Red tonight. Why?

"Were Em's and my desserts Wendy's creations? Is that why you insisted we come tonight?" Victoria asked Marcos, making sure that Garrett knew exactly who was responsible for her being at Red tonight.

"Only the flan recipe on the dessert menu isn't hers, although she's talking about creating a chocolate version."

A server put a plate of enchiladas in front of Garrett, smiled flirtatiously at him—or maybe *knowingly*—then sauntered away. Marcos excused himself, then Emily stood.

"I'll be back in a few minutes," she said.

Victoria was glad for the empty seat between her and Garrett because she wanted too much to sit closer, to brush arms, to straddle him right where he sat. "So, you come in every Sunday night for enchiladas?"

"And to pick up a standing order for a week's worth of dinners."

"You don't cook, I guess."

"I barbecue now and then, and breakfast and lunch are easy, but dinner's a challenge. They freeze individual portions for me. Makes it simple."

"You don't get tired of eating the same things night after night?"

"Nope." He scooped up a mixture of rice and beans then chewed thoughtfully while watching her. After he swallowed, he said, "You okay after today?"

"So far, so good." She couldn't remember being this tempted by a man. She'd had plenty of flirtations in her life, but she craved Garrett. He'd dominated her dreams for months, had held her hand for an hour, kissed her once—but very well—and now he was just sitting there, eating, and she wanted to go home with him.

He eyed her. "Your cheeks are pink."

"It's warm in here."

"You sure you're just not remembering our kiss?"

She angled her body toward him and crossed her legs, pleased that the kiss was on his mind, too. "I told you I was a good kisser."

"It takes two."

She smiled leisurely. "It certainly does."

He gave her a cool look, which made her laugh.

"When do you go back to Atlanta?" he asked.

"Soon. I don't want to overstay my welcome." She leaned closer. "I'd like to see you again."

"Why?" He didn't seem surprised, which annoyed her.

"You interest me," she said.

"And you usually get what you want, I expect."

She thought she should be offended by that, but realized he was speaking the truth as he saw it. She was a Fortune, therefore her life must never hit any speed bumps.

"Most of the time I guess I do," she answered,

although she'd never wanted anything that mattered a whole lot—until now.

He stood, tossed a couple of bills down for the bartender, then swiped his hat off the bar top. Was he going to take off without another word?

"May I come out to your place tomorrow?" she asked, her insides churning. He apparently didn't have a high opinion of her. She'd like the opportunity to change that.

"Not a good idea."

Her brows went up. "That wasn't a no."

He touched a finger to her chin, then dragged it down her neck, his expression intense. "It sure as hell wasn't a yes. Good night, princess."

"See you around, cowboy," she replied, pleased her voice didn't shake.

She watched him walk away and sighed. The skin he'd touched still burned. She'd always wondered what it would be like to want a man like that, really want him. Now she knew.

It probably wasn't smart on her part, trying to get him to meet with her again and see what happened, but an insistent voice in her head—and heart—was telling her to pursue him. She'd always been the resistant one, the person to keep a suitor at arm's length. Now the tables were turned, and she totally understood the frustration of being rejected, or at least being held off.

She wasn't proud of her past behavior, but in her own defense, she hadn't understood it, either.

Emily returned. They put on their jackets and walked back to the Mendoza house.

"You looked like you wanted to gobble that man up," Emily said.

"Too bad he wasn't on the menu," Victoria said, smiling, enjoying the crisp April evening. Life was so different here from Atlanta, so starkly different. "Wendy seems to love living here, Em. I never would've predicted that."

"I'm not sure it's the *where* but the *who*. She loves Marcos. That's all that matters to her. Plus she found a passion for making desserts, so now she has a career. Add in motherhood..." Her voice trailed off. She shrugged.

"Are you envious?" Victoria asked. "I know how much you want to be a mother. It would be good to have a husband first."

"In an ideal world. How about you? Unlike me, you've never talked about—"

"Obsessed about, you mean," Victoria interrupted.

Emily nodded. "I admit to an obsession. Anyway, you've never said anything about wanting a family."

"I've given it some thought, but I'm not in a hurry. I don't think I've found *me* yet. I've got a job that doesn't excite me, but I don't know what else I want to do. I have great friends, but they're settling into relationships and careers, so I feel at a loss a lot of the time. I've gotten restless."

As they left the downtown, the night seemed darker and quieter, and yet Victoria felt safe. She didn't know how safe she would feel at Pete's Retreat. Garrett's desolate location, where animals and humans could be hovering without anyone knowing, made her nervous. What a city girl she was.

Victoria's cell rang just as they reached the house. Emily went inside, leaving Victoria alone on the porch.

"Coward," Victoria said into the phone instead of hello.

"No question about it," her cousin Jordana said. "I'm sorry. I just couldn't stay any longer. Couldn't do what I said I would."

"Your sisters are worried about you. They think you're seriously ill."

"What did you tell them?"

"That they shouldn't worry, because you're not. But you know you'll be showing soon. How long do you expect to keep your secret?"

"I already can't fasten some of my pants."

"Then you can't delay. And Jordana? Tanner deserves to know."

"Soon," she said. "I'm not ready. How about you? Did you meet your rescuer?"

"I did." She told her cousin about her visit with Garrett, although not about the kiss. "As soon as I get home, we'll talk."

"When you were at the airport, did you…"

"See Tanner?" Victoria said, finishing her question. "No. But it's Sunday, and the flight school probably isn't open on Sunday. The building looks pretty much done. It was hard for me to tell without going inside."

After they ended their conversation, Victoria sat on the porch steps. The air felt cooler now that she wasn't moving, but she didn't seek the warmth of the house yet. She set her arms on her knees and rested her chin there, her eyes closed. It'd been a long day, but she needed to examine it, needed to decide if she was truly taken with Garrett or the *idea* of him—what she'd built up in her mind. That he'd added to his list of heroic qualities by taking her to the airport deepened her need to see him again.

It wasn't like her to fall so quickly and so hard. Maybe his resistance had presented her with a challenge, and she didn't have many challenges in her life these days. It was exhilarating. She felt anxious for night to come so the next day could start. It'd been months since that had happened. Maybe longer than that.

Without question, she had to see him again. She couldn't go home with her mind full of him. It would be worse than the nightmares from the tornado. At least those were limited to nighttime. Garrett would haunt her daytime hours, too.

She stood then, her decision made. She would figure out a way to see him again, somehow let him see the real Victoria—at least the one she wanted to become because of him.

Chapter Three

"She's fourteen years younger than me," Garrett said the next morning to his hound as he followed along to the next stall. "Plus she was born with a silver spoon in her mouth. And she's...she's short."

Pete wagged his tail, the dog equivalent of "I hear you, man."

Garrett tossed used straw into a wheelbarrow. "On the other hand, she *is* just passing through. That's a good thing, right?"

Pete cocked his head and whined a little.

"I get it. She's the marrying kind. I need to remember that."

Pete looked away then took off running at the same moment Garrett heard a car coming down his driveway. The rest of the dogs followed. It was probably the straw he'd ordered earlier being delivered. At least he hoped so.

No such luck. He spotted Victoria's car. She tapped the horn twice and the dogs scattered except Pete and Abel. Pete stopped when Garrett did. Abel hurried over to greet her. Garrett didn't call him off.

"Well, don't you look all spiffy," she said, grinning. "Those rubber boots are the height of fashion." She was wearing the same thing she'd worn yesterday, except her shirt was deep purple, low cut and a little frilly. Garrett had a soft spot for feminine frills, even more if they were red, lacy and barely covering a fine female body. He wondered what she was wearing underneath...

"I've been muckin' manure, princess. Wanna help?"

She wrinkled her nose. "Maybe another time."

"Uh-huh."

She made the mistake of stopping downwind of him. After a second, she waved her hand in front of her face. "You weren't kidding."

"You take your chances when you come uninvited." He cupped her arms and reversed their positions.

"I thought you'd like to know that I didn't have the nightmare last night," she said.

He'd had one. It'd been a hell of a night, in fact. "Good. So, now you've come to say goodbye?"

Her eyes sparkled. "Did you think I'd let you off that easily, cowboy?"

"Meaning?"

"I still want to get to know you."

The last thing he wanted was more alone time with her. He turned on his heel and headed back to the barn. "You're welcome to watch me work."

He heard her following him and shook his head. She was like a mosquito. A stubborn, tenacious… and damned sexy pest.

He'd reached the barn door when the sound of a truck stopped him. His order of straw. Great. Lenny, the delivery driver, would spot Victoria and the town would soon be alive with rumor. Hell.

"You look like you want me to hide," Victoria said. "You don't want anyone to know I'm here, I suppose?"

Her insight surprised him. "*Would* you hide?"

"Heck no." She laughed.

He eyed her steadily, resettled his hat on his head and went to greet Lenny, a sixty-year-old man who only seemed slow. He backed his truck to the barn door, hopped down and lumbered to where Garrett stood, waiting, Victoria next to him.

"Howdy, Garrett." Lenny grabbed a bale hook, as did Garrett.

They worked in silence until the bales were unloaded and stacked. Garrett didn't order too much at a time, preferring fresh straw and feed. His barn wasn't huge, just ten stalls, one where he stored straw and another a tack room. Plus his workshop, hidden from casual glances.

When Garrett didn't introduce Victoria, Lenny

made it a point to do the honors. He lifted his gimme cap for a second. "Lenny Paulson, miss."

"I'm Victoria Fortune." She extended her hand as if he'd just washed up for supper, when in fact he was a mess from head to toe.

He hesitated, looked at his hand, then grasped hers for less than a second. "You Fortunes seem to have populated the whole earth."

She laughed. "We have many branches all over the country, that's for sure, and most have been fruitful. I have four brothers myself in Atlanta."

"Whacha doin' with this reprobate?"

"Learning how to muck stalls."

Garrett almost laughed. She'd said it with a straight face.

"That so?" Lenny asked. "Got much call to do that in Hotlanta, do you?"

"You might be surprised."

Lenny guffawed. He pulled a folded piece of paper from his back pocket and passed it, along with a pencil stub, to Garrett, who signed the bill.

"He ain't much of a bargain," Lenny said to Victoria as he headed to his truck.

"'Free' is always a bargain," she countered.

After the truck rumbled off, Garrett went to work finishing cleaning the stalls. She sat on a stool and watched, not saying a word, but not seeming bored, either. He wondered what Lenny would say to people, because he certainly wasn't about to keep this bit of news to himself. No way.

Garrett was aware of her, of every time she

crossed her legs or stretched or sneezed. Once when she was hunched over a little, her shirt gaped and he could see she was wearing a black bra. He liked red best, but black took a close second. It gave him something to fantasize about, anyway. Did she wear some tiny black thing as underwear?

"You only have the three horses?" she asked after a while, having seen them in the corral.

"At the moment. One's been with me a long while. Apple Annie. These others ended up here over the past week. Haven't located any owners as yet."

"And how many dogs?"

"Six. At the moment."

"Do those numbers change a lot?"

"They come and go. Except for Pete. He stays."

"Abel seems pretty entrenched, as well."

Garrett glanced over at the mutt, who'd made himself at home at Victoria's feet. "He's been hard to place. Not that he isn't a good dog. He's just... attached."

"I haven't seen any cats."

"They keep to themselves. Last I counted, there were three. They do a good job of keeping the rodent population controlled." He spread new straw in the last stall and wondered what would happen next. She didn't seem inclined to leave.

"I brought lunch," she said then, sliding her hands down her thighs nervously.

He didn't know what to make of her—of the adoration in her eyes, her sassiness and straightforwardness. It was an odd and fascinating combination, and he needed to be careful. While he felt an almost blinding physical attraction to her, he would never be good enough for a Fortune, not with his past, not even for a night.

"I pictured you slapping a peanut-butter sandwich together for yourself," she went on when he didn't speak. "Thought maybe you'd like something a little heartier."

He ambled over to where she sat. She straightened as he got closer. Her eyes took on a little wariness. "Victoria—"

"Vicki," she interrupted breathlessly. "Most people call me Vicki."

He let a few seconds pass. "Victoria, I don't need mothering."

"I'm not mothering you. I'm trying to be your friend. Friends do nice things for each other."

"I've got all the friends I need."

"Well, then, you're a rare man. I figure I'll meet lots more people in my life who will become friends. Some just for a little while and some forever. You saved my life, Garrett. That's an unbreakable bond between us."

"Yeah? Well, I'm beginning to regret doing that." He stalked toward the door, not knowing where he was going, just that he needed to get outdoors.

She laughed and followed. "Roast beef sandwich, potato salad and apple pie," she said, a coaxing lilt in her voice.

How'd she know his favorite meal?

"Estelle told me," Victoria said smugly, apparently reading his expression. "Emily and I ate breakfast at her diner this morning. She even packed our lunch in a cooler I'm supposed to bring back when we're done."

He reached the stairs to his front porch, stopped and turned around. "So now Lenny and Estelle both know you're out here visitin' me. You might as well have taken out an ad in the weekly."

"Are you hungry?"

Her cheerful, I-am-never-denied-anything tone made him want to shake his fists at the sky. Instead he shook his head. "I need a shower."

"I'll wait. Thank you," she said seriously.

He bit his lip. She'd gotten her way, and she knew it. "We'll eat here on the porch," he said.

"Afraid if I come inside your house, I'll slip behind the shower curtain with you?" Her eyes took on some shine, not so much in humor this time but provocation, as if daring him.

She had it backward. He was afraid *he'd* invite *her* in. Not only would lunch not get eaten, but maybe dinner and perhaps breakfast, too. He wouldn't mind a good, long time in the sack with her.

"I won't be long," he said, then escaped into his house.

"I'll be right here," Victoria called after him then drew a calming breath. Keeping her hands off him had been torture.

She pulled the cooler from her trunk and set out

lunch on a small, rough-hewn table between two unpadded rocking chairs. She couldn't picture him in a rocker at the end of the day, except maybe if he had an ice-cold beer while watching the sunset for a few minutes. Maybe. She would've said he wasn't a sentimental man, except that the way he treated animals said differently.

She wondered if he really deserved his reputation. He'd been gentlemanly with her—unfortunately. She smiled at that, then she loosened a button on her blouse, sat on a rocker with her knees up and waited patiently for him to join her.

Beyond the way her body felt around him, she liked him. He wasn't like anyone else she knew, sure of himself but not in an arrogant way. The way he touched his animals said a lot, too. He knew how to be tender. She figured he was also very strong. Men who worked ranches and farms generally were. She didn't know anyone else who worked physically for a living.

And he seemed comfortable in his own skin, a very good trait.

The screen door creaked open. Pete stood right away then tracked Garrett to the second rocker, sitting next to his master.

"Is Pete one of your rescued dogs?" she asked.

"We sort of rescued each other. The food looks good." His easy change of subject was marked with a tone indicating it wasn't going to be reopened. He grabbed a wrapped sandwich and dug in.

They didn't talk, and that was amazingly okay

with her. She was a curious person, one who asked lots of questions, wanted to know the how and why of things, but this time she just ate and listened to the land, the wind swirling dirt across the property, horses neighing in the corral, dogs yipping now and then. How different were the night sounds?

After they finished eating, she put the empty containers in the cooler, which he carried to her car.

"Have a safe trip home to Atlanta," he said, blocking her from moving beyond the car.

She forced herself to smile. "I'm not leaving Red Rock yet."

"Your choice, Victoria Scarlett, but don't come out here again." His eyes seemed filled with both desire and regret.

Something roared through her—loss, a sense of abandonment and even more, a feeling her future had just zagged onto another path. "How'd you know my middle name?"

"You're splashed all over the internet, the adored daughter of Atlanta."

"I want you," she said impulsively, probably foolishly but honestly.

"Which is exactly why you need to go now and not come back." Tension coated his words. He fastened the button she'd undone, his fingers grazing her hot skin, making her draw a shaky breath. "You can't be with a man like me, Victoria."

"Why? What's wrong with you?"

"I'm too old for you. I like my quiet life. I don't want bright lights and big cities."

"What makes you think I want more than to sleep with you?" She saw that her words surprised him. Maybe he even saw she was lying. She *did* want to sleep with him, but perhaps he could see more deeply into her and know that she felt something more than that. She shouldn't. It was ridiculous, given their short history. But she wanted more. Her dreams had been full of him. She'd been wanting him for months.

"Princess, you've got a little fantasy going based on me saving your life, and maybe because there's an attraction between us. We won't be acting on it. That's that." He walked straight into his house and shut the door.

Pete had followed him, but Abel let her give him a hug, one she really needed.

Rejected. Emily had been right. Victoria wasn't used to it, and it stung a whole lot. Mattered a whole lot.

"Take good care of him, okay?" she said to the dog. "I think he needs someone to love him."

She had to leave him alone, as he wanted. If she pursued him, pushed him, he would only get angrier, and she'd rather he remember her fondly.

Victoria got into her car, then a half hour later she walked into Estelle's diner, cooler in hand, having lost her good spirits. The noon rush was over, only a few customers sat at the counter, sipping coffee. The redheaded, fiftyish Estelle was leaning her elbows on the counter and gabbing with an older man.

"Everything was wonderful," Victoria said to her. "I'll set this by the kitchen door, Estelle."

"That'd be fine, thanks. Oh, Lenny was here for lunch. Said he met you."

"Yup," Victoria answered, drawing a laugh. She would be as tight-lipped as necessary. Garrett would appreciate her discretion, she was sure. "Garrett was kind enough to show me his rescue operation. He's doing good work."

"Rescue operation? I thought he just took in stray animals."

"He also trains them so that they're ready to be good pets for people." Victoria assumed an all-business mode. She owed it to Garrett to protect him from gossip—and maybe to improve his reputation a little. "That's a nice little enterprise he has going. Well, thanks again, Estelle."

"Sure thing, honey."

Instead of getting in her car, Victoria walked to a park a couple of blocks away. She didn't want to face Wendy and Emily yet, afraid the disappointment of being dismissed by Garrett would be visible on her face. That defeat hurt more than she'd expected and was deepening each minute. She was torn between staying away, as she'd first thought she could, and making a bigger effort to tear down his walls of resistance. Could she accomplish that? Maybe if she had more time…

Caught between the challenge of winning him over and her usual don't-make-waves stance, Victoria sat on a park bench to think. A young mother pushed her toddler in a swing across the way, but otherwise it was a school day and therefore devoid of older, noisier children, giving her the quiet she needed.

He was right about some things—fourteen years was a big difference in age. Wendy had told her he'd moved away a couple of times. What had he done during those exiles? What kind of life experience did he have that she didn't? She was accustomed to the men of her social circle. Similar backgrounds helped smooth the path to an easier getting-to-know-you time in a relationship.

Nothing was similar about her and Garrett, not that she could tell, anyway. She did like bright lights and big cities—it was all she knew. When he'd said he didn't like them, it probably also was experience speaking. She'd only visited Red Rock, so she didn't know about small-town living, especially isolated-ranch living. She didn't think she was cut out for it.

So, what could she do?

She rubbed her face and blew out a breath. She focused on the mother and child playing, heard their laughter, smiled as the little one said, "Higher, Mommy. Higher!"

Emily had asked Victoria about having a family, and she'd answered truthfully. She hadn't given it a lot of thought, except in the way she always had—someday, when she was married and the time was right, it would be the next logical step. But she hadn't hungered for motherhood like Emily.

And Garrett certainly wasn't marriage material.

He'd separated himself from daily life among people for a reason. If she could somehow convince him to sleep with her, that would be the extent of their relationship.

Could she live with that?

No. She knew for a fact she would want more. Much more. He appealed to her on levels she'd never experienced before. He was worth fighting for, but at what cost? Not just to her, but to him. Everyone had the ability to be hurt, even him, no matter how hard he might fight it.

She made the decision then to leave him alone, to relegate him to a bittersweet memory and unfulfilled dream. She would finish her vacation with Wendy and Emily, return to home and work in Atlanta, nightmare-free at last, and move on with her life.

And leave him to live his.

Chapter Four

Garrett was about to bang on Wendy and Marcos Mendoza's door four days later when he spotted the "Baby Sleeping" sign hanging on the knob. It didn't cool his ire but it did temper the force with which he knocked. Victoria Fortune had some explaining to do.

She opened the door. Her shower-wet hair had dampened her yellow blouse. No jeans this time, but slim, dark brown pants. Socks but no shoes. No lipstick.

She looked sexy as all get out.

"Well, Garrett, how nice—"

"What the hell did you do?" With his boots and hat on he towered over her. And while he didn't usually use his height to his advantage, especially with a woman, he was furious enough with this one to make a point.

Victoria stepped outside, pulling the door shut behind her. "Be specific, please."

"You told Estelle I run an animal-rescue operation."

"Don't you?"

"Hell, no. I take in strays now and then and rehabilitate them and find them homes. It's not an *operation*. There's nothing official about it."

"Maybe my terminology wasn't exactly right but—"

"Your *inexact* terminology brought me two horses, eight dogs and five cats in the past two days. And I don't expect the 'donations' to stop. Included in that total are a mother dog and four puppies and a mother cat and four kittens, by the way. That's *fifteen* more mouths to feed. And find homes for. Not to mention spaying and neutering and shots. Plus they need to be isolated until they get their vet check."

"Technically, you only have seven new mouths to feed—assuming the puppies and kittens are being fed by their mothers."

He glowered and she held up a hand. "Just trying to lighten the mood."

"Try a different tack."

"I apologize for what happened. What can I do to help?"

"You can tell Estelle you made a mistake and let her spread the word."

"You could do that yourself."

"You need to eat a little humble pie, princess."

She crossed her arms. "I'm supposed to fly back home in a few hours."

"Then you'd better get crackin'." He spun on his heel and took off, feeling her eyes on him as he strode to his truck. By the time he started the engine, she'd moved to the front of the porch, watching him.

She's leaving....

He'd sort of been waiting for her to show up uninvited again, figuring she didn't like being denied something she wanted, and she'd made no bones about wanting him. He'd been flattered and aroused by it. Dreams of her had become jumbled with renewed nightmares of the tornado. He wondered if hers had gone away for good.

He took off for home. It wasn't the dogs and cats that would take up his time, except for finding them homes—it was the horses. They took a long time to work with, especially if they'd been injured or abused. These two new arrivals were skittish, not yet letting him check them out, so he didn't know what he was dealing with. But the time involved in caring for them took away from his work, and his work brought him an income. Without money he couldn't continue to support his animals.

For the moment, however, he needed to make boxes to contain the puppies and kittens, a job that shouldn't have been necessary in the first place.

Why had she done it? Did she think he wasn't

good enough as he was, so she wanted to make him seem more charitable, therefore better, to the citizens of Red Rock?

Cursing the tornado that was the source of all his current problems, he pulled up in front of his barn and unloaded supplies. He spent the next couple of hours working in the barn, surrounded by the sounds of puppies yipping and kittens mewling. Strange and familiar dogs milled around, with Pete asserting himself as alpha dog to settle down the new arrivals and establish their place at the ranch.

Garrett had just moved the mamas and babies into their respective stalls when he heard a car approach. The new dogs barked or hid. The rest went to greet the visitor. Garrett didn't recognize the car—or the one that pulled in behind it. Or the next one, which also towed a horse trailer. But as the people emerged, he recognized several from the Red Rock branch of the Fortune family, and a couple of Mendozas, as well.

An hour later, he was still standing outside his barn feeling bewildered when he spotted Victoria's rental car coming up his driveway. She bounded out of the vehicle, her face glowing.

"Well?" she asked.

"I gave away four dogs, one horse and two kittens—when they're ready. What'd you do? Strong-arm your family?"

"Who doesn't want a well-trained pet? They sold themselves. I think more people will show up in the next week, too. Everyone eating at Estelle's got the

word, and she'll spread it further. You may run out
of animals."

She looked pretty proud of herself—understand-
ably—but she'd also just turned his life upside
down. People would be coming to his ranch, interrupting his life. He didn't want that.

"You've got jeans and boots on again. Aren't you
leaving?" he asked.

"I changed my flight. I needed to right my
wrongs before I left."

He crossed his arms and angled toward her more.
"Why'd you do it, Victoria? Why'd you tell people
what you did?"

She frowned. "I was trying to help you."

"Help me how?"

"I thought to improve your standing around
here."

"Why would that matter to you?"

"Because I know you're a better person than your
reputation."

He couldn't remember a time when someone
had defended him. Certainly no one had mounted
a public relations campaign on his behalf. It made
him distinctly uncomfortable.

"May I see the newest members of your menag-
erie?" she asked.

He figured the puppies were about two weeks old
and the kittens only days. The three new adult dogs
were all mixed breeds and skinny but gentle. Food
and a little attention would turn them into good pets
before too long.

Victoria oohed and ahhed over the babies and cooed to the mothers, telling them what good mamas they were. Garrett watched her crouch low to talk to them, her hair curling down her back, her jeans cupping her rear. He wouldn't mind putting his hands there. Wouldn't mind it one bit.

She looked up at him. "How can I help?"

"I'm gonna give the new dogs baths. They all need to be brushed and have burrs cut out. A two-man team works more effectively than one."

She stood and rolled up her sleeves. "Just tell me what to do."

One by one they bathed the dogs, muzzling them first, washing, rinsing, combing, snipping. He treated their ears, checked their skin, then turned them loose, figuring they'd go roll in the dirt. He was right.

Victoria sighed beside him. "That didn't last long."

"They like to smell like the stuff they like."

She was wet and muddy. At some point she'd twisted her hair into a knot at the back of her neck. She didn't seem worried about the way she looked, however, didn't fret about her appearance at all.

"What do you do for a living?" he asked.

"This 'n that," she answered, giving him a sly grin.

He came close to laughing. "Guess I deserved that."

"Guess so, but since I'm not as secretive as you—"

"Private, not secretive. There's a difference."

"The end result's the same," she countered.

He shrugged at her logic, not giving in.

"Anyway," she continued, "I'm the assistant director of sales for JMF Financials."

"JMF being your father's business?"

"Yes. He started it himself when he was twenty-four. We sell and manage financial portfolios, mostly for corporations, specializing in retirement plans."

"So you sell 401(k)s?"

"Sounds exciting, hmm?" She rolled her eyes.

"It could be, if it's what you want to do."

"I don't know what I want to do." She kicked at the dirt, as if measuring how much she should say. "Actually, according to my parents, my primary job is to find a husband, but I haven't cooperated. I did finish college while I was husband hunting, however. My degree is in marketing, but I haven't been invited into that tight circle at work. My family didn't want me floundering after college, so my dad made my brother Shane take me as his assistant director. I think there's resentment from all my brothers because they had to work their way up. I had a pretty good title to start with."

"But?"

"It's a job. I want a career."

"Being a homemaker could be a career."

"I'm not ready for that, much to my parents' disappointment."

Abel bumped her from behind, knocking her legs

out from under her. Garrett caught her by one arm before she landed on the ground. She laughed and wagged her finger at Abel, who barked and jumped around her until she knelt and rubbed him.

She glanced up at Garrett. He didn't release her immediately, but almost pulled her against him.

"I should get going," she said. "Wendy and Marcos are throwing a little party."

He dropped his hold on her. "Special occasion?"

"Oh, someone they want me to meet," she said dismissively.

The way she said it implied it was a man. He tamped down a surge of jealousy, unfamiliar and unwanted. "I thought you were leaving."

"I extended my vacation a while longer." She met his gaze. "I won't be missed at work, and it's been fun hanging out with my cousins."

He walked with her to her car, not knowing what to say. "Goodbye" would've been the best and easiest choice, but he had a feeling he would see her again.

Or maybe not, depending on how her dinner date went tonight.

She opened her door then turned to him, pulling something from her pocket and shoving it at him. "Here. To help with food and shots and stuff."

He glanced at the check, which was folded in half. He had no idea how much she'd written it for, but he figured it was enough to cover his expenses for a while. She thought he was that poor?

"I don't want your money." Insulted, he held it out to her.

"I got you into this mess. At least let me help pay for what I did."

"I don't need it."

She ignored him and got in the car.

"I won't cash it," he said.

"That's your choice."

When she reached for the handle, he held the door tight, then he shoved the check in her shirt pocket. Her breast was firm and full. He pulled his hand out fast, after barely two seconds of contact.

Don't go. Don't go back to Red Rock for a blind date. Don't go back to Atlanta....

He didn't say any of it. She looked at him the way Jenny Kirkpatrick had twenty years ago. He'd had to leave town because of that look—and what Jenny had wanted from him, which he hadn't wanted in return. He'd made a life for himself finally, a life he wasn't willing to risk, not for a fling—because surely that's all it would be—and he'd given up high-maintenance, demanding women.

"Goodbye," he said to Victoria.

"Bye now," she said cheerfully, then shoved the check under his belt so fast he barely felt it, but his imagination dragged out the moment.

He didn't watch her drive off, not giving her that satisfaction, but Abel looked at him as if to say, "You let her *go?*" before he turned tail and walked away. Even Pete seemed disgusted with him.

Curiosity got the best of him, however, and he

opened the check, whistled at the amount, then
ripped it up. She probably brought in an above-
average salary for someone of her age and experience. He'd bet she got annual bonuses, too, maybe
even had a trust fund.

Well, he wasn't running a charity, but doing
what made him happy. He could afford the life he'd
chosen. He'd been angry at her for what she'd done
and had wanted her to feel guilty.

Apparently he'd been too successful at doing that.
She'd stayed on in town instead of flying home,
would continue to be in the area for however long
and she was about to be introduced to someone her
family obviously approved of.

It was for the best, he decided, especially as his
head filled with memories of Jenny Kirkpatrick.

When he'd been a senior in high school, Jenny
had been one of Red Rock's golden girls, a sixteen-
year-old, straight-A student with a desire to become
a doctor. At eighteen, he was older but really no
wiser, not knowing how the world worked then. He
just knew she was pretty, and he liked her fine and
she liked him, too. Was fascinated by him, in fact.
Kind of like Victoria.

Garrett looked out at the horizon now, taking his
time to think about Jenny, something he hadn't done
in years, knowing it was his meeting Victoria, another golden girl, that was spurring the memories.
He needed to analyze the past now, because it could
have bearing on his future.

After he and Jenny had met, her grades took a

nosedive, and he'd gotten blamed for it. Her parents forbade him to see her. Her father's wrath had struck fear in Garrett, so he'd done the right thing and told Jenny they were through dating until her parents okayed it.

The never-before-denied pampered daughter had rebelled by running away from home—all the way to San Antonio. Without money, she'd shoplifted food at a convenience store, and the owner had called the police and her parents, getting her the attention she'd wanted.

Somehow that had been all Garrett's fault, too. The Kirkpatricks were the richest people in town, and Jenny the most spoiled girl. Garrett was just… Garrett—poor, fatherless and with a mother who didn't care enough to parent him. He'd finished his senior year then joined the army. Jenny had been sent away to a private school.

Pete barked, pulling Garrett out of his thoughts. Another car was coming up the driveway, towing a trailer, a horse inside it.

Maybe he'd ripped up that check too soon.

Victoria yawned as she carried empty dessert plates into Wendy's kitchen, Emily at her heels.

"What was Wendy thinking?" Victoria whispered. "He's such a bore. And so full of himself." He was a high-tech innovator from San Antonio and let everyone know how successful he was.

"She was thinking he would distract you from your infatuation with Cowboy Freud."

"Seriously?" Victoria looked toward the kitchen door to make sure they weren't being overheard. "And she thought that man out there would do the trick?"

"Okay, I can't put this on Wendy. Your mother set it up."

Victoria plunked her fists on her hips. "I haven't spoken to my mother about Garrett, at least not since the first night when I told her I'd been to see him."

"Your mother talked to our mother, who had talked to Wendy. She hadn't thought anything about Mom's curiosity, just answered questions that apparently your mother gave her to ask. Wendy commented that you seemed taken with Garrett. She didn't know she was being grilled, Vicki, although she is worried about you a little."

"She doesn't need to be." Victoria swiped the dessert plates almost violently with a sponge under running water.

"Really?" Em said, coming up close. "Wendy and I both think you're headed down a dangerous path chasing after him, Vicki. You're bound to be disappointed when he doesn't live up to your expectations."

"You've barely met him and you've decided I'm going to be disappointed?" Fury welled inside her. First, Garrett kept her at arm's length, thinking she was some kind of pampered daughter of society, and now her own family wasn't acknowledging her as a competent adult. "What does Marcos say? He, at least, knows Garrett some."

"You'll have to ask him."

"I will." She dried her hands and returned to the living room.

Her "date" stood. "Wendy and Marcos are putting the baby down," he said.

She sat in a chair next to him. "You never mentioned what company you work for, Derek."

He shifted in his seat. "TexTechtronics."

Ah. "JMF Financials handles your retirement plan."

"Oh, that's right. They do."

Like he didn't know that.

"Would you like to go for a walk?" he asked in an obvious change of subject.

"No, thank you." She couldn't get mad at him for doing her father a favor. He'd been used as much as she had. "I enjoyed meeting you, Derek, but I don't see this going anywhere. I'll be headed back to Atlanta very soon."

He looked relieved. "I see." He offered his hand. "I think I'll head out, then. Please thank Marcos and Wendy again for the meal. It was top-notch."

Marcos had brought it home from Red—delicious, as always. He'd taken a break from work to have dinner and would return before closing later. Friday was a busy night. He'd probably been perturbed at his presence being required.

"Where's Derek?" Wendy asked when she and Marcos emerged. Emily came out from the kitchen

at the same time. There was little doubt she'd eaves-
dropped.

"Vicki sent him on his merry way," Em said.
"She got the whole messy plan figured out."

"Oh." Wendy put a hand over her mouth. "I'm
sorry, Vicki."

"I'll leave you all to sort this out," Marcos said,
giving his wife a kiss.

"A word before you go, please," Victoria said.

He stopped at the front door, looking resigned.

"Should I be afraid of Garrett? Or worried in any
way?"

Marcos shrugged. "He lives a quiet life, doesn't
cause trouble. It's true he hasn't made friends in the
sense that we think of. He doesn't have parties or
go to parties. But he's fair in his business dealings,
always pays his bills."

"Why does he have a reputation?"

"He's years older than I am. I don't know what
happened, except he left town when he was eighteen
because of a scandal over a teenage girl. When he
came back he picked fights in bars. He left again.
Since he came back, he's been a hermit." His shoulders shifted. "He does entertain women, I've heard,
but I haven't heard any complaints about his treat-
ment of them. That's all I can tell you."

How often did he entertain? And why did he turn
her down? "And you don't know how he supports
himself?"

"What am I? The town private investigator?"

Victoria crossed her arms. "You run a restaurant. You must overhear stuff."

"Not anything related to Garrett. He's always seemed okay to me. Look, I've got to get back." He kissed his wife goodbye again and rushed out.

"Why are you so protective of Garrett?" Wendy asked Victoria. "He doesn't even have a job. He likes animals a whole lot more than people."

"Maybe he has good reasons for that. Maybe he was railroaded out of town. Injustice makes me angry."

And because I'm falling for him.

Victoria had to sit and let the idea sink in, without letting her cousins see anything they might report to their mother or hers.

"Are you going to see him again?"

"Yes." That much she knew.

"You have to know a relationship with him would only be short-term," Emily said, looking worried. "And if by some chance it does go beyond that, do you really think you could live his kind of life? Or that he could live yours?"

"No, but I'm also not a starry-eyed teenager. Don't worry. I won't come crying on your shoulder."

Wendy reached out and grabbed Victoria's hand. "You can always cry on my shoulder. I won't say I told you so."

"Me, neither," Em said. "And we won't be talking to our mom about it again, either."

"Thank you," Victoria said with a sigh of relief. "I think maybe I should move to the hotel so you can honestly say you didn't know anything. I feel like I'm crowding you, anyway."

"You're welcome here," Wendy said. "But do what makes you feel comfortable."

"I'll think it over. Thank you." She stood. "I'm going to take a walk. Clear my head."

She grabbed a jacket and headed out. Again it occurred to her that she wouldn't do this at home, not at night, although more from caution than experience. It was quiet here, a car passing by now and then, but no one honked. She could look up and see a starry sky.

Victoria kept walking, ending up at Red. She peeked in the window. Almost every table was full, and in a corner booth was Tanner Redmond, a man whose photo she'd only seen once, when Jordana showed his website to her, but she was positive it was him. He was laughing with a beautiful dark-haired woman who touched his arm now and then as she spoke. When he sipped from his glass, his eyes held her gaze.

She pulled out her cell phone and called her cousin Jordana. "Did I wake you?" Victoria asked.

"It's okay. I always seem to be napping."

"How are you feeling?"

"Better. I'm into my second trimester. It's good. How about you? Are you home?"

"I'm taking an extended vacation in Red Rock— where you should be, I might add."

"Have you seen Tanner?" she asked.

"I'm looking at him right now. He's having

dinner at Red with a very attractive woman who's flirting like crazy with him. Jordana, I'm about ready to go in there and tell him he shouldn't be dating anyone since he's going to be a father."

"You can't do that!"

"Then you get yourself down here and tell him the news. You really can't wait any longer."

"I just need a little more time. But I will. Soon."

"What are you waiting for? You are one of the strongest, smartest women I know. It isn't like you to avoid such a major issue."

"You haven't been pregnant and unmarried, so don't lecture me."

Victoria blew out a breath, calming herself. "You're right. I haven't."

"I'll deal with it in my own way."

"All right."

"And you won't interfere."

Someone tapped Victoria on the shoulder. She spun around. "Marcos! You scared the wits out of me."

"Are you spying on someone?"

She held up a finger. "I have to go, Jordana. Talk to you soon."

Jordana was still sputtering when Victoria ended the call—without promising she wouldn't interfere.

"What's going on?" Marcos asked.

"I was out for a walk, and I decided to call Jordana."

"I heard the tail end of your conversation. Wendy's very worried about her, you know."

"She doesn't have to be."

Marcos gave her a long look. "All right. Um, one thing I thought of after I left the house. Garrett had some trouble out at his ranch a couple of years back. Had to do with a woman, but I don't know more than that. The sheriff was called. But you know small-town gossip. The truth is in there someplace, but you'll have to search it out for yourself at the source."

"I will. Thanks. Oh, Marcos," she said as he turned to leave. "Is that Tanner Redmond at the corner table?"

"Sure is."

"And the woman with him?"

"Don't know. I've never seen her before."

Well, shoot. She was tempted to hang around until they left and check if they were cozy or not as they walked to his car, but that could be hours and she wanted to be up bright and early.

She had a big day planned for tomorrow. It was time to start taking some risks.

Chapter Five

It was Garrett's first breakfast at Estelle's since Victoria had come to town. He'd expected to be the subject of a few raised eyebrows, maybe even a couple of comments. What he hadn't expected was to find Victoria seated at the counter, reading the newspaper and eating pecan waffles and ham, maple syrup coating everything on her plate, as if it was something she did every day.

She didn't look up until the whole place went quiet, then she glanced toward the door, saw him standing just inside it, looked surprised and then waved him over.

He nodded at various customers as he headed toward her, then he took the seat next to her. "You're in my seat," he said.

She looked one way then the other. "I don't see anything indicating that."

"Everyone knows that's my place on Saturday morning." He couldn't tell whether she'd planned the moment or was as innocent as she looked. She wore jeans again and red boots he hadn't seen before. Her blouse was new to him—red-and-white stripes with pearled snaps, like something she'd wear to a hoedown. Not that he'd been to one anytime recently....

"Do you want to trade seats?" she asked.

"Hell, no. Not with everyone watching."

Estelle set a mug of coffee in front of him. "Your usual?" she asked.

"That'd be fine, thanks." He waited until she got out of range, then finished his answer to Victoria. "What I want to know is why Estelle didn't say anything about it to you." He cocked his head. "Or did she?"

Her teeth flashed white in a quick grin. "She might have mentioned it in passing."

"So everyone here has been waiting for my reaction."

"You would know better than I. Seems to me the people around here are overly involved in each other's business, so you're probably right. What's your usual?"

He shifted mental gears. "Two eggs over easy, hash browns, a slab of ham and biscuits and gravy."

She gave him the once-over. "I don't see where you put it."

"I don't eat lunch on Saturdays."

She laughed at that, raising her mug in a toast.

"Did you know I'd be here?" he asked.

"I told you before, cowboy. If you have a particular schedule you stick to, I've never been shown it."

Her phrasing was just vague enough for him to take her answer either way. He decided to let it go, figuring it wouldn't be so bad having breakfast with a pretty woman.

"Want the sports?" she asked, holding up a section she'd put aside.

"Thanks." They sat next to each other, reading and eating, occasionally commenting on something in the paper. Their arms brushed now and then. The first time it happened, she froze for a few seconds. After that, he consciously pressed against her every so often, until she finally did the same. It seemed friendly, almost like an inside joke, but it felt arousing. He couldn't remember a time when such a small, innocent touch had made him wish for a private room, a big bed and all the time in the world.

After a while, Estelle came over. "You two need to kiss, start a fight or take off. No one here's gonna go until something happens. I'm gonna start losing business in a couple of minutes."

They looked around. Customers were lining the walls, waiting for a table, because no one had left. Garrett pulled out some bills and dropped them on the counter. "My treat," he said to Victoria.

"Why, thank you." She had a bit of maple syrup

stuck in the corner of her mouth. Licking it off wasn't an option, so he gestured to her.

"What are your plans for the day?" she asked, dipping her napkin in her water and wiping her mouth.

"Errands, then back to see how many new residents have arrived."

She looked contrite for a second or two.

They walked out together, him nodding occasionally, her waving and calling out goodbye. He'd lived quietly in Red Rock for years. He didn't want life to change, yet she was already changing it.

"How did last night's dinner go?" he asked as they neared her car.

"Somehow my mom and dad managed to set me up on a blind date. I love my parents, but they've been pushing too hard to get me married. It's driving me crazy."

"Did you like the guy?" *Say no.* If she liked him and ended up staying in town because of the man, Garrett would have to see her now and then. It wasn't an option.

"No, but he didn't go for me, either, so it ended just fine. Do you have a girlfriend?"

The question caught him off guard. He answered without thinking. "No."

"Good," she said, getting into her car. "See you around."

Good? He didn't want to get caught staring at her as she drove off—especially since everyone in the diner seemed stuck to the window, watching, holding their collective breaths—so he went to his truck without hesitating, putting an end to the crowd's anticipation.

Good? he thought again. She should've figured out by now that he wasn't a man who wanted ties, not even a girlfriend, much less a wife. Maybe he hadn't been clear enough. He'd just have to flat out tell her.

He'd do that next time there was an opportunity so there wouldn't be any confusion about the issue.

When he pulled up to the hardware store, he saw her car outside. This time he was more than a little suspicious. He couldn't imagine a single reason for her to be shopping at a hardware store, but there she was, studying a rack of picture hangers.

"Well, hey," she said, looking surprised, an expression she'd perfected. "Fancy meeting you here."

"Come here often, do you, princess?"

"Wendy just framed a bunch of pictures of the baby. I volunteered to pick up hangers. What do you think? Which ones are the easiest to use?"

He grabbed a package and passed it to her.

"Thanks. What are you getting?"

"This 'n that."

She laughed, then she tapped his chest with the packet. "See ya."

When she was shining it on for someone, she was irresistible. Ray Cleft, who owned the hardware store, got swept up by Victoria's charm to the point where he was blushing. Garrett shook his head, but he also moved to a place in the store where he could watch her get into her car. She had the audacity to smile knowingly and wave, then off she went.

By the time he reached the feed store, he was no longer surprised that her car was parked there. He was a creature of habit—Estelle's, hardware store, pet food, then groceries, every Saturday, like clockwork. Despite what she'd said, someone must've told her.

"Marcos and Wendy get a new pet I haven't heard about?" he asked as she stood contemplating doggy chew toys. "I've been trying to sell Marcos on a dog for a long time. He always says no."

"Hmm? Oh. Yes, you're right about Marcos. I'm getting these for your dogs. You know, so they can chew away their frustrations. And look at these adorable bandanas they can wear. I think I'll get a dozen. The dogs will look even more adoptable when they look cute, too."

Garrett didn't try to talk her out of it, figuring there was no purpose in trying to change her mind. No one said no to her.

He was surprised twenty minutes later when he pulled into the grocery store parking lot and didn't see her car. He even admitted to himself he might be a bit disappointed. But when he came out of the store later there she was, standing next to his truck when he pushed his cart up to it.

"I didn't want you to think I was stalking you," she said, a twinkle in her eye.

He raised his brows.

She laughed. "I know. 'And yet, you're here, princess.' That's what you're really thinking, right?"

"Close enough. What do you want, Victoria?"

"To come out to Pete's Retreat and help with the animals."

He started loading his groceries into the truck bed. "It's up to you."

Her big brown eyes widened comically. "Stop the presses! Garrett Stone didn't tell me no!"

He didn't give her the benefit of even a tolerant look. "You should probably change your fancy clothes first."

"Already in my trunk. Be prepared, you know? I'll follow you." She turned away.

He cupped her arm, made her face him again. "I'm not ever gettin' married, Victoria. Nor am I lookin' for a girlfriend."

An expression crossed her face that he couldn't interpret, then she said, "You know, Garrett, I never would've thought I'd get such a kick out of getting muddy in somebody's barn, either. I'm keeping myself open to new experiences, cowboy. Maybe you should try that yourself sometime. Change can be good."

She was lecturing him? She'd just finished college, had been cloistered all her life, and she was telling *him* how to live?

Regretting he hadn't discouraged her from coming to the ranch, he drove home, his temper simmering. She was right behind him.

Seven dogs greeted them—Pete, Abel, the three

dogs who'd come a couple of days ago and two who'd been waiting in the yard that morning when he got up. He was down to three horses again, one more having been taken yesterday.

"Goodness!" Victoria said as the dogs surrounded her. "You've added more. Where do they come from?" she asked, all innocence.

"I'm sure you'll be pleased to know that word of my *rescue operation* has spread as far as San Antonio."

"As well it should. A lot of people are having to give up their pets because of the housing downturn. Instead of leaving them behind, people are thrilled to find a no-kill site like this. I know I would be." She gave Abel his rubdown as he rolled his eyes in rapture. "Won't the word that you aren't running a shelter spread, too?"

"Probably. It's just being ignored because it's convenient to some people's way of thinking." He grabbed the two grocery sacks with perishables then walked over to her. "Did you get my message earlier? I want to be sure you understand me, princess. I may be set in my ways, but I also know myself well. I've been to hell and back a couple of times and lived to tell about it. Having a woman around for more than a night doesn't sit well with me."

"What happened to you?"

"I try not to look back." He headed toward the house, he could hear her following after a few seconds.

"If you lived to tell about it, why not tell me?" she asked when they reached the door.

He'd set down his grocery sacks to unlock the door. When he glanced back at her, he could barely see her face, hidden behind two bags as she was. Just her eyes. Her beautiful chocolate-diamond eyes.

"It's an expression, you know? I don't talk about it."

"But you just did. So feel free to continue."

He ignored her, leading the way into his house, wondering what she thought of it. He'd seen pictures on the internet of her parents' mansion when it'd been on a holiday home tour for some charitable organization. He could just about fit his place into their living room.

He liked his place a hell of a lot better.

In the kitchen they unpacked the groceries in silence. He couldn't tell if she was mad or hurt. They seemed to have had long periods of silence between them, mostly comfortable. This one had an edge to it.

"I'll get my clothes and change," she said.

"Bathroom's across the living room and down the hall."

After she left, he leaned his hands against his countertop for a minute and blew out a long breath. He'd had women in his kitchen before—women always seemed to want to cook for him, as if showing off their wife potential—but he'd never felt as if anyone belonged, not until Victoria moved around the space with him. Maybe because she hadn't been gabbing the whole time. Maybe because she seemed to know where things belonged without asking.

Maybe because he kept having images of her in his bed, naked and willing...

From the bathroom, Victoria heard the front door shut. Not slam, exactly, but shut more loudly than necessary. What was he so ticked off about? He hadn't seemed to mind her popping up everywhere he went this morning. She'd been testing the waters with him, seeing what she could get away with, and he'd seemed, well, not unhappy, anyway.

One thing she'd learned—when his emotions were involved, he dropped his *g*'s. *I'm not ever gettin' married, Victoria. Nor am I lookin' for a girlfriend,* he'd said. She liked knowing that about him, figured it would come in handy sometimes.

She carried her clothes to the living room and hung them over a chair. His house was about what she'd expected—old, durable furnishings, but the rooms were spotless, a masculine decor with lots of wood, devoid of accessories or art except for one oil painting of his ranch. She got close enough to look at the signature—Liz. Was she one he'd spent a single night with?

Jealousy reared its ugly green head, so she joined him in the barn. Abel had been waiting at the door much like Pete did for Garrett. Abel bounced around her, as if making sure her attention would be on him and not the new dogs or the plethora of puppies and kittens.

She took a deep breath as she walked across the yard, enjoying the open air. Yes, it smelled like dust and animal, but it was a clean scent to her. And the near silence of the place healed something in her she hadn't known needed healing. Usually her head was full of words and images, things she needed to do for work or at home or with friends or family. She rarely had a moment to think, just think.

Victoria found Garrett talking to one of the horses. She was about to tease him about being a horse whisperer when the horse nuzzled him. Victoria sat on a nearby bale, Abel at her feet, and watched Garrett halter the horse and lead him out to the corral. She waited until they were inside the corral before joining them at the fence. Garrett walked him, talking the whole time, his voice soothing.

"Do you ride?" he asked Victoria as he passed by.

"Some."

The next time around, "Do you enjoy it?"

"Mostly."

He gave her a look at her short answers and kept walking.

Next pass by he said, "Ever taken a fall?"

"Twice."

He shook his head, but he smiled, as if he couldn't help it. "Break any bones?" he asked as he approached again.

"My left arm. Now I can tell when it's going

to rain hours before it starts. I also scattered my brains, according to my brothers."

"Ever get 'em back straight?" he asked.

"Depends on who you talk to."

He laughed then. Victoria draped herself over the top railing. She loved watching him walk, loved watching him encourage the horse. He'd be a wonderful father...

The thought blared in her head. *He'd be a wonderful father?* Where had that come from? Since when was that issue of any interest to her whatsoever?

Shaken, Victoria dropped to the ground and headed into the barn. She crouched outside of the puppy pen and played with the puppies, who were awake and crawling all over each other, making yipping sounds. Mama had climbed out of the box for a rest but hadn't gone far. She got a drink of water then seemed to be debating whether to return to her pups or enjoy her freedom a little more. She compromised by coming up beside Victoria but not jumping back into the box.

"Are you worn out, Mama? I can't imagine taking care of one, much less four. And where's the father, hmm? You're here doing all the work, and he's out howling at the moon somewhere."

Garrett would never do that, she thought. He'd be there, come hell or high water. He would protect and support and never turn his back on his responsibilities. Everything about him told her, but especially the way he handled his animals, the permanent ones as well as the strays.

The fact he liked animals better than people was a big loss to humanity. She could picture him cradling an infant in his big, tender hands. She could almost feel him holding her through the night, keeping her safe, making her feel loved.

"You okay?" The man himself crouched down beside her, startling her.

"Yes, why?"

"I called your name five times."

"I'm sorry." She looked at him with different eyes now. He would make a wonderful husband, a loving father, a tender, exciting lover. She'd fallen hard for him, and there was nothing she could do about it. She cupped his cheek, moved closer to him, waited for him to pull back. But he didn't, so she kissed him, a long sigh of a kiss, so exquisite her throat burned.

"I admire you more than anyone I've ever met," she said. "You are so responsible and kind. You have some give to you, but you won't compromise your principles."

He couldn't hide his discomfort at her compliment fast enough. She saw the starkness of surprise and appreciation—and then maybe disbelief. Had no one ever complimented him before? Openly appreciated him?

"That's experience, Victoria. The times I've compromised, I've regretted it."

He stood. She followed suit. "Do you have siblings?" she asked.

"Nope." He headed to another stall.

"What about your parents?"

"Couldn't have been born without 'em."

She laughed. "A few more details, please."

"My father was mostly absentee. He was in and out of my life for a few years, then he disappeared. I've never gone lookin' for him. My mom lives in San Antonio, but I don't see her much. She's a nurse at a doctor's office. I have been a disappointment to her all my life, and an embarrassment most of my life."

He'd recited the words matter-of-factly—except that he'd dropped the *g* when talking about his father. "I heard you left town a couple of times. Where'd you go?"

He talked to the second horse just as he had the first, ignoring her question until the horse calmed. "I went in the army the first time. Second time I worked on an oil rig in the gulf."

"Were you running away?"

"You could say that."

"From what?"

"The first time because I'd been accused of something I didn't do but didn't have the resources to correct. Small towns have long memories, so when I came back, I found no forgiveness, no acceptance. I got into a lot of trouble, bar fights, speeding tickets, you name it. I couldn't find work of any measure, so I left again." He grabbed a rake and worked the dirt floor, his movements taut and quick. "When I came back I had matured. I didn't need to fight anymore. And I'd saved enough money to buy this property. Pete showed up the first night and refused to leave, even though I tried my damnedest to get him to go. Satisfied?" he asked, giving her a look.

"Maybe sometime you'll fill in the gaps, but, yes. It answered questions." She followed as he guided the second horse to the corral and worked with him.

"How about you going first," he said. "I'll bet your childhood doesn't resemble mine much."

"I was doted on all my life," she said, unembarrassed by her upbringing, although sad for him. "After having four sons, my parents were thrilled to have a daughter. I wasn't denied much. I went to finishing school, took piano and ballet lessons, attended a private university, and joined the Junior League as soon as I was old enough."

He got out of hearing range, so she stopped talking.

"I'll bet the whole city of Atlanta knows who you are," he said as he approached again.

"My photo shows up in the newspaper society pages a few times a year, mainly for charitable works. I didn't do anything to earn my status except to be born to James and Clara Fortune, but I hope I've been a good steward of the name."

He circled the corral again. She enjoyed every second of being able to watch him openly. He looked at her with the same intensity, the same desire. It thrilled her, agitated her, excited her.

"Sounds like a good life," he said, coming close again.

"Yes, it has been, and maybe I've been frivolous but I've also volunteered many, many hours for worthy causes, just not jobs where I had to get dirty. But, honestly, Garrett, nothing has made me feel as good as working with you and your animals." She reconsidered her words. "I know I've only helped bathe the dogs, but I'd like to do a lot more, if you'll let me."

He kept walking after her last statement. She couldn't see his reaction, couldn't see if it mattered to him, although he was usually good at hiding how he felt, anyway. At the beginning, she'd thought he didn't care about anything but himself and his own small world, but she was beginning to think he cared too much, and this was how he dealt with it.

"You know, Garrett," she said as he approached again. "You don't have to be what people expect you to be."

"Meaning what?"

"When you came back the last time, people expected you to be the same bad boy as when you left. You've lived a quiet life, not giving anyone fuel anymore, but not really proving you've changed."

He kept walking. She waited what seemed like hours for him to near her again.

"You expected me to be a princess," she said. "Do you still think I am?"

"I don't think you're used to anyone having a bad opinion of you," he answered. "I think it would bother you a whole lot if anyone said something bad about you. Like if my reputation tainted yours, for example."

She considered that as he made another loop with the horse. His expression was questioning when he made the turn toward her. "Are you saying it doesn't bother you if someone says something bad about you?" she asked.

"You're answering with a question now, are you? Very sneaky." He kept walking.

"I do what I find works."

Victoria was having the time of her life. She liked everything about him—except maybe how reclusive he was, which was a big negative. And how resistant he was to anything long-term with a woman, which was a bigger negative.

"This may shock you, but I don't fall into a swoon over such things," he said, coming near again, his eyes sparkling.

She laughed at the image. "I probably would," she said, being honest. "I don't have particularly thick skin."

"What a surprise. Have you ever gone against your parents' wishes?"

She thought about that until he got close again. "Not in a big way. The usual teenage rebellions, but minor ones."

They spent the rest of the day doing chores, most of them having to do with keeping things clean for the animals. She stalled going home for as long as possible, but finally there was no work left, at least for today. Tomorrow it would all start again. Garrett's routine was just that—routine. Except for the changes because of what she'd done, all the additional animals.

Before she left, they sat in his rocking chairs on the porch drinking sweet tea. She was getting hungry, having not eaten since breakfast.

"May I come tomorrow?" she asked.

He hesitated a few beats. "Aren't you leaving town?"

"I haven't booked a return flight."

"Why not?"

"I wasn't ready to." Wasn't ready to give up on him, anyway. She wanted to curl up in his lap, but she knew if she tried he would not only reject her but tell her not to come back. She planned to ask for another week off, giving herself time to let him get more used to her. They'd come a long way today with the revelations they'd shared with each other.

"It's been a while since I had a real vacation," she said.

"You call this a vacation?"

She smiled. "If you think of it as a change of scenery and change of pace, yes, this has been one. Plus my nightmares have gone on vacation here, and I'm not ready to test them back home yet. So, may I come back tomorrow?"

When he didn't answer, she said, "I've got your back, Garrett."

He gave her a sharp look. "Meaning?"

"Meaning whatever we say or do here, stays here. This relationship is precious to me. If rumors start around town, it won't be because of anything I've said or done."

"I don't need a champion, Victoria."

Yes, he did, but she wouldn't defend him again. His hurts were buried deep. She didn't want him to relive them. "You've made that clear. I won't try to boost your reputation for the general population again. Actions speak louder than words, anyway. I'll prove that to you. So, knowing that, may I return and help?"

He nodded, not looking at her.

It was enough for now.

Chapter Six

"I already talked to Shane, Dad," Victoria said on the phone the next morning. She was lounging in a chair on Wendy's sunporch, waiting to leave for the ranch. "He's fine with me being gone another week. I haven't had a real vacation since I started working for JMF."

"I don't have a problem with you taking more vacation, Victoria. I just want to know why. Why there? Why now?"

"I'm having a good time with my cousins and the new baby." Which was the truth, although she hadn't paid all that much attention to the baby. Victoria had never babysat; her brothers hadn't married and had children yet, either. She wasn't used to being with an infant so tiny.

"Here's your mother," her father said abruptly.

"Hey, sugar. What's this about staying on an extra week? Does it have to do with a man?"

"No, ma'am."

"How was your dinner the other night with that friend of Marcos?" Her tone was perfect, just the right amount of curiosity and innocence.

"Let's just say it wasn't a match."

"Oh? Why not?"

"How can anyone define such a thing? No sparks, on either side."

"Have you seen that…cowboy again?"

"It's a small town." She couldn't wait to get out to the ranch again.

"I've been thinking I might like to join you girls for a few days. I'm sure Virginia wouldn't mind seeing her new granddaughter again."

Victoria saw through the ruse. "It's a full house, Mom."

"You and I could stay at the hotel. Let Wendy and Em have their mother to themselves."

Victoria had always found it interesting that the two Fortune brothers didn't get along but their wives did, even to the point of socializing quite a bit. However, Victoria absolutely did not want her mother to fly in, with Aunt Virginia or alone. Victoria had no doubt at all that her mother would somehow ruin what was growing with Garrett. But if Victoria fought it…

Maybe a little reverse psychology? "That would

be fun, Mom. I'm sure we can figure out *something* to do here that would interest you."

A few seconds of silence ensued. "I just remembered. This week I've got the hospital guild luncheon. I'm co-chair this year, you know."

"What a shame." Relief rushed through Victoria. She'd dodged a bullet.

"Sugar, you know your father and I want what's best for you, don't you?"

"Of course I do."

"Every girl falls for a man once in her life who isn't exactly right for her."

"Your point, Mom?"

"I know you well. Your silence about that cowboy is saying more than you think."

"Even if I were interested, he's not. Does that set your mind at ease?"

"Why, yes, it does, sugar. Very much so. You stay in touch now, you hear? You've been too quiet all week."

Like most of her girlfriends, Victoria checked in with her mother at least once a day. Her current lack of communication had probably been the trigger for her mother suspecting something was going on with Garrett. She would try to phone more often.

"Oh, there you are," Wendy said, breezing into the room carrying the baby, who was bundled in a knit blanket. "Marcos just left for Red, and Em's blow-drying her hair. Can you watch Mary-Anne for a few minutes? I want to grab a shower myself. Thanks." She put the baby in Victoria's arms and left.

The seven-week-old infant usually slept a lot—or cried a lot. But her eyes were open now and she was peaceful. Her mouth was puckered, her hands closed into tiny fists tucked under her chin. She smelled… pink.

After a few minutes Emily joined them. Mary-Anne had drifted to sleep. "Want me to take her?" Em asked.

"We're fine, thanks. You can take her when she's colicky." Victoria snuggled the baby closer. "How goes the Baby Plan?"

"Adoption's starting to seem more and more unlikely. They want couples, at least the private agencies I've contacted. They can afford to be choosy. I think I'm going to make an appointment at a fertility clinic. If they can't find a match for me, I don't know what I'll do."

"Maybe your list of requirements is too exact."

"I'm entitled to that." She moved to stand at the window, looking out at the garden.

"I still don't see why the rush, Em. You're only thirty."

"If I meet a man, go through the courtship process, plan a wedding and *then* get pregnant, I'll be thirty-two at the very least—and I want several children. I want to be a young mom, with energy. I've been looking for a man, you know that. No one's ever been the one."

Victoria thought that no real man could ever

measure up to the ideal that Emily had created in her mind. Even a sperm donor probably couldn't. She was setting herself up for disappointment in a big way.

"I don't know how you aren't craving one of your own," Emily said, coming close.

Victoria was starting to understand maternal need a little, but she figured it had more to do with a certain man. A man who made her want to have children with him.

Wendy joined them before Victoria could answer. She handed over the baby. "I don't know when I'll be back," she said, hugging her cousins.

"Call if you're going to be gone overnight," Em said with a wink.

A girl can dream. "Cell coverage is spotty out there, you know."

"That and 'My battery was dead' must rank one and two in the most-clichéd-excuses book," Wendy said, her mouth twitching.

"I'm a big girl."

"You're on the Pill, right?" Em asked.

"Yes, Mom." She hadn't really considered they would sleep together today until Emily and Wendy made it seem like a real possibility.

It all depended on what the man in question wanted. Or *allowed.* She was pretty sure he wanted. Everything about the way he looked at her said so.

The drive to the ranch sped by, then she had to wait while a pickup truck drove toward her up Garrett's driveway. She didn't recognize the driver as she waved back to him. She also couldn't see a dog crate, either empty or full.

"You're my fourth visitor today," Garrett said as she climbed out of her car, trying to calm a joyful Abel at the same time.

"Down," she said. He jumped up. "Why does he listen to you and not me?"

"Abel," he said. The dog looked at him. Garrett made a quick motion with his hand and the dog sat.

"That's all it took?"

"He'll stay there until I release him. Like this." He made a different gesture. Abel popped up. "He's a smart dog. He picked up commands in a couple of lessons."

She bent to scratch his ears. "Who were the other visitors?"

"First one wanted the remaining two kittens once they're weaned. Second one was looking for her own dog who'd disappeared. Didn't find him here, but if hers doesn't come back, she'll take one of the new dogs. She'll wait until he's gone through training. The last one was from a San Antonio television station."

"I'll bet that went over well."

He tossed his head. "Right. I got my shotgun out."

"You didn't!"

"You're so gullible." He grinned at her then headed for the barn. "'Course I didn't. I just threatened to get it."

"Because you're nobody's headline."

"You got it. So, how was your morning?"

"Nice. Wendy made us some amazing French toast with strawberries."

"Do you cook?"

"I get by. Nothing fancy, but I enjoy it."

"What's your specialty?"

"Pasta with whatever vegetables I have on hand."

He opened a stall. "I put all the horses in the corral. If you're game to clean stalls, I wouldn't mind the help."

"Sure. Let me greet the rest of the animals first."

Soon she grabbed a mucking fork and got to work. Because he mucked twice a day, it took him about fifteen minutes for each stall, which meant he finished two to her one. She sang along with the country music playing from a boom box he kept nearby. He cocked his head at her a couple of times when she sang dramatically loud and off-key, but they didn't talk.

"How often does an owner find their lost dog here?" she asked when they were done.

"It's happened a couple of times. In both cases, the dogs wore tags, so it was only a matter of making a call."

"Do you crate them?"

"I've never had to contain a dog except to quarantine when necessary. Once they pass the vet test and are released, they seem to like it here. Never had any get into big fights, either. Pete puts a stop to 'em right away."

"Are you always successful in finding homes for the strays?"

"I can be persuasive when I want to be."

She smiled at that. "I don't doubt that a bit. Plus you don't let them go until they're trained. That's a bonus for most people." She rubbed her arm. "It's been a while since I've done physical labor."

"Or it's gonna rain."

"That's it! That's what it feels like. How'd you know?"

"It's in the air, a couple hours out."

"So, what else needs to be done before the rain hits?"

Victoria had spent a lot of time being a team player—in high school, college, on charity committees and at her job. She was a self-starter, but was usually okay with being part of a collegial group. Working side by side with Garrett felt productive and satisfying. He led, she copied. She tried to anticipate what he needed from her as they got the horses back into their stalls, cleaned out the puppies' and kittens' pens and put out fresh food and water for the rest of the pets.

"Rain's about here," he said as they left the barn.

She sniffed the air, acknowledging the distinctive scent. "Maybe I should just head home before it hits."

"Your choice. I was just going to offer you lunch. Although I guess we worked through lunch. An early dinner? I've still got a couple of portions from Red."

"That would be great, thanks."

She was surprised to find fresh vegetables in his refrigerator and made a green salad while he heated enchiladas, rice and beans. They sat at his small dining table in the kitchen nook and looked out the window into his back acreage, filled with brush starting to green out for spring, and tumble-weeds. It was stark but not ugly.

He offered her sweet tea. It was a perfect meal. Once again they didn't talk much as they ate, and it was okay with her. Comfortable. The rain started, noisy and cocooning. She didn't mind it a bit.

She leaned back when she was done, pressing her hands against her stomach. "I'm stuffed."

"No dessert?"

Her interest perked. "What kind?"

"What would make you feel not too stuffed?"

"Pie."

"What kind?"

"Pie."

"Well, then, you're in luck." He set their plates in the sink. "Blackberry pie. Want coffee?"

"No, thanks. And just a sliver." She wondered where he'd gotten it. The pie plate looked like it came from someone's kitchen, not store-bought.

"Ice cream? Whipped cream?" he asked before he brought her the plate.

A few fantasies came to mind at the image of whipped cream. "Just plain, thanks."

The first jolt of thunder hit when she took her last

bite, followed by a crack of lightning. Then the rain started pelting down, loud and hard.

He jumped up. "Thunderstorm. Hadn't expected that. I need to make sure everyone's inside and shut the barn doors."

"I'll help."

He eyed her briefly but thoroughly. "It won't take me long. No sense both of us getting drenched." He grabbed a rain jacket then rushed outdoors.

Victoria followed, deciding to watch from the porch. She'd never seen a Texas storm—except the tornado, of course. When she pushed open the screen, it hit Garrett in the back.

"What's wrong?" she shouted, as thunder rumbled.

He turned around holding a puppy in his arms. "It was on the rocking chair, along with this note. It's wet. I can't read all of it. Just take it inside for now."

She gathered up the frightened, shaking puppy, who looked a little older than the ones in the barn. She glanced at the note then. "Wait! Garrett, wait a second. It looks like the note says, 'I can't keep the pair of them. Their mama died.' There's another puppy."

Garrett cursed a blue streak the likes of which Victoria hadn't ever heard. It fascinated her, all those words strung together like that. "You go tend to the rest," she called out. "I'll put this one in the house and hunt for the other."

"No, I'll do it."

"I won't melt in the rain, cowboy. Just go."

He hesitated, then he said, "There's a flashlight on the kitchen counter and a jacket by the front door. Look around the perimeter of the house first, through the lattice. It couldn't have gone far, and it probably wouldn't venture into the open."

By the time she was armed with flashlight and jacket, the rain had intensified to sheets. Thunder cracked and pealed. Lightning flashed in the distance, but was inching closer. She shined the flashlight at the foundation, behind the shrubs that lined the front of the house. If a puppy cried out at all, she couldn't hear it above the pounding rain. Rain soaked her jacket, weighing her down and running into her boots, filling them and making it hard to lift her feet.

Still she kept looking, panicking a little more each second, hoping she wouldn't be too late. She'd noticed yesterday that Garrett had been digging along the perimeter of his house, as if he was going to plant more shrubbery. It wouldn't take too deep a hole to trap a puppy. If it filled with rain…

She was on her hands and knees calling, "Here puppy, puppy, puppy" for the hundredth time when Garrett dropped to his knees beside her.

"Go inside," he shouted. "I'll take over."

She shook her head. She had to find this puppy. She had to. It had become critical to her. "I've checked both sides of the front. You take the right side. I'll go left."

He didn't argue but scrambled up and away. In

time they met at the back of the house. The thunder and lightning had moved on, their noise in the distance now. The rain continued, although not as hard or loud. She heard a sound that froze her in place. Then she heard it again, coming from nearby.

"Garrett!" she yelled. "Over here."

He slid on the mud, ending up next to her as she shined her flashlight toward the sound, under the raised foundation. Fortunately the lattice only covered the front and sides of the house, but it left the back open for the puppy to tuck himself farther under. Now he was mired in mud, trying to dig his way out, his cries breaking Victoria's heart.

"Move," Garrett said, shoving her, trying to dig an escape route for the dog but only creating more mud. He shifted his body parallel to the house, but the puppy remained out of reach.

Victoria ripped off her jacket and copied him from the other side. "I'm smaller," she said. "I can get under there."

"Stop! You could get trapped in the mud," he yelled.

She didn't say anything. She inched her way closer, then suddenly felt Garrett's hands on her legs, his fingers wrapped around her calves, holding her tight. "Come here, baby. Come on," she urged the puppy. His eyes shined back when she spotlighted him, but he didn't, or couldn't, move.

"Push me closer," she shouted to Garrett, keeping a hand out. Her clothes sucked mud as he pushed her a few inches, until she could grab the pup by the scruff of its neck and drag him to her. "Got him! Pull me out!"

Out she came, mud coating her. She didn't care one bit. She shook some of the muck off her shirt then wrapped the dog in it.

Garret put his arm around her and guided her to the back door, which led into the laundry room. Her mud-filled boots were hard to walk in, weighing a couple of pounds more than usual. Once they were inside, he told her to stay put, moved past her then quickly returned with towels. He yanked off his jacket and pulled his shirt over his head. Then he took the puppy from her, wrapped him up and held him close to his chest.

"Drop your clothes in the set tub, then you can go shower. I'll rinse everything before I dump it all in the washer." He turned his back to her, giving her privacy.

Getting the boots off was the hardest. It was like her feet were stuck in cement. Huge sucking sounds accompanied her efforts, then she was free. She dragged her clothes off and tossed them into the open tub, added her bra and panties, then wound a towel around her body.

She started to pass by Garrett.

"Are you okay?" he asked.

"I'm exhilarated. My adrenaline is sky-high. We saved him, Garrett. We saved him." She rubbed noses with the puppy then pulled Garrett down for a kiss, mud and all.

"I'll put some clothes inside the bathroom door

for you," he said, touching foreheads, a surprising depth of emotion in his voice. "If you dig around in the cabinets, you'll find a blow-dryer, I think."

"Thanks." She hurried down the hall, anxious for a warm shower, even more anxious to get back to Garrett and the puppies.

She'd just climbed into the shower when she heard the door open. "Here you go," he said.

Want to join me? The words stayed trapped in her throat. "Thanks," she said instead.

She didn't linger to dry her hair, knowing he needed to shower, too. She put on the shirt he'd left, a soft flannel plaid, and rolled up the sleeves. His sweatpants were way too big around and long, and his shirt covered her almost to her knees, so she just wore that. The fact she was naked underneath made her feel vulnerable but also excited.

Victoria found Garrett in the kitchen, still shirtless, gently bathing the puppy while its littermate romped across the floor and back. An old-fashioned towel rack held her bra and panties.

"I figured you wouldn't want them in the wash with your jeans and all that dirt," he said, trying to contain the wriggling puppy who probably hadn't seen a bath before. He eyed her lingerie. "Pretty in pink, princess?"

"I own every color of the rainbow, cowboy. What's your favorite?"

"Red."

"Predictable. Black is probably second."

"You've got me figured out, I guess."

"Just going with the odds." She felt her nipples hardening at his interest, was aware of straightening her spine some, arching her back a little at the direction of the conversation. "I'll bet you sleep in the buff."

"You'd win. You? Tell me you don't wear some old sorority house T-shirt, or former boyfriend's football jersey."

"I've never quite managed being comfortable sleeping naked. What if there's an emergency in the night and there's no time to get dressed?"

"How many times have you had an emergency in the night?"

She felt her cheeks heat. "Never."

All he did was smile.

"Do you really think it feels different?" she asked.

"I can't speak for anyone else." He settled the puppy in a clean towel. "You did good out there, Victoria. Better than I could've. Here." He put the bundle in her arms. "I need a shower."

She watched him go, thought she heard him say "A cold shower," but wasn't sure. She sat at the kitchen table and dried the ball of fluff, then set him—her?—on the floor with its sibling. They pranced around, their tiny nails clicking against the wood.

Thirsty, she poured two glasses of iced tea and carried them into the living room, keeping an eye on the puppies until Garrett returned.

When he did, he was wearing a T-shirt and

sweatpants, for the first time not looking like a cowboy, but comfortable…and ready for action.

Victoria was ready, too.

Chapter Seven

The cold shower didn't work. Garrett took one look at Victoria seated on the couch with her legs tucked under her and knew he was a goner. She was naked under his shirt, her breasts moving whenever she did. Plus she was brave and caring—and not nearly the princess he'd originally assumed she would be.

Because she kept her gaze locked on his, he avoided the couch and headed to the kitchen. "The pups are probably starving."

"Do you think they're weaned?" she asked after a slight pause.

"I doubt it, or else the person who dropped them off wouldn't have brought them here. I figure they're about four weeks, given their behavior. I've got some bottles and formula. I'll have to get some puppy food tomorrow. Would need some soon anyway for the other pups."

"May I feed one?" She'd followed him into the kitchen. The pups bounded in, too, whimpering.

"Sure."

He'd had to feed pups and kittens before, so he had a stock of appropriate bottles and formula. Soon they were settled on the floor with towels and cushions, the puppies sprawled on their bellies, drinking noisily. Victoria never stopped smiling, especially when her pup wriggled closer, its tail wagging. After they'd emptied their bottles, they both fell asleep. Garrett made a bed in a cardboard box for them, one they couldn't escape. They didn't even open their eyes when he set them inside.

"Would your other mama dog nurse them, do you think?" Victoria asked, taking a seat on the sofa again and picking up her glass. "She's only got four puppies, after all, and room for more."

He sat in a chair across from her and took a long drink himself. "I thought about trying, but she's a small dog. She couldn't produce enough milk right away. These two can be weaned soon probably. Plus, they need to be checked by the vet before I introduce them to any of the others."

"Did you take the new dogs to the vet?"

"He comes here. It's easier. Yeah, he checked them out early this morning. By the way, the one you rescued is a boy. The other's a girl. Want to name them?"

"Dee and Dum," she said right away. "Dum's the boy, of course, for getting himself stuck like that."

"I'd say he was adventurous and not content with the status quo."

She laughed. "Of course you would. Do you name all the animals that land here?"

"The dogs for sure, so they'll respond to commands by name. It's part of their training." He looked at his mantel clock, surprised it was only eight-thirty. He'd thought it was at least ten. It was still raining hard, although the thunder and lightning had moved on. "Guess I'm not going to make it to Red to pick up my meals," he said. "I checked the phone lines a while ago. Nothing."

"I checked my cell. No signal. Won't they guess that the storm kept you from coming?"

He nodded. Now, what to do about Victoria? "I don't want you out there trying to drive home," he said finally. "Flash floods can happen in an instant, and it's already muddy and wet."

"That's okay with me. I want to help feed the puppies during the night."

"I don't expect they need to eat during the night anymore. How will your family react to your not coming home?"

"They'll figure it out. I'll check my phone for service now and then, but they'll know what happened."

"I don't have a guest room. Only my bedroom and an office."

She patted the couch. "Here's just fine. I'm easy."

She smiled then, her eyes darker than usual and heavy-lidded—which could be arousal or exhaustion.

"Easy?" He doubted it. "Complicated, I think."

"Good. I like that you think that."

He stretched out his legs, crossed his ankles. "I appreciated your help." Especially since he didn't usually accept help from anyone. Of course, she hadn't let him reject her offer, either.

"I got you into this mess," she said.

"Yes, you did."

She grinned. Her hair wasn't dry yet, and it had begun to curl, a lot. She wasn't wearing makeup. Her toenails were painted a deep purplish color. She looked even younger than twenty-four. It was a stark reminder of just one of their differences.

He went to the front door. "I need to do a final check on the animals. Make sure everyone weathered the worst of the storm okay. There's a blanket chest in my bedroom. You'll find bedding and pillows."

Garrett shrugged into his still-damp rain jacket then a dry pair of boots. Pete came out of his doghouse at the end of the porch to walk to the barn with him. Abel greeted them and tagged along as Garrett made the rounds of the stalls and boxes. The new dogs were still wary, but they seemed to be getting along all right. The two new horses tossed their heads at his approach. He took a little time to talk to each of them, calming them.

The storm had probably upset them, as well as

being in new surroundings. They would adjust soon.
The mother dog and her puppies were snuggled together in a heap, Mama giving Garrett an I'm-so-
tired look before tucking her head among her babies
again. Mama cat gave him a similar look. They
should all do well until morning, he decided. The
light of day would bring new questions and problems, but also answers and solutions.

He and Pete returned to the house. Garrett had
given up years ago trying to convince Pete to come
indoors. Even during cold and rainy nights he liked
his doghouse, always seemed to want to stand
guard.

Garrett gave him a thorough rubdown before returning to the biggest question and problem, the one
on his sofa. He hoped she'd gone to sleep.

He had a feeling she hadn't. Even if she was
bone-tired, it wasn't late enough for bed.

The couch was empty. He glanced in the kitchen.
Not there. He couldn't hear a sound of movement
anywhere. He hoped she hadn't taken it upon herself to climb into his bed.

He hoped she had....

Garrett found her in his bedroom, bent over his
blanket chest and pulling out linens, his shirt riding
up her slender thighs. He found it hard to believe she
hadn't heard him come inside. He leaned a shoulder
against the doorjamb and admired her.

Her arms full, she turned around. "Oh! I didn't
know you were back. That was fast."

"They didn't require any work, just a once-over."

"I'll get out of your way." She started to pass him. He didn't budge. "Except that you're in my way."

It'd been a long while since he'd spent intimate time with a woman, and this one was more than willing. How long was he supposed to resist her eagerness? She was a modern woman who'd already pointed out that she was only interested in sleeping with him, so what was holding him back? It was exactly the kind of relationship he liked.

In bed, none of their differences would matter, not their ages or social statuses, not their upbringing or life experience. She would head back to Atlanta, their curiosities satisfied, the tension gone. She could return to her ivory tower, and he to his animals and—hopefully—peace and quiet.

"Garrett? What's going on?"

He cupped her face. "Would you share my bed tonight?"

"Why?"

Her question so caught him off guard that his mind went blank.

"Because I'm here and convenient?" she asked. "Because we just saved a puppy's life and we're high on adrenaline from the experience?"

"I think the answer's more basic than that," he said finally. "You said you wanted me."

"That was yesterday."

What had he done to lose his appeal to her in a day? He didn't know how to respond to that. He backed away, giving her space to get past him.

"Now I know you better," she said, not budging. "And like you even more. I'm attracted to the whole man now. That could complicate things. For me, anyway."

She was right about that. It could be a big complication. "Well, girl, that's a decision only you can make. I'm drawn to you for you, not because you're standing here bein' willing. If that's enough, okay. If not, I'll see you in the morning."

"First of all, I'm a woman, not a girl, so don't call me that again. Second, this is all getting too unromantic to me. It's losing its passion and spontaneity."

"If everyone took the time to think things through, we'd have fewer problems in the world—and fewer surprise babies."

Victoria didn't want to lose the spark, didn't want this to become some kind of business deal. She wanted to get carried away, to get lost in his arms, but she didn't want to leave with regrets, either.

Won't you regret more giving up the opportunity to make love to him?

Yes. A great big yes.

He took her by the shoulders and turned her toward the hallway before she could tell him yes. "Good night, Victoria."

Angry at herself for blowing the opportunity, she marched down the hall into the living room. She didn't bother making the couch into a bed, just tossed a pillow down then yanked a blanket over her.

She heard a puppy whimper for a few seconds then stop. *I know just how you feel,* she thought. She squeezed her eyes shut. Her day had been long and tiring. Sleep should come easily. Instead, she lay there imagining what she was missing, hoping he was having trouble getting to sleep, too. She tossed herself onto her side, punched her pillow. He was probably sawing logs already. Naked.

Men.

Victoria rolled onto her stomach and groaned into the pillow. Suddenly she felt hands on her back, large, competent hands.

"Relax," he said, bending close to her ear.

"What are you doing?"

"What I should've done earlier."

He was romancing her, she realized. Caressing her.

She did relax. His hands felt wonderful on her back. He had strong fingers that massaged out kinks she hadn't known she had. He found every one of them. He didn't push her shirt up, but worked through the fabric, even over her rear. The blanket slid down and off her legs, then his hands were touching her skin at last as he worked his way down to her feet. His thumbs pressed into her instep, making her groan with pleasure.

He slid his palms up her legs again, this time pushing up her shirt over her rear, which he kneaded and stroked. He dragged his tongue over her, bit lightly into her flesh, as he slipped his hand between her legs and caressed with featherlight touches. Fire raced through her body, fast and liquid. Sounds came from her mouth that she'd never heard before. She'd known he would be gentle. She hadn't guessed how sexy gentleness was.

He rolled her over, put his mouth on the hot, aching core of her. *Backward,* she thought. *We're doing this backward. We shouldn't have started this way.* She needed his mouth on hers first. And yet…

She'd never felt like this before, the center of complete attention, complete adoration. His tongue did exquisite things to her, making her rise to meet him then making her wait, almost there, then cold air washing over her for a few seconds, then his warm mouth again. She shook uncontrollably, grabbed his hair, arched her back. He rose up before she could climax. She wanted to curse and praise him at the same time.

His mouth finally came down on hers, his tongue meeting hers, dueling, demanding and yet not making her feel dominated. His chest was bare. She ran her hands over his flesh, felt the ridges of muscle and bone. He sat up and slowly, so very slowly, unbuttoned her shirt, spreading it open, cupping her breasts, running his thumbs over her aching nipples.

"You're perfect," he said just before he sucked a nipple into his mouth, his teeth dragging along the hard flesh. He pulled her onto his lap, her legs straddling him, then he carried her down the hall to his bedroom, his big hands cupping her rear. By the time he set her on the bed and pulled the shirt off her, she felt light-headed but the rest of her body felt full and heavy. She'd wanted passion and romance. She was getting it.

He didn't wait for her to help him take off his sweatpants, but he shoved them down and off, grabbed protection from his bedside table, then joined her in bed, stretching out beside her. He fanned out her hair, ran his fingers through the curls, dragged them over her breasts.

"How can you hold back like this?" she asked. Every nerve was aflame with need.

"When something's important, you do it right." He looked into her eyes.

"You're making a memory."

"Damn straight."

Why? she wondered. Why did it matter to him that she take a memory with her? She laid a hand on his chest and memorized him, too. He wasn't bulky like a weightlifter but he was strong and muscular, his way of living enough to keep him fit. She had to use the gym in her building.

Finally he put a hand over hers, stopping her exploration, pressing it against his chest. Then he kissed her, tenderly, thoroughly, passionately, moving over her without stopping the kiss, sliding into her slowly, filling her then pausing. His body went rigid, he made a low, guttural sound as he pulled out then thrust in. It was all it took for both of them. The mutual explosion was loud and fast and long…and excruciatingly beautiful. She felt connected in every sense of the word, heart, soul and body. A memory, indeed, framed in her mind forever.

She hoped he felt the same.

He gathered her close and rolled with her, settling her on top of him, wrapping her up, both of them struggling to breathe, to settle, to relax. She wanted to cry, so she burrowed her face against his neck and squeezed her eyes shut, staving off tears of magnificent fulfillment. She wanted to stay in his arms forever.

After a while he pulled up the covers but didn't let her go. She wanted him to say something. She wanted to know he felt the same things she did.

Eventually he climbed out of bed for a few minutes. When he returned, they lay on their sides looking at each other. He pulled her leg over his, then draped his arm over her hip, splaying his fingers over her rear, the tips teasing her, making delicate circles, keeping her level of desire high.

"Nothing to say?" he asked.

"I'm pretty sure you could tell I enjoyed myself." She ran a finger across his mouth. "Would this have happened if I hadn't been stuck here?"

"Yes." His gaze held hers. He didn't even blink until she broke the contact herself.

It was exactly what she'd wanted to hear.

"Think you can sleep as you are, or do you want a T-shirt or something?" he asked.

She smiled leisurely. "I'll let you know if I start feeling uncomfortable."

"Are you sleepy?"

The sound of rain on the roof lulled her, as did the steady feel of his heart pumping against her hand. She could easily fall asleep, but she didn't want to give up a moment in bed with him. "Sleep isn't what I'm craving at the moment."

"Craving? Hmm. That's a good word." He moved his hand over her breast, cupping her, running his thumb over her nipple. "There's a lot more to you, it would seem."

"I don't flaunt." Which wasn't entirely true. She'd unhooked an extra button with him more than once. She let her hand drift down his body, finding him ready and willing. "I could say the same for you."

Garrett sucked in a breath and savored her exploring touch. He shoved her hair aside, pressed his lips to her neck, tasted the perfume that was Victoria, distinctive and tempting. As their bodies warmed, he threw back the covers, sat with his back against the headboard and straddled her in his lap. He barely felt her weight, yet she was settled heat to heat on him. He lifted her, guiding her onto himself, letting her take him inside then go perfectly still.

"We fit," she said breathlessly.

Too well, he thought. *Far too well.* Even knowing the consequences, he accepted what she offered and gave back in full. They merged and melded, found pleasure and satisfaction. Her mouth was hot on his, demanding yet yielding. Giving and receiving. Powerful beyond measure. Twice would not be enough. One night would never be enough.

She arched back, squeezed him tight, let out a

long, low sound that reverberated through him until he couldn't resist and climbed atop the same peak of pleasure. She collapsed against him, breathing hard.

It struck him then what he'd done—or, rather, hadn't. "I didn't use protection," he said, panic twisting inside him. However well they fit together physically, it was all they could have.

"I'm on the Pill."

"I don't take chances. Ever."

"It'll be fine, Garrett. Really."

He had to believe her, had to hope there weren't any consequences for his carelessness. And for a long time he stayed awake, holding her and wondering just what kind of hole he'd dug for himself.

Chapter Eight

Garrett was gone when Victoria woke up in the morning. They'd made love somewhere around five-thirty, then he'd tucked the blankets around her and got out of bed. "Go back to sleep," he'd said.

She had. For hours.

Victoria stretched, pulled his shirt on and went in search of him, not finding him in the house. The puppies jumped and whimpered at her, making her laugh, then she poured herself a cup of coffee and took it with her to the shower. Maybe he'd be back by the time she was done.

Her cell phone rang as she passed through the living room. She picked up the phone, saw it was her mother calling and noticed there were seven messages awaiting her, as well. All from her?

"Good morning, Mom."

"Finally. Victoria, I have been scared out of my mind. I was about ready to book a flight. Where have you been?"

"I'm right here in Red Rock. We had a big storm and it wiped out phone service." Victoria picked up a magazine from the coffee table, *Saddle and Rider.* Then she noticed her fingernails. Not only was her polish chipped, she'd split two nails.

"Well, I worry. Mothers do that."

"If something happened to me, don't you think Wendy or Emily would let you know? Unless you hear otherwise, assume I'm fine, okay?"

"You don't have to get snippy about it. I thought the vacation was doing you some good, but you're still uptight."

Victoria closed her eyes for a moment. Her mother was right. She was being defensive because she knew she was doing something her parents wouldn't approve of. It had made her secretive, and she was usually open, especially with her mother. "I apologize, Mom."

"I'll be glad when you're home again and I can see for myself how you're doing."

"Despite apparent evidence to the contrary, I really do feel good."

They ended the call on a happier note, then Victoria showered and went in search of Garrett.

Everything was quiet. His truck was in the yard, the horses in the corral, but no dogs were out and she couldn't hear music or him talking to the animals.

She almost tiptoed to the barn door, then heard the sound of metal hitting metal, but light taps not hammering. Abel spotted her and woofed, then others followed suit, including Pete. Garrett came out from behind a wood divider wall she'd never paid attention to before. He looked guilty...or something. Definitely uncomfortable. Was he regretting making love with her?

"Good morning," she said, not moving toward him.

"Sleep well?" He stuffed his hands in his pockets, something she'd never seen him do.

"Never better." What was going on? He was the most self-confident man she knew. He couldn't have any doubts about whether she'd enjoyed herself last night, so why did he look so hesitant? "You were up early."

"My internal alarm clock never changes. The braid suits you."

Her hair always kept falling in her face—and sometimes into muck. It seemed sensible to get it out of the way. "It's practical."

"You need a hat, then you'd be set. The Cowgirl Princess."

She gave up waiting for him to make a move. She hugged him. His arms came around her, loosely at first then all enveloping. "Are you hungry?" he asked after tipping her head back for a lingering kiss.

"For food or you?" she asked.

"Given the number of surprise visitors I have these days, I would say food. I waited to have breakfast until you woke up."

"How about I fix breakfast and you go back to whatever it was you were doing. Give me about twenty minutes."

"Sounds good."

"What *were* you working on?"

"Um, just doin' a little work on a saddle."

The *um* threw her off. When he chose to speak, he spoke well, without hesitation. It was almost as remarkable as the dropped *g*. "May I see?"

He made her wait a good thirty seconds. Finally he said, "What happens at the ranch, stays at the ranch, right?"

"Of course, Garrett."

He took her by the hand into a room largely hidden from the barn section and reached only by a small doorway ingeniously blocked by another fake wall. She hadn't thought about how much wider the barn seemed from outside than inside. Now it made sense.

And what a room it was. Organized chaos, she decided. There were saddles on racks, long tables with tack laid out, shelves full of boxes and tools, lots of tools, few of which she could put names to.

"What is this?" she asked, wandering around.

"It's how I make my living. Custom saddles and tack. A few other items."

"You make saddles?"

"I embellish them. These are for show and parade horses. I also repair museum pieces. That's what I was picking up at the airport that day. A museum in Montana had sent some old leather pieces they'd received." He rested his hand on a saddle next to a worktable. "I've been working on this one all morning. The horse and rider will be in the Rose Parade this year. Actually, I'll be doing four saddles and other paraphernalia for her group."

The work was detailed and exquisite. He did leather tooling, but also set gems in silver, intricate work, especially for a man with such large hands and long fingers. "Remember that bolo tie you wore at the airport? Did you make that?"

"One of my first pieces. Most show people want jewelry to match their saddles, so I learned how. I do belts, too."

"You're an artist." She picked up a necklace of hammered silver and orange jade. A saddle with matching silver and jade was perched nearby. "This is stunning, Garrett. I hope you're charging what this is worth."

He shrugged. "It pays the bills and keeps the animals fed."

"How does word get out about you?"

"Through satisfied customers."

"You've never advertised?"

"Wouldn't know where to start."

"How much time do you put into it?"

To give himself something to do, Garrett straightened a few tools. "A couple hours a day." He could sense the wheels turning in her head, the business-woman coming to life. To distract her, he tugged on her braid. "Breakfast?"

She left reluctantly, looking over her shoulder. Now that his secret was out, he could go back to work hammering silver for a belt. It was an original design, his own take on the Navajo conchos but with a Texas touch, more a look of mesquite, intricately carved.

He worked with all kinds of gems, precious and semiprecious, his well-hidden safe containing a treasure trove of stones, including some chocolate diamonds a client had sent to be made into earrings and a necklace. They were the diamonds he likened to Victoria's eyes, especially when they'd glittered as he'd made love to her.

Garrett worked until she showed up with a plate in each hand piled with country-fried potatoes, scrambled eggs, bacon and toast.

"I would've come to the house," he said, making space on a counter.

"I didn't see a dinner bell," she said. "And I figured it'd stay warmer if I just brought it."

"Plus you want to use this setting to push some kind of plan you hatched while you were cooking."

Her cheeks turned pink. "That's how my mind works. My degree is in marketing."

"I remember. These are great," he said after sampling the potatoes, which had just the right amount of crisp. Personally, he would've left the skins on, but he wasn't complaining.

"I could create a global network for you on the web," she said earnestly. "You could command top dollar."

He aimed his fork at her. "You know, princess, I may live in the middle of nowhere, and I never did set foot in a classroom after high school graduation, but I figured out what the market would bear. I negotiate now and then, but I've always been willing to walk away from a job. It's all been on my terms. I have no interest in changing that."

"I get that, Garrett, I do. Most artists just want to be left alone to ply their craft. That's where I would come in. You wouldn't have to do a thing except produce the final product."

"Nope. But thank you for your interest." He said it in way that meant the discussion was over.

"You haven't even heard my ideas."

He hadn't seen her this animated before and didn't want to dampen that excitement. Nor did he want to mislead her.

"Okay, here's the deal," he said after giving it some thought. "You put together a solid, workable business plan and we'll talk about it." That ought to keep her busy—and happy—for a few days. She threw her arms around him and thanked him again and again, so he figured he was doing the right thing, at least for her.

"What are your plans for the day?" she asked as they finished their meals.

"I need to fix a better box for the new pups."

"Oh! Do they need to be fed? I didn't even think about it."

"I fed them. They're good to go awhile longer. It'll give me time to get to town and pick up my meals at Red. They'll be wondering."

"They're closed on Monday, but I have an in with the manager, you know. I'm sure Marcos would meet you at the restaurant if you give him a time." She looked away for a second. "Or I could pick up the food when I go to town."

"I wouldn't want to trouble you."

"I need to change clothes. And get my laptop." She met his gaze, a challenge in hers.

"Why?" he asked.

"So that I can work here. It would be much more efficient if I could put together the plan with you available on the spot for questions. Plus I could help you with the animals so that you could spend more time in your shop."

"Are you talking about staying overnight?" Although the idea of her being here with him all day, every day, excited him, her staying went against his personal rules, rules that had worked fine in the past.

But she didn't answer, putting the burden on him to say which way it would go.

"It's not a good idea," he said finally, picking up his silver mallet and starting to work again so he wouldn't have to see the disappointment in her eyes. "What would people say, Victoria?"

"Does it matter?"

"It does. It should matter to you, too."

"I haven't been mingling with people much, mostly just my family. Who would know except them? It's not as if I have a reputation to maintain here."

"But I do."

"Oh! Of course you do. I'm so sorry, Garrett. Truly. I was only thinking of myself. It was just so good last night."

Damn good. Excellent. Satisfying in ways he had never been satisfied. Still, he couldn't give in to the temptation of her spending every night in his arms. He wasn't sure he could give her up.

"Okay," she said. "Let me do this much. I'll go to town and pick up your meals. Only Marcos will know about that. And I can stop by the feed store and get the puppy food you need. I can take the pups to the vet, too. Anything else you can think of?"

He was probably making a big mistake, but he said, "Go ahead and bring your laptop and work here, at least during the day. As long as no one sees your car too early in the morning, it should be fine."

She kissed his cheek. "My parents would love you."

He doubted that. "Why?"

"You're a gentleman. They would appreciate that."

"You don't normally hang around with gentlemen?"

She cocked her head, as if considering that. "Not like you. You're old-school."

"I slept with you out of wedlock. And it wasn't the first time I've done that," he said, giving her a look.

Her eyes widened. "You weren't a virgin? I'm shocked, cowboy. Shocked."

He lifted her onto the workbench. She opened her legs, letting him get close. "You shocked me a little last night."

"How?" She went all flirty on him, fluttering her lashes, her lips curving in a totally sexy way.

That you matched me so well, in every respect. "I'll take the Fifth on that."

"Chicken." She grinned. "I enjoyed you, too. You have excellent moves."

He hadn't felt as if he'd been using moves, but just reacting and responding. As she'd said last night, they fit.

She wrapped her legs around him as he kissed her. He'd enjoyed this morning beyond any in his memory. It was nice to wake up to a beautiful woman by his side, exciting to be kissing her in his workshop, where no other human had been. And way too easy to get used to.

"I'll clean up the kitchen then take off," she said, finger combing his hair. "Call me on my cell if you think of anything else I can pick up."

"I will, thanks."

He lifted her off the workbench then followed her to the big barn door.

"Sure I can't interest you in a quick roll in the hay?" she asked.

Before he answered, the dogs started barking. A vehicle was coming up the driveway. "It's your fault we can't," he said, taking the empty plates from her and setting them aside.

"Guess I can't clean up the kitchen, either. Too bad."

He laughed. They went into the yard as a county sheriff's car pulled up.

"Garrett," the man said, hitching up his pants. He left his hat in his car, which Garrett decided was a good thing. Not an official visit.

They shook hands. "Cletus. How's it going?"

"Can't complain." He looked at Victoria expectantly.

"This is Victoria Fortune," Garrett said. "Victoria, meet Deputy Cletus Bodine. He was my arresting officer a few times in my wild youth."

"The days of the bar fights?" Victoria asked, shaking the deputy's hand.

"He grew up. Been walkin' the straight and narrow for a long time. Except…"

Now what? Garrett thought, figuring Victoria had to be somehow responsible for whatever came next.

"It's come to my attention that you're running an animal shelter. You gotta have a license for that, you know?"

Garrett gave Victoria an I'll-handle-this look before she could pipe up. "I'm doing the same as I've always done, Cletus. Strays just end up here. A misunderstanding arose about this over the past week, but it was just that, a little communications snafu. I've been trying to let people know it isn't true. Meanwhile, more animals have landed here than usual, but I've also found more homes."

"Mind if I look around?"

Although it was phrased as a request, he wasn't really asking. Garrett knew he didn't have to comply, but felt he should, proving he had nothing to hide. "Don't mind at all." To Victoria he said, "Thanks for taking the pups to the vet." He figured she'd slip into the house for her purse and the dogs as soon as he and Cletus went inside the barn.

She held out a hand to Cletus. "Nice to meet you, Deputy."

"Same here, miss."

Garrett had forgotten the empty breakfast plates sitting just inside the barn until he spotted them. He saw Cletus take a look, too.

"A Fortune gal, Garrett? Really?"

Garrett said nothing. He knew the ridiculousness of it without being reminded by someone else. Pete came protectively to Garrett's side, as if sensing something was amiss. Abel sat and watched, attentive. The other dogs were unusually quiet as well, picking up on the tension.

The sound of Victoria's car leaving relaxed Garrett. He told Cletus what had happened to set off the influx of animals.

"I don't think I've been out here since you called to have Crystal evicted. That woman sure did want to stay."

"Not a high point of my life," Garrett said.

"We're all entitled to one crazy woman, I suppose. Me? I had more'n you." The deputy chuckled, gave him a slap on the back and took off.

Crystal had been the straw that broke Garrett's back when it came to women. He'd only intended to spend one night with her, but he'd enjoyed her and let her stay two more nights.

Then he couldn't get her to leave—and then she'd revealed her true colors. She'd pulled everything out of his kitchen cabinets, broken what could be broken, destroyed his home, as well as his fleeting affection for her gender. He'd thought she was different. He'd been right. She was worse.

He'd had to call the sheriff to tame her. The embarrassment of it still haunted him, so he'd put his old rules back into place and had held steady to him. No girlfriend. No wife. Lesson learned.

Or so he thought. He was involved with another woman who wasn't right for him, although in an entirely different way. He couldn't picture Victoria destroying his house, but he hadn't thought so of Crystal in the beginning, either.

Frustrated, he took the empty plates into the kitchen. As he washed the dishes, including the many pans she'd used, he considered Victoria's suggestion for his business. Did he want to expand? Maybe not become a shelter, but a sanctuary? There were good ones around the country, but there was room for more. And if his designs could bring in enough money, he wouldn't constantly have to be fundraising, which was one of the biggest headaches of such endeavors.

Realistically, could he do that?

Not without a plan. And not without help. He also couldn't see himself spending an entire day working on saddles and jewelry. He liked being with his animals too much for that. But if he hired someone to clean the stalls and crates, maybe do the feeding, then he could work with the animals, playing and training. It would depend on what kind of animals he took in. There were circus animals always in need of homes, and Hollywood actor animals. Did he want to take in anything exotic? Elephants? Tigers?

He didn't think so. He was a basic man.

Basic, as in he didn't mind dirt or living without an electric dishwasher or a swimming pool. He liked his air conditioner, though, and the internet and satellite TV for all those long, quiet nights.

Basic, as in he enjoyed hearty, filling food. And sex.

Victoria's face came to mind, not at all a basic woman. He'd spotted her checking out her fingernails while she'd been eating breakfast, recalled how perfect they'd been when they'd walked through the terminal that first day. He'd bet a month's income her nails had never looked like that before.

Her mind fascinated him. She was bright and competent. And game, he thought, for just about anything. He never would've pegged her as adventurous.

No, not basic at all, but multifaceted and complex. How long until she tired of her foray into ranch living and its isolation? This extra week of vacation? Less than that?

Those were the biggest questions of all.

Chapter Nine

When Victoria returned to the ranch, she planted herself in Garrett's workshop with her laptop and got to work. She would need to confer with a CPA and probably a tax attorney, but first she needed a general plan. A plan Garrett would agree to, where he wouldn't have to be concerned with involving himself in the day-to-day operations. He only wanted to create. She understood that. And he wanted time with his animals. He wouldn't be Garrett without that. She would figure out a way.

He'd brought Dee and Dum into the shop, giving them playtime away from the other dogs.

The sounds of Garrett's tools were almost rhythmic. His presence alone soothed her. Every once in a while she found the chance to just stare at him and enjoy the sight. Every so often, she could feel his gaze on her, as well.

After a few hours, he said, "Cletus noticed the breakfast plates," as he polished a silver piece.

"Is that a problem?"

"I don't expect he'll spread the word, but I wanted you to know, in case you run into him again."

"Okay." She saved her work, stretched and rolled her neck. She'd had enough for one day. "Do you want me to bring in the horses?"

He stopped what he was doing, stared at the counter for a second or two then looked at her. "I'm done for the day. If you'd like to bring the two new horses in, that'd be great. Apple Annie could use a ride. We usually spend some time on the property every afternoon. Thanks."

"You're welcome. I'll put the pups and my laptop inside the house first."

She was aware of him saddling the mare as she brought one of the other horses into his stall, then he grinned at her, looking like a kid as he took off at a canter. He'd been right—he couldn't spend all day working at his trade. He needed movement, action and freedom. She needed to build that into his plan.

She wondered how he would feel about having help.

Hired help or…her? She was more excited by working on this than any project she'd been given at JMF Financials. It may have a lot to do with the man, of course, but beyond her attraction to him was the challenge the work presented. She could finally use her education, apply it to a real-life situation, even though she didn't really know what she was doing.

But she did know what he needed.

Garrett didn't come back for an hour, then didn't come inside for another half hour, probably grooming Apple Annie. Victoria fixed a salad, slipped a tray of Carne à la Mexicana, a Red specialty, into the oven and then set the table. She'd even bought napkins to replace the paper towels he normally used. His face was windburned but relaxed as he leaned against the kitchen doorjamb.

"Dinner'll be ready in about five minutes," she said. She could smell horse on him, not a bad smell but a strong one.

"No time for a shower first?"

"Go ahead. Everything will keep that long."

"Thanks."

She was tempted to join him. The only thing that stopped her was the possibility that someone might drive up and interrupt them. Since her car was out front, one of them needed to be able to answer the door.

When he joined her in the kitchen he didn't give her a kiss or hug or even a pat on the rear. He walked past her, opened the refrigerator and pulled out a beer, holding it up to her.

"Yes, thanks," she said, so he grabbed a second, opened it and set it next to her plate.

"How far did you ride?" she asked after several minutes of their usual silence.

He looked startled for a second, as if he'd forgotten she was there.

Which totally annoyed her.

"Out to the river, then along it for a while. Everything's greening up." He dug into dinner again. He didn't gaze longingly at her or reach for her hand or indicate in any way that he wanted her to stay.

Even after dinner while they were doing dishes, he didn't touch her. Finally she folded the dish towel over the oven handle and plunked her fists on her hips. "So, one night was enough for you?"

"Pardon me?"

"You slept with me once and the need is gone?"

He stiffened. "Did I say that?"

"You haven't kissed me since breakfast." She craved him.

"What is it you want?" he asked, crossing his arms.

"To make love with you again." Really, was he that dense? "Wasn't last night good enough?"

"Last night it stormed. We didn't have to worry about anyone driving up and seeing your car."

"Which doesn't answer my question."

"Hell, yes, it was good. Unless you were in a coma, you already know that."

"So, it's only worry about getting caught that's stopping you now?"

He leaned toward her. "Victoria, if I lay a hand

on you right now, I won't stop. I can't take that chance."

It was all she needed to know. She grabbed her purse and headed outside. He followed and watched as she got into her car. She didn't head for the driveway, however, but the back of his barn, where her car would be well hidden unless someone paced the entire property.

She came back up to him and waited expectantly for his reaction.

His eyes glittered as he scooped her into his arms and carried her into his bedroom, dropped her on the bed, then landed on top of her. "You're a problem solver."

"When I have a need."

He dragged his lips along her jaw. "A need. That's a good word." He kissed her then, finally, with heat and demand and a need of his own. "What do you think your cousins would say if you stayed here with me?"

She pulled back a little. Had she heard him correctly? "You want me to?"

"When you got in your car I realized how much I didn't want you to leave. If your car stays where it is…"

"My cousins had mixed reactions."

He rolled onto his side, although he kept his body close and his hand on her arm. "Had?"

"I packed all my clothes and brought them with me." She pressed her fingers to his mouth. "I was hopeful. Let's not overcomplicate things. It's a week, cowboy. Six days, actually. That's all."

"After that we do business via phone and email between Atlanta and here?" he asked.

"If you decide my plan will work for you."

"How will you handle your parents?"

"I'll call a lot. Do you lead off every round of lovemaking with unromantic conversation?" she asked, a little exasperated. "Do I need to go out to the living room and have you come get me again?"

He smiled, a slow, sexy smile, then worked the snaps of her shirt and pushed the fabric aside. "Red," he said, sliding a hand over her lacy bra. "Thank you."

"I aim to please."

He laughed then. She didn't know why nor did she care. She only knew she would get to spend the rest of her vacation with him—and that he appreciated the things she did for him.

She reached for his buttons. He grabbed her hand and eyed it. "You got a manicure."

"And a few pairs of gloves."

"Like I said, a problem solver. So, what are you gonna do about this problem I seem to have developed in the past little while?"

"I thought you'd never ask." Time marched by. She had no idea how many minutes passed, but at some point she was able to say, "Problem solved?"

He pulled her up and planted a kiss on her mouth.

"Damn, you're good." Then he rolled her flat on her back and said, "But I'm better."

And then he proved it.

Days passed. Spring took hold; the countryside came alive with bluebonnets, red-orange Texas paintbrush and yellow gorse. Victoria's vacation was coming to an end, but her business plan wasn't ready yet.

Maybe she'd stalled a little, spending more time with the animals than on the computer. Dragging her heels wasn't usual for her, but she'd mastered it in the past week. If Garrett noticed, he didn't say anything. He spent a lot of time working with the adult dogs, getting them trained so that he could find them homes. Two new dogs had joined them. Garrett was running out of room in a hurry.

Victoria had made two trips into San Antonio to speak to financial experts, but the trips had resulted in producing even more questions. Maybe she was in over her head. She didn't doubt her marketing abilities. What she doubted was coming up with an estimate of costs for him, both start-up and ongoing. He needed to know exactly what he would be getting into. That was critical to her.

It was Saturday afternoon. They'd gone to town to run errands, but not together. She'd visited her family, catching up, surprised to find Emily still living at Wendy's.

And now Victoria and Garrett were in his workshop, working independently. She watched him don magnifying glasses so that he could insert small stones into earrings. He'd finished a saddle with matching stones earlier in the week. The client would be picking up the items on Monday. Victoria wanted to be there to see her reaction.

Actually, she wanted to be there to see every client's reaction to every item he worked on. She'd fallen totally, completely, forever and always in love with him. How that could happen in two weeks was a mystery, but she knew it with all her heart. He was everything she hadn't known she was looking for.

"I'm going to tell my parents I'm staying on another week," she said, testing the waters with him. Since she could only see the back of his head, she couldn't tell what his reaction was—except that his shoulders jerked a little.

"Why?"

"I haven't completed the plan, and there are aspects of it that I can't take care of in Georgia. I need to be in Texas." Which was sort of the truth. It would be easier being able to talk to her sources in person rather than through some form of technology, but it wasn't absolutely necessary.

"Your parents weren't happy when you took a second week. What do you think they'll say to a third?"

"My father could fire me, I suppose, but I've decided that wouldn't be a bad thing."

He set his tools aside and spun his stool to face her. "In what way?"

"I haven't been happy there, at least not with the

work. I've enjoyed hanging with my family more, but selling 401(k) plans isn't what I went to college for. Plus maybe the lesson I've learned these past couple of weeks is that working for and with my family is too easy. I haven't stretched. No one has asked me to or expected it of me. I've been stagnating."

"Stagnating? Really?"

"Now that I've seen a different side of the working life, I can identify what I've been feeling. You're happy with your work. It's obvious in everything you say and do. I want to be happy with my work, too." She shut down her computer and closed the lid.

"Do you plan to stay with me?" he asked.

"That would be my preference." It felt as if they were making a business deal, no emotions involved in their decisions. "Would you mind? Things have worked out okay here, haven't they? We haven't argued. I cook. I clean up after myself."

"You do pretty up the place. I've never had place mats before. Or flowers on the table."

Or a willing woman in your bed every night, all night. "See? I do have value."

"I never denied that." He came up to her. "How much of your decision is personal and how much is business?"

"It's mostly personal."

"Is 'mostly' fifty-one percent or more than that?"

She sat a little taller, prepared to hear him tell her she had to go after he heard her honest answer. "Closer to ninety-five percent."

He looked more serious than he ever had. "You know marriage will never be part of the equation with me."

"I know."

"Do you really? I don't mean this to come across as egotistical, but I see the way you look at me. I know that women think they can change a man's mind. Mine's set."

He was standing right in front of her now, his gaze not wavering from hers. "Okay."

"Okay what?"

"Your mind is set." The words dragged painfully along her throat. It wasn't what she wanted to hear, but it was better that she knew the truth. And maybe, just maybe, she could change his mind.

"I've had a good time, Victoria."

"Me, too." Her heart began to ache. She wanted—no, needed—this extra week with him, even if she left with a broken heart.

His kiss wasn't soft or tender, but flatteringly uncontrolled. She gave it back to him and took more for herself. He wrenched open her shirt, taking only a second to admire her hot-pink bra before he had her naked from the waist up, his hands and mouth busy until her breasts felt heavy and her nipples hard. He managed to get her jeans down to her ankles, then unzipped his own and joined with her in a powerful thrust. The planes and angles of his face were sharply defined, his mouth a serious line, his jaw like iron as he slipped his hand between their bodies and brought her up fast and hard. He pulled her close as he reached climax at the same time, their bodies one, their satisfaction mutual.

In the quiet aftermath, they held each other until their breathing quieted and slowed. Only the sound of the dogs barking, indicating someone was probably arriving, got them moving. He shoved his shirt in his pants, kissed her hard, then picked up her cell phone from the bench and put it in her hand.

"Call your parents," he said. He grabbed his hat on the way out.

She scrambled to get dressed, although she wouldn't go out into the yard unless he came and got her. She took a deep, shaky breath and dialed her mother.

"Hi, sugar," her mother said. "I was just about to call you. What time does your flight arrive tomorrow? We'll pick you up."

"I've decided to stay another week." Victoria's pulse was pounding in her ears. "I got involved in a project here and I want to see it through."

"You have a job, Victoria. People are counting on you. Hold on. What, James? Yes, it's your daughter. She's not coming home."

"Victoria," her father said a second later. "What's this nonsense?"

"I need one more week, Dad. I'm helping someone get a business started."

"Your cowboy?"

"He's not my cowboy. He's a very talented artist. I'm helping him develop a web presence." Emotion crept into her voice. "He saved my life, Dad. I wouldn't be here if it weren't for him."

A long stretch of silence followed. When he spoke again, he'd lost his irritated tone. "All right, sweetheart. I understand. But one more week is it. You're putting a lot of extra work on your brother."

"Count on me for Sunday brunch," she said.

"I'll send the jet Saturday afternoon," he said, making sure she'd come home.

"Sunday morning."

"Saturday night," he said. She didn't argue.

Victoria pushed the off button and cradled her phone against her chest.

"You played the he-saved-my-life card," Garrett said from the doorway, startling her.

"It was the only reason that would work with him."

"But is that how you feel? You're not doing this... You're not here now because of what happened at the airport?"

"That was originally why I came, but it's not why I stayed. Who's here?" she asked, changing the subject.

"Estelle's son Jimmy. She asked me this morning if I might have part-time work for him. He's nineteen and going to college, studying to be a vet. Knows horses. I figure whatever plan you're making, it'll include having to hire some help."

"It's the only way you can increase your time in the shop." *Unless you take me on permanently.*

"Well, then, come talk to him with me and see what you think."

They found him hanging over the stall of the most skittish horse, talking in a soothing voice. Garrett wondered if that was how he sounded, like a new father trying to calm a crying baby. Victoria went up beside him and introduced herself.

So. She was staying for another week. He'd been geared up for her taking off tomorrow. This change of plans was a blow to his self-control, as evidenced by the way he'd made love to her in the workroom. He was still a little shocked he'd done that in the middle of the day. It was damned satisfying, too, the way she wanted it as much as he did. The way she was ready so fast, as if she'd been thinking about it already.

As she talked to Jimmy, Garrett studied her. He could look at her naked forever. She hadn't worn anything to bed the whole week, even though he'd told her it wouldn't bother him if she did. She said she was surprised at how good it felt not to get tangled up in anything—except him, she'd added, slipping a leg between his.

She was a pretty good cook, too. Better than he was, although she didn't know the first thing about barbecuing steaks. She never seemed bored in the evening, never complained about how dirty the work was taking care of the animals. He did notice she looked at her fingernails now and then with a little yearning glance, and he hadn't seen her hair not in a braid all week. He missed the dark curtain it had made when she was on top, how it cocooned them in their own private world.

She'd already turned his world upside down. After one more week with her, would he be able to right it again? Would she stay in touch because of the business? Would she come back to visit now and then—and expect to share a bed again?

Could he handle that?

That night he showered with her, shampooing her hair then towel drying it after. She'd brought her own products when she moved in, so her hair smelled exotic to him now, not the same as his. She wore a short silk robe that looked completely out of place in his humble home as he brushed her hair, drawing sounds of pleasure from her the whole time.

After a while, he lowered her robe and massaged her back, tracing her spine, bone by bone, her body so incredibly delicate and yet so strong, getting stronger every day.

She wasn't a princess. His expectations had been all wrong. Maybe she was used to the good life, an easy life, but she carried her own weight on his ranch, worked hard and without complaint.

What had she told him before? "You don't have to be what people expect you to be." She wasn't. And for years he'd been doing exactly that himself— living up to expectation. Not showing everyone how much he'd changed, preferring to be alone rather than trying to change people's minds about him.

Maybe they'd changed their minds on their own,

however. No one seemed afraid of him. No one crossed the street rather than walk past him like they'd done years ago.

He knew he hadn't been that person for a long time, but who else did? A few. The vet. Estelle, probably. Other merchants he did business with.

Victoria—although her view of him was from behind rose-colored glasses. He knew he was still her hero. He hadn't done anything, intentional or otherwise, to change her mind about that. As she'd said, they hadn't argued. Their many, many differences hadn't come into play much during the week, probably because they were both blinded by passion. He hadn't felt so much older or less educated. He'd stopped thinking of her as being short, but enjoyed the way he could tuck her under his chin and hold her there.

Knowing they had another week, he could slow down a bit, figure her out more.

Or maybe he needed to speed things up. He was struck by the feeling that something was going to happen to take it all away.

"You have the best hands," she said with a sigh, bringing him back to reality. It would have to do for now.

Chapter Ten

At the sound of a car coming up the driveway several days later, Victoria hurried the final two steps into the barn. She'd helped feed the animals, then had showered and spent the morning in the house making phone calls, but had taken a break to bring Garrett some iced tea. She set down the glass as he emerged from the workroom to look out of the open barn door.

"Looks like your cousin Wendy's car," he said.

Victoria peered out, too. "It is. I hope everything's okay." She stepped into the yard as Wendy parked. Emily sat beside her. They both waved.

"Until you got here, it was rare for anyone other than the vet or Lenny to come by, and that's only business," Garrett said.

"Your point is?"

He gave her a look teetering between humor and exasperation. "It's just an observation."

"Well, when I've gone home, you'll have your peace back." *And how do you feel about that?* she wanted to ask. Every day they were becoming more of a team, the rhythms of doing barn and household chores a routine now. She did get a little lonely for her girlfriends and a little frustrated with the drive into town when she wanted to buy something, she admitted that. It was a huge change for her. But she had so much to make up for it.

"We brought MaryAnne," Wendy said, hugging Victoria. "She's been cleared to appear in public. Hi, Garrett. I haven't seen you in ages." She hugged him, as well.

"Since before you gave birth," he said. "Are you going back to work at Red?"

"Part-time."

Emily got the baby out of her carrier. MaryAnne was awake and alert.

"Nice to see you again," Emily said to Garrett.

"Same here." He touched his hat. "I'll leave you all to talk."

"We brought lunch," Wendy said. "Enough for everyone."

Victoria left the decision up to him, not wanting to push him into socializing.

"I'm sure Victoria would like to spend time just with you, but thanks."

"We'll leave you a plate," Wendy said as he

strolled away. He acknowledged her words with a raised hand.

"I can bring another chair onto the porch," Victoria said, happy to spend time with her cousins.

"Can't we eat inside?" Emily asked. "What?" she said when Wendy made a noise. "I'm dying to see the place Vicki can't seem to quit. Aren't you?"

"I'm curious."

Victoria hoped Garrett didn't think she was taking over, making his house hers. She didn't figure he was embarrassed or anything, but it was his personal space. People sometimes got uptight about such things.

They moved the party inside. As Victoria got out plates for the sandwiches and coleslaw, Wendy and Emily explored.

"Very quaint," Emily said, passing the baby to Wendy. "Manly."

"It suits him," Victoria said.

"At least he has internet and satellite TV."

"A thoroughly modern man," Victoria said, smiling.

"Is he?"

"About some things. Most things, actually," she said after thinking about it.

"Is the couch comfortable?"

"It is."

"To sleep on?"

Victoria ignored the question and took a bite of a chicken sandwich layered with pancetta, sun-dried tomatoes, arugula and parmesan shavings. "This is incredible, Wendy. Is it from Red?"

"No. Just a recipe that looked good."

"Come on, Vicki. Give us a little dirt," Emily said. "Is he good?"

"I'm still here, aren't I?"

"Which is one of the things we came to tell you," Wendy said. "We've been fielding calls from your mother."

"Really? I talk to her every day." She took another bite as she figured out what else to say. She wanted to keep the extent of her feelings for Garrett to herself. The last thing she wanted was for people in town to change their opinion of him because of anything she said or did. "She understands why I've stayed. Dad, too."

Or so they'd said, although her mother had commented in her often cryptic way, "A mother knows every nuance of her child, Victoria. Her voice, her demeanor, even her laughter. You'll see for yourself someday."

"We just thought we'd give you a heads-up," Wendy said. "There's also been a little talk around town. Just a little," she added in a hurry. "Nothing bad, but even though you haven't been flashy about it, your daily presence here has been noticed."

Victoria groaned. He was never going to forgive her for that. "The last thing I want is for his reputation to suffer because of me."

The sisters exchanged glances. "Well, actually, it's improved because of you."

"Seriously? That's good, then." Although she couldn't tell him that. It would sound egotistical.

"Maybe," Emily said hesitantly. "But maybe it's going to cause him problems when you leave. You know, like he wasn't a good guy, after all. There'll be gossip."

Appalled, Victoria dropped her chin to her chest. Once again, her good intentions had taken a wrong turn. She shoved her plate forward a little, planted her elbows on the table and looked out the window at his property. She'd been envisioning a new structure, a huge shelter with lots of dog runs and places to train them. Several areas to quarantine new animals until they passed their vet checks. She'd been thinking maybe he could teach obedience classes, too. He had such an easy way about him.

And now look what she'd done—wreaked havoc for him every step of the way. He would think she was a jinx, that anything she touched turned sour. How could she overcome that?

"Um, we need to talk to you about something else," Wendy said.

"There's *more?*"

"Not about Garrett," Emily said. "We need reassurance that Jordana is okay, Vicki. I know you told us a few weeks ago, but according to everyone at home, she's been taking a lot of sick days or coming in late to work. She isn't showing up for family events, and you know how much she loves them."

"Well, maybe you should finally go home and

check her out for yourself," Victoria fired back, tired of keeping Jordana's secret. After a few seconds of shocked silence, Victoria blew out a breath and said more calmly, "She's not sick. Does she have something on her mind? Yes. She's at a crossroads just like I am. While I have to put up with you because I'm here, she has the luxury of privacy." She flashed a smile.

"I guess I understand that, but she's never left us in the dark before," Wendy said.

Victoria picked up her fork and took a bite of coleslaw, but her appetite was gone. She had to figure out how not to hurt Garrett with her actions. She had to figure out how to keep Jordana's secret when Victoria didn't believe in keeping the pregnancy from the father. Jordana and Tanner needed to talk and reach decisions, and soon.

"May I hold MaryAnne?" she asked Wendy, giving up on eating.

"Not hungry?"

"We had a big breakfast. It's delicious. I'll finish it later." She lifted the baby out of Wendy's arms and sat back in her chair again. "We can go out to the porch and rock when you're done eating."

"Go now, if you want," Wendy said. "We'll finish up and stow the leftovers."

"Okay." Victoria wanted a few minutes to herself, anyway.

The weather was a perfect seventy-five degrees with a slight breeze, but not enough to stir up dust. MaryAnne stared at Victoria, which made her regret not having spent more time with her. After all this time, she should be seeing a familiar face, not that of a near stranger.

She started to fuss. "No. Oh, no, don't do that," Victoria said, jostling her, which only turned her fussing into crying. Her cousins were probably having a big laugh at her expense about now, since neither of them bothered to come outside and help.

"What'd you do to her?" Garrett asked, climbing the porch steps.

She'd never been so happy to see someone. "Nothing! I was just holding her. Shh, baby. Shh."

"Is she hungry?"

"How would I know?"

"Need her diaper changed?"

Victoria lifted her up and sniffed. "I don't think so."

Garrett sat in the second rocker, enjoying seeing Victoria out of her element. *Competent* was usually her middle name.

"You seem to know a lot about babies," Victoria said, her expression one of bewilderment. "You take her."

"Can't. I've been working with the animals too much."

"Go shower and change."

He laughed. "Try a different position. Put her on your shoulder."

That only made things worse.

"Hold her in front of you, her legs against your stomach, then bounce her, using your arms," he suggested. He'd never pictured Victoria with a baby. Himself, either, for that matter, and yet he wanted to cradle the crying infant, to soothe her.

"It's working," Victoria said, relief in her voice and body language. "She's not crying. You're a genius."

"Not much different from soothing a scared animal."

MaryAnne turned toward Garrett, her fists tucked under her chin. He took off his hat. She seemed to study every part of his face. She was probably used to being with women most of the time. His voice was so much deeper, like her father's.

"She's a pretty little thing," he said.

"When she's not crying."

He smiled. "You haven't spent much time with babies, I guess."

"Well, I didn't earn a merit badge in babysitting. Man. My arms are getting tired. She's heavier than she looks."

"Lay her down in your lap. Maybe she's just tired of being held. Maybe she needs a little freedom to move."

He watched Victoria carefully place MaryAnne on her legs, itching to pick up the baby himself. His thighs were longer, would provide a better, more secure cradle.

He looked away then, surprised at his thoughts, which were definitely a first for him. Then a movement caught his eye. Wendy and Emily were peeking out the living room window, watching them.

"We have an audience," he whispered.

Victoria jerked her head toward the window and stuck out her tongue.

They retaliated with funny faces in return until Victoria cracked up.

"You've missed them," Garrett said, enjoying seeing this side of her.

"We've always been close, but even more so as adults. Wendy's only two years younger, so I've been closest to her. It's been hard for me having her move away."

The sisters came out the door, laughing like kids, making him wonder what kinds of gestures they'd been making through the window after he'd turned away. He didn't have a sibling, or even a cousin that he knew of, didn't have that kind of relationship with anyone. He'd made a friend in the army, one who'd helped him get through the long days, made longer by never getting a letter or package from home. Then on the oil rig, an old-timer named Ned had become his mentor, not just about the job but life. Ned had died a few years back.

Garrett only saw his mother if he went to San Antonio with the sole purpose of seeing her. She never contacted him. He'd never known what having a close family meant until he listened to Victoria talk fondly about her brothers and cousins. What would that be like, having someone who mattered for your entire life? Someone who had some of the same memories as you?

He figured Wendy and Marcos would give Mary-Anne more siblings. They each had four of their own. She would have lifelong connections. Lucky girl.

A hand waved in front of his face. "You in there?" Emily asked. "We must be boring the heck out of you."

"Maybe if we'd been neighing or woofing, he would've been paying attention," Wendy said, a teasing glint in her eyes. "Garrett, Marcos asked me to tell you that a man's been asking questions about you around town. It sounds like he's interested in your animal interests."

"I hope it's not another reporter. What'd he look like, do you know?"

"Marcos said he was short and wiry, and he wore a Resistol that was too big for his head."

The description screamed outsider to Garrett.

MaryAnne started to fuss again. "Guess that's our cue to leave. It's too early for her to eat. Maybe riding in the car will soothe her."

She picked up her daughter, said goodbye then walked to the car. Victoria followed, talking to Wendy as she buckled the baby in her carrier. Emily remained behind, watching them.

"Do you believe in destiny, Garrett?" she asked.

Not until recently. He didn't say the words, couldn't trust her not to tell Victoria. Besides that, he needed to figure it out for himself. "I guess *you* do."

"I'm not sure. I only know that you happened to be in the right place at the right time to save Vicki's life. I've been hoping destiny would find me, too, but now I've come to realize that I'm going to have to make my own destiny. I don't have time to wait anymore."

"Well, that's crystal clear."

"Sorry. I was mostly thinking out loud." She touched his arm. "Enjoy your final days with my sweet cousin. All good things must come to an end, as they say."

Final days. Talk about bursting a bubble, which was obviously her intention. What had Victoria told her?

After waving her cousins off, Victoria came up the porch steps. "Are you hungry? They brought great sandwiches and coleslaw."

"Maybe in a bit." *Final days*. The words were already starting to haunt him, a countdown to lift-off and an unknown journey. This was Wednesday. They had until Saturday afternoon. How much could happen in those few days?

Not much, he figured. Or possibly too much. He didn't think there would be a happy medium.

Maybe he should give it up to destiny and see where they ended up. It wasn't like him to leave things alone to happen...

No sooner had the women left than a pickup rumbled up the drive. Painted on the door was the name of a feed store on the outskirts of San Antonio.

The driver hopped down, a clipboard in his hand. "Garrett Stone?"

"That's me." He tried to see what was clipped to the board.

"Got a delivery for you."

"I didn't order anything."

"It's okay, Garrett. I was expecting it," Victoria said.

"You know I use Jensen's. It's local."

The driver waited, but not patiently. He tapped his toe and sighed.

"It's a donation," she said. "Just show the man where to drop the bags, please."

As they unloaded bags of pet food, Garrett kept glancing at Victoria, who never met his gaze. He considered how appropriate it was that they'd been brought together by a tornado, because she *was* a tornado. She whirled into lives and disrupted them. He cleaned things up. She instigated. He handled.

"You'll get a monthly donation," she said idly as they watched the driver leave.

"How did you manage that?"

"Made a few phone calls. It's something I'm good at, Garrett, getting people to donate things. It's just the beginning."

He didn't know how he felt about it. "I didn't realize we'd already started the new venture."

"Not officially, but I wanted to show you a little of what I can accomplish."

Another vehicle was coming down the driveway. "My life was so peaceful before."

She had the audacity to grin. "You didn't know what you were missing, huh?"

A small man with a big hat approached. "Howdy. You Garrett Stone?"

"That's me."

"Been hearing about your place. Thought I'd take a look at what you've got, if you don't mind."

"Are you interested in a particular kind of animal?"

"I'm fond of dogs."

"We've got a few," Garrett said, leading the way, his instincts shouting at him. If he was the same man who'd been asking questions in town, he was interested in Garrett personally, and Victoria, not the ranch animals.

He proved it a while later when he said he'd think it over and be back.

"He won't be back," Victoria said.

"No."

"What do you think he really wanted?"

"Don't have a clue. I don't owe any money beyond the usual debts. Nothing from my past is unresolved." He'd memorized the license place. Maybe Cletus would do him a favor and run it.

"I'm really sorry for all these disruptions to your life, Garrett."

He'd gotten kind of used to it now, but he wasn't about to give her the satisfaction of knowing that.

He called Cletus later, explained he was worried because of Victoria. The Fortunes had, well, a fortune. Garrett wanted to make sure she wasn't a target of some kind. She had the protection of family at home.

"P.I. firm outta San Antonio," Cletus said when he called back with the information.

Garrett didn't know whether to relax or not. A P.I. firm wasn't going to kidnap her for a ransom, but he wasn't comfortable, either, having someone snooping around, whether it was because of him or Victoria.

He would step up his usual vigilance. Nothing would happen to Victoria Fortune on his watch.

Chapter Eleven

Victoria waited until Saturday morning to present her plan to Garrett. She could have done so a day earlier, but she didn't want her last night with him to end up with her sleeping on the couch.

They'd had an amazing three days. Jimmy had come to work with the horses, giving Garrett more time in his shop. She felt confident—and worried. It would be a big change for him. She didn't think he adapted well to change, but it was exciting to think about what he could accomplish. That would be her selling point.

Garrett was seated at the kitchen table across from her. She passed him a binder, then opened her matching one.

"The first page shows what the ranch will look

like." She tapped her freshly manicured fingernail on the mechanical drawing of the new structure she thought would be necessary. "This would allow for the barn to be remodeled so that your workroom could be enlarged."

He didn't lift his gaze from the drawing. "Why would I need that?"

"In case you want to hire help at some point to do some of the basic work."

"I can't ever picture letting someone else do work that has my name on it, Victoria. That would be lying."

"You could have apprentices or interns. Lots of businesses do that."

"Not me. My product, my name. Anything else would be dishonest."

"That's fine." She'd figured he would argue that point, so she moved on. There would be time down the road to try to change his mind.

"You'll need a real office space, not just a computer on top of a desk in your second bedroom. It could be set up in the new structure, where there'd be room to have a shipping and receiving station. Streamlining would save costs down the road."

"Where are we coming up with the money for all this?"

"Take a look at page four. You'd be making more profit from your own work, because you'll be working more and charging more. You may think you've been getting a fair price for your work, but I've done a ton of research into it. You could easily double your prices. Plus you'd get donations, like the pet food."

"I don't want or need to be fundraising, Victoria."

"You wouldn't." She took a steadying breath, because this was the tricky part. "I would. Just like I did with the food, only on a bigger scale."

"How could you do that from Atlanta?"

"It would be possible, but it's not what I'm proposing. I'd run it from here."

He finally looked up.

She explained the various ways she would promote his work and the sanctuary and the legal hoops he would need to jump through. The media push via the internet would be all-consuming at first. "I would take on all the business roles. You could just work. I'd not only run your saddle-and-jewelry business but all the things related to the care of the animals, ordering feed, straw, medicines, whatever is needed. You could still work with the animals, but not have the daily responsibility for their upkeep. Again, we'd use interns, apprentices, even volunteers to help. It would free you to do only the work you choose to do, whatever that may be."

He sat back and stared at her, his expression unfathomable. "You would move to Red Rock? Give up your life in Atlanta? For this?" he asked, gesturing to the space around him.

"In a heartbeat." Did she have doubts? Yes. But not enough to stop her from making the move.

"Why?" he asked.

Because I love you. Because I hope that by being in your life all the time, you would come to love me, too. I'm counting on that. "I've told you I haven't been happy at my job. I've found purpose here, doing something that's important. I can be indispensable, not just a cog in a wheel. I've never wanted anything this much. I'd do a great job for you."

"I don't doubt that." Garrett got up and went to the refrigerator. He grabbed some orange juice and poured himself a glass, stalling.

He couldn't take it all in. He needed time to think about it. The intrusion into his life would've horrified him a few weeks ago, maybe even as little as a week ago. Then he would've said no and walked away. Now he was considering it. That was a shock in itself.

But a crucial question needed to be answered first. "How could I afford you?" It would no longer be their final days. She wouldn't be gone forever.

"I'd work for room and board for now. I'd sell my condo in Atlanta and use the equity from that. My maternal grandmother left me a trust I'll have access to on my next birthday. It's not huge but it'll help. And I figure I'll form a business of my own and take on clients."

Her workload sounded overwhelming to him. As for him using her trust fund, well, they would deal with that impossibility later. No way. "Wouldn't you have enough to do here without adding other clients?"

"I'm leaving the doors open, that's all. At first this would be all I do."

He studied her, looking for insecurities or doubts. He saw none. "In your mind, does that mean we'll be living together? Sharing a bed? Being a couple?" he asked.

"That would be my choice, yes."

"You'd stay without marriage? Because that's not something I can ever offer you." At some point, he would disappoint her. It'd always been so. Or maybe she'd even disappoint him. He was already breaking his rules for her.

She came up and wrapped her arms around him, burrowing close. "I know."

And when you tire of that kind of relationship, what then? he thought. "I see your vision, Victoria. You want bigger and better. I don't know that I do."

She started to argue. He put up a hand. "But I'm willing to give it a shot."

Her arms tightened. When she finally leaned back, he could see the happiness in her eyes.

"Thank you," she said. "It'll be good. You'll see."

He kissed her. It felt different somehow, as if sealing an agreement.

"Now for the hard part," she said, not leaving his arms.

"That was *easy?*"

"A snap." She grinned. "I need you to come home with me tonight and meet my parents. Let them get to know you. I need to explain why I'm leaving the family business and why I'm joining forces with you. Meeting you in person will help."

He understood her reasoning. He also knew it would be an uphill battle. A father didn't take well to a man taking his little girl away, especially when that man lived a thousand miles from home, wasn't college educated, had some jail time under his belt, didn't have many friends, much less a social circle, and could not provide a lot of extras in life. Not yet, anyway.

But then, that was thinking like he was a potential husband when he was only a potential business partner. Would her parents acknowledge the difference?

"What do I need to wear to meet your king and queen?" he asked.

She actually squealed as she leaped up on him. He caught her and held her tight.

"You must own one pair of dress pants," she said. "If not, you have time to shop."

He set her down. "I am that civilized, yes."

"And the bolo you wore when you rescued me. It'll bring good luck."

"Fine. But you need to do something for me."

"Anything."

"If you want your parents to believe this is only a business deal, a partnership in the making, you need to not look at me like you always do."

She smiled. "And how is that?"

"As if I single-handedly saved the world instead

of one woman. They'll think I'm taking advantage of you."

"Oh, but you have." She toyed with the buttons on his shirt as she spoke, sidling closer. "In wonderful, satisfying ways."

He wouldn't have to give her up. Give this up. His bed wouldn't be empty. He'd been awake most of last night thinking about it. For the past week he'd been secretly creating a bolo tie for her as a going-away gift. He could save it for another occasion now. Something special.

"Same goes for you," he said.

She looked pleased with his answer. "I'll accept all the blame, if that makes you happy, cowboy."

He was afraid to feel happy, wasn't really sure what all it entailed. He only knew he'd felt different since she'd come into his life.

Her cell phone rang. He reached into her back pocket, pulled it out and passed it to her.

"Hey, Em," she said. "Six o'clock. Why?"

Garrett went back to the kitchen table and thumbed through the rest of her plan. Even without studying it, he could see it was ambitious.

"Emily's hitching a ride with us on the jet," Victoria said, coming up beside him. "She decided she should give Wendy and Marcos a few days alone. It's about time."

"She said something cryptic the other day. Something about making her own destiny."

"I know you'll keep this confidential, so I'll tell you. Emily's been baby-obsessed forever. All she's wanted is to be a mom, and she'll be a great one, for sure. Since she turned thirty, she's decided it's never going to happen the usual way, so she's tried to adopt, which isn't working out, or at least not fast enough. Now she's going to register at a fertility clinic. I think that's why she's going home. There's an excellent facility in Atlanta. I also think she wants to check on Jordana for herself."

"What's wrong with Jordana?"

"She's pregnant with Tanner Redmond's baby."

Garrett took a step back, which made Victoria laugh.

"Now you know the family secrets that I've been having to keep. Whew. Sharing that felt good. I haven't been able to confide in anyone."

He shook his head. Family secrets were new to him, but he knew how important it was to Victoria that she be able to confide in him. "I've got your back, princess. Your secrets are safe with me."

Tears welled in her eyes immediately. "Thank you," she whispered.

He didn't know how to deal with her tears, so he picked up his kitchen phone. "I need to get Jimmy to take care of the place. We'll be back tomorrow, right?"

"Even if we have to hitchhike."

He hesitated before he dialed. "Do you think your parents will disown you over this?"

"I think it may make things tough for a little while, but disown me? Never."

"Will your brothers challenge me to a duel?"

"Honestly, I don't know how they'll react. Shane may even be glad to have me gone. I think it's been hard for him being my boss. I didn't take orders well."

"What a shock." He dialed the number, talked to Jimmy, then went into his bedroom to check his clothes. She wasn't packing much at all, having appropriate clothes at her condo to wear.

He'd seen her family's house online, but he'd been wondering what her condo looked like. She would've chosen it herself, decorated it, made it her home. What kind of information could he glean about her by seeing it? Plenty, he figured.

While he was packing, Victoria lay on the bed, not making a comment unless he asked a question. He was glad she wasn't trying to dress him beyond what she'd already told him. He wanted to make a good impression for her sake. For himself, he was okay with who he was, who he'd become, especially recently. He could stand eye to eye with anyone. What he wore mattered little.

"Have I told you what a fine figure of a man you are?" Victoria said.

"Sort of." She stared at him a lot and touched him constantly, even during the night. Her hands would roam over him, even when she seemed sound asleep, as if she couldn't help herself. He simply enjoyed it.

"You are. Lean and strong. Sexy. I love your shoulders and arms best, I think."

"The better to lift you with, my dear."

"What do you like best about me?"

"The rare times you're humble."

She tossed a pillow at him, pretending fury. He tossed it back, then immediately threw another, but that was all he had on his bed. No frilly decorative pillows for him.

"I like everything about you," he said.

"Everything?"

"Maybe you're a little bossy now and then."

"You don't seem to mind if I take the lead in bed sometimes."

"True."

"Or on the sofa."

He remembered that particular moment fondly. "Also true."

She grabbed his shirt and yanked him down, dragging the tails from his jeans. "Or that time on the washing machine when it was on the spin cycle."

"Stop, stop," he said, caught between laughter and fresh desire. "Uncle. I agree that 'bossy' can be a good quality." He glanced at the bedside clock. "Jimmy will be here in fifteen minutes."

"Which is enough time for me. How about you, cowboy?"

"I think I can manage."

Hours later, they picked up Emily and headed to Red Rock Airport. After Emily climbed out of the truck, Garrett looked at Victoria before she hopped down, too. "You okay?" he asked. She hadn't seemed to balk at flying out from the memory-filled airport, but he wanted to make sure.

"You're here with me. What can go wrong?"

He didn't want her believing that. Didn't want her to think everything would be perfect as long as he was with her. She had to be realistic.

But she leaned over and kissed him so that he couldn't—or maybe wouldn't—contradict her.

"Everything's good," she said.

He wished he could believe that. Instead dread invaded him finally—realism. They'd left their fantasy world at the ranch behind and were facing a big unknown, except that he could pretty well predict what her parents' reaction was going to be. He'd gotten enough hints of how they felt when he'd listened to Victoria's side of the many phone calls.

She would be tested by her parents. *Are you strong enough to stand up for yourself, Victoria? Or will going home remind you of how much you would be giving up?*

Garrett needed the answers to those questions.

Chapter Twelve

Everything looks so sterile, Victoria thought as she and Garrett walked into her condo hours later. Her furnishings and art were contemporary; she'd never been a frills and flowers person. Her mother had been taken aback at the way Victoria had furnished her condo, had offered pieces from Victoria's late grandmother's estate, which were in storage. None of them had appealed. Now she could see their value.

"Great view," Garrett said, noticeably not commenting on her condo. He laid his suit bag over the streamlined sofa and moved toward the window. The sky was almost dark, so the skyline was lighting up.

"That's the main reason I chose this place. That

and the in-building gym, so I wouldn't have to go somewhere else to work out. There was a unit available on the third floor, but the fifteenth suited me. Are you hungry?"

"I could eat."

She took a binder out of a kitchen drawer and passed it to him. "What're you in the mood for?"

"What's this?"

"Menus of every place nearby that delivers. I haven't been home for three weeks. Cupboards are bare." She felt uncomfortable around him, showing him the way she lived, the granite countertops, cherrywood cabinets and stainless-steel appliances. The brown leather sofa that held center stage on the hardwood floors.

There was no softness, except a few throw pillows and a shag area rug.

"Let's go out," Garrett said, closing the binder. "We've never been to a restaurant together."

"We've been to Estelle's and Red."

"But we didn't really go together, did we? So, what's your favorite place?"

She came up to him. "We won't run into anyone you know, but we could run into people I know. Are you okay with that?"

"I am if you are." There was challenge in his eyes, as if daring her.

"Garrett, I'm happy to take you anywhere."

"Okay, then. You choose, princess."

He'd almost stopped calling her that. She hadn't missed it.

"Do you dance?" she asked.

"I'm somewhat competent."

"Then I know just the place. Wanna see my bedroom first?" She waggled her eyebrows.

"Sure." He grabbed his suit bag and followed her into her bedroom, which was a little more feminine but still uncluttered and without a floral print in sight.

"I wouldn't have pegged you as a minimalist," he said, looking around. "I never would've walked into this place and thought it was yours."

"It isn't anymore. This belonged to an entirely different person." Her comforter was sage-green. Other than that, there was little color. She watched him open her closet door and hang up his clothes.

"There's color in here," he said. "Lots of shine and glitter, too." He whistled long and low. "Look at all those shoes."

She'd had the closet customized for her. She did like shoes—and purses. She dressed up a lot, too. It was part of how she lived, how she was raised and what people expected of her.

He pulled a garment off the rod and held it up. "Where'd you wear this?"

It was white, strapless and designer. "My debutante ball."

"Debutante," he repeated quietly. "How about this one?"

It was stuck way back in the closet, a yellow, full-skirted, off-the-shoulder number. "One of six bridesmaid gowns. My mom is storing the others in my old bedroom. This one was from a wedding in March. I hadn't taken it to my parents' house yet."

"You live a fascinating life, Victoria."

She couldn't read his thoughts. Didn't have a clue what he was thinking. He was a fish out of water here in her space—and she felt like one now, too.

Suddenly he grinned, moved in on her and backed her to the bed, making her fall onto it, following her down. "At least your bed's a good size. We'll make good use of it later."

Her fears that he was discovering a woman he no longer liked were allayed. He'd just been, well, surprised, probably. Taken aback. He'd found his bearings again.

They didn't linger on the bed but headed out to a club a few blocks away, one that showcased a new band every week. Sometimes it was hard rock, sometimes rhythm and blues, rarely jazz and occasionally country. They got lucky tonight with a local country band, so she figured Garrett would be happy.

After weeks of a steady diet of country music in his house and workshop, she'd developed a feel for it, too, especially the songs that told a story.

For dinner they shared a platter of ribs, corn on the cob and potato salad. Then they danced it off. He taught her a simple line dance and tried unsuccessfully to teach her a more complicated two-step. But when a ballad started, she knew exactly what to do. She moved into his arms, laid her head against his chest and closed her eyes. The dance floor was so crowded, they barely moved their feet. *Foreplay at its finest,* she thought.

"Someone is staring at us," Garrett said, dipping low to whisper in her ear.

"What does she look like?"

"He."

"Move us around so I face him." In a moment she saw who he meant. "That's my brother Shane. When the song's over we can head back to the table. He'll follow. I'm not missing out on a second of this dance."

Garrett didn't want to miss out on anything, either. He didn't know why they hadn't danced before, except it hadn't entered his mind. He would make sure they did from time to time at home, now that he remembered how it could feel.

If she came home with him.

He was beginning to have some doubts about that. He'd taken one step into her condo and realized they were going to face some issues he didn't think had occurred to her. There was lot for her to leave behind.

She was right about her brother. He slid into the booth next to her as soon as they settled in.

"Welcome home, Vick." He held out a hand to Garrett. "Shane Fortune."

"Garrett Stone." He decided to let them lead the conversation. Victoria didn't look at all uncomfortable. In fact, she was grinning at her brother as if challenging him to ask whatever questions were on his mind. Apparently she wasn't going to volunteer information, either.

"So you're home," Shane said.

"A couple hours ago." She took a long swig of water, and her eyes sparkled over the rim.

"You must be her cowboy," Shane said to Garrett. "The reason my workload doubled the past few weeks."

"Mine halved. Sorry," Garrett said with a shrug.

Victoria laughed. "He's my hero, Shane. Be nice."

"We all do appreciate what you did, Garrett. I know I'd sure miss doing this." Shane grabbed her in a headlock and knuckled her scalp until she hollered for him to stop.

"Fortunately, he doesn't do that at the office," she said. "I really am sorry I left you with all the work, but the time away did me a world of good."

"I can see that. You look rested again. Happy. It's been months since I've seen that." He glanced at Garrett. "I guess that's your doing."

"With help from some puppies named Dee and Dum," Victoria answered. "And a dog named Abel, among others. I've found that mucking stalls is good for the soul, too."

"Mucking stalls? You?" Shane said to Victoria. "The original I-can't-stand-dirt-under-my-fingernails girl?"

Which confirmed Garrett's city-girl suspicion about her. "She got herself covered in mud in a storm to save the puppy named Dum. Head-to-toe mud."

Shane eyed her more seriously. "You did?"

She shrugged. "I couldn't let him die, could I?"

"No." He caught a server's attention and asked for a beer, then ordered another one for Garrett.

"Are you here alone?" Victoria asked.

"Nope. Marnie's in the restroom, but she's always there a good fifteen minutes. Why do women take so long?"

"Is she with a girlfriend?"

"Yes. Oh. Right. They've got to analyze the evening so far."

"We enjoy it."

"I take it you haven't seen Mom and Dad yet."

"Tomorrow morning."

"You'll be joining us for brunch?" Shane asked Garrett.

"That's the plan."

Garrett couldn't interpret Shane's expression, something between "Good luck" and "Is your estate in order?" Neither was good.

"There you are!" A curvy blonde came up beside Shane. "We didn't know where you went, sugar."

Shane introduced everyone as he stood. The server showed up at the same time with the beer order so that a bit of chaos ensued, then Garrett and Victoria were alone.

"See you tomorrow," Victoria had said.

"Wouldn't miss it for the world," Shane had answered.

"That was interesting," Garrett said. "Will he warn your parents that I came with you?"

"Oh, no. He loves drama. He'll want to see it unfold. I figure we can show up fifteen minutes before the others usually arrive. That'll get the initial introduction and Q and As over."

The gap between her world and his continued to widen. There was only one place where their world didn't matter, and he wanted to go there right now.

He reached across the table and grabbed her hand. "I have a hankerin' to make love to you."

"A hankerin', hmm? Well, cowboy, I'm all yours."

In her dark bedroom a while later he could imagine they were at his house, in his bed—except that the bed felt different, the room smelled different and it was completely quiet. No puppies whined from their box in the kitchen; no wind blew. He didn't have to keep an ear open for anything unusual happening.

It should've been a vacation for him, but it only made him more anxious to get home.

Victoria made a sleepy sound next to him. He maneuvered her closer, wrapped her in his arms and tried to sleep. He had the terrifying feeling he'd seen his last sunset, eaten his last meal, made love for the last time....

If the I'm-glad-I'm-not-you look in Shane's eyes was any indicator, that is, and Garrett figured Shane knew his parents well. They were a tight-knit family. Shane didn't even know Victoria planned to move to Red Rock, and he was worried for her. All her life she would've been expected to bring home someone suitable. Even her job at JMF was secondary to her job of finding a suitable husband.

Garrett had little hope that the Fortune family would find him suitable.

He turned toward Victoria, heard the steady rhythm of her breathing as she slept.

"I love you," he whispered into her hair, the first-time-ever-spoken words freeing him of every question in his mind about the mixed emotions he'd been experiencing. He couldn't tell her, however, couldn't let that influence her choices. She had to decide what she could live with.

Or without.

Victoria didn't ring the bell on her parents' door. She opened it and went right inside.

"You don't even knock?" Garrett asked. Forget the internet. In person it was even grander. It seemed like a place where one should knock, like a uniformed butler would come to the door.

"I never do, so if I did today they would know something was up."

"I'm not invisible, princess."

She smiled, although it was shaky. He wished he could hold her hand, not only to settle her but himself.

"I'm home!" Victoria called out.

"You're early," her mother said, coming up a long hallway. "I—" She slowed upon seeing Garrett. Victoria's father came out of his den at the same time.

"Mom, Dad, I'd like you to meet Garrett Stone. Garrett, this is James and Clara Fortune."

Because civility was rooted deeply, her parents welcomed him politely, this king and queen who reigned supreme in the family.

"Welcome to our home, Mr. Stone," her father said.

"Garrett, please."

James nodded, but didn't offer the same in return.

"Coffee's ready," Clara said. "Shall we go into the living room?"

A coffee service was set up. At least there were mugs, not cups and saucers, Garrett thought, although the mugs were more dainty than he was comfortable with.

"I'll get yours," Victoria said to him, indicating he should sit on a love seat nearby.

"None for me, thanks." He remained standing. He was a man of action, didn't like putting off anything, even those things that might cause discomfort. He wanted to get it over with.

She gave him a curious look, poured for herself and her mother, then sat on the love seat. Clara settled in a delicate chair. James also refused coffee and didn't sit. They looked like a snapshot out of an Agatha Christie play, intrigue abounding in an elegant drawing room.

"We should have thanked you long ago for saving our girl's life," James said. "We can't thank you enough."

"Right time, right place," he said, tired of all the gratitude. It'd been destiny, just as Emily said.

"So, why have you come here with my daughter?"

"I wanted you to meet him," Victoria said before Garrett could answer. "I also wanted to let you know in person that I'm quitting my job at JMF and going to work for Garrett."

"In Texas?" Clara asked, sounding surprised and resigned at the same time.

"In Red Rock, yes, ma'am."

Garrett heard a tiny quaver in Victoria's voice. Her eyes had gone wider, too, her back stiffer. In fact, her posture had been different from the moment they stepped inside the house. She set her mug aside. It rattled against the coaster for a second.

"I've never been as excited about working on a project as I have been these past few weeks. I need to be part of the completion."

"And is Garrett part of being excited about it?" James asked, as if Garrett weren't in the room.

"Of course. There wouldn't be a project without him. Daddy, we're going to build an animal sanctuary where—"

"Will you be living with him?" her father continued.

"Yes, sir."

"Sharing a bedroom, as you have been for a while now?"

"How do you know that?" Victoria asked.

Garrett had eased over to where Victoria sat. "He

hired a private investigator to look into me," he said, keeping his voice steady and polite. "It's all right, Victoria. I would've done the same thing in his position. Fathers protect daughters."

"I had to be sure. Marry a Fortune and you marry the Fortune family."

"We haven't mentioned marriage," Victoria said. "We're entering into a business deal. That's all. Please give Garrett a chance. Please get to know him. I know you'll come to like and admire him as I do."

James focused on Garrett then. "I'm all ears. What do you have to say, Mr. Stone?"

Garrett realized he'd been kidding himself. He couldn't take her from this life, this world. It was just a fairy tale to her. He could see the future clearly, and she couldn't. She didn't have enough life experience. Once the excitement wore off, it would be tedium to her, and she might not be willing to tell him that she'd made a mistake. Not too many women would be happy living his kind of life.

More important, he couldn't be party to creating a rift between her and her family, be the cause of their disapproval and disappointment. He'd lived with his mother's disappointment his whole life. He knew what that was like.

He turned to Victoria and said what needed saying, not taking the chance of going somewhere private to have a discussion. He'd been losing discussions with her. He couldn't lose this one.

"This isn't going to work," he said. "I'm sorry,

Victoria. I can't do this." He gave a slight bow to her parents and took long strides across the room, then the foyer, then out the door. He didn't look back, not even when she called his name.

He never should have stopped trusting his instincts.

Victoria rushed to the window and watched him walk away. They didn't live on a bus line. He didn't have a cell phone to call a cab. What was he going to do?

"He's gone. Are you happy now?" she almost yelled.

"If it takes so little for him to give up," her father said calmly, "then you're better off without him. You need a real man."

"A real man?" She flung her arms up. "What does that mean to you? Because to me a real man is one who fulfills his responsibilities, keeps his word, protects those who need protecting, doesn't complain about working hard so that others can be more comfortable, whether they're human or animal. A real man cares more about others than himself. He does an honest day's work. He lives by a code he sticks to, come hell or high water.

"You know what he told me? He said he doesn't need bigger and better, but that I do. Maybe he's right. Maybe I came up with this plan because I wanted more. I fell in love with him because he's a real man. And he didn't fall in love with me because

I'm not a real woman. I'm spoiled. I'm pampered. I'm not worthy of him."

"Nonsense," her mother said. "You're worthy of anyone in the world. We were ready to accept him, sugar. We found nothing in the investigator's report that would've stopped us from welcoming him."

"If I hadn't approved," her father said, "you would've been home a week ago. He had youthful indiscretions. He paid for those long ago."

"Why didn't you tell him that?" Her heart was breaking. She didn't know who or what to blame. She needed to blame something.

"He didn't give me a chance, now did he?"

"What am I supposed to do now? He was all I wanted. I wanted to marry him." Tears were flowing unchecked. Her mother tucked a tissue in her hand. One wasn't nearly enough.

"Victoria, my dear," her mother said. "The best thing we can do is to marry the man we need, not the one we want."

"What? I don't even know what that means, Mom. Please, I have to go home." She grabbed her purse and raced toward the front door.

Her mother caught up to her as she fumbled with her car keys. "You can't drive in this condition, Victoria. Stay here with us, sugar. Let me take care of you."

"I need to be alone. Please don't call me. I'll get in touch when I'm ready."

"Here come Shane and Wyatt. One of them

can drive you home in your car, and the other can follow. You really shouldn't be on the road."

"I don't want to explain what's going on to anyone else."

"I'll take care of it." Her mother walked up to her sons, said something, then Shane came over and took her keys out of her hand as he urged her toward the passenger seat. Her big brothers had always watched over her. It made her cry again.

"I'm quitting my job. I'll work until you find a replacement."

"We'll talk about it. There's no need to make a hasty decision."

"It's well thought out, Shane, believe me." She didn't know what she would do next, but it wasn't going to be selling retirement plans. She needed to do work with a purpose, something satisfying. She needed to find a job on her own, not be given one.

She got her keys from Shane, thanked both brothers and made the long, lonely elevator ride up fifteen floors. Once she got inside her condo she stood and stared. His suit bag was draped over her couch. They'd planned to fly back tonight but were going to take a cab to the airport so they hadn't loaded their things in her car.

Victoria went straight onto her balcony, flinging the slider open so hard it bounced back. She shoved it then, stepped out, tried to draw enough air to fill her shaky lungs. With the door closed she rarely heard a sound, but now she could hear sirens and a car horn. The air wasn't pure enough, didn't feel clean inside her chest. Abel hadn't greeted her at her front door. She couldn't bury her face in his fur and find comfort there.

She made her way back into her living room, kicking off the high heels that had been hurting all morning. Boots. She wanted her boots.

She unzipped his bag, pulled out his shirt and pressed her face into it, trying to find his scent. After a long while, she picked up the phone.

"Em? Is there any chance you could come over?"

"What's wrong? You sound terrible."

"Remember when you asked if I'd ever been rejected?"

"Yes." The word came out slowly, asking a question at the same time.

"I told you yes, but I really didn't have a clue." Her head ached from so much crying. Her heart compressed into a hot ball of fire. "Now I do."

Chapter Thirteen

"Um, you've recovered?" Emily asked Victoria a few days later. They were sitting on Victoria's balcony enjoying margaritas and the view.

"I have," Victoria said. *Except for the nightmares.*

"So, why haven't I seen you smile once?"

"I'm not saying I've fully recovered, but I'm on my way. Something my mom said helped a lot. She said, 'Marry the man you need, not the one you want.'"

"What does that mean?"

She squeezed Emily's hand. "I'm so glad I wasn't the only one not to understand. It took me a while, but I figured out that we are supposed to marry the man who's good for us, who'll take care of us, who'll provide a good life. He's what we need. But wanting is physical and ephemeral. It doesn't last."

Emily didn't say anything for a while, then finally said, "What if that's not what she means at all? What if she means we're supposed to marry the man who sees us as we are and accepts us as is? Don't we need a man like that more than one who just wants to sleep with us all the time? Of course, in an ideal world, the two combine and life is good."

"Well, of course. Ideal would be good." She had to give it more thought. She'd thought that Garrett did see her as she was, did accept her as is. The wanting was strong, too. But in the end, he hadn't proposed, had even walked away without discussing it with her. He'd also taken away the opportunity to work together, the chance to let love grow.

"Here's an easier question. What are you going to do for work?" Emily asked.

"I don't know yet. I'm exploring my options."

"What do you want to do?"

I want to create the Pete's Retreat Foundation with Garrett. The words popped into her head without a moment's thought. It was what she wanted more than anything.

She wanted to be with the man she needed *and* wanted.

"What are you thinking, Victoria?"

"That it's time for a road trip."

"Where?"

"To Red Rock. Wanna come along?"

"You've been after me to come home, which I

finally did, and now you're trying to get me to go back?"

"We both know you only came home for a visit, and with a specific purpose in mind. As soon as you're inseminated, you'll move to Red Rock. I've decided to live there, too."

"I haven't even started the paperwork at the clinic. And you've lost your mind, Vicki. I think you've had too many margaritas."

"I've had three sips of one."

"Well, it's gone to your head. Why would you go back to the place of such heartache?"

"Because I felt alive there." Which was the tip of the iceberg for her. Yes, a lot of it had to do with Garrett, but a lot didn't.

"What will you do for work?"

"I can commute to San Antonio if I have to. I'll find something, Em. I can't stay here anymore. Too many people. Too many cars." Not enough Garrett.

"Are you going to try to rent this place or sell it?"

"I'm going to cut ties. I'll be home to visit often, but I can stay with any number of family members. So, do you want to come along?"

"When will you leave?"

"Saturday. I can spend the night midway. Where would that be? Jackson, Mississippi, maybe? I'll drive the rest of the way on Sunday."

"I couldn't be ready by then," Emily said. "I can't believe you're doing this."

She needed to end the nightmares again. If she stayed in Atlanta, they would never go away.

She was haunted by visions of Garrett's animals wandering loose or getting caught in storms. She dreamed about him getting hurt with no one there to see, much less be able to help. If only he'd get a cell phone—

"You're going after Garrett again," Emily said, narrowing her eyes.

Victoria shrugged. "We'll be living in the same town, shopping in the same stores, eating in the same restaurants. It'll be hard to avoid him completely."

Emily grabbed her hand. "I don't want to see you hurt again. You haven't even recovered yet, no matter what you say."

"He's worth fighting for."

After Emily left, Victoria called Jordana and made the same offer of a ride to Red Rock.

"No, thank you." Her answer was quick and light. "Drive safe."

"Do you ever plan on telling Tanner?"

"Of course I do."

"Well, maybe you should do it before he gets married to someone else."

There was a brief, tense silence, then, "He's getting married?"

"How would I know? But there's nothing to stop him, is there?"

"That was mean, Vicki."

"It was the truth. Honey, I know you're scared. I would be, too, but you can't wait any longer. Pretty soon your family is going to storm your doors, your secret will be out and they'll force you to tell him. It'll be better if you do it."

Victoria hung up feeling strangely energized. Once she'd made her decision, she had stopped grieving. She had a plan, a goal. She would not live the rest of her life regretting that she hadn't tried hard enough.

She wasn't even nervous about telling her parents.

Four days later, her car packed full and with more to be shipped later, she hit the road, alone, excited and feeling a freedom she'd never felt before. She knew what she wanted. Now she had to go get it.

Red Rock, here I come.

Garrett arrived at Red at his usual time on Sunday night. Marcos looked up from the podium and smiled. One hurdle jumped. At least Marcos wasn't going to shun him for hurting his wife's cousin. Or maybe he didn't know yet.

"How's business?" Garrett asked.

"Can't complain. Thanks for letting me know you'd be in to pick up last week's order tonight."

"I would've paid for it regardless."

"I know. Your usual tonight?"

"Sounds good. No, wait. How about some Carne à la Mexicana instead?"

"Shaking up your life, huh?" Marcos asked.

Is that what he was doing? He headed into the main dining room and bar. The bartender spotted him and started pulling a draft. Garrett had almost reached his usual bar stool when he spotted a woman sitting a few seats down, her shiny brown hair cascading in soft curls down her back. His heart stopped for a couple of beats as he was reminded of Victoria. He didn't even want to sit near the woman.

But then she turned and spotted him. "Well, hello there, cowboy," Victoria said as if nothing had happened between them. "I was hoping I'd run into you tonight." She patted the stool on the other side of her. "I brought your things."

Numb, he took a seat, leaving one chair between them.

"How's it going?" she asked.

"What are you doin' here?"

She'd changed in ways he couldn't define yet. She smiled a kind of a secret smile, like she knew something he didn't. She nodded, too, as if he'd said something she'd been waiting to hear. What the hell was going on?

"I moved here," she said. She might as well have been telling him she was running an errand, something routine and normal, her voice was so calm. This was not normal.

"Why?"

"I'm looking for what I need, not just what I want."

"You are making no sense."

"I came to love Red Rock, so I quit my job, packed my car and here I am."

She sipped some frothy concoction, which left a bit of pink foam on her lips. Rather than use a napkin, she ran her tongue across her lips. She had to know it would drive him crazy.

"A bunch of your stuff is still at my place," he said.

"I know. I'll get it all sometime. Or you can drop them off at the Red Rock Hotel. I've got a room there for now. If Emily moves here—and I don't know that she will—maybe she'll rent a house with me. We'll see what happens."

"Is she pregnant?"

"She hasn't started the process."

"And Jordana?"

"Still hiding out."

Maybe he should give her a call, give her a man's point of view about her keeping that critical information from Tanner. "How do your parents feel about your move?"

"They want me to be happy."

He stared at her painted nails, which reminded him why he'd left her in the first place. "Do you really think you'll find happiness here?"

"This town has felt like home almost since the first day I got here."

He didn't know what to say. It changed everything and nothing. "Have you eaten?" he asked.

"Yes." She stretched and yawned. "And I'm wiped out. I drove four hundred and fifty miles today. I need sleep." She tucked some bills under her glass and climbed off the stool, then slid his suit bag onto the chair next to him.

"Guess I'll be seeing you around town, cowboy." She patted his arm, then looked over his shoulder. "Do you believe in destiny, Garrett?"

"Sometimes."

She looked at him and laughed. "That is so you. Well, in this case, I'm looking at Tanner Redmond, who just walked in." She dug into her purse, pulled out a business card and turned it upside down on the bar. He watched her write Jordana's name and phone number on it.

"Bye, Garrett," she said. She went right up to Tanner, who'd taken a stool at the bar. "You need to call her," she said to the surprised man. "She has something important to tell you."

She held up her hands toward Garrett, her fingers crossed. She was taking a big risk, and the possible unforgiving wrath of her cousin for interfering, but Garrett approved.

After a minute she passed in front of the window and didn't look inside at all. She was over it? Over him? Just like that?

He'd been afraid he'd hurt her, but apparently she'd recovered better than he had.

He sipped his beer, considering her. He'd never known loneliness. Even though he'd spent most of his life alone, he never would've called himself lonely.

And he wasn't lonely now, he decided…

No, he was forlorn. And desolate.

Marcos set his hot plate on the counter in front of him.

"You might have mentioned that Victoria was here," Garrett said.

"I didn't know it mattered." He smiled grimly and walked away.

Was that the response he would get from everyone in town now? Did everyone know? She'd made herself a welcome part of the community in less than a month. He'd lived here most of his life, and he didn't figure anyone would champion him like that, although Victoria had seemed to from the start, even without knowing the details of what had happened with Jenny Kirkpatrick. After all these years, did he need to explain it? Her family moved away years ago.

When Garrett arrived home later, he went straight to his bedroom and opened the closet door. Her clothes were still hanging there. He'd ignored them all week, even though he knew he should pack them up and ship them to her.

One by one, he took her clothes off the rack. Out of his dresser he withdrew the rest of her things, a rainbow of lacy lingerie he loaded into a paper sack. Her perfume wafted from the bag. He rolled it down and took it to the living room along with her clothes. He would take them all to her tomorrow. Get it over with.

He tripped over her boots when he returned to the bedroom. He'd brought them in from the porch a few days ago, had cleaned and polished them so that he could mail them with her clothes. He'd been methodical and unemotional, doing a job that needed doing.

But he clasped them now as he remembered the way she kicked the dirt when she was getting ready to tease him or tick him off. The way she pitched dirty straw into the wheelbarrow, her feet planted. The way she'd saved Dum, her boots filling up with mud so that she could barely walk.

Indelible memories. And now she'd moved to town. He couldn't escape the memories—or her. She would probably start dating, in time get married and have children. Another man's children.

Garrett threw the boots across the room, rattling an old cross-stitch sampler on the wall that said Home Sweet Home. It had come with the ranch, and he'd never taken it down. The sampler tilted for a second then fell to the floor, the old wooden frame breaking into pieces.

It seemed like an omen—or a sign of what his life had become. No home sweet home for him.

Garrett picked up the four wooden pieces, then the cloth sampler itself, which disintegrated at his touch. Dust must've been holding it together, and now it had turned to dust.

He shoved his hands through his hair, then he went to his shop and got out the bolo he'd created for her from his safe. He set it on the counter, pried out the stone, then threw the silver into a crucible. He could melt it down, reuse it. He didn't want reminders of a farewell gift to her.

He turned the stone over and over in his hand. He needed to do something else with it, something that made a statement.

The idea came to him in a flash of light. He settled in and got to work.

It would be his best work yet.

Chapter Fourteen

"He hasn't even had the courtesy to return my clothes," Victoria complained to Wendy after eating dinner on the sunporch after Marcos went to work. "It's been *days*."

"Maybe he wants you to come to him. Come to the ranch. Victoria, you are bouncing MaryAnne like you're on a trampoline. Please sit down."

Victoria stopped bouncing and looked at the baby in her arms, all wide-eyed and beautiful. "She looks fine to me."

"She's getting green around the gills. You're making her seasick!"

Victoria sat in Wendy's rocking chair. "Why would he want me to go to the ranch?"

She hadn't come up with a clear plan about winning him back, but she knew it had to start with contact, and she thought for sure he would bring her clothes to her at the hotel. Make contact. She'd counted on that.

"I don't know. I'm just trying to think like a man," Wendy said.

"Men like the chase. Are you listening, sweetheart?" Victoria said to MaryAnne. "Don't make yourself too available. They'll drop you like a hot poker."

Wendy threw up her hands. "Will you please not poison my not-yet-three-month-old daughter?"

"You're right. She has plenty of time to learn about heartache on her own."

Wendy rolled her eyes. "So, when you told me you were moving here no matter what happened with Garrett, was it a lie? If you're going to spend years being angry at him, what's the purpose of a new beginning here?"

Which was an excellent question, Victoria decided. "I'm not ready to give up, that's all. I'll adapt when I have to."

"In the meantime, we all have to listen to you moan and gripe?"

"Pretty much, yes."

Wendy laughed, then Victoria joined in.

"So, now what?" Wendy asked.

"I guess I'll go out to the ranch and collect my stuff. I've been feeling like a walking neon sign wearing my Atlanta clothes instead of my jeans and boots."

"Let me know how it goes."

"I will." Victoria kissed MaryAnne's cheeks then passed her to her mother. They'd spent enough time together in the past few days, and without Emily there to hog the baby, that Victoria had started feeling comfortable not just holding her but changing her diaper and getting her in and out of her baby carrier, with all its complicated straps and fasteners.

Dogs were easier, but they wouldn't let her cuddle them for long.

"What are you smiling about?" Wendy asked as they moved toward the front door.

"How incredibly my life has changed in a month. Just one month. Can you believe it?"

"Since the same thing happened to me, I *can* believe it. I hope you have the same happy ending I did."

Victoria debated whether to go back to her hotel room and change into something more alluring than the blouse and slacks she wore or just go straight to the ranch. It would be dark in an hour. She should wait until morning—

No. She needed to get it over with.

The drive seemed incredibly long. She hadn't driven the route in more than a week. As it became more desolate, with fewer houses, she began to question herself. Was she still so sure she wanted this life? Would it satisfy her?

Could she satisfy him? Not in bed, that was easy, but as a partner?

Apparently he didn't think she could. She wanted

the chance to prove him wrong, maybe even prove herself wrong. The niggles of doubt would be settled with time.

She pulled into the driveway. Her heart thundered so loud, she thought it would open her chest. She didn't see his truck, but saw Jimmy's pickup.

Where could Garrett be? He didn't have a regular place to go on Thursday nights.

"Howdy, Victoria," Jimmy said, coming up to her. "I didn't recognize the car, but I guess it's your own, not a rental. Heard you moved to town for good."

Abel shoved his head into her, his tail and hindquarters wagging like crazy. Pete watched, looking somber. "I did. Where's Garrett?"

"He didn't say. He had me come before the crack of dawn. Want me to give him a call?"

She was giving Abel a rubdown that he was thoroughly and noisily enjoying. "If you don't know where he is, how can you call?"

Jimmy grinned. "He got himself a cell phone. Can you believe it?"

No, she couldn't. What did that mean? "It is hard to imagine. Anyway, it's okay. Um, I just came to pick up a few things I left. I'll just go in the house and get them."

"Sure thing. You want to see the animals? I'm about ready to get them bedded down for the night, so now would be the best time. Just put Dee and Dum in the house, in fact."

"Yes, I'd love to."

She kicked up dust as she walked next to Jimmy into the barn. She peeked into the stall with the mama dog and puppies. "Look how they've grown," she exclaimed, tears springing to her eyes. Babies grew so fast. The kittens had their eyes open and were stumbling over each other and their mama. There were a couple of new dogs, a few were gone. Apple Annie held court in her stall, but only one other horse was in residence.

Changes could happen in the blink of an eye.

"Somebody brought a boa constrictor the other day," Jimmy said. "Garrett about threw a conniption fit. I took the snake home with me. Figured I could find it a permanent place somewhere."

She couldn't imagine Garrett throwing a conniption fit over anything. He was patience personified. "That must've been something to see."

Jimmy shrugged. "He's been pretty edgy lately. I didn't know him before I started working here, but I'd heard from my mom that he wasn't one to shift gears real easy, you know? Pretty mellow guy. I haven't always seen that."

"Everybody has problems now and then."

"That's what I figure. He keeps his mouth shut pretty good about stuff, though."

Except when he tells you it isn't gonna work and walks out, she thought.

She headed into the house and reached for the light switch. The room lit up. Dee and Dum started making noises, knowing someone was there.

And right smack in front of her on the sofa were

her jeans and shirts on hangers draped over the back, and a paper sack that probably substituted as a suitcase for her undergarments and toiletries and her boots, polished to such a shine she could see her reflection.

She felt the blow of rejection as hard as she had at her parents' house, maybe harder, because this time she had no doubts whatsoever. She knew she wanted to be his wife, the mother of his children, his partner in everything.

She stood staring at the couch until she was dizzy. She staggered into the kitchen, leaned over the sink and cried. She couldn't go outside and face Jimmy until she got herself under control. He would tell Garrett. She couldn't have that. Garrett only needed to know that she'd gotten her things, and that made it over and done with.

The puppies were whimpering, having seen her. She reached into the box and picked up Dum, who wriggled even more than Abel had. He licked her face until she laughed and cried at the same time, then she tucked him under her chin and felt his soft fur against her neck. She'd missed this so much. All of them. Even the stinky dogs who liked to roll in manure.

The front door opened. "I'm just getting a drink of water," she called out to Jimmy. "I'll be there in a sec."

But Jimmy didn't come into the doorway. Garrett did, and he was all dressed up—or dressed up for him, anyway. It was the same outfit he'd worn when he'd met her parents, although a different bolo. This one had more detail and a large blue stone, maybe a sapphire. He held his black Stetson, turning it in his hands.

"Victoria," he said.

"I got tired of waiting for my clothes." She put Dum back into the box and started past Garrett. "I'll be out of here in a second."

She wanted him in the worst way. He looked good. Really good. Relaxed. How ridiculous was it that she wanted him when he didn't want her at all? Or need her.

He set a hand on her shoulder, blocking her way. "You've been crying."

She didn't look at him. "I hadn't realized how much I missed the animals, you know? When Dum's old enough, maybe I can adopt him. I'm trying to find a house to rent that has a yard. Maybe Abel, too."

"We'll talk about it."

Fresh tears stung her eyes. She hated that he was seeing her so emotional. "You're probably tired from your trip, so I'll get going. Bye, Garrett."

"I'm fine. Don't hurry on my account, Victoria," he said. He tossed his hat onto the sofa, landing it next to her belongings. Usually he was fastidious about hanging it on a rack by the door.

She made a move to go again, then noticed his shirt pocket. "Why did you get a cell phone?" she asked.

"I was feeling too out of touch with the world."

"I thought you liked that."

"Changed my mind. You look good."

It wasn't her imagination. He really was in a happy mood. "I— Um, thank you."

"You're welcome."

"And you're dressed up," she said.

"Would you like something to drink?" he asked as he went into the kitchen. "I've got a powerful thirst."

"I'm okay, thanks. What's going on with you? You're not yourself."

"No, I'm not, am I? I've changed." He grabbed a bottle of water—bottled water, really?—and drank most of it in one gulp, the only indication he wasn't as relaxed as she first thought.

He's nervous, she realized. It steadied her a little.

He finished the water and set down the bottle carefully. Then he said, "This wasn't the way I planned it, but I think destiny's taken hold again."

"Planned what?" Whatever he was about to say would be momentous, that much she knew. *Tell me fast,* she urged him silently.

"I'm dressed up because I flew to Atlanta and back today."

"Why?"

"I needed to pay a visit to the king and queen."

"Why?" she asked breathlessly, afraid to guess the answer.

"I had some explaining to do. Let's go sit on the couch."

With one end of the sofa piled high, they were

forced to sit close to each other. Garrett could've moved everything, but didn't, making sure she wasn't too far away.

"My parents actually let you in the house?" she asked.

"They seem to have accepted the fact you want to be in Red Rock, whether you're with me or not. Your mother, in particular, gets it." In fact, she'd told Garrett that she'd never seen Victoria so happy, especially after months of seeing dark circles under her eyes and a weight loss she couldn't afford. "I took your business plan with me and showed it to your father. He was highly impressed, by the way, and regretted not realizing himself that your talents should've been used better at his company."

"I did a great job because it was personal and important," she said, but she looked pleased at the praise.

"I finally read the whole thing, Victoria. It was amazing, from beginning to end. I made a few notes, though."

She laughed. The sound was shaky, in a good way, a way that said her emotions were involved. "Of course you did."

He opened the folder and showed her the changes he would make.

"So, you're going to do it?" she asked.

He shrugged. "Depends on a few things falling into place." He pulled out a sheet he'd tucked in the back and showed it to her.

She examined it. "This looks like a house."

"It is. It'll be built right in this spot, although it'll take up more room than this one by far. Figure we can live in a mobile home for a little while."

"We? You and me?" Her fingers were linked into a white-knuckled knot. He cradled her hands in his until she opened hers, then he clasped them.

"I asked your father for permission to court you. He gave his blessing. Now I'm asking permission from you. I know I hurt you, Victoria. I'll never forgive myself for that." He stood then, needing to move. "And I need to tell you about Jenny Kirkpatrick, before you give me your answer."

"Is she the source of the scandal?"

"Yes."

"I don't need you to tell me, Garrett. I know the man you are."

"Maybe you do, but you don't know why I fought being with you, why I didn't believe I was good enough. Maybe this will explain it."

"Okay."

He told her the story and discovered the memory no longer hurt.

"Since I was a teenage girl myself once," Victoria said, "I'll wager that she's the one who pursued you, even though you were doing the standup thing when her parents put a stop to things."

"Yeah. No one believed me, and I got tired of justifying it. I joined the army."

"Yet you came back after that."

"I didn't know anything but this place. It was home. When I left the second time and came home,

I'd seen more of the world, knew I could live alone and not be bothered by what people thought. But when it came to you, I cared what people thought. And I've been prejudiced, too. I figured the Fortune family would be just like the Kirkpatricks. I was wrong. I'm eatin' crow, big-time."

She pressed her fingers to her mouth, her eyes welling with tears. "And now you're going to court me?"

"I've been givin' that a lot of thought as I made the trip home." He finally sat beside her again. He took her hands again. "See, your father said I could take it a step further if I wanted. That I had his blessing to ask you to marry me, if I wanted, but I thought I should do the right thing. You know, start from the beginning. Do better."

"I don't see how you could do better, cowboy."

He wanted to kiss her, but he needed to finish what he had to say first. "I told your father not only could I provide for you, but I could provide well. I'm not a poor man, Victoria. Not anywhere near it. You've changed my life in just about every way, from how I think to how I act to how I feel. I'm carin' about things I never cared about before. I'm in love with you, princess. I'd like to have a passel of kids with you. Will you marry me?"

"How many is a passel?" she asked, her eyes going wide.

"More'n a few. I want my kids to have what I didn't—lifetime connections, the bonds of family. Are you game?"

"I love you, cowboy. With all my heart. I'm game for anything with you. Do you know why?"

"Tell me."

"Because you're the man that I need."

He kissed her then, tasted her hot, salty tears, then pulled her into his arms for the longest, hardest hug of his life.

"Your father only asked one thing," he said, not letting her loose. "That you have the wedding you deserve."

She leaned back a little and combed his hair with her fingers. "Do you mind?"

"If it's important to you, I can do anything. Victoria, I've been lost without you here. Utterly lost. I know you need more of a social life than I do, and I'll work on givin' you that."

"You keep dropping *g*'s for me, and I'll be plenty happy."

"Huh?"

"I'll tell you later. Or maybe I won't."

"You've been home for half an hour and you're already teasing me. Wait here a minute." He went outside, was gone less than thirty seconds and returned with a gift bag. First he handed her a framed cross-stitch piece like the one that hung in his bedroom, but without explanation. Then he gave her an envelope with a gift certificate inside for fifty-two manicures. "I had to get Gwen to open up her shop tonight. Every year on our anniversary I'll give you fifty-two more. You need to keep your nails nice. I know it means something to you."

She laughed and kissed him. "I didn't know you were so observant."

"When it comes to you? I notice just about everything." Then he dug into the bag for the final item, a small velvet bag. He reached inside and fished around for a particular piece. "Maybe you noticed I didn't bring your clothes to you, even though you told me I could."

"I was devastated. I thought you never wanted to lay eyes on me again."

"I didn't want to see you until I was done with this." He held up an intricately carved silver ring. Woven into the design was a chocolate diamond. "I got you a chain, too, because I figure you won't want to wear it doing all the dirty work around here."

"Oh, Garrett! It's beautiful! I'd never heard of chocolate diamonds until I met you."

He slid the ring on her finger. "That's one of the things I remembered from the airport, how your eyes looked like these stones." He tipped the rest of the contents of the bag into her hand. "There's two wedding bands." He'd spent the better part of three days creating the three rings.

"Pretty sure of yourself, cowboy."

He almost told her he hadn't been sure at all, but decided she didn't need to know that. "I was hopeful."

"I was hopeful, too."

"Would you really have stayed in Red Rock, even without this?"

"It's home, Garrett. But this is my world, right here. I love you."

"I love you, too." He framed her face with his hands. "Remember a while back when you told me we don't have to be what people expect us to be?"

"I do."

He paused at the words. He would hear her say those words soon, too, and she would legally be his forever. "I realized I'd been doing that, figuring everyone had a certain opinion of me that I was sure I couldn't change. I'm not that uncivilized jerk people thought I was, not anymore. I deserved the title once, but not now."

"I didn't have anything to do with that change, you know," she said, her gaze never wavering. "You'd done it for years before I came along."

"But I didn't know it. You think I saved your life? Well, you saved mine in ways you can't begin to imagine."

"Let's go to bed, cowboy."

"It'd be my pleasure."

* * * * *

A sneaky peek at next month...

Cherish™

ROMANCE TO MELT THE HEART EVERY TIME

My wish list for next month's titles...

In stores from 15th February 2013:

❏ Her Rocky Mountain Protector – Patricia Thayer

& The Soldier's Sweetheart – Soraya Lane

❏ Fortune's Unexpected Groom – Nancy Robards Thompson

& Fortune's Perfect Match – Allison Leigh

In stores from 1st March 2013:

❏ Resisting Mr. Tall, Dark & Texan – Christine Rimmer

& The Baby Wore a Badge – Marie Ferrarella

❏ Ballroom to Bride and Groom – Kate Hardy

& Cindy's Doctor Charming – Teresa Southwick

Available at WHSmith, Tesco, Asda, Eason, Amazon and Apple

Just can't wait?

Visit us Online

You can buy our books online a month before they hit the shops! **www.millsandboon.co.uk**

0213/23

Special Offers

Every month we put together collections and longer reads written by your favourite authors.

Here are some of next month's highlights— and don't miss our fabulous discount online!

On sale 15th February

On sale 15th February

On sale 1st March

Save 20% on all Special Releases

Find out more at
www.millsandboon.co.uk/specialreleases

Visit us Online

0313/ST/MB407

MILLS & BOON® Book Club

2 Free Books!

Get your free books now at
www.millsandboon.co.uk/freebookoffer

Or fill in the form below and post it back to us

THE MILLS & BOON® BOOK CLUB™—HERE'S HOW IT WORKS: Accepting your free books places you under no obligation to buy anything. You may keep the books and return the despatch note marked 'Cancel'. If we do not hear from you, about a month later we'll send you 5 brand-new stories from the Cherish™ series, including two 2-in-1 books priced at £5.49 each, and a single book priced at £3.49*. There is no extra charge for post and packaging. You may cancel at any time, otherwise we will send you 5 stories a month which you may purchase or return to us—the choice is yours. *Terms and prices subject to change without notice. Offer valid in UK only. Applicants must be 18 or over. Offer expires 31st July 2013. **For full terms and conditions, please go to www.millsandboon.co.uk/freebookoffer**

Mrs/Miss/Ms/Mr (please circle) _____

First Name _____

Surname _____

Address _____

_____

Postcode _____

E-mail _____

Send this completed page to: Mills & Boon Book Club, Free Book Offer, FREEPOST NAT 10298, Richmond, Surrey, TW9 1BR

Find out more at
www.millsandboon.co.uk/freebookoffer

Visit us Online

0113/S3XEb